COMPLICATED

ALSO BY COLIN ALEXANDER

Starman's Saga: The Long, Strange Journey of Leif the Luck
Accidental Warrior: The Unlikely Tale of Bloody Hal
My Life: An Ex-Quarterback's Adventures in the Galactic Empire
Lady of Ice and Fire
God's Adamantine Fate

COMPLICATED

The Interstellar Life and Times
of Saoirse Kenneally

COLIN ALEXANDER

COMPLICATED:
THE INTERSTELLAR LIFE AND TIMES OF SAOIRSE KENNEALLY
Copyright © 2020 by Colin Alexander

All rights reserved, including the right of reproduction in whole or in part in any form. No part of this book may be used or reproduced in any manner whatsoever without written permission except in the case of brief quotations embodied in critical articles and reviews.

ISBN: 978-0-9993257-8-0

This novel is a work of fiction. Names, characters, places, and incidents are either the product of the author's imagination or are used fictitiously and are not to be construed as real. Any resemblance to actual events, locales, organizations, or persons, living or dead, is entirely coincidental and beyond the intent of the author.

Cover art by Alejandro Colucci

This one is for Liz, and for Jess

PART I
THE BOTTOM

Many shall be restored that now are fallen and many shall fall that now are in honor.
HORACE
"ARS POETICA"

There is nothing permanent except change.
HERACLITUS

ONE

"Kenneally! Saoirse Kenneally! You have a visitor!"

At the shout, the young woman on the narrow bed rolled over. She opened her eyes, but they did not want to focus immediately. She blinked and looked away from the glaring light strips embedded in the ceiling. Too bright. At least her stomach wasn't threatening to heave, even if it rumbled. Her head was still pounding.

"Kenneally, you getting up or are we telling him you won't see him?"

"Wait. Wait. Just give me a second." Saoirse's voice sounded like a croak to her ears. Her mouth tasted like stagnant ditch water. When was the last time she had brushed her teeth?

She swung her legs over the side of the bed and sat up. Her feet recoiled from a floor chilled by air-conditioning. She held her head in her hands, elbows on knees, then forced herself to stand up.

She saw a steel toilet across from her bed, a tiny sink with a metal mirror above it next to the toilet. Stark gray walls. Not a hospital.

Jail cell.

Again.

She tried to think back, to remember what had happened. She recalled being brought in, but maybe that recollection was invented, existing only because it was obvious she was in jail. She couldn't remember when that might have been. The air stank, a sour odor that was strongest in the direction of the toilet. She remembered throwing up in it multiple times, but she had missed more than once. They had made her clean it up from both the toilet seat and the floor. She definitely remembered that.

Saoirse tottered over to the sink and looked in the mirror. There were stains on her T-shirt and jeans, some from throwing up. Some looked older. Some of the odor was coming from her clothes. Nothing she could do about that. Not at the moment. She regarded her face: Pale skin with scattered freckles across her cheeks and nose. Upturned lips opened to draw in a gasp. She closed her eyes. She didn't want to look at her teeth. When she opened them again, she saw deep blue eyes gaze back at her from the mirror. They were steady enough, she decided. She ran her fingers through her hair; they snagged on tangles. It fell straight past her cheeks and shoulders, dark to the point of being truly black, except for where she had colored it. She couldn't recall when she had done that, but it was sufficiently long ago that the natural black had grown out on top and partway down the sides. It would do; she would do. At least she wasn't fat.

"If you're done beautifying yourself, let's go."

"Yes, Mx.," Saoirse said.

There was a click, and the field that had formed the door of her cell shut off. On the other side stood a Black woman wearing the gray pants, blue shirt, and badge of the Kenosha County Sheriff's Department. She was a good three inches shorter than Saoirse's five foot nine, but next to her burly form, Saoirse felt like the smaller one.

"My arm is sore." Saoirse rocked her left arm back and forth and grabbed at the deltoid with her right hand.

The guard laughed. "I'm not surprised. They told me that last night you were thinking your uncle Patrick was sitting on the toilet in your cell, doing his business. You had to get meds and you didn't make it easy. Twisting and fighting is not a good way to get an injection. You remember any of that?"

Saoirse stared glumly at the guard. "No."

"Thought not," the guard said. "Look, now put on your slippers and let's go. You've got the vid room for a twenty-five-minute visit. That's all you've got; your visitor is here and the clock's ticking."

Saoirse nodded. It would be Tim Duncan, her father's lawyer, although he should be in person, not vid. Didn't matter. She needed to talk to him. Obviously. He would know how to handle this. It wasn't the first time.

She found elastic slippers that had rolled up into a ball on the floor, and stretched them over her bare feet. The soles, if they could be called that, weren't thick enough to block the cold from the floor. They must have taken her shoes when they brought her in. She didn't remember that either. She wasn't even sure if she'd had shoes.

Saoirse shrugged and walked out with the guard at her side. Talking to Duncan was all that mattered.

· · ·

Donal Kenneally sat in the vid visiting room and fidgeted. Saoirse was late—so what else was new?—and the timer at the top of the grayed-out vid wall showed that three minutes of his visiting time had already gone. He berated himself again for choosing to come to the pretrial detention facility in person, to visit instead of doing it remotely on his comm from his apartment in the Loop. He wanted to be anyplace except here.

It was a gorgeous summer day outside in Chicagoland. He could have been in Grant Park enjoying the sunshine, sampling food from the vendor booths, listening to the street musicians, and gawking at the art and exhibits set up for the celebration of Wormhole Day.

This year would be the grandest holiday in his memory because it was the one hundredth anniversary of the day the *Irrational* out of Titan Station made a wormhole and dropped through it to emerge at Tau Ceti, twelve light-years away. That had set off a land grab among the stars that made the opening of the American West look like nothing more than the subdivision of one of the old lots in Highland Park. Now the Interstellar Reach of Humanity, or the Reach, stretched out roughly five hundred light-years in all directions from Earth, although who knew how far some ships had really gone once wormhole transits close to one hundred light-years became possible. The Stars and Stripes—and other flags—waved proudly against strange skies on God only knew how many other worlds. Planets like Lincoln, the most glorious vacation destination for anyone who could afford to go, where he remembered the air tasted like sweet wine.

He sighed. He would still make it to the lakefront for the symphony. Dad had a front-row box because it was Kenneally Systems that designed and built the hardened computer systems that could go through those long-distance wormholes and still function. Those computer systems had fueled the explosive growth in commerce in the Reach over the last twenty years. Pundits claimed the Reach would double again in size over the next twenty. Dad's genius in designing those systems while staying within the bounds set by the anti-AI and anti-cyborg laws that had followed the end of the Forty Years' War built the family business, Kenneally Systems. It was a triumph for the poor Irish refugee who had arrived in the United States thirty-seven years ago with nothing but the clothes on his back after the collapse of the Irish economy. Ireland recovered—she always did—but Dad had stayed in the US, married well, and raised five children, four of whom were successful in their own right. And here was Donal, waiting on the fifth, sitting in the vid visiting room of a jail and staring at a gray screen.

Why had he thought that he could be physically in the room with Saoirse? The answer, of course, was that he hadn't been thinking. This was yet another Saoirse debacle and he had reacted instinctively without paying attention to details. The information about how visits were conducted was posted on the Sheriff's Department page, and no amount of pleading after he arrived could change that. Yes, the vid at the facility was life-sized and 3D instead of the flat image he would have gotten from his comm, whether on its own screen, linked to a wall unit, or projected in front of him, but still . . . He wanted to be able to reach out and hug his baby sister, even though he knew she wouldn't like it. At least, he *should* want to. Saerie was . . . complicated.

Light flashed around the perimeter of the vid wall, and a voice informed him that audio and video recording of the visit were about to start. Then the screen cleared to show a room identical to the one he sat in. It looked, in fact, like an extension of this room, as though he could get out of his chair and walk over to it. Only yellow stripes around the edge of the screen served to remind him that he was looking at a vid screen. The door at the back of the other room opened and Saerie walked in, followed by a female guard in police uniform. Saerie sat in the chair near the screen, while the guard took a chair behind her.

Saerie looked awful. How much weight had she lost? She had always been slim, but now the memory denim of her jeans could not contract enough to be snug; there was a noticeable gap around her waist, and the jeans seemed at risk of falling down. A stained shirt hung loosely from her shoulders. Her always pale skin verged on translucent, except for the dark circles under her eyes. And her hair! At some point she had apparently dyed it red, but the natural black had grown out to cheekbone level, with an irregular band of red below that. He realized she was staring at him.

"Saerie . . . ," he started. She grimaced at the nickname. He found his voice again. "How are you? Where have you been staying?"

She let out a short laugh, closer to a snort. "I'm fine, as you see, Brother." She spread her arms wide. "As to where I've been, I've been here and there. This shelter or that. Or, this street or that. You know."

"Jesus."

"Well, what the fuck do you expect when they take your Benefit away?" Saoirse went on in a falsetto, "'Your Benefit is suspended for a minimum of six months, or until you demonstrate you can live by society's rules.'" She switched back to her own voice. "What a piece of fucking bullshit! How am I supposed to live by 'society's rules' with no money to live on? I thought Guaranteed Benefit meant 'guaranteed,' but I guess not. Not that I'm getting any help from you."

"Dad said we can't give you any more money."

"So what are you? A fucktard with no mind of your own?"

Donal drew a long, slow breath. Saerie could be so . . . challenging. "Where did it go the last time?" *Don't start a fight*, he warned himself.

She ignored the bait. "I thought Duncan would be here, not you," she said. "I need him to get me out of here."

Donal swallowed, his carefully planned conversation gone from his mind. Saerie had had this effect on him since she was twelve. It was ridiculous. He was ten years her senior.

As best he could get the words out, Donal said, "We heard. You were arrested. Dad and Mom . . . Dad, well . . . Dad sort of detonated."

"Because I called him a fucking idiot the last time I was home? Well, he was."

"That may be part of it," Donal said. "But also, you stole—"

"I was in a bind," she snapped. "I'll pay it back."

Donal stifled his next words.

"Look," Saoirse added, "I need Duncan to work this. I know I need to go back to rehab. I'll get sober, stay sober. This time, I mean it."

"You're a lousy liar, Saerie." At the flash of anger on her face, he wondered how he had managed to say that. Words started to tumble out. "No. You're not a lousy liar. Actually, you're a really good one. It's just, we've heard them all before. That's why I came. Dad said he's had it. He doesn't want to have anything to do with you, doesn't want to know you. You're out of the family. Dad doesn't even know I'm here."

She scowled. "Dad will get over it. But why isn't Duncan here?"

"Saerie, Duncan's not here, because Dad won't pay for him to do it. Not anymore. He said you're on your own now."

"What?" The stare from her blue eyes drilled through him, even though she was looking into a camera and not directly at him. "I need a lawyer here. I need a *good* lawyer here. I've got to get out of here. I want to go into treatment."

Donal took a breath. "Saerie, they'll give you a public defender. That's all. Someone will come. I don't know who. I'm sorry. There's nothing else I can do. Nothing else I'm going to do. You own this."

At the glare from his sister, Donal Kenneally cut off the vid even though there was time remaining. Then he fled the room.

TWO

It took two days before anyone else came to see Saoirse Kenneally. Two days that she spent thinking about all the ways she was a failure, all the ways she had fucked up, all the very good reasons no one liked her. She also spent those days hating Donal for being an idiot, hating Dad for not helping her, hating Mom for letting Dad not help her, and hating herself most of all. Her stomach did settle down over those two days and her headache eased, too, except for when she bashed the back of her head against the cell wall in frustration at all the things she'd failed at and all the things she hated. That had not ended well.

    A drink would have fixed the situation, would have made it so that she did not have any of those feelings. Well, it would have been more than one drink. Right then, she hated herself for needing it and hated the drink for making her need it. Anyway, none of that mattered, because she couldn't have a drink until she got out of jail. So she sat on her bed except for when they took her out for mealtimes, and then she mostly sat in the dining hall and looked at the food on her plate.

    Late in the afternoon of the second day, a guard announced over the speaker in her cell that her lawyer had arrived to meet with her. The cell door blinked out to reveal a different guard, who escorted her to a small conference room. He remained outside as she went in.

    Inside, a small brown-skinned woman with wavy brown hair trapped in a bun sat at a table barely big enough for two. She wore a white shirt over a red skirt, the first bright color Saoirse had seen in days. Dark-brown eyes in an unsmiling face watched Saoirse as she took the seat opposite.

"My name is Madeleine Mariam," the woman said. "I have been assigned the duty of defending you." She picked up an unrolled comm from the table and looked at the screen. "How do you say your first name, Mx. Kenneally?"

At least she asked. "Two syllables. *Sear* followed by *shuh* is the way I say it."

"Do you have a nickname you'd prefer?"

"I hate nicknames."

That brought Mariam's eyes up from her comm to lock with Saoirse's. She shrugged. "No matter." She glanced back down at her comm and said, "The law requires them to give us in-person meetings, not just a vid, and the same law does not allow the authorities to monitor or record our conversation. Not audio, not video. But I guess you know all that." She reached into the pocket of the red jacket that hung on the back of her chair and pulled out a small black puck. Her forefinger tapped the puck, and a blue light flashed on its top. She set it on the table and allowed herself a tight grin. "Since they are not allowed to monitor us, they can hardly object to a scrambler." She leaned forward. "I've read through your record. Seriously, Saoirse, how have you managed to get into so much trouble?"

"Shit happens."

That brought a frown. "Look," Mariam said sharply, "I actually will do my job, not like most who get assigned these cases and just check the boxes and don't care where you end up—because it's not like the system gives us grades on this. And I'll bet you know that too. If you want me to help you, you're going to have to help me."

Saoirse nodded. The lawyer was right.

"Okay," Mariam went on. "The biggest problem we have is the attempted robbery and assault charges. The police are accusing you of grabbing a woman's bag. When she struggled, you hit her."

"It's a misunderstanding," Saoirse said. "We just bumped into each other on the street and got a little tangled. I never hit her. That's for damn sure."

"All you have to do is make physical contact with someone for it to be assault. And the person you 'bumped into' was an off-duty police officer."

Saoirse closed her eyes. "I guess that's a problem."

"Dammit!" Mariam snapped. "It would serve you right if I got up and left!"

I'm sure it would serve me right. Why don't you?

Saoirse said nothing.

Mariam turned back to her comm screen. "You're not even twenty-one."

"Not for six months." She took a breath. "I'm sorry. I need your help. I'll shut up."

"Yeah." Mariam's eyes were on the comm. "It's not like you haven't had opportunities. You went to boarding school for high school. Those are expensive. Good school, right?"

"It's famous, if that's what you mean."

"In Dublin? Your parents paid for you to go to school in Ireland?"

Saoirse shrugged. "We're Irish, obviously, first generation here. Mom and Dad wanted me to go to school back there." *And get me far out of the house*, she thought but did not add. "It's a great place to send a kid who drinks."

"But you won a European award in computer science. CAST?"

"Coding and Systems Technology," Saoirse said. "We called it the Hacker Races. My dad built a computer company and my mom was his top programmer. I'm good at that stuff."

"And you played sports, too, it says. What is this? Camogie?"

"Say it with a hard *g*," Saoirse told her. "It's an old sport in Ireland for girls. You need good hand-eye coordination. Like a mix of field hockey and lacrosse."

Mariam looked up again at Saoirse. "So you're pretty tough, playing a game like that, right?"

Saoirse's lips curved in a wan smile. "I don't know about that," she said. "I never played sober."

Mariam sighed. "Yeah. So you had offers from universities for computer engineering programs. Real school, with professors, not the online stuff almost everybody does. And where are you instead? Six arrests. Two convictions, although no jail time. Yet. Five different inpatient rehabs. All that in less than three years out of high school."

"What's not in the records you've got?" Saoirse asked. "I drink. I'm a fucking alcoholic. I'm sure it says that. Been drinking since I was twelve.

I do drugs too. I need to go back to treatment. This time I'll stay sober. I know I can." She needed to go someplace for a month or two, she thought, that wasn't the street and wasn't jail. After that, it would be a different story, but for right now, a rehab was where she wanted to go.

"I thought about that," Mariam said. "Plead to something and go to rehab instead of jail as part of the deal. You've done that before, for all the good it hasn't done." She sighed. "I've called the places you've been. All five of them. They won't take you."

Saoirse sucked in a sharp breath and her hands clenched into fists on top of the table. "What? Why not?"

"One of them cut me off when I couldn't guarantee your father would pay. Three of them said you got into fights and they don't want you back. One said you hacked their computer system, never mind what you did with it. I guess you are good at that. I called some others I know. No-go, once they heard your background. I can tell you the prosecutor won't buy any of the outpatient thirty-day wonder programs."

"Wait a minute." For the first time, Saoirse felt fear creep in. "What are you telling me? That I have to go to jail? I didn't really do anything. I told you that."

Mariam drummed her fingers on the table. "Do you want to tell the court you really didn't do anything? You've got priors, and she is a police officer."

Saoirse shook her head.

"Good thinking. Which, for all your brains, you don't do much of. I've got one possibility, if you'll listen to it."

Saoirse leaned across the table. "I'll take it. What's the program? Where is it?"

"One thing I have to know first," Mariam said. "Do you use zombie?"

"No." Saoirse was emphatic. "I drink; alcohol is my drug of choice, although I'll use whatever sometimes, but I don't do that. I know people who've used it, even back in school. They say it's not really addictive, is the perfect high, comes from something legal." Saoirse favored Mariam with a little grin that could have been a smirk, which said she knew better. "I know what it does. It changes your brain wiring and it can be permanent. Use it long enough, you become, well, a zombie. No recovery from zombie. That shit scares me. Never used it and I'm not going to. What do you think I am?"

"I know what you are." Mariam frowned. "And I know about zombie. It's made from something called zombipterisin, which comes from somewhere in the Reach, and you can make a schizophrenia drug from it, so, yes, at that stage it's legal. But it doesn't matter what you think you know about it. I just need to know what you use because what I've got in mind won't take anyone who uses zombie. And if you're lying, they'll find out."

How much clearer could she have been? "I told you I don't use it!"

Mariam shrugged. "As long as you pass the screening, you're good. Here's the deal: As you know, the Solar Council and Assembly of Worlds are responsible for administering the Reach. So all the nations on Earth and the independent member worlds of the Assembly have the responsibility to provide people to staff that administration. The US is always behind on its quota, and our region, here in the Midwest, is way behind. So if you volunteer for off-planet services, and you make it through the ten-week training program and you take a position, the charges will be dropped and you can do—well, I don't know what, somewhere other than Earth. It's a two-year commitment, but you won't be gambling on how hard the prosecutor wants to push the assault charge. If you don't make it through the program, or you turn it down, I'm certain you're looking at jail time. I can't be sure how much, or where you'd serve it. What do you say?"

Saoirse stared at her. "Yes. Obviously. I'm a volunteer."

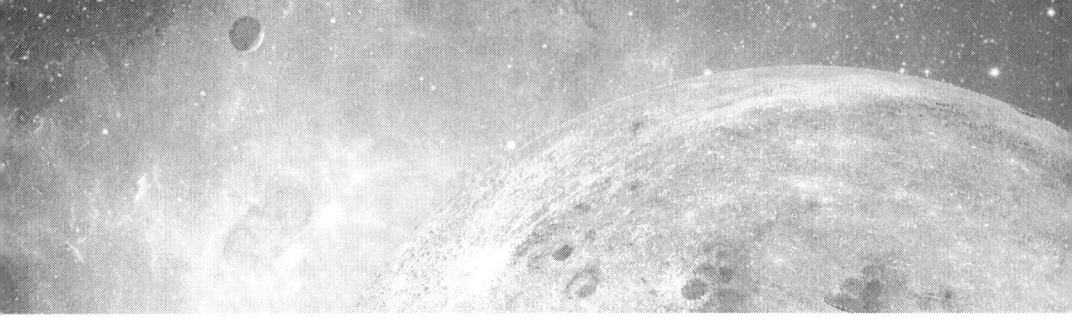

THREE

By midmorning the next day, the deal was done. Mariam informed Saoirse that the court had accepted her plea of abeyance and that the charges would be dismissed if she completed training for, and accepted a position with, the uniformed service of the Solar Council Off-Planet Personnel, the SCOPP.

Not that she was free to go, of course. The Sheriff's Department would escort her to training. Saoirse accepted the escort with a silent shrug. She had nowhere else to go. Anywhere other than jail was fine with her. She left the jail in the same T-shirt and jeans she had been wearing through most of her detention. Those were, at least, freshly laundered so the stains were less evident and the odor was gone. Apparently they were all she'd had on her when she was arrested, except for a pair of sneakers they returned to her on departure.

Their first destination was Union Station in Chicago, a sprawling edifice that had been at the hub of the city from the Second World War through the Forty Years' War. It had last been renovated in the early twenty-first century and now, in the early twenty-third, was in serious need of another face-lift. Saoirse and her escort made a dash through the maze of cranes, bots, workers, and drones to reach the maglev to Charles City, Iowa, before the doors closed. The officer who was stuck with the duty of escorting her was kind enough to buy her food once they were on the train, which she appreciated. With jail being left behind, she was rediscovering her appetite. She accepted with thanks the sandwich and soft drink and then sat silently for the ninety-minute trip.

With nothing else to do, she stared at the vid screen at the end of the car that rotated ads every fifteen seconds for products she had no money to buy. At least, it rotated ads until its system froze with one ad on display for nearly an hour. That ad showed a star field with bold white letters superimposed. The words crawled up the screen, disappeared at the top, and then started again from the bottom in an unending loop.

CAN'T GET A REAL JOB?
DON'T WANT THE JOBS THEY DON'T BOTHER MAKING BOTS FOR?
TIRED OF LIVING ON YOUR GUARANTEED BENEFIT?
GO OUT INTO THE REACH!
JOIN A PLANETARY COLONIZATION FORCE TODAY!
BE THE ALPHA YOU WERE MEANT TO BE!
HIGH FRONTIER COLONIZATION, LTD.

A comm contact scrolled continuously across the bottom of the screen. Saoirse didn't feel very alpha, but she suspected that SCOPP would send her out into the Reach.

· · ·

In what had once been a cornfield in northeastern Iowa stood Solar Council Base Dag Hammarskjöld. It was a small city more than a base, one of five, the others being in Russia, China, Kenya, and Earth Station in orbit. The people at those bases oversaw affairs across a thousand worlds and stations—give or take; the number kept increasing—none of which could be contacted in real time.

As Nicholas I, a tsar of the old Russian Empire, was reputed to have said, "Russia is not ruled by men but by my forty thousand clerks." So, too, the ever-expanding Reach was ruled not by the Solar Council and Assembly of Worlds but by their forty thousand clerks and their computers, many of whom occupied this once-forgotten niche of the American Great Plains. By treaty, the base, like its counterparts, was not national territory but the property of the Solar Council. The flag at the main gate was the sunburst on black of the SC. The Stars and Stripes was nowhere to be seen, a fact that often raised the ire of Americans posting in various online fora. Even the name of the base could be seen as a dig at its American hosts, who had never lost their disdain for the late and unlamented

United Nations even 148 years after its demise at the outbreak of the Forty Years' War. Of course, what happened on Earth was not the business of the Solar Council. Its writ might reach across half a thousand light-years, but it did not extend to Earth.

One small part of the base—a pimple on the butt, as locals referred to it—was fenced off as the training area for personnel newly recruited to the uniformed SCOPP. The buildings there were low and plain and could have been taken from a vid set for a story about the twentieth century. No paving covered the ground around those buildings—just bare dirt. Away from the buildings, grass grew out to the perimeter fences.

One of those buildings, identified by the sign HQ, was occupied by three men and one woman in a back office. Behind the desk Mohammed Desai, representative of the Solar Council, slouched in his chair, the brightly colored patterns of his shirt a glaring contrast to the US Army camouflage of the three who sat facing the desk. All three of them wore sergeant's stripes.

"Again, let me thank you in advance," Desai said, "for your effort to come in and train our new recruits. It is much appreciated."

"You should thank the US Army, not us," First Sergeant Orestes Adelayo said. "We're just following orders."

Desai waved one hand in the air, unfazed by the remark. "However you wish to view it," he said. "It is an agreement with your army, the same as we have recently established with other armies. May I assume that you have read the SC manual *On Delivery of Training*?"

"Yes, of course," Adelayo said. The other two nodded.

"Any questions?"

A brief silence followed. Then Adelayo spoke. "More of a comment than a question." Desai gestured for him to continue. "I have been a drill instructor for the US Army for five years. I know how to train soldiers. This manual," he held up a comm with the SC sunburst on the back, its screen facing Desai, "won't work. You can't build teams like this. To be a team that will function under stress, in combat, every member of that team has to value the team above their individual self. This almost does the opposite. You can't train soldiers this way, at least not ones who are any good."

"They are not soldiers," Desai said quickly, forestalling whatever else Adelayo had been about to say. "They are recruits for the Solar Council

Off-Planet Personnel, the uniformed SCOPP, and most of them will serve unarmed, as privates and specialists in administrative roles. Therefore, the SC has determined that their training is to be conducted in a civilized manner. They are guaranteed downtime each day for relaxation or activities they choose. Their individuality is to be respected. None of the *this recruit* third person you use in your army. They may refer to themselves as *I* and have their choice of pronouns." Desai paused to clear his throat and looked from one hard face to another. "It does bring me to a request," he said. "By our agreement with your army, the recruits are not permitted to have any personal communication or computation device—that is, their comms. Young people find it difficult to do without their comms. Frankly, I think that has been true for every generation back to when comms were called phones, wherever that word came from." He gave a little chuckle but did not see a positive response. "Anyway, would you consider allowing them their comms during the unstructured-activity part of the day, after dinner? I cannot insist, so I am asking."

Adelayo fixed him with a cold stare and said, "No." Silence stretched out for a minute before Adelayo spoke again. "That is a civilian mentality. We know that many of these youths, these *children*, would sooner part with the hand holding the comm than the comm itself. We have even heard that some in this generation have openly wished for the days of a century and more ago, when these devices, the *chips*, could be implanted. Civilians!" His voice rose sharply as though he was giving a speech. "They have forgotten all about what happens when someone else has control of an implanted chip. We soldiers, on the other hand, do not forget. *We* remember the soldiers *compelled* to make suicide missions, *compelled* to defend a useless position to the last man, *compelled* to commit atrocities. We remember the Seattle War Crimes Trials at the end of the Forty Years' War, when having an implant was no better defense than following orders had been at Nuremberg. No government today would survive its own soldiers if it didn't follow anti-cyborg and anti-AI laws. No electronic device is legal unless a person can put it down, turn it off, and leave it away from themselves. These recruits need to learn to cope without electronics."

Desai was flustered; his hands moved purposelessly across the desk as though straightening something on its clear surface. "I would never consider violating those laws," he said. "I was only talking about comms, they are compliant, and only for a part of the day."

"Mx. Desai," Adelayo said, "if you don't want us to train the way we know how to train, why bring us in at all? Why don't you hire a bunch of elementary school teachers who will teach them how to add when they don't have a comm, and call it done?"

"Because they may be posted anywhere in the Reach, and the Reach continues to expand. There are worlds where we see armed conflict—thanks to your army and others—worlds with dangerous predators, and worlds where social breakdown exists. Even schoolteachers and clerks need to be in good physical condition and able to shoot a rifle. And some of these recruits may be selected for an additional ten weeks' training for the Off-Earth Armed Peacemaker units."

"Peacers," said Adelayo. "We know them. Some of their units know how to fight, although my understanding is that those are units raised mostly out in the Reach."

"Some of their troops are from Earth," Desai replied, "as are many of the officers. We concluded two years ago that the recruits from Earth, specifically, are in need of more rigorous training, especially physical training. Hence our agreement with your army. And so, Sergeants, we expect and appreciate your best effort. Your captain, who will arrive in a few hours, has been briefed in detail and understands completely."

．　．　．

The bus from the maglev station had pulled into Hammarskjöld and discharged its passengers onto the packed earth in front of the HQ building by the time Adelayo and the other two sergeants came out the front door. Fifty young men and women stood, singly or in clumps, uncertain what to do next. Nearby, identical duffel bags, also fifty in number, sat on the ground in a square-bottomed U. Adelayo had supervised their placement before he went into the HQ building for the conference with Desai. It took only a simple order, although more time than Adelayo would have liked, for each recruit to find the duffel with their name on it and stand next to it. That put them into a rough formation, the men on one side and the bottom of the U, the four women on the other side.

Adelayo stepped to the open top of the U. "I want to hear your names," he said. "Shout them out so everyone hears. Starting with you." He pointed at the nearest man. Adelayo had memorized the pictures and thumbnail bios of all of them. He did not need to check his comm as they spoke.

He took them in at a glance as they called out their names, more mumbles than proud shouts. All of them ill at ease, all unimpressive. The men were a mixture of browns and whites; more browns, but that was typical of army recruits as well. Most of them looked soft and pudgy, whatever their color. Baby fat. Wannabe gamers, not good enough to support themselves, not satisfied to exist on their Guaranteed Benefit, or maybe useless extra mouths their parents had finally kicked out. A few looked lean and hard. Street criminals. Of the four women, three were brown and one was so pale it was hard to say she had enough color even to be called white. That one wore an insolent smirk. Trouble for sure.

The first of the women was Alexandria Lopez, the second Ruby Jones. Their bios included a history of prostitution. Adelayo stopped the roll call to deliver a warning. If he found any business being conducted, they would be gone faster than the speed of light. Jones looked down when he said it; Lopez was stone-faced, hard-eyed hatred looking back at him. Augusta Gray was the next woman, almost as dark as he was, her black hair buzzed close to her scalp. He stopped the roll call again.

"New Anabaptist," he said. "Answer me now: Will you train with weapons? If you are assigned to an armed unit, will you carry a weapon and use it? If you say no now, you may leave without prejudice. If you refuse later, discipline may be severe, depending on the circumstances."

"I'm fine with weapons," Gray said.

Her eyes were straight ahead. Did he believe her? If she was lying, it would be her problem. The last one was Saoirse Kenneally, a drunk and an addict. That was trouble to start with. Her bio had the notation "plea deal." That was trouble for sure, trouble Adelayo did not want in his training company, trouble the army would never have put up with.

"There is no alcohol and no drugs here," Adelayo said. "Use either and go straight to jail." He neither asked nor waited for an answer.

Kenneally swayed as if the force of his words was enough to make her fall over, but the goddamn smirk was still there. He would have to deal with that. What quirk of fate had stuck him with this ersatz military and these ersatz soldiers?

"I am First Sergeant Orestes Adelayo, US Army," he said in a voice that boomed out across the men and women in front of him. He put extra emphasis on the *US Army* at the end of the sentence. "I have been ordered here by the US Army," again the emphasis, "to be the senior drill instructor for the 5233rd Training Company of the uniformed Solar Council Off-Planet Personnel. That is you. Assisting me will be Sergeants Jennifer McDonough and Calvin Jackson, also US Army."

Adelayo looked around the U, letting his eyes rest for a few seconds on each man or woman in the formation. He could not believe that the Solar Council expected disciplined and competent teams to emerge from this bastardized training approach, or that the army had ordered him to do this. However, orders were orders.

"I am going to instruct you now in how we will address each other," he said. "You have all been taught since childhood to call any adult Mx., a gender-neutral honorific. That is a civilian mentality and it will not do here. Now, this is not the US Army and do not think for one second that this is the US Army, or that you are soldiers. But you are no longer civilians and you will address everyone with appropriate respect. I am First Sergeant Orestes Adelayo and you will address me as First Sergeant, which is the rank I have *earned*. You will address any officer as *sir*. That is the term of respect for officer rank and is not to be confused with any specific gender by either biology or preference. *You*," he paused, "until graduation will be called Recruit and referred to, to the extent possible and consistent with your training . . . by your preferred pronouns." He wanted to spit that last phrase out onto the ground and grind it under his boot. "Are there any questions?"

Most of them were silent. A few mumbled responses could be heard at various places in the U.

"The answer to that question is 'No, First Sergeant,' if there are no questions. Now, are there any questions?"

The response was correct in form, if lacking in volume. He proceeded to give them a brief lecture on what would be expected of them: the behavior that would be demanded, when to salute and when to say *sir*. Then he went on to read them their rights, as the saying went: what their protections were, what *they* could demand. He would have done the same for recruits to his beloved US Army, but it would have been a different and shorter list. Here, he was guaranteeing their free time and their individuality, down to pronouns and how they wore their hair. Well, hair was "within reason." That red-and-black mess on the girl with the smirk was not within reason. That was coming off.

He wanted to shake his head while he spoke. The whole point of basic training, beyond the physical conditioning and learning the skills a soldier had to have, was to *get rid of* the individuality. That was the only way soldiers would be part of a team and put the team first. That was what he had tried to tell Desai in the office. That was the difference between success and failure on the battlefield. Adelayo had been in combat. He knew.

"You are not soldiers," he said, "not now, and not when you finish this training, if you do. You are scopps. But we will do our best. Now, you are not permitted any personal communications or computing device while you are in this program. Sergeant McDonough is going to walk along your line now with the comm box. You will put your comm in the box. At the time you leave, whether you withdraw, are dismissed, or graduate, your comm will be returned to you."

He watched the recruits struggle with that simple act as McDonough walked along the U. Adelayo had turned thirty only recently, but he scoffed mentally at these children who could not separate from their comms. His musing came to a halt when McDonough and her box came to a stop in front of the girl with the smirk. She stood still, her hands jammed into the pockets of jeans that looked ready to fall off her.

"Let's go, Recruit," McDonough said. "Your comm has to go into the box."

"I don't have one," the girl said finally.

"That's, 'I don't have one, Sergeant,'" McDonough snapped, "and what do you mean you don't have one?"

"I don't have a comm, Sergeant." She looked off into the distance. "Stolen, maybe. Lost it, maybe. Maybe, I sold it . . . sir."

"Get your hands out of your pockets!"

The hands came out. Empty.

"All right, Recruit," McDonough said. "You don't have a comm. Just remember. If it turns out you do have one, it's immediate dismissal. Understood?"

"Yes, sir," the girl said.

Adelayo did not care if he believed her. He did not like the smirk on her face. That would be for later. He got back to business. "Your uniforms, boots, and gear are in those duffels. You have thirty seconds to change. Here and now. Anybody not changed in thirty seconds will do push-ups."

That set off a scramble by the recruits to rip open the duffels and start changing. A few stared at Adelayo. That lasted until he ostentatiously tapped his wristband and stared at it. At the end of the thirty seconds, only the girl with the smirk was not changed. One of her boots lay on the ground. The other was still in the duffel. Her shirt hung out. Her gear belt was on but not buckled. At least the smirk was gone.

"Push-ups, Kenneally," Adelayo said. "Thirty. Now."

Saoirse Kenneally went down to the ground, hands wide, knees on the dirt.

"No!" Adelayo barked. "Hands next to your sides at the bottom of your sternum. Knees off the ground. Back straight. We don't do girl push-ups. Not even scopps do girl push-ups."

Saoirse struggled to do five, shoulders rising first and hips lifting only later. Then she dropped to the ground facedown. "I can't do any more," she said.

"You can do them and you will do them," Adelayo said in reply. Part of him hoped that she would stand up and tell him to fuck off. That would be adequate reason to dismiss her. She did not do that. She lay on the ground and started to cry.

"Sergeant McDonough," Adelayo said. "Line up the company behind you and take them on a run. Around the perimeter." He indicated the fence in the distance. "Keep them running until Kenneally gets her thirty done properly."

FOUR

The rest of the first day was spent on drill, marching, running, exercises, and what seemed like a hard drive's worth of facts to be committed to memory and spouted back on command. Lunch was vacuumed down between physical conditioning periods, with the only concession to digestion being a thirty-minute quiz on facts they had been given in the morning. Dinner vanished from trays at the same rate. After dinner was their mandated free time, but by the time it arrived, no one wanted to do anything except go to the barracks.

The training facility had separate barracks for women and men. They were identical long, narrow single-story structures of poured concrete with a door—an old-fashioned pull-the-knob swinging door—at each end. The women's barracks was painted stark white on the outside. As soon as the four women went through the door, they could see it was the same color on the inside. A line of fifteen metal beds with thin mattresses ran along each wall, under three windows set at identical intervals. In front of the far door, a room was built out from one wall and labeled BATHROOM. There were no visible electrical outlets, no charging discs, no device ports, no screens. The building had, in fact, nothing to suggest that it belonged in the twenty-third century instead of the twentieth, if not the nineteenth. The only remotely modern item was the light strip that ran the length of the peaked roof. The room's emptiness was accentuated by the echoes of their footfalls on the concrete floor.

The door closed behind them, and for the first time since the bus from the station had let them off, no sergeant was on top of them. Lopez glanced at the door, then rounded on Kenneally. "Motherfuckin' asshole," she snarled. "Think you're so goddamn smart, or do you just like to see the rest of us run? I bet that asshole Adelayo added extra to everything because of you." She shoved Saoirse's shoulder.

Saoirse was past tired. She didn't think. Emotion boiled. "Fuck you!" she screamed back. "You think I knew what he was going to do?"

"Don't care what you thought, bitch!"

Lopez followed the words with a left jab that caught Saoirse on the cheek. Her head snapped back from the impact, and any control she might have had vanished. She let out a wordless yell and lunged forward, her right fist coming around in a wild haymaker punch. Lopez blocked it and laughed. She stepped in close to Saoirse and shoved her backward with both hands. Saoirse fell against Jones, and the next thing she knew, her arms were pinned behind her back.

"Now we're gonna watch you suck for some air!" Lopez yelled. She stepped close and drove a right uppercut into Saoirse's gut, then a left-handed one just below the short ribs.

Saoirse had no air, couldn't breathe, thought she was going to retch.

"Goddamn it! All of you! Enough already!" Gray forced herself between Lopez and Saoirse and pushed Lopez back toward the door.

At that moment, the door crashed open, smashing against the wall, and a voice roared, "What is going on in here?" First Sergeant Adelayo stood in the doorway, hands on hips, eyes narrowed, and a portent of more thunder on his face.

The instant she saw him, Jones let go of Saoirse. Saoirse dropped to the floor on her hands and knees, gasping for breath. None of the other three said a word.

"I'll ask the question one more time," Adelayo said, "and if you want to fight in your free time, we'll set up a ring outside and spend the evening working on those drills. Now, what is going on?"

Saoirse found enough breath to speak. "Nothing really, First Sergeant," she said from the floor. "I was ... tired. I fell onto a bedframe. Knocked the breath out of me. Recruit Jones was just holding me up." She got one foot under her, put her hands on the knee, and pushed herself upright.

Adelayo crossed the space between them and peered at her face. "And what is that?" He pointed at the reddish blotch that had blossomed on Saoirse's cheek. "Bad makeup?"

"No, First Sergeant." Saoirse licked her lips. "I walked into the door when we came into the barracks. That's why I fell onto the bedframe. Like I said before, Recruit Jones was only holding me up."

The expression on Adelayo's face said without words that he doubted the veracity of Saoirse's story. "Is that what happened?" Adelayo's stare fixed on each one of them in turn. "Recruit Kenneally is clumsy. Is that the answer?"

"Yes, First Sergeant," Saoirse said. "That's all that happened."

The other three stayed silent.

"I see," said Adelayo. "Then all of you had better make sure there is no further clumsiness from Recruit Kenneally. Or we will find a way to work on your coordination. All of you. Is that clear?"

"Yes, First Sergeant," said four voices together.

None of them moved or spoke until Adelayo was out the door and it had closed behind him.

"Idiot," Gray whispered to Lopez. "You want to get yourself jailed or thrown out of SCOPP, I don't care, but you don't take me with you. I can't go back where I came from. No way."

"Fine," Lopez ground out. "If any of us wanted to be where we came from, we wouldn't be here. And what do we do with her?" She pointed at Saoirse.

"Nothing," Gray said. "Didn't you hear what Adelayo said? He's made us all responsible for her. Anyway, she didn't say anything. She could have." She turned to Saoirse. "Why didn't you?"

"'Cause I'd beat the shit out of her after," Lopez broke in.

"I've had the shit beaten out of me by people a lot tougher than you," Saoirse said. "You got shit." She made a point of turning her back on Lopez. "The answer to you, Gray, is that I don't snitch."

Fine words, Saoirse, she told herself. Not true, of course. *If Adelayo had thought to offer you a drink or a high, you'd have sold out Lopez and Jones and Gray and Donal, too, in no more time than it would have taken you to open your mouth.* That was the truth. She hated herself.

"Look," Saoirse added, "that crap before, with the push-ups and shit. That won't happen again."

· · ·

Of the thirty available beds, Lopez and Jones took the two nearest the front door, Gray the one next to Jones. Saoirse retreated to the far end and took the bed next to the bathroom. That was fine. She didn't fit in with the other three in the same way she never fit in anywhere. That is, she never fit in unless she was drinking.

The arrangement lasted until Adelayo arrived with McDonough for morning inspection. The four of them were a team, he told them. There was no room for people who wanted to be individuals. Those who wanted to be individuals should pack and leave. He was looking at Saoirse as he spoke. She knew leaving was not an option, not really, so she moved her gear to the bed across from Gray. Then the four of them stood at attention in front of their beds while McDonough found all manner of deficiencies in their dress, the state of their beds, and the organization of their gear.

Saoirse kept her face clamped into immobility, her eyes fixed on a spot behind Gray's head. She moved only to correct the errors McDonough pointed out, although her heart and stomach sank through the floor as she did. She was sure that McDonough found more wrong with her than with any of the others. She tried to keep count, but lost track quickly because each mistake needed an immediate correction. They were singling her out. She knew it. She didn't fit, wouldn't fit—and they knew it. They would throw her out. She didn't care about being thrown out, but she did care about going to jail. She didn't want to go to jail.

Even Adelayo and McDonough had limits to the items they could find that needed fixing, but that did not mean they were done with Saoirse. They ordered all four of the women outside and announced that it was time for Saoirse to demonstrate that she had learned how to do push-ups. Fifty of them. Hands close by her sides, at the level of the bottom of her sternum. Back ramrod straight as she lifted. Incorrect ones had to be repeated. By the time she reached thirty, the muscles that held her shoulders to her chest felt as if they were ripping apart. She looked up, saw Lopez smiling. That stoked the anger inside. She no longer cared if the muscles did tear apart. She kept lifting. Sit-ups followed the push-ups. Those also had to be done properly, exactly as they had been demonstrated, while

McDonough timed her. Then it was time for jumping jacks, to be sure that her arms and back hadn't stiffened, as Adelayo said. When she finished, it was back to attention, fighting to keep the trembling in her muscles from showing.

Saoirse hoped that the morning torture would be followed, at least, by breakfast, but that was not next on Adelayo's agenda. He had them march to the firing range to join the men and Sergeant Jackson. There they sat on ground still wet with overnight dew while Jackson reached into a truck parked nearby. He pulled out a rifle and handed it to Adelayo.

The rifle was a monotone in metal and plastic, more black than gray. In Adelayo's hands, even with the barrel pointing at the ground, it exuded menace and danger. Saoirse had seen real firearms before, once too close for comfort, but those had all been handguns. By comparison, this was vicious, a beast. Fascinated, she stared at it.

"The musket," Adelayo was saying, "was introduced in Europe in 1521 and is the ancestor of all modern firearms. The US Army began using the M16 in 1964, in the fighting in Vietnam. You will memorize these facts the same way you will memorize all the information I am about to give you, because when the enemy is shooting at you, there is no time to look up the answer on the children's toy you call a comm. Is that clear?"

A chorus of "Yes, First Sergeant" followed.

"Good," he said. "This," he gestured with the rifle, barrel still pointed at the ground, "is the MK32, direct descendant of the M16, and it is the standard rifle in use by the US Army and all English-speaking peacer units in the Reach. It fires a 5.2 millimeter bullet from a one-hundred-round magazine at a rate of two thousand rounds per minute with a muzzle velocity of three thousand two hundred feet per second. In the hands of an expert marksman, it will kill an unprotected target at two thousand yards and a target in body armor at four hundred." He paused and glared at the SCOPP recruits. "Now, can anyone tell me why, in the Year of Our Lord 2232, we are firing bullets from rifles to kill our enemies?"

No one spoke. No one even stirred.

"Because," Adelayo intoned, and his voice became very loud in the stillness even without shouting, "for all our fancy tech and lasers and plasma jets and sonics and nerve tanglers, there are ways to defeat all of them. The fastest, most reliable, most efficient, hardest to defeat, and cheapest way to kill another human being is with a bullet propelled by exploding gunpowder. And make no mistake: we kill other human beings, and you will learn to do this. Today you will be taught how to disassemble, clean, and reassemble your weapon so that it will function properly when you need it, because a clean weapon is the difference between a live soldier and a dead one." He paused. His glare returned. "You can be sure it is the difference between a live scopp and a dead scopp as well."

Adelayo proceeded to take one of the rifles apart in front of them, naming each part and giving its purpose. Then he cleaned the weapon meticulously and put it back together.

Saoirse watched intently. The MK32 was a puzzle. Take it apart and put it together. She liked puzzles, and she was very good at that kind of puzzle. She decided she was going to be perfect with this.

They spent hours with the rifle, each recruit taking one from the truck to be their own, repeating back the facts about it, learning how to carry it—never point it at anything you do not plan to shoot—and how to present it. They disassembled their rifles, cleaned them, and reassembled them, trying to do it exactly as Adelayo had. If Saoirse wasn't perfect at the routine by the time they were done, she was close. She picked up speed with repetition, fast enough that Adelayo timed her at the end of the session. A minute and a half.

"Almost good enough," Adelayo said.

Then it was time to shoot. They would each fire ten rounds at a simple bull's-eye target at a range of fifty yards. In the future, they would train and be tested on pop-up and moving targets that resembled soldiers with twenty-five rounds a test, but this was an introduction.

Saoirse liked the feel of the rifle as she leveled it and sighted the target. She was grateful that her hands were steady. It had been enough days since she had anything to drink, and she had eaten enough meals. She was not going to shake. The target sat at the end of her sight.

Slow breath. Gentle pull on the trigger. The first round blasted out of the rifle with a satisfying bang. Her shoulder felt only a minimal kick, not enough to spoil her aim. She fired her ten rounds quickly and wished she had more. The target bot whirred and rolled up to her firing position so she, and everyone else, could see the results. Six holes were clustered tightly and overlapped in the small bull's-eye at the center. The other four bullets had hit the target; they were scattered within the concentric circles around the bull's-eye. Saoirse's heart sank. She needed to be perfect. She hated herself.

Adelayo removed the target from the post on the bot. He stared at the bull's-eye, then looked at Saoirse. "Good shooting, Recruit Kenneally," he said.

· · ·

Shooting was followed by more drill, classroom work, and physical training. By the time dinner was over and free time arrived, all they wanted to do was drop on their beds in the barracks, even before the lights went out. Saoirse hoped that with the long day and the fatigue, the others would ignore her.

"Fuck it, Kenneally," Lopez said, spoiling that hope. "Where did you learn to shoot like that?"

"Never learned," Saoirse said. "That was my first time."

"Shit." That word came in triplicate.

"It wasn't that good," Saoirse said. "I missed the center with four shots."

"The other six were in the goddamn bull's-eye," Lopez said. "Nobody else shot anything close to that, even that lyin' son of a bitch from Minnesota who said he used to hunt. You saw Adelayo look at it."

"That doesn't mean anything," Saoirse said.

"Sure as shit does," Jones put in. "They'll send you to peacers for sure."

"Yeah, that will be perfect." Lopez gave a nasty laugh. "They'll ship Kenneally to some mudball where they haven't worked out distilling alcohol yet. That work for you, Kenneally?"

Saoirse pulled her pillow over her head and rolled to face away from the other three.

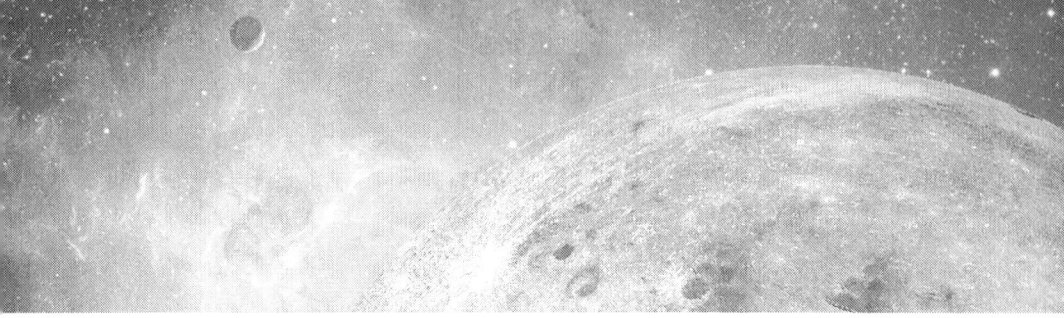

FIVE

The rifle became Saoirse's project. If she concentrated on the rifle, she didn't need to think about the other women, or the men, or everything she didn't do right. At night, when the lights were out and the barracks was dark, she took the rifle into her bed and practiced taking it apart and putting it together. She decided that even the minimal amount of light in the barracks was too much, so she practiced with the rifle under the blanket, forcing herself to do it only by feel. She ignored the snickering from the others, Lopez in particular, and the remarks about knowing where she was sticking the barrel and what she was doing with it. She would have moved her bunk back down to the other end of the barracks, but if she did that, Adelayo would scream at her again, so she concentrated on blocking out the comments. She demanded that she do the disassembly, clean, and reassembly three times perfectly before she allowed herself to go to sleep. Any mistake and she had to do all three times over again.

She took the same approach with shooting. When they had their free time after dinner, she went to the rifle range, begging every extra round she could get from whichever sergeant she could find. She used the pop-up and moving targets, and her goal was for every round to hit a kill spot on the target. As she improved, her goal was to pick a kill spot in advance, and every round had to hit the spot she had picked. Every round had to be perfect or she would chastise herself, because only perfection counted.

She could hear her father in her mind, teaching her about computers—how to code, how to dissect a system. A computer is literal, he would say. It does what you program it to do. If there is a mistake in the program, the computer will not work properly. Only perfection counts. Maybe her father hadn't actually said that. Maybe she only imagined he'd said that. Maybe she had told it to herself, and it was easier to blame him. It didn't matter. Like the computer, she had decided to learn the rifle, and perfect was the only satisfactory score. Sometimes she wished she could hide from herself.

The physical demands of the first two weeks left little energy in the evening, and little thought of anything but sleep once they reached the barracks. They were all young, however, and with the combination of hard physical training and plenty of food, youthful bodies toughened quickly. They still had to be in their bunks at lights out and the lights still went out, but talk replaced snores. Among the women, one focus was the men and their attributes, both real and imagined. But when the topic got away from the men, it usually drifted to what they were going to do when they graduated from training.

Saoirse's riflery and the likelihood of her ending up a peacer, with any one of a number of dismal and gory endings, was a favorite with Lopez and Jones. Her studied silence did nothing to discourage them.

"Actually, you're both full of shit," Gray said one night, breaking into the dialogue. "I'd take the peacers; I want the peacers. I just don't know that I can get it."

"Oho!" Lopez hooted. "Now it's little Augusta Gray who wants to be a peacer. Not happening. The only safe place when you're shooting is the target."

"Fuck you," said Gray. "Damn little justice on Earth and probably less in the Reach. Maybe the peacers can make it right sometimes."

"You think that, Gray?" Lopez said. "More likely you'll just be guarding another set of bosses and putting down riots by the people they're bossing."

"I'll take my chances on that," Gray said.

"Then you're a fool," Lopez said. "I've said it before and I'm saying it again. All being a peacer gets you is being shipped to some fucked-up planet where the colony's messed up and you spend your time running from hut to hut, trying to stop them shooting each other, and all that will get you is that they'll shoot *you* in the back and leave you in the mud. Or maybe they sent settlers some place without really knowing what lives there, and it will eat you. Or poison you. That what you want, *chica*?"

"Plenty of civilized colonies now," Gray retorted. "Towns, cities, hell of a lot better than here."

"Oh yeah, right," Lopez said. "Nice, peaceful places don't need peacers. Oh no. They'll send you where there are national armies and you're in the middle, the fuckin' meat in the sandwich. Whether it's Americans and Chinese or Indians and Pakis, they're gonna go through you to get at each other. You want to face Adelayo and his buddies for real? That's bullshit, Gray."

"Actually," Jones put in, "Gray just wants to be a peacer so she can carry a gun and blow the balls off a guy who won't pay up."

"Fuck you," said Gray. "The whole universe isn't like goddamn here. What do you think you're gonna do, Lopez? Live the high life at SC HQ?"

"Damn straight," said Lopez. "I'll be admin for Solar Council at Earth Station. All the comforts of Earth and none of the crap about your Benefit getting suspended. Leave on Earth for shopping, and credit in my account. I'll probably process your death certificate, Gray."

"Bullshit," Gray replied. "You think Earth Station is all fun and games; it's not. Twist your head off trying to watch your back."

"I know what goes on," Lopez said. "I'm goin' in with my eyes wide open."

"With your legs wide open, you mean," Gray said.

Lopez chuckled, but it was a nasty sound. "Ya gotta do what ya gotta do to get what you need, *chica*." She raised her voice a little. "Ain't that right, Kenneally? She ought to be able to tell us all about getting what she *needs*."

Saoirse stuffed a corner of her pillow in her mouth to keep from screaming out what she thought Lopez should do and what she should do it with.

Lopez wasn't ready to let go of the conversation, though. "Kenneally is at least smart enough not to want to be a peacer, but Gray's going to do it. Gray's going to win that big peacer medal. The PLM. Right?"

"What's that stand for?" Jones asked.

"It's French," Lopez said. "Hey, Kenneally, you know any French? Learn any in that high school you went to? Did you finish high school? Do you remember finishing high school?"

Saoirse said nothing, pretended she wasn't there.

"Well, do you know what it stands for?" Gray demanded.

Lopez laughed. "I don't know. Maybe *Pour la Madame*. Right, Gray?"

"So, Gray," Jones said, "you know the difference between a peacer with the PLM and a corpse in the morgue?"

"I'm sure you're going to tell us."

"One is a dead body. The other is a dead body with a pretty medal."

"Why don't you both get fucked raw," Gray said.

. . .

The next day, Gray stopped Saoirse as they were leaving dinner.

"Kenneally, you got a minute?"

Saoirse stopped, waited but said nothing.

"Listen, are you going to ask for extra time again on the firing range?"

Saoirse nodded, still without a word.

Gray stuffed her hands in her pockets and managed to look everywhere except at Saoirse. "Listen, if I ask for time also, will you help me with the gun, with shooting? I see what you do on the range. Lopez and Jones may be cunts, but they're right about my shooting. I know I have to meet standards to make the peacers. Will you help me?"

Saoirse stood there, waited until Gray finally looked at her. "Yeah. I'll help you."

"Thank you. What do you want for it?"

Saoirse hesitated. There was a lot she wanted. "I don't want to hear about what I do or what I've done."

"That's it?"

She was quiet for a moment. "Nothing else."

Gray gave her a sharp look, then put out her hand. "Okay, then. We've all done crap we're not proud of and don't need to hear about. Call me Gusty, though."

They shook on it.

After the third day of their evening target practice, Saoirse and Gusty sat down on the ground by the firing line, their rifles on the ground in front of them. Every round they had been able to get for the evening had been fired, but neither of them was ready to go back to the barracks. Gusty was improving. Most of her shots hit the target now, even if it was the stationary bull's-eye target and not the pop-up moving ones.

"You're getting better," Saoirse said. "By the time you have to pass the checks at the end, you'll be okay."

"Thanks." Gusty had her arms on her knees and was staring at the ground between her boots. "I didn't realize how long this was going to take. Or how tiring it would be."

"It doesn't make me tired." Saoirse thought about how she felt when she raised the loaded rifle to aim at a target. It was as though all the rest of the world disappeared except for the target. Sounds vanished too. Nothing existed except the target and the crack of the rifle. "I wish we could shoot more."

"Why? I mean, God knows, I need the practice, but you're damned near perfect."

"Damned near perfect isn't perfect," Saoirse said.

Gusty raised her head. "Why do you have to be perfect?"

"I just need to," Saoirse said. The words sounded odd in her ears, so, reluctantly, she told Gusty about how it felt to have the world vanish when she was firing, how wonderful it was to see and hear nothing else.

"That's a little strange," Gusty said.

Saoirse tossed a rock. Sure, she was strange. "It's not as strange as being a New Anabaptist. Are you really a New Anabaptist?"

"Was."

"And they're really pacifists? No guns, won't fight? Won't participate in government, hate computer networks, don't drink, don't smoke?"

"Yeah, that's us."

Saoirse shook her head. "Never met one," she said. "Certainly wouldn't expect to meet one here."

"Well, you still haven't, 'cause I quit. Or got thrown out. That's why Adelayo made such an issue that first day. Would I use a weapon; will I follow orders? I will, but *they've* got to believe it. That's why I wish I was as good as you with that." She pointed at the rifle. "It's twice as hard for me to make the peacers."

"You'll get good enough," Saoirse said. "How many New Anabaptists are there? Like I said, I've never met one and I've, well, lived around."

"Not many today," Gusty said, "not for decades. Used to be a lot, though. It was very popular back toward the end of the wars. People were scared shitless of cyborgs and AI and all the fighting. Jarrett Minor was head of the church then. He used to preach all the time about the evils of cyborgs, AI, and war. That's why people joined. But they banned all that electronic crap and we've had peace on Earth for a century, so who wants to put up with such a strict church? My parents, I guess. I couldn't stand it and they couldn't stand me."

"I can relate to that," Saoirse said.

Gusty waited for a moment, then looked over at Saoirse. "I know what I promised, but I just told you about me, so can I ask?" Saoirse gave a minimal nod. "Is what they say true? That you're a drunk and a druggie who came here 'cause you made a deal with the court? We heard Adelayo on day one—and you hear it all around, not just Lopez and Jones."

"True," Saoirse said, and stopped. She looked over and saw Gusty studying her. She didn't want Gusty to get up and walk away. "Look," she said, "this was the best I could do."

"So, that's the plan?" Gusty asked. "I come here and stop being a New Anabaptist and you come here and stop being an alcoholic?"

Saoirse shook her head. "It's not like that, Gusty. It doesn't work like that. I can stop drinking and using. Yes. I could stop for ten years and go to a meeting every day and do all the shit I'm supposed to do—but after all of that, all I'd need to do is have a drink and I'm right back where I was. I can't change what I am. It's not like they can rewire my brain so I'm not an alcoholic anymore. We used to be able to do things like that, back before the wars, but not now. I guess that's some of what your Jarrett Minor preached against that's gone now."

Gusty shivered. "Oh my God, brain hacks. That's what you're talking about. Brain hacks. Be glad those are gone and all the cyborg crap is illegal, so they can't put a chip in and take over your mind."

"I don't know, Gusty," Saoirse said. "Sometimes I do wish they could put in a chip so I could stop being me. I hate being me."

Gusty spat on the ground between her boots. "Oh, are we going to have a pity party now?"

"Fuck you. That's how I feel."

"Really?" Gusty put a hand on Saoirse's arm. "Let *me* tell *you* something. Maybe you can't stop being an alcoholic and a druggie, but there is something you can stop. Completely under your control."

"Yeah? What?"

"You can stop acting like an ass."

"What the fuck are you saying?" Saoirse felt her anger flare. "You're saying I'm an ass?" She tried to stand up, but Gusty had an iron grip on her arm.

"No. I said you act like one. And it's only my strong religious upbringing that stops me from using more descriptive words. I didn't say you *are* one—I don't think you are—but you act like one a lot of the time. You come on like you're smarter than everyone, better than everyone; you've always got that little smirk on your face like you know better about everything. It's not just Lopez and Jones. You do it with me. You do it with the sergeants, and that's not smart. Why do you need to do that?"

Saoirse's first impulse was to tell Gusty to fuck herself, break free of Gusty's grip, and walk off. But she didn't. Finally she said, "Maybe it's because I feel the exact opposite. Ever think of that?"

"No," Gusty said. "I didn't."

Neither spoke for a few minutes.

"I'm sorry I upset you," Gusty said. "I didn't mean to. I want to like you."

"It's okay," Saoirse said, surprised she was still sitting there to say it. "Maybe I needed a kick in the ass. I don't know. No promises, but I'll work on it." She held out a hand. "Friends?"

They helped each other up and headed back to the barracks.

SIX

Saoirse had told Gusty she would work on it, and she meant it. However, it seemed that there was always one thing or another that rubbed people the wrong way. Most of the time, Saoirse couldn't see how she could be blamed for acting the way she did. For example, the ropes course. She'd always been athletic, even as a young child, and her strength had increased rapidly with all the conditioning work. So what did the men expect her to do on the timed runs up and around the ropes? Deliberately slow down, or fall into the mud under the ropes? And there had been a mistake in one of the sims, in the programming. How could she not point that out? And the stupid artillery problem they had been given about how the World War I German army had fired long-range artillery at Paris and had to correct their aim to keep the shells from falling a mile west of the city? Obviously, the earth rotated and the correction for that was straightforward, not something that needed a computer or a comm. Hell, the Germans had worked it out in 1918 without any computers. Was it her fault she could solve it in her head when the numbers were all laid out?

But Gusty's face would get that look that said, *You've done it again.* No one but Gusty liked her at all. Nothing new about that, she told herself. The thought would pop into her head, randomly it seemed, that if she could have a drink, she could fix that, but that wasn't happening at Camp Hammarskjöld.

She was brooding about the unfairness of life at dinner after the artillery problem. It was the end of the fifth week of training, the halfway point. The 5233rd Training Company was a substantially shrunken group from the one that had started, more the size of a platoon at that point. They occupied only two of the long tables in the dining hall, instead of four.

"You would think," said DeShawn Abbott, "that we would have something special to mark the halfway point. Something with a little seasoning." The food they were eating was no different than it had been: nutritious, high in protein, and completely tasteless.

Saoirse sat across from him. Abbott was tall, six foot three, and lean. She had noted his muscle definition even at the beginning of training; he had stood out among the ill-defined blobs that constituted most of the men. Those muscles made him look tough, and he looked even tougher after five weeks of hard physical work. His close-cropped hair was black like hers, in his case only a little darker than his skin. She thought his eyes and his face were kind, although he had boasted about running with a gang and having been arrested. Saoirse was sure she had been arrested more often, but she wasn't going to bring that up.

She was sure that Gusty was looking at him, too, and unlike her, Gusty was not the wrong skin color—but that didn't stop her from daydreaming. If nothing else, she was taller than Gusty. That might matter, she thought.

"Pizza would be good, don't you think?" Saoirse said. As soon as she said it, she looked around as if someone else had said it. She had been *thinking* it.

"Pizza, is it?" Abbott gave her a broad smile.

Saoirse liked his smile.

"That's a good idea, Kenneally," he added, "but how do you suppose we are going to get it? I can't see asking Adelayo to put in an order."

"I can get it for us," she said.

Oh my God! Did you actually say that? You must have; everyone is looking at you. Stupid, stupid, stupid. Like usual.

Saoirse heard the little voice inside, what she thought of as "inner Saoirse" and what her mother had termed her excuse for a conscience. It would always chastise her, point out her failings, and remind her of the consequences of what she had done. She hated it and often told it to shut up—mentally, at least—but it was always there and she could never manage to ignore it.

"You're full of shit, Kenneally," said Lou DeSantis, one of the other men. "You always show off, but this is pure bullshit." DeSantis had hated it when she beat him on the ropes course.

Saoirse felt her stomach sink to the floor. All the stares made her anxious. She didn't want to feel any of it. Too late now.

"After dinner is free time," she said. "Get me into the computer building where we do sims and practice the admin shit. I'll set it up." She was making it up as fast as she was saying it. Nothing unusual about that, but how the fuck was she going to do it? They would all laugh at her. Worse than usual.

Lopez was sitting at the end of the other table, but she had been listening to the conversation. Now she came over to stand behind Abbott, staring at Saoirse over his head.

"Get into the computer building, Kenneally?" DeSantis sneered. "It's not exactly locked. But those comms only connect to the base system. Remember they told us we were welcome to try? Although I'd like to see what Adelayo comes up with for you when he catches you. Maybe we'll get to watch you run around the base twenty times."

"Just make sure nobody bothers me for fifteen minutes," Saoirse said, still talking without thinking. "After dinner, we're dismissed for free time right after formation. The sergeants go back to the HQ building. Surely your little mind can think of ways to keep them from snooping around."

"Oh, you're on, Kenneally," DeSantis said. "I want to see what genius girl comes up with, and it better be pizza."

"Enough of that," Gusty said. "All you're going to do is attract attention now and give one of the sergeants an excuse to find a 'more productive way to use our time' this evening. Lopez, you're not supposed to be up until dinner is finished. Sit your ass down before there's a problem."

"My, aren't you the perfect little police." Lopez flipped a middle finger in Gusty's direction, but went back to her place at the other table.

Dinner soon ended, and evening formation took almost no time, as there were no announcements. Saoirse, Gusty, and DeSantis headed for the computer building, a one-story concrete structure that looked no different from the other buildings at the training facility. It was, in fact, unlocked.

"You two just hang around outside and make sure no one comes in," Saoirse said.

"The only reason anyone might come here in the evening would be if they saw some of us hanging around," Gusty said. "No one is going to think you'd come here to run sims in your free time, and they probably wouldn't care if you did. *Think* before you come up with these ideas, Kenneally." Gusty had that look on her face again.

If you thought before you came up with these ideas, you wouldn't be here at all. Not at this building, not on this base. But you're an ass, and you don't think—do you, Saoirse?

"Just keep a watch," Saoirse said. Then she went in alone.

The inside was spartan. Rows of bare wooden tables were fronted by chairs without cushions. Each table held a large viewing screen and a comm. Those comms simply rested on the tables; they were not tethered, not locked down in any way. That was how useless they were outside of that room. What they did do was allow a learner to simulate any administrative job in any SC office. But that was the problem: they simulated. Saoirse stared at them and tried to think. What was she going to do?

Wait, her mind said. The comms did interface with inventory control at the base. She knew that because they had practiced managing food supply against consumption for a colony, with the training facility simulating the colony. They had been told one of the links was live—not which one, of course—and would, in fact, control the food ordering for the week. If the recruit with the live link had screwed up, they could be living on popcorn. Or nothing. Or pizza.

She shook her head to clear it. If the sim comm could interface with inventory control in the supply area, well, inventory had to interface with the main system for Hammarskjöld. That meant a route to the main system could exist from the sim comms.

She sat at the table and hit the screen of the nearest comm. It showed her the system eye. She stared at that, unblinking, with her thumb pressed to the touch point for the required five seconds. Once her face and thumb logged her in, she played with the settings, looking for the underlying operating system. Yes, it was nothing more than a variant of a commercial system in common use, the same system that LiveClean rehab ran on when she had been there. When she was a kid, her father had given her hack tests using the then current version of that OS. Like most systems, it had a back door in case the recognition login got corrupted or a tech needed to get into the system. Or someone like her. She wished she had a coder's keyboard; it was so much easier for this type of work. But she could do it with only the comm. Slender fingers helped.

A few minutes' work confirmed that the back door was there. Less than a minute after that, she had Adelayo's access. A few seconds more, and she was looking at the page for Pat's Pizza in Charles City. Yes, they delivered. Figure four slices per person. She chose the toppings and ordered fifteen pies to be delivered the next night, at dinnertime. Then she confirmed the name on the order: Orestes Adelayo. With a sigh of relief, she closed down the comm and left the building.

· · ·

The next evening, shortly after the training company had queued up inside the dining hall, a truck bearing the logo of Pat's Pizza rolled up to the entrance. All it took was for one person in the company to spot the van. The food queue was abandoned as all of them rushed outside.

Sergeant McDonough reached the truck first. In response to her question as to how the truck had been allowed into the training facility, the man from Pat's Pizza said only that he had told the scopp at the gate that the order came from Sergeant Adelayo. That name had been enough for him to get through.

"And what did Sergeant Adelayo order?" asked McDonough.

"Fifteen large pies," said the man. At a touch on the truck's dash, a side panel slid open to reveal three stacks of five boxes each, each box labeled as containing a large pizza. "Can I leave these with you?"

McDonough blinked. "Not so fast."

Everything stopped until Adelayo had been called over from the HQ building. On arrival, his eyes took in the truck and the recruits crowded around it. He did not look pleased. "I did not order any pizza."

The driver unrolled a small comm, poked at it, then turned the screen to Adelayo. "There's the order," he said. "It's paid for, so no need to argue about it."

"We're not going to argue about it," Adelayo said. "Why don't you just stack them on the ground here." He pointed to a spot next to the truck.

After Pat's Pizza rolled back to the main gate, leaving a stack of fifteen boxes of hot pizza, Adelayo turned to the company. "You are not on unstructured time until after dinner, and even then, unstructured time does not mean no discipline. Sergeant McDonough, send three of them to supply to get shovels. Then have them dig a hole and bury this stuff. Deep. Now." He paused while his eyes flicked from face to face. "Who did this?"

The first thought through Saoirse's mind was that the rest of them would give her up in an instant. If they didn't, Adelayo would run them around the base until they did and then they would beat the shit out of her afterward. Did Abbott look even a little bit sympathetic?

You are such an idiot. You never think, do you, Saoirse? Never, never, never. And this is what you get.

"I did it," she said.

The base did have a jail, but it was no worse than others she had been in.

. . .

"First Sergeant, it seems that you threw quite a pizza party for the recruits. To celebrate an excellent first half of the training program. Apparently, the pizza was coded as ammunition in the supply ledger." Captain James Houston, US Army, leaned as far back in his desk chair as it would go and clasped his hands behind his head.

Across the desk from Houston, Adelayo stood at rigid attention, his eyes locked on the wall behind Houston. "Sir." It was remarkable that even that one word came out past his tightly clenched teeth.

"Do we understand exactly how she pulled it off?" Houston asked.

"Failure of supervision on my part," Adelayo said. "I should have dismissed her from training before this. I request to be relieved of my duties here. I request a disciplinary hearing to examine my conduct."

"Denied," Houston said. "At *ease*, Sergeant."

Adelayo shifted into an at ease stance every bit as rigid as his posture had been at attention.

"For God's sake, Orestes," Houston said, "we've known each other too long to be doing this. I specifically requested to have you here as the senior drill instructor."

"You may have made a mistake, sir."

"I don't think so." Houston sighed. "Look, this isn't the US Army and this isn't army basic. We're not even starting with the human material we would get in the army."

"I understand that, sir," Adelayo said. "SC can't seem to decide whether we're supposed to train soldiers or be counselors for kids at summer camp."

"Well, maybe it is a hybrid of basic and summer camp," Houston said, "but these are scopps, not US soldiers, and this is what the Solar Council, in its infinite wisdom, is willing to accept. And there are good reasons for us to go along with it." He swung back to an upright position at the desk and tapped on the comm that lay there. A hidden computer projected an image of a document in the air off to his right. He glanced at it, then turned back to Adelayo. "You are recommending that we dismiss Recruit Kenneally for this act."

"Yes, sir."

Houston sighed again. Longer this time. "I've reviewed your fitness reports on the training company, hers in particular. She has improved steadily since arrival and physically meets standards. Your notes. Correct?"

"Yes, sir."

"In fact, looking at these," he turned again to the midair document and scrolled it, "she would meet standards for the army, wouldn't she? The regular standards, not the watered-down ones the women have to meet."

Adelayo gave a grudging assent.

"And how did she do on the last timed marksmanship test?"

"Twenty-five out of twenty-five, sir. All head shots."

"Right." Houston's face turned grim. "So, let's talk about some different numbers. Orestes, we started with fifty: forty-six men and four women. We're down to twenty-eight now. Track record for SCOPP recruits in the US says we'll finish with less than half, and I think we'll be lucky if it's more than a third. These men come in such awful shape, they've never done anything more strenuous than a vid game, and I don't think anyone has demanded that they do anything since toilet training. At least we haven't lost any of the women. With only four, we really can't afford to."

"Yes, sir. Four women. Two whores, a pacifist, and Kenneally, who's an alcoholic and a drug addict for good measure. And Kenneally is a problem even without that. Damn cocksure and individualistic. Dammit, sir, we wouldn't even waiver her to let her into the army, never mind keep her. You've seen her record, sir. Multi-time loser. You know what will happen, sooner or later, and that's how a lot of good men and women get killed."

"Maybe." Houston stood up and walked around the desk to stand next to Adelayo. Houston had streaks of gray in his hair and might have been a shade lighter than Adelayo, but otherwise, they were similar in size and physique. "Look, we all know what's happened since the genius boys and girls figured out how to open a wormhole. We exploded out of the solar system like a cork out of a champagne bottle." Houston sighed. "I think, if we'd found aliens, we'd have all pulled together to fight them, but it doesn't look like there's anyone else out there. So, all the countries signed the Treaty of the Solar System that set up the Solar Council, SCOPP, and the Peacemakers to manage the settlements and keep the peace among ourselves. Or make the peace since there's damn little peace to keep. But the Solar Council needs people. Any nation that puts colonies in the Reach has to contribute people each year to staff SCOPP, both civilian and uniformed, and the peacers. A quota, if you will. The US is behind, has been behind, is always behind. Americans with real jobs won't go, and too many of the ones that don't work are happy to live on their Guaranteed Benefit and play games. We have enough trouble recruiting for the US armed forces, and we get the best of what's available, never mind SCOPP. However," his voice hardened, "the treaty says that if a nation fails to meet its quota, its voting right in the Solar Council can be suspended. Russia and China are pushing to have us suspended. And that is why, First Sergeant Orestes Adelayo, the army has agreed to take over training American scopps, and why you and I are working as hard as we can to send as many qualified Americans as we can to SCOPP and the peacers. As long as they meet the standards the SC sets, it's fine. Am I clear?"

"Yes, sir," said First Sergeant Adelayo.

SEVEN

Like all things, training finally came to an end. Adelayo assembled the company—those who still remained—on the final Friday night and informed them that they would be granted liberty in Charles City on Saturday. After morning inspection, a bus would arrive at the facility to take them into town and drop them off at the old Independence Hotel. Curfew would be 2:00 A.M. Sunday. A last bus pickup at 1:30 A.M. from the hotel would be available if they did not come back earlier on their own. With that glad news, he dismissed them for dinner.

The Saturday liberty was the only topic of conversation during dinner. None of them had been off base in ten weeks, and the prospect sparked their imaginations.

"They always do this. It's a tradition," one of the men said. "I've got a cousin who's a scopp. They had it when he went through here three years ago. Said the bars all discount; it's a crazy night."

"I've heard the same," said Abbott. "From people I know back home. They said the best place to party is called the Leprechaun's Pot. It's down by the river, just off Main Street. I've got it all in my comm, and we'll get those back when we get on the bus."

Any of the company who had heard about places where drink and fun could be found in Charles City began to chip in their ideas. As they did, the voices around the tables grew louder and the company grew raucous.

Saoirse stayed silent and kept her eyes on her plate. She hoped she was shrinking and becoming invisible. She felt that way. This was a bad idea. She didn't want to go into Charles City, but at the same time, she wanted to. She knew what would happen, but she told herself it wouldn't. She ought to leave the table, but she didn't. None of it mattered anyway, she thought sourly. She had no money to go out on the town. Sure, the company would get their comms back when they got on the bus, but she didn't have a comm. She would not have the means to find her way around or access her money even if she had any in her account.

"Hey!" Abbott's voice rose above the others. "I don't know about all of you, but I'm going to the Leprechaun's Pot. Now, that's an Irish name, so it's got to be an Irish bar." He looked down the length of the table and found Saoirse staring at her plate. "Hey, Kenneally, you're Irish, right?"

Saoirse's head could not have snapped up faster if an electric shock had been applied to a sensitive area. She nodded mutely.

"Okay, Irish girl, you coming to the Leprechaun's Pot with me?"

Momentarily, Saoirse froze. She hadn't spoken to Abbott since the day of the pizza incident. She had stayed away from him and out of his line of sight as much as possible. But now, *he* was asking *her*.

"Fuck yes!" she said, loud enough to be heard over everyone else.

"Oh yeah!" Lopez yelled across the table. "It's going to be party time with Kenneally. You're going to show us how it's done. Right?"

Saoirse smiled, not even mad at Lopez in that moment. She would manage it without money of her own. It wouldn't be the first time. She would manage without the comm too. She owed herself the party. She'd had two and a half months of nothing more interesting than coffee in the morning. Women her age had a right to party. It was the normal thing to do.

Saoirse looked for Gusty and was surprised to see an odd expression on her friend's face. She was not joining in the merriment of this last dinner of training and anticipation of liberty. Well, Gusty had talked to Saoirse about Abbott, and now Abbott had asked Saoirse to go with him. Without meaning to rub it in, she gave Gusty a broad smile.

Abruptly, Gusty stood up and left the table and the dining hall. Surprised, Saoirse watched her go. Why was her friend so jealous? Then she shrugged it off and turned back to the party planning. It was all right. She could handle it. This time she could handle it.

. . .

Inspection the next morning should have been brief because the bus was already on the base and waiting. It should have been brief, but Captain Houston was present along with Adelayo and the other two sergeants. From the time they entered the women's barracks, it seemed to stretch out forever.

When they reached Saoirse, everything was wrong: Her bed was not properly made. But it was! The belt buckle on her pants was not centered, the shirt pulled out at the waist. Saoirse struggled to see these imperfections while standing at attention, and couldn't do it. They couldn't be there, but Adelayo kept finding them. Then he turned to her rifle. They had not inspected any of the other rifles. Adelayo took it apart, ran an ultrafiber through the barrel, and pronounced it dirty. That wasn't possible! That rifle was cleaner than Saoirse herself!

Adelayo turned to Houston. "Multiple infractions, sir. Out of uniform. Weapon has not been cleaned."

"So I see," Houston said. "Recruit Kenneally, you are confined to base. Your leave is canceled."

Saoirse almost shouted at him. Almost.

Before a word came out, Houston said, his eyes drilling into her, "It can be confined to base or confined to the base jail. Your choice."

She stayed silent.

. . .

Saoirse was lying on her bed, staring blankly at the ceiling, thinking about everyone else being at the Leprechaun's Pot, when Captain Houston entered the barracks. He did not announce his presence the way one of the sergeants would have done, so she remained on her back until the moment beyond which she could not fail to recognize him. Only then did she pull herself off the bed, come to attention, and salute as slowly as it was possible to get away with.

"At ease." Houston gazed at her as though debating whether to comment on her dilatory movement. In the end, he said, "With the company enjoying liberty in town tonight, I have been keeping in touch with the

Charles City Police Department. As a consequence, I have heard about, call it a situation, in town. It does not involve our company, but the police are busy and could use some help with, shall we say, cleaning up. I offered your assistance and they accepted."

"I can't do that, sir," said Saoirse. "I am confined to base for the weekend, sir."

Houston took another long look at her. "I believe that I mentioned the possibility of being confined to the base jail for the weekend. We can still do that until the time of the graduation ceremony, if you prefer."

"No, sir."

"Good. Then you will spend the remainder of this evening doing a good deed, helping the officers in Charles City. Possibly, you will help yourself in the bargain."

Saoirse wanted to ask him what he meant, but Houston had already turned and was headed for the door of the barracks before she could say anything. Shouting at his back did not seem like a good idea, so, perforce, she followed him out.

An olive-drab vehicle with US Army markings was parked close to the barracks. It was a ground effect multipurpose all-terrain vehicle, a Gemav in slang. Houston pulled himself into the driver's seat as she walked up. He indicated that she should take the front passenger seat and waited for her to belt in. Then he started the Gemav, its wheels retracting to leave it on its cushion of air, and drove off, autonomous vehicles being proscribed, of course, by the AI laws.

The twenty-minute drive went by in silence—or Houston was silent, and after questions that did not receive an answer, Saoirse was quiet as well. Finally, Houston turned the Gemav off the road at a sign for Brady Townhomes that proclaimed, THE WAY 23RD-CENTURY LIVING SHOULD BE. Even in the dark, the condition of the exteriors and the litter strewn around the grounds belied the claim of the sign. Blue flashers signaled a police presence. Houston stopped the Gemav by one of the police vehicles, where an officer was standing.

"Thank you for offering to help," the officer said. "We're a little stretched tonight with your boys and girls downtown. The investigators are finished here, so it's cleanup time. Your person can help."

Houston nodded. "Do you know what happened?"

"Not much more than when you spoke with our captain. Woman, her daughter and a boyfriend. All killed. Whether there was an argument over drugs or a buy went bad, can't tell. Drugs involved, though. We found zombie, among other stuff."

Houston nodded again and walked toward an open ground-floor door where another officer was standing.

Saoirse hurried to keep pace with him. "Captain. Sir," she said, "what is this about? What am I doing here?"

"You're helping to clean up," he said without looking at her.

As soon as she stepped through the door, the bodies riveted Saoirse's eyes. A man, possibly in his thirties, lay flat on his back on the living room floor, three bullet wounds evident in his left chest. A woman of about the same age was seated on a couch nearby, a bullet hole in her forehead. A small body lay near a toy chest at the rear of the room. Two men and a woman in uniforms were packing memory cards and forensic samples into labeled bags.

The uniformed woman walked over to them. "Glad you're here for this," she said. "We're done, so you can start with the kid."

She led them to the back of the room. Saoirse felt as though she were being dragged along by an invisible force.

"Her name was Caitlyn," the female officer said. "She was eight years old."

Saoirse looked down in horror, her eyes as wide open as her mouth. Caitlyn lay on the floor, her long brown hair loose under her shoulders, freckles across her cheeks, her open mouth showing some missing teeth. Her throat had been cut so deeply that her head flopped back. Blood had poured down her chest, partially blotting out WORLD FRIENDSHIP on her T-shirt and soaking the fur of the stuffed bunny rabbit she hugged to her chest.

The officer was speaking again. "We don't know if her throat was cut to persuade those two to do something," she pointed back at the other bodies, "or whether the killers were simply drugged-up sadists." She shrugged. "Too soon to tell."

"What?" Saoirse started. "What," she started again, "am I doing here?" She turned to Houston, but he was silent, his face grim.

"The three of them need to go to the morgue," the woman said. "Put them in the body bags, get them on the gurneys, and wheel them out to the ambulances. You'll want gloves." She held out a pair.

Caitlyn's eyes were open, fixed sightlessly on the ceiling, but when Saoirse bent over the girl, those eyes seemed to bore into hers. Saoirse could not move. She could not move her eyes from Caitlyn's. Her stomach twisted. "I'm going to be sick."

"Use the bathroom. Back there to the left." The woman pointed. "Don't worry. It won't affect anything. We're finished."

Even after Saoirse's stomach had emptied itself into the toilet, she felt sick. She heaved again, but nothing more came up. Still nauseated, she wiped her mouth with toilet paper and made her way back to the body. Houston was still there. She was going to have to put Caitlyn's body in the bag. She had to look at those eyes again. *You failed me*, they said to her. *It's your fault.*

Saoirse couldn't shake the accusation in those eyes. She pulled the gloves on, but even with those, it strained the limits of her control to touch the body. She could not bear to take Caitlyn's bunny away. It went into the bag along with its owner. She dealt with the man and woman next.

When the business of removing the bodies to the ambulances was over, Saoirse sat, shaking, in the passenger seat of the Gemav. Her left leg rocketed up and down from the ball of her foot to her thigh, the heel tap-tap-tapping on the floor.

"Want a cig?" Houston said from the driver's seat.

Saoirse nodded. Her voice did not want to work. Houston reached back to the rear seat and pulled a cigarette from a small pack that rested there. He held it out to her, directly in front of the lettering on the dash that proclaimed SMOKE-FREE ENVIRONMENT.

Saoirse accepted it without a word. She inhaled to ignite the tip and it glowed orange. She inhaled again, deeply this time, and blew smoke into the interior of the Gemav.

"I find it interesting," Houston said, "that they send us into combat with scarcely a moment's thought, but obsess about smoke-free environments."

"What the fuck, sir?" The smoke down her throat helped Saoirse find her voice. "What the fuck was that about?"

Houston started the Gemav. He didn't speak until he had turned the vehicle onto the road back to Hammarskjöld Base. "You have a friend in the company—you actually do have a friend—who let me know what you were planning for your end-of-training liberty. That's why you were confined to the base. Because both you and I know what would have happened if you had gone into Charles City. Correct?" He looked over at her.

Saoirse concentrated on dragging on the cigarette. The shaking in her hands had stopped. The leg still went up and down, but the amplitude had decreased.

After three more drags, she found her voice again. "Why should you care, sir?"

"Fair question," Houston said. "I could say that I need to deliver as many graduates of this program to SCOPP as I can and I did not want to lose another one the day before graduation, and that would be true. I could also say that I have seen you in training and I think there is the possibility you can amount to something. If you don't self-destruct first. Which brings me to tonight." He paused. "As I said, I stay in touch with local police when there is liberty, because things happen. That's how I heard about that disaster back there. And it occurred to me that you should see that, deal with it, because the way you're going, that's going to be *you* dead on the couch along with your kid, if you live long enough to have one. Or somebody you've killed, along with their kid."

"That's bullshit! Sir," Saoirse said, "they said they found zombie; you heard it. I don't use it, never used it. And I would never do something like that. Not ever."

"You're what's bullshit, Kenneally, and I think you know it." He was quiet for long enough that she began to think he wasn't going to say anything else. Then he said, "You tell me, Kenneally. You tell me that if you're drinking, or using, and you needed something, *needed it*, you tell me you wouldn't do whatever it took to get it. You tell me that. *You* tell *me* it could never happen."

Saoirse knew the lie to give him. But she couldn't say it, for once. She couldn't tell that lie to Houston; she couldn't even tell it to herself. All she could see were Caitlyn's eyes staring at her, the small hand clutching the stuffed bunny rabbit, and the blood.

So she didn't say anything else, all the way back to the base.

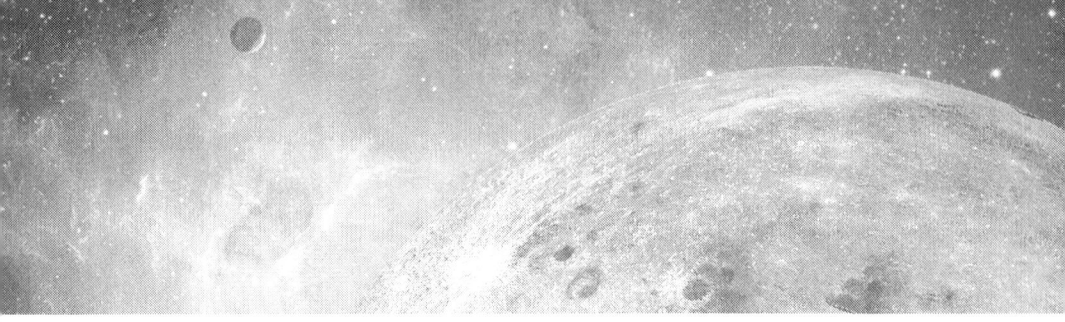

EIGHT

Graduation day dawned gray, with thick, low clouds a portent of rain to come. The company assembled in formation in front of a reviewing stand with a vacant podium. It was now a very shrunken company. Less than half the number who had started were present—and they were, additionally, one fewer than the previous day. DeShawn Abbott sat in a Charles City jail and never would graduate.

While they waited, a drizzle started. They stood there, wet splotches beginning to show on their new uniforms, waiting to be called by their new ranks and receive their assignments. Four of the men wore the light-blue shirts and gray pants of the Off-Earth Armed Peacemakers. They were the only ones who had been selected for the peacers and would leave immediately for further training. The rest wore the dark-blue shirt and matching pants of the uniformed Solar Council Off-Planet Personnel, the scopps. Less than half of them had family or friends there to see them graduate and wish them well on their assignments out in the Reach, so Saoirse was not unique. No one was there for her.

Saoirse stood, lost in thought, in the gradually strengthening rain. She heard the drops patter on the bill of her cap and felt them soak through her uniform. She wouldn't mind the rain if it could wash away the previous night, but it couldn't. She could still see Caitlyn and her bunny as clearly as she saw Captain Houston standing not twenty feet away, seemingly indifferent to the rain. More clearly, in fact. Her mind kept cycling through images of Caitlyn as she'd manhandled the girl's stiffening body into the black bag. She kept hearing Houston's words in the car. She wished never to want a drink or a pill again. She didn't want to die over drugs, and she didn't want to think she would kill for drugs. She wanted Houston to be wrong.

She glanced along the line, at the other recruits standing miserably in the intensifying rain. She was drenched. If only the rain could wash away everything she had done before, her entire life. But it didn't do that either. Life was never that simple or easy.

Mohammed Desai of the SC was the first speaker to the podium, and determined to do his duty, he droned on about the service to humanity the graduating scopps were going to provide. Humanity's future, he said, was in the stars, and it would be the people in SCOPP who would build the homes, the businesses, the transport, and the administration to make it all possible. His soft monotone gave no hint of enthusiasm for the venture he was describing.

Saoirse shifted her weight furtively from foot to foot, hoping not to be noticed fidgeting, wondering if interstellar exploration could die of boredom. Listening to Desai made it seem possible.

At long last, Desai wound up his talk. "This is our mission," he declared, "and the one you have now committed yourselves to: Bringing Peace to the Reach."

"Well, that's not goddamn likely!" came a shout from the stands. There was more emotion in that one sentence than Desai had shown in his entire speech.

Saoirse saw her fellow scopps struggle to suppress laughs. Then Captain Houston strode to the podium to call the roll.

When Houston called out, "Specialist Saoirse Kenneally, Titan Station, Operations," she saluted and responded with a quick "Yes, sir." That was all she had to do until Houston finished with Private Arthur Zang. She supposed she should focus on how remarkable it was that she had reached this point, but she couldn't do it. Images from the previous night kept intruding.

Finally, the roll call completed, the company was dismissed for the final time, and the formation broke up. Those with family and friends received hugs and congratulations; the rest walked back to their barracks to retrieve their duffels and wait for the bus that would take them to the maglev station.

Saoirse caught up with Gusty before the door to the barracks and pulled at her sleeve to get her to turn around. "I'm sorry you didn't get the peacers," Saoirse said. "Really, I am."

"Thanks." Gusty let out a sigh. "I met standards on the range, and thank you for that. I thought . . . well, who knows. They look at my file and probably figure I'm a pacifist with a distaste for authority, no matter what I say. It's hard to outrun your past, you know."

"Yeah." Saoirse wiped rain off her face. That was what the liquid was. "Gusty, I know what you did the other day."

"Thought you would figure it out." Gusty stepped aside to let Lopez and Jones out as they left the barracks. "I had to do it."

"No, you didn't, actually," Saoirse said. "I'm glad you did, though. Last night I hated you, but now I'm glad you were there. I needed you."

"Thanks. Still friends?"

Saoirse nodded. With a sudden move, she wrapped Gusty in a bear hug that picked the shorter woman off her feet and whispered, "Thank you."

After Gusty had been released and recovered her breath, she said, "Look, I got Titan Station, same as you, and we're the only ones who get to stay there. And I got Station Security. That's working with the peacers assigned there. Maybe I can transfer."

"Yeah." Saoirse smiled. "These girls are going to Titan Station! It will never be the same! Life could be worse."

Sure, life could be worse than going with you. Of course, that might depend on whom you ask. You know hanging around with Saoirse Kenneally isn't encouraged. Plenty of parents wouldn't let their kids hang out with you. And, of course, they had good reason— Goddamn it, Saoirse, shut up and get out of the rain!

"Hey," Gusty said, "all we're doing now is getting wet."

Saoirse forced a smile this time. "Let's go get our stuff."

·   ·   ·

SCOPP seemed determined to get its newest members off-planet quickly. There was no leave, no chance to go home for those who had homes that would take them, and no opportunity for second thoughts. They were bused to Charles City, put on a maglev to O'Hare, herded onto a flight to

Quito, the closest city to the base of the Western Hemisphere space elevator, and then taken up the elevator to Earth Station. With the exception of a few assigned to Earth Station, an in-system ship was waiting in orbit to take them to Titan Station.

· · ·

The *Marquis de Lafayette*, which would take three weeks to bring the scopps out from Earth Station, was a ship that took working middle-class families out to Titan Station for the middle-class version of the vacation of a lifetime. It was nothing like taking a luxury interstellar, the ships that took wealthy families out into the Reach for grand vacations to planets like Lincoln. Those ships had entertainment scheduled around the clock and crews whose job it was to keep the paying passengers entertained, much like the oceangoing cruise ships of a bygone era.

The *Lafayette* reminded Saoirse of a comment she had read that had been attributed to Winston Churchill: a boat was like a prison with the added consideration of drowning. She remembered the line because she hated boats. They made her seasick. They were like being seasick in a jail cell. Maybe drowning wasn't a consideration on a spaceship, but asphyxiation might be. Or exploding. Or dying of boredom.

The one time she had been in space was when her father had taken the family to Earth Station for a vacation, and Saoirse's sole memory was of being bored. The *Lafayette* at least offered round-the-clock vids, including the immersible VR vids that put the viewer into the viewpoint of one of the characters. But hours of vid left Saoirse feeling as if her brain had turned to mush, and the VR characters always dealt with life better than she did, which was depressing.

Like all spaceships, the *Lafayette* had a well-stocked bar open twenty-four seven. That was where most passengers parked themselves, especially the new scopps. With the care of an ancient traveler detouring around a plague-stricken city, Saoirse avoided the bar, the corridor that led to it, and, to the extent possible, the entire deck where the bar was located. Caitlyn was too much on her mind, and the best way to avoid temptation was not to have it in front of her.

Out of sight was not out of mind, however. Troubling thoughts and cravings would pop into her head at random times, especially when she was bored. She had only one rule, and that was to stay away—she could deal with the cravings if she couldn't actually put her hands on anything.

Having Gusty along on the trip made it easier to avoid trouble. New Anabaptists did not drink, just as they were pacifist and had nothing to do with governmental institutions. Gusty had broken with the drinking prohibition, as she had with all the others, but to help a friend, she was willing to give up alcohol again. She made it a point to keep Saoirse out of trouble and as far from the bar as possible.

This meant they ended up spending almost all their time together in a search for something to do. At first, they pretended they were kids again and staged a game of hide-and-seek, the bar being off-limits, of course. That was fun, but in retrospect, areas marked ENGINEERING should have been as off-limits as the bar. The game ended in a confrontation with the crew and the warning that a repeat performance would lead to a reprimand in their files.

That led to a search for activities that the ship offered. The first one they agreed to try was yoga classes. Unfortunately, while Saoirse had the flexibility and strength for it, Gusty found it uninteresting.

"I can't see how turning myself into a pretzel and seeing how much pain my joints can stand qualifies as a good time," she told Saoirse. "If there is going to be pain, I want to inflict it on someone else, not on myself."

That led Gusty to suggest meditation, but it went badly for Saoirse. Thoughts always crowded into her head, and too many of them were ones she did not want to have.

The next option on the ship's list was Muay Thai.

"A gym in my neighborhood taught this," Gusty said. "I started sneaking there when I was sixteen, and it was a lot of fun. Of course, New Anabaptists are pacifist, so that made it more fun." She sighed. "Until my mom caught me. She went down there and made me say I was quitting and then she screamed at the guy to give back my money and, oh my God, what a scene. But it was fun while it lasted. Want to try?"

"Sure. I went to a place to study Muay Thai also." Saoirse had done that, a few times anyway, during one of her sober interludes. "I know how to fight."

The ship had a well-equipped gym with a class they could take and was happy to rent them headgear and gloves and sell them tape for their hands. Saoirse and Gusty made a variety of comments about the instructor, mostly behind their hands, as he taught the class. They were sure that Adelayo, or any of the sergeants, could reduce him to hamburger in ten seconds. They were not so subtle as they had thought, and the instructor invited them to take a far corner of the gym and work out on their own. They took him up on that and went at it enthusiastically, with an equal lack of skill and control.

"You know," Gusty said afterward as they stood by a sink in the locker room unwrapping their hands and comparing matching bloody noses, "you know shit about Muay Thai."

"What I said was I know how to fight, not Muay Thai specifically."

"Hnnh. I might believe that if I were deaf, my implant failed, and the comms were down."

"Well, I got you good enough." Saoirse pointed to Gusty's nose and cheek.

"One lucky punch," Gusty said. "Although there is no way a rich white girl like you is supposed to have fists that hard."

"I'm not rich," Saoirse said. "I'm disowned."

"Yeah, well, you're still white," Gusty replied. "That fist is like a rock in your glove."

"It's my Irish heritage. We're all great fighters, back to the mists of time. That's my excuse. Where does a Black New Anabaptist pacifist get a right cross like yours?"

Gusty grinned. "That's why they threw me out. Well, one of the reasons."

"We should do this again," Saoirse said.

"Yeah. You'd look better if I got you on both sides of your face. That'd put some color in your cheeks. Since you can't afford makeup, I mean."

Then they both winced as they daubed at their noses, smiled as they touched fists, and giggled at their images in the mirror. "Look out, Titan!" they said together. "The bad girls are comin'!"

PART II
TITAN

O, what a tangled web we weave when first we practise to deceive!
SIR WALTER SCOTT
Marmion: A Tale of Flodden Field

In any moment of decision, the best thing you can do is the right thing, the next best thing is the wrong thing, and the worst thing you can do is nothing.
ATTRIBUTED TO THEODORE ROOSEVELT

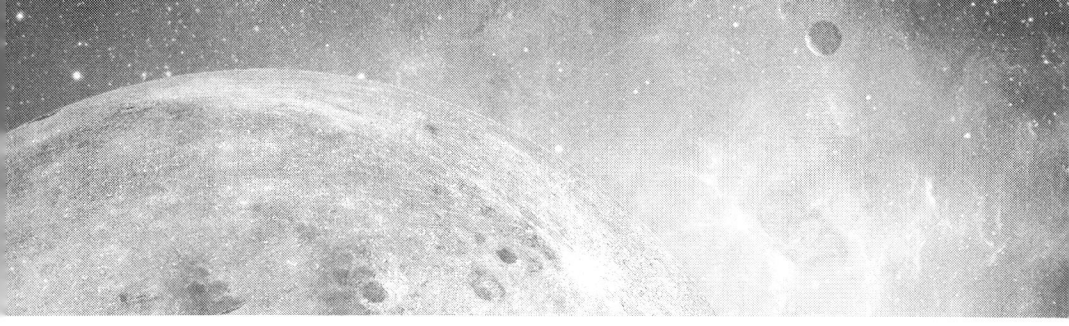

NINE

The *Marquis de Lafayette* had a lounge with a wall-sized screen where its passengers congregated to watch the approach to the Saturn system and to Titan. It wasn't the same as looking out a window, of course. The *Lafayette*'s telescopes picked up the view of Saturn as the ship came into the planetary system, and then the computer system synthesized the data into images for display on that screen. Saturn, with its rings and its bands, grew larger against the pitch-black backdrop of space as they approached, but it was the computer, generating ever-larger images, that made it feel as though the ship were zooming into the planet. When Saturn reached full-screen size, the computer restarted the approach, as if from a great distance.

People watched the show over and over, even if they had been to Saturn before. Saoirse could see why; she found it mesmerizing. Those rings were so gorgeous, with their different shades and dark divides in between. Then the focus shifted to Titan itself, an enigmatic, hazy orange orb set against giant Saturn and the rings, now on a knife edge. She could feel Gusty next to her, staring just as raptly at the incredible images. Strange to think it was really happening outside the ship, and not just a mind-blowing vid.

Soon, the *Lafayette* came close enough that Titan Station became the star of the show. It was a brilliant white cylinder, gleaming in front of orange Titan with the light of the distant sun. The cylinder was hollow; men and women lived and worked at the outer layer, where the spin of the cylinder created a comfortable one gee of centrifugal force to match the gravity of Earth. Essentially, the station was a stack of rings like a can of sliced pineapple, each ring a deck, all of them spinning around a central shaft.

The *Lafayette* cruised past one end of the station. Lights on the station showed the central shaft and the spokes that ran from it out to the inhabited rim.

"It's weird to look at this and think that it's all an accident," Gusty said. "Do you know what I mean? Do you know the story?"

"I know the history," Saoirse said. "I did go to school. At least, through high school. At least, some of the time."

In fact, she had heard more of it from her father than she had in school. The original Titan Station, much smaller than the one they were approaching, was built back in 2123 as part of the Titan Research Base project. The objective then had been to explore the strangest moon in the solar system, the only one with an atmosphere. It was from this original Titan Station that the negative mass experiments had been carried out and the first wormhole opened. From that time, Titan Station became the port from which starships left for the Reach, and the port they returned to when they came back to Earth.

Of course, that port didn't have to be Titan Station specifically. That was what people meant when they called the station an "accident." Space-time was flat enough to open a wormhole anywhere from halfway between Jupiter and Saturn and on out. That was what the physics underlying those negative mass experiments had correctly predicted. You didn't need to be at Titan Station to open a wormhole; you didn't need a station at all. A ship could leave Earth, head out under Mach effect drive until space-time flattened enough, and then open a wormhole. That was what ships did out in the Reach, where few systems had stations.

But people piloting commercial interstellars did not want to spend weeks running from a wormhole to Earth and then weeks more running back out. No profit in that. And the Solar Council, not to mention the nations of Earth after the Forty Years' War, didn't want ships popping into the solar system and going straight to Earth with no controls, carrying God only knew what. It was better for everyone if the interstellars transferred their cargoes and cleared customs at Titan Station. That was the public, agreed-upon position of the SC and the nations of Earth. Hunter-killer missiles in wide orbits around Earth were the unspoken reinforcement of that position.

"There was logic to it," Saoirse said out loud. "That's why the station grew and grew and why they built this new one. Even if people call it an accident. Even if, when Krishna Venkataraman was appointed first station executive and secretary of interstellar trade, they called him His Accidency. That's how the SC keeps the peace and controls trade. It's not an accident, even if they never talk about the real reasons."

"Why do you always have to make things sound like a plot?"

Saoirse elbowed her. "Because they usually are."

   ·   ·   ·

The *Lafayette* docked, not at Titan Station itself but at the Titan Spacedock, a large, thirty-degree arc of metal and graphene supercoils floating in space one mile away from the station in the same orbit around Titan. As many as four in-system or interstellar ships could berth at the Spacedock at the same time. Once docked there, passengers transited from the ship into the Spacedock and followed signs that directed them to the small pusher ships that could dock directly with the station.

While they moved through the dock, the passengers disembarking the *Marquis de Lafayette* heard a repeated overhead announcement in a bland, synthetic, androgynous voice stating that they were in zero gee and must always maintain a handhold. No flying was permitted, and parents were responsible for ensuring that their children behaved or used a track tether.

Saoirse decided that she did not like zero gee and would be happy never to experience it again. There was no up or down, at least to her stomach, which insisted that it was falling. Symbolic human figures on the corridor walls showed head and feet with the message ORIENT YOURSELF THIS WAY in multiple languages, but that did not help her middle ear. It was with a sigh of relief that she reached the hatch to the pusher ship.

The pusher was little more than a large box filled with rows of seats. The overhead announcement urged passengers to take any available seat and belt themselves in, because the pusher would not move until sensors indicated that everyone had complied. Attendants stood by, waiting for the inevitable: a passenger losing their handhold and then, floating in the compartment, losing their composure—or their lunch. Saoirse watched them fish one woman out of the air and maneuver her to a seat, and tightened her grip on each handhold that came her way. She was afraid if she floated loose, she would vomit.

That would be so like you, you know, a mess everywhere you go.

Even worse, nearby, Gusty seemed to be enjoying herself.

The pusher left the Spacedock under the shove of a dozen small thrusters and crossed the void to Titan Station in a few minutes. A gentle bump and clank heralded its docking at the station's rim. As it did, Saoirse felt weight return. The overhead announcement stating that they were now in a one gee environment was totally superfluous.

The hatch opened and the overhead voice told them to walk through it onto the concourse of Titan Station. A large screen that hung from the concourse roof read, WELCOME TO TITAN STATION, GATEWAY TO THE REACH, in a language that changed every ten seconds. Saoirse ignored it. What caught her eye was a much smaller sign on the wall past the hatch. TITAN STATION IS SMOKE-FREE, it read. NO PRODUCTS THAT RELEASE SMOKE OR VAPOR ARE ALLOWED.

"Great," she muttered. If she was going to be sober, she would need cigs. Immediately, she felt anxious.

She stared into the glass front of the immigration kiosk so the camera behind it could scan her face and retinas while she put her thumb on the pad below. In response, the screen flashed a green check mark and a voice intoned, "Admitted."

Admitted was fine, but where to go? She was already tense.

Gusty came through right behind her. A man in a Peacemaker uniform was standing just past the kiosk. He collected Gusty and walked her toward one of the corridors that exited the concourse. Gusty waved and called, "Good luck!"

Then Saoirse was alone in the crowd. She stood in one place and turned in a circle, trying to orient herself. The station immigration kiosks were behind her. They were set for admissions; there was no exit through them even if she wanted to leave. Numbered corridors labeled A-RING led away from the concourse, but nothing in the labeling told her where they went or which one she should take. She still did not have a comm, so she couldn't even look up which corridor might lead to Operations.

Oh yeah, think of it as a new beginning, just like every other new beginning you've had. This is so like you. Out of place. Awkward. No idea what you're doing— Shut up, Saoirse!

A voice behind her said, "Specialist Saoirse Kenneally?"

Saoirse said, "Yes," even as she was turning around. The speaker was a short, stocky woman wearing a *shalwar kameez* of deep purple, with blue-gray squares set in a broad beige band at the cuffs and hem. Black hair, streaked with gray and pulled into a ponytail, framed a brown face seamed with wrinkles.

"You are to join us in StatOps," the woman said. "We messaged you with where to go and so on, but it bounced. I checked the passenger list and you were on it, so that did not make sense, so I said to myself that I should go myself and see what was happening. And, indeed, here you are."

"I don't have a comm," Saoirse said reluctantly. "I'm sorry."

"You don't have a comm?" The woman cocked her head and looked up at Saoirse, who was more than half a foot taller. "I've never heard of anyone off-Earth not having a comm. How did that happen?"

"It's a bit of a story." Saoirse sighed. "By the way, who are you?"

The woman looked surprised at first, but recovered quickly. "Oh, of course—no comm, no information. I am so sorry. You poor child. My name is Mamta Jhosi, and I am in charge of all computer systems and communications for Titan Station. So, as I said, my name is Mamta Jhosi, but everyone calls me Mom." She reached out and took Saoirse's hand. "You seem troubled, child. What is wrong?"

Saoirse reflected that the word *troubled* could be applied in many different ways, and this was not the first time it had been applied to her. As for what was wrong . . . she could not think of where to begin. But none of that was what this "Mom" was talking about.

Saoirse searched for something to say and came up with, "I'm surprised the head of computer systems came to find me."

"Oh, that is nothing." Mom waved her hand in front of her face as though to brush the concern away literally. "The message bounced, as I said, and we are so short-staffed, and I selected you myself when I saw your file on the potential match list for our openings. So of course I came myself. You have such an interesting background."

Saoirse thought, but managed to avoid asking, *Is my background interesting for the amount of booze I've drunk or the number of different drugs I've taken?*

When Saoirse stayed silent, Mom spoke again. "We need to get you straightened out and set up properly. Don't worry about your bags. A bot will unload them from the pusher and leave them in your room. You come with Mom now. We'll go to my office at StatCent. You will sit with me and have a cup of chai and I will get you settled."

With that, Mom walked her, hand in hand, through the maze of corridors beyond the immigration kiosks. They stopped at a set of deck-high doors marked ZOOMCHUTE, A-RING STATION. When the doors opened, Mom ushered her into a small car with seats. After the usual "Please fasten your seat belts" announcement, the car moved off. They traveled four lettered stops ending in E-Ring Station; then when the doors opened, Mom led her out.

More corridors, intersections, and turns followed. Saoirse lost all track of where she was. Without a comm showing her destination on a map, she would have wandered aimlessly. She could see herself, meandering through the corridors until she finally dropped from exhaustion, people stepping over her and cursing. Her mind dredged up a memory of a street, in Milwaukee perhaps, where something like that had happened. She fought to suppress it.

Her inner Saoirse wanted to continue making trouble, but the gentle pressure of Mom's hand kept her anchored on Titan Station and not drifting back to Milwaukee. Or Chicago. *Shut up, Saoirse, and keep walking*, she told herself firmly. She did not let go of Mom's hand. She had not walked holding her mother's hand since she was little, and back then, all she wanted to do was drop the hand and run ahead on her own. Now it was . . . easier.

StatCent was cavernous. Strip after strip of LEDs in the high ceiling lit the entire area as brightly as a desert under the noon sun. Workstation after workstation filled the area, clustered into groups, each with computer screens and keypads. Mom led her past them to the rear.

"This is where the sysadmin sits." Mom indicated a seat before a bank of twelve screens that reached up the wall from the desk, angled so they could be seen from the chair. "You'll be one of our assistant sysops, but I am sure you can actually handle the admin position. The last person had an accident a few months ago and went back to Earth. It has been hard to replace him."

Saoirse looked at the screens. She didn't know if Mom expected her to be awed or intimidated, but she wasn't. Not at all. She saw computer screens, a comm port, a keyboard and touchpads in front of the seat. This position might access every part of the computer system of Titan Station, but it was still only a computer. Computers ran on code that people wrote. The laws placed restrictions on how computers could think or learn. She was comfortable with computers. They weren't judgmental.

Mom gave a little tug on Saoirse's hand and led her past the sysadmin's position to a small office at the very back. That had its own computer screen and keyboard on a compact desk decorated with pictures of children. Mom caught Saoirse looking at the pictures.

"My children, when they were young," she said, tapping several of the pictures, "and now their children." She tapped a number of others. "Sit down, child, and let me get you some chai."

Saoirse could not remember the last time anyone had called her *child*, but somehow, it did not bother her. She sat while Mom busied herself with a pot and cups at a corner of the desk. The tea was sweet with a hint of spice. She could get used to it.

Mom told Saoirse to wait and bustled out, returning a few minutes later with a small box. She pulled a comm out and handed it to Saoirse.

"It's a Peach." Saoirse turned it over and over in her hands. "This is the new model. These are expensive." She wanted it. She knew she didn't deserve it, but couldn't bring herself to say that she couldn't take it.

"If you are going to be one of my group," Mom said, "you need to have a comm, and I have good equipment for my people. Do you know how to set it up?"

Saoirse nodded.

"Of course you do. I'll download your schedule to you and we'll see how you do on the system. Then you can go find your quarters. And remember, child, you can always come back here for a cup of chai and talk to Mom."

Mom gave her a gentle pat on the shoulder and left her with the comm.

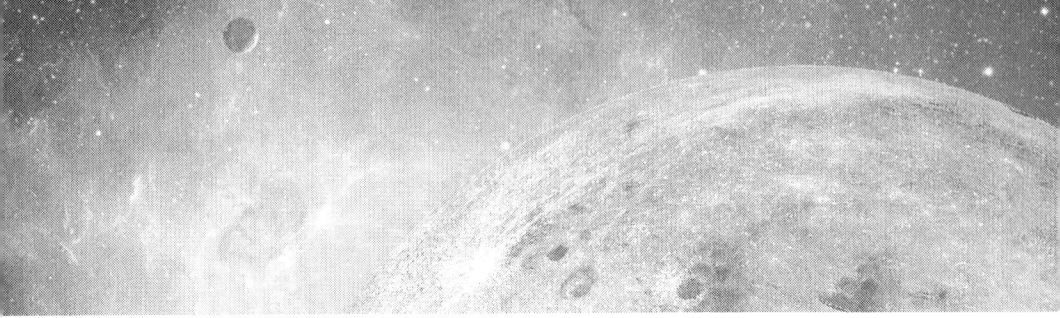

TEN

Mom put Saoirse right to work. Officially, she was the most junior assistant sysop for the computer system that ran the station, handling the communications with ships headed out to, or in from, the Reach, and with in-system ships going to and from the inner planets. She couldn't have any posting higher than that, because she had only a high school diploma and no certification of any kind in computer systems. However, the sysadmin position was vacant, and the sysop and more senior assistant sysops, all civilian SCOPP, kept their seats warm but did little else. The system showed the lack of attention, and Mom said she was tired of doing all the day-to-day work.

Saoirse could see problems from the day Mom gave her a tryout on the boards. The station was supposed to establish communication with an incoming interstellar within five seconds of observing its exit from the wormhole. That was crucial to efficient course correction. However, the cross talk between key systems in that loop would drop at random intervals. Then C-Ring, where the Mall with its shops and restaurants and bars was located, was supposed to be kept cooler than the rest of the station because of the crowds that occupied it. However, for three weeks prior to Saoirse's arrival, it had been too warm, which had been blamed for a greater than usual number of bar fights.

Saoirse might lack degrees and certifications, but from the day she could read by herself, her father had set her system problems the way some parents set up arithmetic problems for their children. She could hack. In a situation where Mom granted her any access she asked for, playing with the system was easy. From her third day, she was the *de facto* sysadmin.

Saoirse loved that job. She could sit at her boards and watch the screens display every activity at Titan Station, right down to who was accessing which file and when. She spent time reading the documentation Mom gave her and dived into the system to fix the corruptions and glitches that had accumulated over time. These were all puzzles to solve. She spent long hours in that chair, often working double shifts communing with the computer, with little need to interact with other staff. She had one friend: Gusty. The two met for breakfast on occasion, although Saoirse began to feel a strain there. Gusty was, after all, StatSec, and they were the police for Titan Station. Saoirse did not have a good history with police.

More important, Saoirse had a mentor for the first time in her life. She had Mom. They met several times a day for chai in Mom's little back office and talked about everything Saoirse was doing—not just with the computer but also with her life, although, in truth, there wasn't much of the latter to talk about. When she wasn't working, she retreated to her room. There she started to keep a journal, another first for her. This was an actual little book of bound paper, and she wrote in it with an ancient ink pen. She had found both in an odds-and-ends bin in Gartner's Salvage Store in the Mall on C-Ring. She printed her words slowly, laboriously, but it seemed to help her get her thoughts out properly. Other than that, she would read, usually the system documentation. All in all, the less time she had off, the better. It kept her from getting bored and thinking about all those bars in the Mall.

She did find one other way to use her time: she could snoop. Titan Research Base, the scientific station on the surface of the moon, sent message after message complaining that all the food sent down was the same meal package, no variety at all. The SCOPP crew responsible for supply ignored them, so Saoirse intervened. She noticed her system did not extend to the research base, but she could reach out through the station system and change the meal packs. Soon, the research base was getting what Saoirse would have wanted to eat, but at least there was variety.

Then Technician Rogers, a civilian SCOPP, was not, in the colorfully expressed opinions of his shift mates, washing frequently enough. She set an alarm in his quarters to ring at 2:30 A.M. to remind him of the importance of hygiene, and solved the problem in two days.

She only snooped a little, in her estimate. At first she thought Mom would be upset when she found out, but only a minor scolding ensued. It was okay from that point on, as long as Saoirse was careful to tell Mom exactly what she was doing. After all, whatever Saoirse learned went no further than her and Mom.

"Titan Station can be a good home for you," Mom said. "Everything you need or want can be here. But you need to be careful. You need to learn your way around."

The words *learn your way around* got Saoirse's attention. That had been the key to getting along and staying safe in the shelters and on the streets. Maybe Titan Station was nothing but a very big shelter. The cup of chai stopped halfway to her mouth, and she leaned forward. "What do I need to know? What do I need to be careful of?"

"Many things." Mom paused to sip her chai. "I will teach you, and you can always talk to me. Talk to me about everything you do, and I will let you know if there are, well, delicate matters. But first: always, always, be careful of Captain S."

"Captain S? That's their name? Who are they?"

"If you spent time learning about the people on this station as more than simply file and folder labels, you would know. But then, I suppose, you would not be so efficient for me, so I should not complain." Mom put down her cup with a distinct clink. "I can never pronounce his name." She pulled out her comm and tapped at the screen, then held it up for Saoirse to see.

The caption under the picture read, TOMASZ SZCZECHOWICZ. The face in the picture was pale and hard. Pale blue eyes, as hard as the face, seemed to drill into Saoirse from the image.

"It is easier to call him S, and that is what most people do," Mom said. "He commands the peacer detachment on Titan Station, and he is the head of StatSec, Station Security."

Police. Where Gusty worked.

"I understand," Saoirse said. "Intercourse with police is always difficult and usually painful."

"Do not joke, child." Mom's mild eyes flashed hard for an instant. "Do not joke about him. I have read your file. He is death on, shall we say, certain types of people. You know what I mean, I am sure. I cannot afford to lose another person, even an assistant sysop, to say nothing of someone who can be sysadmin even if you lack the degrees. But worse than that, always remember that he is Concannon's man."

"Concannon? Do you mean the head of Titan Station? If this S heads security, I would think he reports to Concannon."

Mom hesitated as though debating how much to say. "Yes, Abel Concannon is the chief executive officer of Titan Station, head of StatEx, and also the current minister for interstellar trade of the Solar Council. Mx. Concannon is a very powerful man, and not only on the station. You will probably not see him, although occasionally he dines at Titan's Rib in the Mall. He spends much of his time on Earth. As you said, Captain S reports to him as the head of StatSec, but it is said that S uses his position to manage . . . other matters for Mx. Concannon. It is best not to speak too much of these things. Titan Station is not a security state, but there are cameras and bugs. My system should know what is there, of course, but still, I would not wish to be too confident of that." She paused. "I would not speak of this except that I need to keep you safe, child. It is not simply that I cannot afford to lose a person with your talent—although, as I said, that is true. I am becoming fond of you and do not wish to see harm come to you. On Titan Station, it is often best to be neither seen nor heard. Simply run in the background like the operating system. You do understand me, child?"

Mom's eyes and tone were as mild as ever, but Saoirse read the meaning. It occurred to her that this Captain S was Gusty's boss and maybe she should warn Gusty. But if she did that, it might get back to Captain S. That might be a very bad idea.

"I understand."

"Good." Mom moved over to the pot. "Would you like some more chai?"

⁂

Saoirse developed another form of entertainment by using the direct data feeds from the astronomy and gravimetric instruments that monitored space around Titan Station. Those data flowed through the computer system to Space Traffic Control, which used them to monitor and direct all the craft around the station and Titan. Saoirse put the feeds on her screens in StatOps. She loved the star fields from the astronomy feed: jet-black space dusted with a million tiny sparks, sometimes the moving track of one of Saturn's moons or a ship, and sometimes the ringed giant itself. Those scenes were soothing. Actually, she liked the gravimetric fields even more. They displayed a negative image of the sky. Space was white, the stars faint gray points. Superimposed on the negative skyfield was a grid that gave a representation of the curvature—or flatness—of space-time. Out around Titan, unless you were looking at Saturn, space-time was pretty flat, which was the whole point of Titan Station. The generators in the ring of an interstellar that unmasked negative mass to generate a wormhole needed flat space-time in order to function properly. The screen, with its grid, was only a visual depiction, of course; the true description of space-time were the tensors in the computer. Saoirse liked to look at the screen and daydream about the math.

You could have learned that math; you could have handled it. If you weren't such a fuckup. Still are a fuckup. Goddamn it, Saoirse, get over it!

She was sitting as sysadmin one day when she noticed a dimple forming on the gravimetric screen. A dimple, a little puckering in space-time, was the first sign of a wormhole forming. She took a deep breath and held it until it hurt. She had never watched a wormhole form from the start. That dimple would widen and deepen until it became the throat of a passage. A passage to another star system. The astronomy screen showed nothing, of course. Black space and bright points of light. You couldn't *see* a wormhole. Only the math told you it was there. The astronomy screen wouldn't show anything until the wormhole was fully formed, and then—pop!—an interstellar would be there.

Saoirse wondered where the ship would come from and who would be on it. There was no way to know in advance. Ships did file schedules, of course, when they left Titan Station, but they were approximate. Delays occurred. Ship captains could and did change their plans. None of that could be communicated to Earth. Any transmission from another star was limited by the speed of light and would take years to arrive. Nothing was faster than a ship dropping through a wormhole, so the actual arrival was the first notice the station would have. That was why Space Traffic Control monitored the fields so closely. Wormholes were not innocuous, and there was plenty of traffic around Titan Station.

She was watching and daydreaming when she noticed something odd on the astronomy screens. A ship was there, moving toward where the wormhole was forming. Her first thought was that this was the outbound ship that was making the wormhole for its passage, but that couldn't be right. A ship formed the wormhole around itself. If that ship was setting up the wormhole, it should have been centered in the dimple—and it wasn't. It was flying toward it. She sat up straight. This couldn't be good.

Space might be vast and space might be empty, but interstellars would plan their passage to transit—outbound or inbound—as close to Titan Station as possible. It saved time and ship resources. All interstellar traffic came and left in a fairly compact spherical zone around the station, and wormholes disrupted a large volume of space. Flying at a random vector across the developing throat of a wormhole was dangerous. Trying to open a wormhole in the vicinity of another one that was already open had been the basis for numerous horror vids. Space Traffic Control was vigilant. They had to be.

Saoirse connected to the Space Traffic Control system. The ship whose course she had picked up was the *Bay of Fundy*, but she found no communication from the ship or from Space Traffic Control to the ship about the wormhole. That was odd.

Saoirse watched a little longer. The *Bay of Fundy* kept flying toward the throat of the developing wormhole. Space Traffic Control did not send a warning.

Saoirse opened a comm channel. "*Bay of Fundy*," she said, "this is Specialist Saoirse Kenneally in StatOps. I'm sitting as sysadmin. Your course is going to cross an opening wormhole. You need to change course. Traffic Control, check that."

"This is Controller Matthis," said a male voice into her ear. "We're tracking *Bay of Fundy*. What are you looking at, Kenneally? There's no wormhole."

Sanae Nakagawa, navigator on the *Bay of Fundy*, was on the channel an instant later. She was not picking up a wormhole on her feed from the station either.

"It's there," Saoirse insisted. "It's there."

"Negative. There is no wormhole," Matthis said. "I have no idea what you think is a wormhole, Kenneally. Stick to your system and leave space traffic to us."

Saoirse went from concerned to boiling mad in a flash, just as she always did when someone put her down or, sometimes, only disagreed with her. She was going to find Space Traffic Control on the station and kick Controller Matthis in the balls. She was going to ram her fist into his mouth and pull out his tonsils. She was going to . . . She looked back at her boards and screens. The *Bay of Fundy* was going to be a flying cloud of scrap metal. Soon. How soon? That depended on *Bay of Fundy*'s course and the wormhole. It could be calculated, but she couldn't handle the math, because she'd been such a fuckup. She pounded her fist on her leg so hard it made her wince. Was there some reason Matthis didn't see the wormhole, other than that he was a fucktard?

The data from the astronomy and gravimetric instruments were transferred from the instruments themselves into the main computer, processed, and then transferred into the area of the computer that Space Traffic Control used, and to directories the ships accessed. Saoirse was different. From the sysadmin position, she was accessing the direct data feed from the instruments. She had access to every nook and cranny of Titan Station's computer.

It took very little time to look at the data flow. The problem was obvious. The data from the instruments scanning that region of space were not going to the directories accessed by Space Traffic Control or the *Bay of Fundy*. Somehow, Space Traffic Control and the *Bay of Fundy* were seeing old data from that region of space. The real, the current data were going . . . somewhere else. It looked as though they were being exported to a directory out of the system, somewhere Saoirse did not have access rights to. That was impossible, but it was true. She spent only a second thinking that, then discarded the thought, because it didn't matter. What mattered was changing the data flow.

She had to get this done, even though she felt like a miserable excuse for a human being. Felt? No, she *knew* she was a miserable excuse for a human being. She hated her feelings. Wished she could make them go away. *Goddamn it!* she thought. *Stop with the fucking feelings! Fix. The. Fucking. Computer.*

How much time did she have? No idea. Could be minutes, might only be seconds. She could see the throat of the wormhole forming, even if no one else could. The *Bay of Fundy* was flying perilously close. How close was too close? No idea.

She keyed in the list of changes. Prayed that fucktard Kenneally had it right. Hit Send.

Matthis' voice exploded in her ear. "Holy motherfucking Christ! Where did that wormhole come from?"

Saoirse Kenneally smiled.

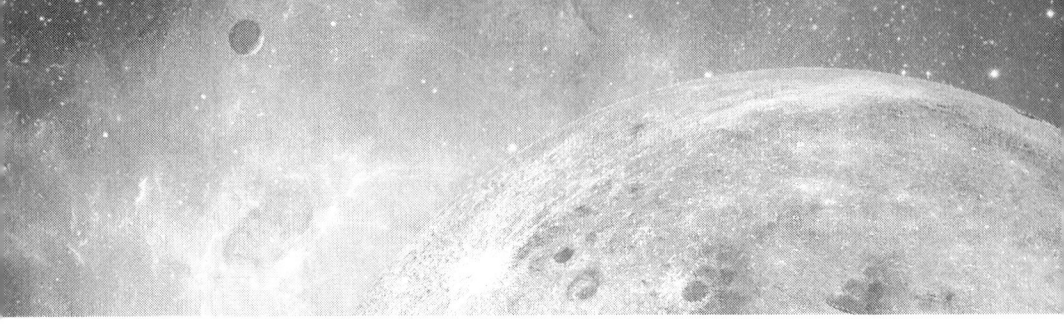

ELEVEN

In the aftermath of the *Bay of Fundy* incident, Saoirse received a message from Captain Szczechowicz, or S, as she tried to think of him. She was being officially commended for her action, which, in his determination, had saved the *Bay of Fundy*. Gusty came running into StatOps, nearly smothered her with a hug, and dragged her to lunch in the Mall, where she showed off the station's hero, while Saoirse's face turned the color of a beet. Mom made a fuss and held an actual party in StatOps, which Saoirse found even more embarrassing. Despite all the congratulations, she knew, inside herself, what she really was. Nothing had changed there.

Mom announced that she would conduct a review of the system to determine what had happened and to make certain it was fixed. She was going to do this personally, just as she took personal responsibility for the fact that there had been a problem in the system. All of that made Saoirse feel bad because of all the work that Mom had to do herself, although Mom pooh-poohed that over chai in her office, insisting that Saoirse should not feel bad about it. This only made Saoirse feel worse. What Mom wanted to know was every detail of what Saoirse had seen, how she had traced the data flow, and how she had fixed it. Mom kept pouring chai and said she would take care of everything, and if there was going to be blame for the defect in the system—well, that came with her position. Saoirse felt even worse when Mom said that. None of it seemed to bother Mom, though. Well, one thing did: Mom was upset that Saoirse had, as Mom put it, brought herself to the attention of Captain S.

"No good can come of that," Mom said. "You did the right thing, of course, child. You saved a ship! Everyone is grateful to you, and that is true. But now S knows who you are, and that is not a good thing. It makes me afraid for you. That girl from StatSec who came to see you. I am sure she is your friend, she seems nice, but please be careful."

Saoirse assured Mom that she would be careful, although she saw nothing that would require any special care. She threw herself into making certain that Mom had every possible detail of what she had found in the system. While that was more work for Mom, it kept her from worrying about Saoirse. Saoirse wasn't comfortable with Mom worrying about her. She wasn't worth it.

Despite the fuss and the attention, Saoirse went back to her routine as soon as possible. Routine was comforting. She worked her double shifts and snooped in various places, although she was careful not to do that when Mom was working in the system. One day she noticed a cargo transport inbound to Titan Station with a container of J&Lizzie brand clothing for shops in the Mall. The manifest was downloaded to the station's computer on approach. She accessed it in the Cargo Receiving section and saw the brand name. J&Lizzie was a line of clothing by a superhot celebrity duo who had moved from wearing and reviewing fashion to creating it. Their line was sleek and modern, and the stores in the Mall that were lucky enough to get some would probably sell out in a day or two.

J&Lizzie wasn't cheap, but it looked great on tall women, and Saoirse's pay had been accumulating in the Bank of Titan Station almost untouched. For the first time since her parents had cut off her credit, she had money she could spend. She absolutely had to have a pair of those jeans.

She left StatOps as soon as her shift ended and headed for the Mall instead of hanging around as she normally would. She knew when the ship had docked; she knew the estimated time for cargo off-loading and transfer from the information in the Cargo Receiving section. She had calculated in her head how long it would take for the container to be unpacked. She was going to be in the Mall at Schiffer's Clothing when the clothes were put out, and she would have first choice.

StatOps—and all of StatCent, for that matter—was located in E-Ring, the opposite end of the station cylinder from the dock concourse in A-Ring. The Mall occupied C-Ring, right in the middle. Saoirse made her way from StatOps to the ZoomChute. The Chute was like a cross between a trolley and an old-style pneumatic tube. It ran from the A-Ring dock concourse to StatCent on E-Ring and was the fastest way to traverse multiple rings, although since it took up almost all the height available in the ring, there was only one Chute. Two would have cut the rings in half. That also meant that not everyone found it convenient, especially those who had to walk halfway around a ring to reach it.

Saoirse hustled to the Chute station, determined to be the first customer for the J&Lizzie shipment. The car slid into the E-Ring station, and the doors opened just as she walked up. She slithered her way through a bunch of people who filled the open door, then grabbed an open seat before the rest of the group was in the car.

Two stops later, she got off at C-Ring and was greeted by a holographic banner, three-dimensional letters suspended in midair: WELCOME TO THE MALL AT TITAN STATION. LAST CHANCE TO SHOP BEFORE THE REACH! She walked through the letters, which took no notice and re-formed as soon as she had passed.

All travel guidebooks said that the Mall at Titan Station was one of the wonders of the world. In that, they were wrong, of course. The Mall at Titan Station orbited Titan, which in turn orbited Saturn, and was nowhere near Earth. Still, to have a shopping mall there was a wonder, and the Mall tried to live up to its reputation. Its wide main corridor started from the C-Ring Chute Station and went two-thirds of the way around the ring, the rest being reserved for storage. Smaller cross-corridors ran from the main corridor out to the sidewalls of C-Ring. A visitor could choose among restaurants that varied from cheap breakfast places to fine dining. An even greater variety of bars catered to everyone from construction workers to the tourists who could afford high-priced drinks. All manner of shops filled the spaces between bars and restaurants. Some, like the giant Schiffer's Clothing, took up the entire space between the main corridor and the ring sidewall. Schiffer's was famous for its slogan, TAKING FASHION TO THE STARS, that hung holographically in the main corridor. In truth, most high-end clients visited Schiffer's on the way home from the Reach to be sure their wardrobe was properly updated after spending months away from Earth. Other, smaller shops, usually on the cross-corridors, were dedicated to used equipment, as it was cheaper and quicker to repair almost anything than obtain a replacement from Earth.

Polished wood carvings from Middle Kingdom in the Reach competed for attention with the prosaic laundry detergent that stationers needed. In the Mall on this day was a shipment of J&Lizzie clothing. Saoirse knew exactly where she had to go.

She was close to Schiffer's Clothing when she walked past the front of Brian Boru's Harp, with its sparkling green harp hanging in the air of the mall corridor, advertising the Harp's Titan-famous food and drink. The Harp's reputation owed far more to its drinks than to its food. It also had a reputation for a loud and rambunctious crowd that often crossed the line from animated discussion into fisticuffs. The peacers knew the Harp well; Saoirse had read some of the reports. What stopped her at the sparkling harp was the person who crossed in front of her and went into the bar. Gusty.

Gusty wasn't in her SCOPP dark blues, but wore a white shirt with flowers and gray pants. Well, Gusty off-duty had no fashion sense. They hadn't spent any time together since the day of the *Bay of Fundy* incident. Suddenly, Saoirse needed to talk to Gusty. But Gusty had gone into the Harp, into a bar. Saoirse decided she could handle it.

She followed Gusty inside the Harp. It took her eyes a moment to adjust to the dim lighting and the noise level, an indecipherable babble of too many conversations in too small a space. Gusty had disappeared, but the bar was directly ahead of her. A burly man sat there, right where she was looking. Dark shadows on cheeks and pate implied thick hair shaved off for his helmet, and that meant someone who worked outside in a suit most of the day, maybe dock or construction. He fit in with most of the individuals around him, and there was nothing special or pleasant about him. What held her eye wasn't the man, but what he was holding. It was a flextainer with a cap and a nipple, exactly what someone would use in zero gee. According to the flextainer's logo, it held Saturn's Rings Lager, a station-brewed beer. Saoirse had never thought of beer in a flextainer. The idea was intriguing. Beer in a flextainer.

The man saw her looking and probably thought she was looking at him. He winked. Saoirse was focused on the beer in the flextainer. She had never had beer out of a flextainer.

She needed to leave. But she could have a beer in a flextainer.

She had to get out of there. But she wasn't going to leave, was she?

She knew better than to stay, but she also knew she wasn't going to leave. She took a step closer to the man at the bar, who smiled.

"Saoirse, are you okay?" A hand touched her wrist. It was Gusty, her face concerned.

"Yeah, I'm fine," Saoirse said. "Just came in for some water. I'll see you around." She took another step toward the bar.

Gusty's touch turned into a tug. "Saoirse, you should come with me. Now."

That snapped Saoirse's mind back to where she was. She needed to leave. Except the man at the bar had stood up and was closing the distance between them. Saoirse turned to leave, to follow Gusty.

"Hey," he said, "you don't stand there staring at me like that and then you just leave the moment I get up. You sit down and have a drink with me."

"No, I'm sorry," Saoirse said, scrambling for an excuse that didn't sound insulting. "I thought you were someone else."

"I'm better than someone else," the man said, leering. "Stay and drink with me." He reached out as though to touch her.

Saoirse realized she had lost contact with Gusty. "No." She raised her hand to fend him off, and he clamped on to it with a grip like a vise. She twisted her arm but couldn't free it. She swung her free hand at his face, but he just batted it away.

"I saw you looking. C'mon and have a drink and you can get to know who you were looking at."

Saoirse's answer was a vicious kick aimed at his groin. He blocked it with a beefy hand that hit her knee and left her feeling like her leg had snapped, while still keeping his grip on her wrist. Off-balance, she tried to punch him with her free hand, but he grabbed that wrist too.

He laughed. "Seems we're gettin' real close now. Time to give ol' Bulkhead Bob Deroach a kiss, for starters."

She opened her mouth, then thrust her face forward like a piston. Her teeth clamped around his nose and bit down as hard as she could. Bob roared and tried to shove her away. She kept her grip on his nose and tightened her jaws, feeling cartilage crack under her teeth. The taste of hot blood and mucus filled her mouth. She bit deeper. Bob screamed.

She felt herself picked up off the floor, then slammed down on her back on something hard. The bar? There was a crack in her back as she hit. Hands grabbed at her.

A claxon rang out overhead. Multiple voices shouted, "Peacers!" and then the shouting blurred into a wordless cacophony. She was no longer clamped on to Bob's nose. She tried to raise her head to see, screamed, and struck out wildly. That was when a big hand grabbed her face and smashed the back of her head into the bar.

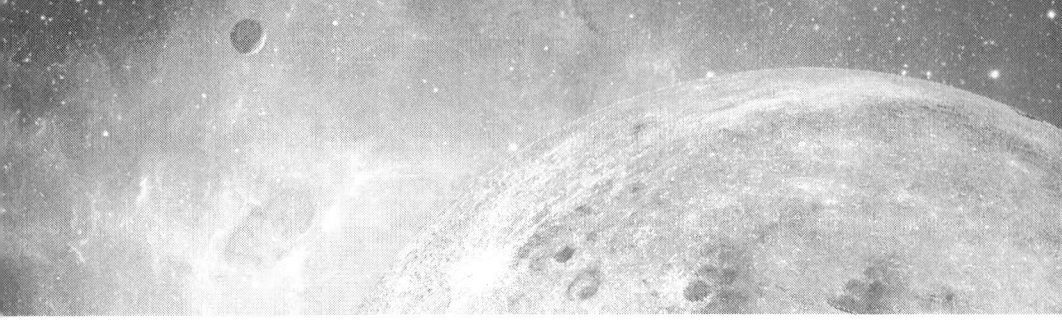

TWELVE

Saoirse awoke on a narrow bed. She sat up, put her feet on the floor, winced, and tried to take stock. The middle of her back hurt, but she could move all her limbs. It couldn't be that bad. Gingerly, she explored the back of her head and found a tender lump that matched up well with her throbbing headache. A bandage had been wrapped around her left hand. No idea why that was there, but it hurt under the bandage when she clenched her fist or wiggled her fingers. All her muscles tingled, and she felt pins and needles in different places, which would vanish only to reappear elsewhere almost immediately. She knew that sensation. Nerve tangler hangover. She had been stunned. Why?

Saoirse looked around her. Except for the bed, the small room was empty. A doorway past the foot of the bed was blocked by solid gray. A force field, not a door. She was in a holding cell. She was a connoisseur of those. But why?

After a few minutes of sitting on the bed, wondering about the situation, she saw the field go transparent and heard a click as it turned off. On the other side stood a man in a blue SCOPP uniform with a StatSec patch.

"Would you come with me, please?" he asked.

"Like there is a choice?"

Saoirse walked with him down the corridor outside her cell, then turned right with him where the corridor ended in another hallway. A short walk from there brought them to a door, where he stopped, looked into the faceplate, and put his thumb on a separate pad. The door slid open. The scopp gestured for her to go in but did not accompany her.

Inside was a spartan office dominated by a large desk. Half a dozen screens sat on the desk, along with a keypad and an open comm. The man behind the desk stood up when she walked in. He was about her height. Sandy hair was cropped short over a face the color of a fading summer tan. Pale blue eyes framed a nose that could have served as a straightedge. Thin lips held no trace of a smile. Suddenly, it registered that he was not wearing SCOPP dark blue. Instead, he wore the light-blue shirt of a peacer uniform, captain's bars on the collar. A small star, composed of four smaller red stars topped by a gold one, adorned the left breast of his shirt. His name badge read, SZCZECHOWICZ. Saoirse recalled his face from the image on Mom's comm. This was Captain S, the one Mom had warned her to stay away from at all cost.

He introduced himself in a voice surprising for its softness. His name sounded like *Sheh-co-witz*. "Most people call me Captain S," he added. "At least to my face." His lips twitched into a smile.

Saoirse ignored the pleasantry. "Why the fuck am I here?" The best defense was a good offense. "I'm the one who got attacked. For no goddamn reason."

"You punched the scopp who tried to help you up," he said.

Saoirse didn't remember any of that. "Well, what the fuck did they expect," she said anyway. "Mess like that."

"You broke one of her teeth," S said. "The doc had to pull the chip of her tooth out of your hand. That will heal up fine. It'll just leave a small scar to go with the other ones on your knuckles."

Saoirse looked at her bandaged hand. "I'll tell her I'm sorry," she said.

"The rest of you scanned okay," he went on. "Your back is bruised where it hit the edge of the bar, but nothing is broken. You've got a concussion to go with the contusion on your head. Doc gave you a dose of anti-tau to prevent any long-term effects. You can go back to full activity, but there's nothing we can do about the headache. It will clear in a couple of days."

"I know about concussions," Saoirse said.

"I'm sure you do."

"Okay, thanks for the medical report. Now, am I being charged for busting one of your pretty faces?"

"No." S paused. "I've watched the vids from the security cameras in the Harp. I've seen what happened. You're lucky Gray is your friend. She's the one who messaged StatSec when it got nasty in there, and since she works for me, it got attention a lot faster than if it had been a typical bar fight and gone through the scopp on monitor duty. Incidentally, Gray talked with the scopp whose face you busted. Again, you're lucky."

"You don't want to know about my luck," Saoirse said. "What about that asshole who started it?"

S sighed. "Well, we're charging him. But let me tell you something, Kenneally. Concannon has used him for, shall we say, dirty work in the past. Charges don't end up going anywhere. He'll be fined. That's about it. Of course, you nearly had his nose for dinner, so I won't say he gets off free."

"Food's better in the other restaurants," Saoirse said. "I'd send that back. What should get torn off are his balls. And then I'd serve them in a soup, along with his nose."

"Can't say I disagree with you," S said, "but I can only bring the charges. Then it goes to StatEx and I'm just telling you how the politics will work."

Saoirse said nothing. Mom had said S was Concannon's man, did his dirty work. Was S the one who fixed it so the charges wouldn't amount to anything? Some people could spin complicated lies with a perfectly straight face. She should know.

S looked down at his comm and tapped the screen. Then he said, "Answer me a question, Kenneally. You're the one who saved the *Bay of Fundy*. We still don't understand how you did it, unless Mom has figured it out and isn't telling anyone. You obviously understood what was going to happen and you put it together and made it work under pressure. Yet you barely made it through high school. How did you do it?"

"You fuckin' know why I 'barely' made it through high school. Even if that's the first time you've looked at my fuckin' file."

He raised his eyebrows. "All the more reason I'm asking the question."

Saoirse looked at the floor, then back at S, who was watching her calmly. "I was looking across the feeds and saw what was happening," she said. "I could extrapolate, shit, guess, what was going to happen." Then she told him about a childhood spent hacking every system two programmer parents could throw at her. "I don't need to go to school to know how to make computers do what I want them to do," she finished. "Give me a little time, and I'll make that computer," she pointed at the screens on his desk, "suck your dick."

His face twisted into a grimace. "Kenneally, is there some reason you make such an effort to come across as coarse, low-life scum?"

"I'm told I have issues."

"Yeah." He actually grinned. "If you're going to continue having 'issues,' I'd like to give you a little advice. Something I know a lot about. You need to learn how to fight."

"I know how to fight!"

"No, you don't." S put his hands on the desk and leaned forward, looking up at her. His voice became earnest. "You fight just well enough to get yourself killed. Somehow, that would bother me. Meet me at the station gym tomorrow night after work. I'll show you what I mean, and maybe, if you'll do it, I'll teach you."

Saoirse laughed, but without humor in it. "Sure. Convenient way to get your hands in my pants."

S laughed in return. "Don't overrate your attractiveness, Kenneally. If I really wanted to do that, I had you here and stunned, and I have control of the monitors. Show up or not. Up to you."

・ ・ ・

"He said he would do what?"

Mom paused in the middle of pouring hot chai into Saoirse's cup. She'd pulled Saoirse into her office the moment she showed up after her release from StatSec. It had taken little urging to get Saoirse's version of the evening before. She was well into the tale before she sat down, and continued while Mom prepared a fresh pot of chai.

"He said he would teach me how to fight," she repeated.

Mom shook her head. "You should stay out of places like Brian Boru's Harp." She finished pouring Saoirse's cup and poured one of her own. "I cannot say you should work more hours, because you already work more than anyone but me, and I appreciate that. I follow what you do and you are good about keeping me updated and I rarely have anything to correct. But you do not need to go to places like that. It is not safe for you."

"I know that." Saoirse wondered *how* Mom meant it wasn't safe. Was she referring to more than the physical attack? She decided she didn't care. StatOps was where she was safe, particularly in Mom's office. Sometimes, though, Mom could be like a mother hen. "I'm not that fragile."

"Fragile or not, you should not be in places like that. And I have warned you about our Captain S. He is a strange and dangerous man."

"You told me he was Concannon's man. Do you mean something else?"

"Well." Mom pursed her lips, then took a sip. "Captain S is a combat peacer. Do you know the expression? What it means?"

Saoirse shook her head.

Mom drank more chai before she continued. "There are two types of peacers," Mom said. "Not officially, but there are. The regular ones, the type we usually have on Titan Station—they are like the police on Earth. Not much different from the uniformed SCOPP, only that they carry weapons and enforce the rules. As long as you follow the rules, there is no trouble. The other type are the combat peacers, like S. They are the ones sent out into the Reach to do the fighting. They are soldiers, really, and that is what they are used for. Violence to them is like, well, having a cup of chai is to us. That is what they do."

Mom shook her head. "Captain S has been in combat, years of it. He has been wounded two times, maybe three, and after the last time, he was assigned here, where he works for Mx. Concannon. He is not a good person for you to be around. There will be a reason he wants to do this teaching you to fight, child, and it will not be a good reason."

Saoirse smiled at Mom over her raised teacup. "I'm sure there's a reason, and I'm sure I know the reason. I'm not such a child, Mom. I know how to fight and I know how to take care of myself."

She said it smoothly, easily, and with assurance. She took a sip of her chai and knew what she had said wasn't true. Well, she did know how to fight. Of necessity. But she had never taken care of herself.

You cried when the kids called you names in school when you were little. You remember that time in Dublin when they dared you to run across the quad naked and you did it for God knows what reason and they had hidden your clothes and laughed at you and took pictures and the school called your parents and made out that it was your fault— Stop it, Saoirse!

Saoirse refocused her eyes on Mom. She was on Titan Station, not in Dublin.

"I'll be okay, Mom."

Mom's eyes looked worried, the way they often did. "If you see this man, you let me know what happens with him. You tell me everything, child. Mom will take care of you."

"I know that, Mom, and I appreciate it." Saoirse stretched her legs out and relaxed. If she never had to leave Mom's office, that would be fine.

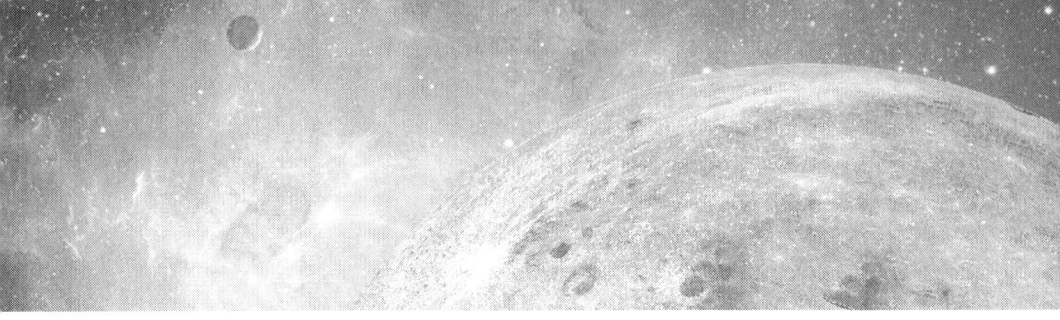

THIRTEEN

Saoirse left work, in her estimate, only a little late. She had dithered, ready to claim that she hadn't cleared all the issues, but she really had nothing left to clear. She hovered by the sysadmin chair, as ready to sit back down as she was to walk out, and watched the time on the clock. S was going to think she was scared of him, or too sure of herself, or an idiot, or an asshole, and he would probably share his opinion of her with Gusty. With a string of curses that would have made Mom wince, she spun on her heel and left StatOps.

The gym facility for station personnel was on E-Ring as well, so she arrived no more than five minutes late, breathing hard from having run through the last few corridors. It took several more minutes to locate S. He was not in the workout area where most people congregated, with rows of exercise machinery and weights lining the sides of the room. Far to the back of the gym, though, was a separate room, its floor covered by a firm mat with a ring layout printed in the center of it. S was standing in the center of the ring. He wore a skintight, short-sleeved workout shirt and pants to match. His feet were bare. That shirt was tight enough that Saoirse could see the definition of his abdominal muscles, although she told herself she was imagining that . . . and why was she even looking? He seemed to be checking the time on the clock mounted near the entrance.

"Didn't think I would show up, did you?" She thought she managed an insouciant tone.

"Maybe I was only wondering how late you would be." He didn't smile. "You should take your shoes and socks off."

"Why? Are you going to teach me kung fu?" She struck a mock pose, balanced on one foot.

He did not smile at that, either. "No. It just helps keep the mat clean." He pointed at a sign by the door that read, BARE, CLEAN FEET IN THE MAT AREA.

"Oh." Saoirse pulled off her station shoes and socks and left them in the designated area next to a pair that, she assumed, belonged to S. It gave her a moment to turn away from him and try to control her blush. Then she turned back to him and walked to the center of the mat.

"Now what?" she asked.

"Now I show you why I think you don't know how to fight."

"I told you, I know how to fight," Saoirse said. "I've done enough of it." The last was true, but she had to admit to herself that the results had often been bad.

"Really?" said S. "It didn't look that way in the camera feeds from the Harp."

"I was doing fine until one of your SCOPP drones hit me with a nerve tangler."

"I think we may have different concepts of 'doing fine.' Tell you what. Hit me. Anywhere, however you want. Hit me hard."

Saoirse stared at him. He looked relaxed and stood with his hands down at his sides. His face held no expression, but she was sure he was laughing at her. He probably didn't believe she would actually hit him. Wrong.

She stepped forward and threw a hard right cross at his nose. S made a little sidestep; his left arm swung up and blocked her punch. Saoirse winced at the impact. She rubbed her wrist, shook out her hand, and clenched and unclenched her fist. S said nothing.

"Damn you," she said under her breath. She could feel the anger rising inside her.

She attacked again, this time with a left hook that hit only air as S moved just enough to dodge it. She followed it immediately with a right, but he stepped the other way this time, and a soft tap with his left hand directed her punch into the air past his head. She recocked her fist, punched again with her right. He blocked it just as he had the first time, but this time his right hand struck out so fast she did not see it move. His open palm connected with her cheek, hard enough to make her vision flash white, if not hard enough to knock her down.

"What the fuck?" she yelled at him.

"The most important thing in a fight is not to get hit," S said. "You need to learn how to take care of yourself."

By this point, Saoirse was furious. She wanted to knock him on his ass. She lunged forward with a roundhouse right-hand punch that had all her strength behind it.

S stepped in, blocked it. Dimly, she was aware of his right leg swinging up high behind her shoulder. The next instant, his leg slashed down, catching both her legs below and behind her knees. Saoirse felt both her feet leave the mat. His arm hit across her chest, propelling her down. She smashed into the mat, flat on her back. Whatever air was in her lungs whooshed out. She struggled to draw breath and felt as if she were suffocating. She wanted to cry but she was not going to do that in front of S. Yet wetness gathered at the corners of her eyes. It was awful.

"If you want to learn, I can teach you," S said, looking down at her as she gasped. "I will teach you, but you have to want to do it."

Saoirse's eyes did not want to focus; it was hard to find enough breath to speak. "So you proved a point," she said finally. "Good for you. Why are you bothering?"

"There was a time I thought I knew how to fight," S said. After a moment, he added, "It's a peacer thing. I think you're worth it. Meet me here tomorrow night, same time. We'll train every day. Or don't. Up to you."

He reached down to help her up. Saoirse ignored his hand, rolled over, and got to her feet herself. That way, he couldn't see her wipe at her eyes.

· · ·

Saoirse was on time the next night. S was waiting for her.

"Surprised I'm back?" she asked.

"Maybe a little." He checked the time and grinned. "I was prepared to wait awhile."

"I'm here to work." She paused. "Asshole."

They worked for the next two hours, practicing blocks and throwing punches and kicks. Blocking S's arm when he threw a punch felt like hitting a metal pipe with her arm. Both her arms hurt long before they finished, but she refused to look at them until she got back to her room. What she saw then was a continuous row of overlapping reddish blotches from wrist to elbow. When she ran her finger over them, she felt a string of bumps to match the blotches.

She was back the next night, and added to the bruises, and then each night after that. The drills progressed to more complete techniques, then to locks and throws and to sparring, bare fist and bare foot. As the days passed, the blotches and bumps turned purple and green and then faded away. Even though she was hitting as hard as ever, her arms stopped bruising.

・ ・ ・

"Do not let anyone grab you," S said one night. "Any man you fight is likely to be bigger and stronger than you—and you can hold off on the 'fuck you' and how you know how to grapple, because I'm right, and you better know it." His voice harshened and he pointed a finger at her, nearly stuck it in her face.

His blast caught Saoirse with the expletive on the tip of her tongue. She stopped, mouth agape, then stuck her tongue out at him as though that had been her intent all along.

"Your leg is longer than your arm," he said, ignoring her expression, "so kicks can help you keep your distance, but don't only go for the groin. Most men have a near-automatic defensive reflex there. We'll drill kicks." And they did, until Saoirse could barely walk and thought her legs would fall off.

S moved on to teach techniques that were vicious and nasty. "Eyes, throat, knees, those are the weakest points," he said. He showed her open-hand attacks that would crack a larynx, finger strikes that would rip out eyeballs, and throws that would break a neck in the process.

Saoirse had to concede that she was learning how to fight, hard and dirty, and she had to admit that she liked it. But where was all of this going? Logically, when a guy paid this much attention to a girl, there was only one place it could go. Yet, it *didn't*.

Nor was it a situation where S was a guy who simply got his kicks out of knocking her around on the mat. Saoirse's skills improved with all the practice, and improved fast. The tipping point came one night when they were sparring. She faked a roundhouse kick at his ribs; he bit on the fake. She pulled the kick back and, without putting her foot down, angled her leg up high and whipped him across his face with the bridge of her foot. From then on, he was as likely to sport a black eye or split lip as she was.

But when they finished working out, all they did was go to the refreshment area and get smoothies—S was partial to Smooth as Silk avocado and açai—and then sit at one of the tiny tables to drink their smoothies and talk. About fighting techniques, or Titan, or a million other inconsequential things. Yes, the tables were tiny, so their fingers touched or their knees bumped. Yes, they made eye contact. But that was *it*.

When their eyes met, she saw a longing in his. It was there, even if he would break off the gaze. Color would rise in his cheeks that had nothing to do with sparring contact. When their hands touched by accident, sometimes they lingered. His touch was warm and welcome and she kept her hand next to his deliberately. She knew he was going to stroke her hand then, but he didn't. He would look down with a little blush, and then take a drink of smoothie.

Finally, Saoirse couldn't take it anymore. She arranged to meet Gusty for coffee and raised the issue, very obliquely since S was Gusty's boss. Gusty's comment was, "Then *you* tell *him* you like him. For God's sake, Saoirse, are you telling me you're almost twenty-one and you can't do that?"

Saoirse hastened to say that wasn't true, of course it wasn't true. What she didn't tell Gusty was that she had never done it sober. Drinking, she reflected after they finished breakfast, had covered for deficiencies in some social skills. She felt paralyzed. Mom would be no help; there was no way she could tell Mom what she was thinking about S. She was left to figure out her own way forward.

The following night, as they sat down with smoothies in hand, she leaned across the table and asked, "So, S, what's the deal here? Are you gay?"

"Huh?" For the first time, Saoirse saw him look confused. "No, I'm not. Why would you ask that?"

"Why?" Her voice slid up an octave in the course of that single syllable.

Don't lose it, Saoirse. Don't lose it like you always do, and then you end up looking like a jerk even when you had every right to say what you said and— Shut up, Saoirse!

"Why?" she repeated. "Because there's a way the boy-girl thing works, and this isn't it. You picked me up. You know you did, even if that was the weirdest and worst pickup line in the history of male-female relationships. I went along with it, and what do I have to show for it except a remarkable set of bruises that, somehow, I seem to have agreed to . . ." She ran down, like a comm out of battery, and threw her arms in the air.

He looked startled. "What are you talking about, Saoirse? I said I'd teach you how to fight, which will hopefully keep you alive. And, yeah, the bruises go with the territory. But you're tough enough to do it, and I admire that."

"Admire," she said, then paused. "That is not a boy-girl word. You're obviously a bio male and you said you're not gay, so the way this works is you pick me up, I agree to get picked up, then you try to get into my pants while I worry about whether the word *commitment* is in your vocabulary and how I'll feel about it next week. It's not about sitting here and playing finger touchy and a little footsie underneath the table."

His look changed back to confusion. "I like working out with you, Saoirse. I thought you liked it too."

"Yes, I fuckin' like working out with you!" she shouted. "That's not the point. The point is, where is this going?" *Good going, Saoirse. How to ruin it with the one guy whose one and only objective isn't sex.*

S turned bright red. "Saoirse, I'm head of StatSec. You're a scopp. We can't . . . I mean . . ."

"Maybe we could go to a real dinner," she said. "Let's do that. You pick the place and let me know." Then she bolted for the exit before he could turn her down.

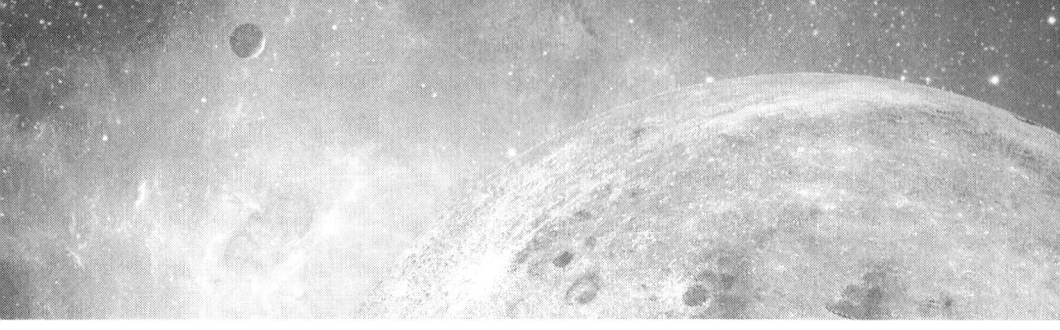

FOURTEEN

Saoirse was pretty much useless the next day. If she wasn't checking her comm for a message—which she didn't need to do, because it was set to alert her when one came in—or staring at its screen, as if staring at it would make a message come in, she sat looking blankly at the StatOps screens and boards and doing nothing. She didn't do her maintenance checks; she didn't even do any snooping. All the systems of Titan Station could have locked up and crashed, and she would not have noticed until the light, heat, and oxygen went out. Maybe not even then.

It was all very un-Saoirse-like, so much so that a message from Mom arrived asking what was wrong. Saoirse tossed off a quick response, blaming it all on her period, but that triggered an avalanche of advice—the virtues of chai as a remedy for cramps and headaches, how dwelling on it made it worse while keeping busy could distract the mind, and why in this day and age and as bright a girl as she was, why didn't she have an implant to prevent this, and Mom could jump over any queue to get her an appointment in Medical.

Saoirse fended off each succeeding message with whatever came into her head until the one about the implant. That pulled her out of her daze. She knew the system well enough that she could jump the appointment queue as easily as Mom, but it made her realize that Mom could peek into her medical file and see that Saoirse already had an implant. That set off a more complicated lie, in case Mom looked. That was the problem with lies: they were complicated to maintain.

Still, she wasn't going to tell Mom the truth. She knew her opinion of S. It was bad enough to be cautioned every other day about working out with the man. A dinner date? Sometimes working with Mom was as bad as having a parent.

Of course, given the slime you used to date, who in their right mind would approve of what you did or the choices you made? But who else was going to date you when all you were interested in was— Stop that, Saoirse!

She became caught up in the memories of everything she had done wrong, datewise. All she could think about, when she wasn't fending off Mom, was that she had pushed S when he didn't want to be pushed. There would be no message, no dinner, no more workouts. She realized she would miss them when that happened. How did she manage, with such precision, to say the wrong thing every goddamn time?

She was so busy stewing that it was a good fifteen minutes before she noticed her comm screen had a message indicator.

"Fuck!" She jabbed at the screen with her thumb with enough force that it blanked. That almost caused heart failure. Fortunately, the screen came back.

MEET ME AT TITAN'S RIB FOR DINNER AT 19:00. S.

Well, that's a bit terse, she thought. *Real happy to take me to dinner, aren't you?* No *Dear Saoirse*, not even *Hey, Kenneally*, no cute avatar to blow a trumpet and have the message unroll from the trumpet. He probably put more enthusiasm into posting the duty roster. Serve him right if she did have menstrual cramps and had to go off sick. Or just ghosted him.

Don't be your fucking idiot self, Saoirse, the way you usually are.

She managed to interrupt her inner diatribe. She'd asked for dinner; she'd gotten it. And this wasn't Olga's, the twenty-four seven breakfast place where she hung out with Gusty. This was Titan's Rib, where Concannon would take visiting luminaries from Earth; where you couldn't tell that the thick rib-eye had even seen the inside of the ultralow freezer. This was *dinner*.

No sooner did she have that thought than her mind moved on to what it implied. A man didn't take a date—a first date—to this sort of dinner without expecting something. He had to know there was no way she could pay half of it. Dinner was the *quid* that went with the *quo*. But hadn't she almost suggested that herself? *Suggested?* All her talk about the boy-girl thing? Like S didn't know? What had she gotten herself into? *You know exactly what you've gotten yourself into, Saoirse. Just like usual.* Maybe the air lock was the best way out.

When her shift ended, she literally ran out of StatOps to avoid the risk of Mom corralling her for a soothing cup of chai and a talk. She did not head to the air lock, however. She went back to her room.

It took only thirty seconds to realize that she had nothing to wear to a place like Titan's Rib. She had never gotten any of the J&Lizzie clothes after the fight in the Harp. By the time she had been released from StatSec, everything she wanted had sold out. The old jeans and shirt she had worn in jail in Kenosha had been cleaned and were in her closet, but she could still see stains and smell vomit, even if the smell was in her mind. Those had been from a donation pile at a shelter, anyway. Junk. The best she had was the SCOPP uniform, she realized to her horror. Oh my God. No help for it, however.

That left her having to dash for the Mall, because after all her anguish over the clothes, she was late. It would serve her right if he left. Of course, she wasn't that late, and only a real jerk would leave that quickly. Saoirse made a mental note to put a kick upside his head the next time they worked out, as payback for what he had put her through.

Her mad dash came to a halt in front of Titan's Rib, an undistinguished storefront on the main corridor of the Mall. No hologram projected into the walkway, no lights, no sound. Only the restaurant's name in black letters above the doorway. She stopped there to catch her breath, oblivious to passersby who stared at the panting scoppy. She was not going to walk into there looking as though she had run halfway around Titan Station, even if that was the truth. Better to be a little later. That gave her an opportunity to glance at the menu that was physically posted on the wall by the entrance. Her eyes shied away from the prices and lit on the wine list. Wine list! Of course he would have ordered an expensive bottle of wine. She was late, no way to stop that. It would be uncorked by now. What was she going to say? What lie could she come up with? And a glass of wine on the table, under her nose . . .

You're going to handle it, Saoirse? After how well you did in the Harp? Maybe the air lock is the best idea after all.

Somehow, she walked through the door.

Titan's Rib was quiet inside, a contrast to the noisy buzz that filled the corridors of the Mall. All three interior walls were covered by a panoramic hologram of a tropical island beach of white sand fronting a blue lagoon. Human waiters attended customers at tables covered in pure white linen. Saoirse knew about the human staff the same way she knew about the quality of the steaks: she had examined Titan's Rib on the system from her chair in StatOps. Reading was one thing, though; seeing was another. She gaped.

"Hey, Kenneally, wake up!"

S sat at a small table that looked as though it had been set in front of a clump of palm trees. Saoirse walked over and saw that two glasses of water were the only objects on the table, aside from the flatware.

"You can sit down, you know," S said. She sat. "I'll apologize in advance—with the price of these steaks, all we can drink is water."

In a way, she was mad. He was cheaping out on her dinner. But she managed to catch herself before any words came out. If she complained, he might order wine—and then what? She said, "I'll take your marker for the future."

S grinned. She liked his grin. The blue eyes that could be so cold held a twinkle. And he was in uniform too—the light-blue peacer shirt with the small Star of Stars over the left breast.

Say something, Saoirse! "How did you get your stars?" she blurted.

The grin vanished. "Something to learn, Saoirse. Peacers don't *get* stars, because that sounds like someone gives them to you. We say that we 'make' our stars, because we have to earn them in combat."

She swallowed hard. Always saying the wrong thing when it mattered. "I'm sorry."

He was waving the apology away almost before her words were out. "Don't look like your pet just died," he said. "Almost everyone who's not a peacer says it wrong. We're particular about it, though; all the more so because they're unofficial."

"What?" Saoirse pointed at his chest. "They're on your uniform. How much more official can they get?"

S smiled. "Peacers started wearing stars around 2159 or 2160. Nobody's sure of the date, the same way nobody is sure which unit started it. The stars spread from one unit to another out in the Reach as the interstellars went from one star to another. Nobody except peacers paid attention until peacers wearing stars started to come back to the solar system. That set off—what's the word?—a ruckus. The US claimed that the peacers' Star of Stars looked too much like the insignia for a top-rank American general and demanded we change it. Predictably, the peacers refused. People used a lot of words and a lot of bandwidth on it for a couple of years. They called it the War of the Stars, although, thankfully, no real weapons were used. In the end, the US blocked the Solar Council from recognizing the Peacers' Stars as an official honor and we keep wearing them right where everyone can see them. It's one of those peacer things that makes us different. Always remember, when you speak to a peacer, the stars mean a lot—maybe more than anything else."

"I'll remember that," Saoirse said. "Let me start again. How did you *make* your stars?"

The twinkle in S's eyes returned. "On Freya," he said. "Pretty planet about four hundred light-years out. We were sent to keep the American colonists from fighting the Russians who were there. Ended up fighting both of them at the same time."

"Sounds crazy," she said. "And why are your stars red, all except the top one?"

"We wear red stars if we've been wounded in action," he said. "In my case, three times, but it only takes once to wear red."

"And the gold star on the top?"

He waved his hand in the air between them. "That's just an award."

"Just an award? An award for fighting?"

"One not worth discussing," S said. "But, yes, it's about fighting. There's always fighting in the Reach."

"I know. I've read about it, seen the newsfeeds."

"Actually, you don't know," he said sharply. The grin was gone. "Nobody knows, not really, because most of what happens in the Reach never gets into the databases on Earth, and so much of what does get into the databases is crap. Nothing goes in the databases at all unless a ship comes back and downloads, and who's to say whether what they download is true? Maybe if someone went through all the units' reports at HQ, maybe then you could put it together, but it would still be incomplete. So accept that nobody knows. Like the old, old days. Before computers, before the internet, like it was when we sailed around the world in ships and you knew only what the ship brought." He put his hands on the table, looking into the air over her head. "The Interstellar Reach of Humanity," he said slowly, "with the Solar Council and Assembly of Worlds in charge. The Reach. Some people call it an empire, others a commonwealth or a network. It's none of those."

"What is it?" Saoirse asked.

"It's chaos." The intensity in his voice rose. "Chaos. Constant warfare on more worlds than I can think of. Little bubbles of peace and prosperity that allow people to delude themselves that life is good out in the Reach."

"But that's what the peacers are for, isn't it?" Saoirse asked. "What's the slogan? Bringing Peace to the Reach?"

"Yeah. We try." S let out a sigh. "The one thing the Solar Council did right, maybe the only thing, is keep control of all the interstellars and their crews. So at least nobody is dropping through wormholes with nuclear bombs, and we don't have ships gunning for each other with missiles. Not yet, anyway." He shook his head. "Otherwise, none of the philosopher geniuses who set up the SC had a clue what humans are like in their natural state. They should have read Thomas Hobbes. I did, a few years ago; I've spent plenty of time in hospitals. Did you know that when interstellars first went out, there were no peacers, not even SCOPP? That people somehow assumed humanity would go to the stars and build one utopia after another?"

Saoirse shook her head.

"Well, they did. But it became obvious really fast that the colonies needed administrators and teachers and people to manage logistics. So they set up SCOPP. You can look all that up. But then some scoppies got themselves butchered. It happened more than once. So they sent out what they called protection squads. With weapons. Until someone pointed out that *armed protection squad* translates into German as 'Waffen SS.' The stench of that name hadn't worn off — still hasn't, and probably never will." He shook his head. "The idiots couldn't even name an organization properly. They changed it to the Peacemakers, with a formal name that means nothing in any language, and we're damned near an army today. That history has been cleaned from the databases. You won't find it anywhere. But we fly from star to star and try to put out the fires."

The intensity in his voice seemed to reverberate inside her and she liked that feeling, but she was also aware of the strain in his lean face as he spoke. "I'll tell you something," he added. "If there is a God and he's looking down on the galaxy, he'd see the Reach as an abscess that's burst, uncontrolled infection spreading in all directions. That's what we humans are. God might think the galaxy needs a spiral arm amputated."

She blinked. "Christ, S. That's dark."

"Sorry. I don't talk about this much." He glanced to the side; a waiter was approaching. "Enough with depression," he said. "Order the biggest steak on the menu as compensation for listening to me go off like that."

Orders placed and the waiter gone, Saoirse looked at the man across the table. The strain she had seen in his face was gone, but he did not look happy. Not the way she wanted him to look while having dinner with her.

"Why don't you tell me your story?" she asked. She had listened to many stories over the years and had told her own, with varying degrees of truthfulness, many times as well. It was comfortable ground.

He took a sip of water. "I joined the peacers when I was sixteen. Been one for eight years now, spent maybe a year of that in hospitals recovering from, well, those times. Was posted here about two years ago. The rule is, after three wounds, your next post is administrative."

"Sixteen?" Saoirse said. "You can't join at that age."

Her words brought a wry smile to S's face. "You're thinking like an Earther," he said. "I wasn't born on Earth, and it's different in the Reach. Rules are different, when there are any rules."

"Okay. You were born in the Reach. Now we're getting somewhere. What planet? What's your family like? How did you grow up? Why did you join the peacers at sixteen?"

"The peacers are my family," S said. "Sergeant Baker, James Andrew Baker, he was my sergeant when I joined. He made me grow up, made me read books, taught a kid who thought he knew how to fight how to really fight. You know, training in the early days of the peacers was pretty rudimentary. If you were lucky, someone took you on and showed you what you needed to know. That became a tradition. The way I'm teaching you."

"Where is your Sergeant Baker now?"

"Dead." S paused. "Dead, except that I remember him, and won't forget. That keeps him alive. That's two important things you've learned about peacers: our stars and the ones who taught us."

The conversation was not going in a good direction, Saoirse thought. "But before Sergeant Baker. What about your first sixteen years?"

"There is no before," S said. "My story starts with the peacers." He took another drink of water. "What's your story, Saoirse Kenneally?"

"Joined SCOPP when I was twenty, came to Titan Station, and I'm learning to fight from Captain Szczechowicz, Tomasz Szczechowicz, so I can teach someone else someday. There is no story before that."

S let out a laugh, loud enough that the other diners in Titan's Rib looked over. He relaxed and his smile returned. "Touché," he said. "But tell me, if nothing else, a nickname. What did your family call you when you were young?"

Saoirse did not want to answer, but she was afraid that if she refused completely, the conversation would stall. "My family always called me Saerie. They thought it was cute."

"It is," S said.

"No, it's not. When I was in grade school, the kids made fun of it." She slipped into the singsong chant she remembered. "Saerie's a fairy, Saerie's a fairy; her mom is Tinker Bell, God do her feet smell."

S started to giggle, couldn't stop himself. The giggle turned into a loud laugh that brought attention from other tables again. Saoirse's face froze. Her dark-blue eyes bored into his pale ones.

"Fuck you!" she said. "What are you laughing at?"

The laughter stopped, but S's face kept a smile. "Saoirse, you said grade school, right? That means you were what, seven, eight, maybe nine years old? Are you actually going to tell me that it still bothers you?"

Well, it did bother her. She hated that nickname. She should never have told him. Having said it out loud, though, made it all sound silly. She settled for saying, "What if it does?"

"I would say it's silly. But let's leave that. You don't like it. Still, a person should have a nickname—an easy handle. You need a nickname."

"I do not."

"If you hate Saerie so much, pick something else. Pick any name you want."

"No. I'm not going to." Her anger had leached away, but stubbornness remained.

"All right." S put his hand to his chin. "If you won't do it, I'll pick one for you."

She opened her mouth to protest, but he waved her to silence and, for a wonder, no words came out of her mouth.

"Your file says you went to school in Ireland," he said, "and you're the first person I've known who has lived there. I like the sound of it. So that's it. You're Irish."

"Of course I'm Irish," Saoirse said. "My name is as Irish as it gets. What does that have to do with anything?"

"No, no, no. That's your nickname. Irish."

Irish? He was going to call her *Irish*? "You are out of your fuckin' excuse for a mind. I'll kick the shit out of you!"

"Want to go to the gym and see if you can? Irish?"

"Oh, for God's sake." Saoirse found she couldn't be angry anymore, wanted to giggle herself. It *was* silly. She met his eyes and laughed.

After that, they talked of techniques and blocks and bruises. When the food came, they kept talking, occasionally muffled by chunks of steak that reminded Saoirse of the best steak restaurants in Chicago, where her father had taken the family back when she was still part of the family. When the meal ended, S put it all on his account and they walked out together.

"We'll work out tomorrow?" he asked.

"Sure." Now they'd maybe go for a walk, head back to his place for some tea, move to the next phase.

But he said, "Good night," gave her an elbow bump, and left her standing in front of the restaurant.

Saoirse stood there a minute and looked at her elbow. An elbow bump? Seriously? She was definitely going to put a kick upside of his head.

FIFTEEN

The next day was too busy for Saoirse to spend much time thinking about her dinner with S until shortly before she left StatOps. Then she closed all her open windows, pushed her chair back from the boards, and tried to think. Him and his stupid elbow bump. She should never talk to him again. She should never see him again. Righteous anger flooded through her in a sudden rush.

Somehow, though, the idea of not seeing him again left her unhappy. What was it with that man? She could not figure S out. Did he like her? Probably, stupid elbow bump or not. That whole business of teaching someone to fight sounded special. Those eyes of his looked so cold, except when they looked at her. And why insist on giving her a nickname? He had to like her. Of course, he had never actually said that.

But the other issue she couldn't figure out was what kind of man he was. His insistence that nothing had existed before he joined the peacers eight years ago; that didn't sound like a peacer tradition. Gusty had never mentioned anything like that, and she was practically in love with the goddamn peacer uniform. Saoirse checked the databases, but found no mention of his long-ago past. So whatever his life had been, S didn't want to discuss it. She came back to the red and gold stars on his chest, the gold one in particular. An award not worth discussing. She keyed the query into the database.

Valor Star. A single gold star as the top star of a Peacemaker's Star of Stars (commonly called Peacers' Stars) is called the

Valor Star. This is awarded for exceptional heroism under fire and is unique because it must be proposed by a member of the awardee's unit (any rank may propose) and be confirmed by a two-thirds majority vote of the members of that unit (all ranks have one vote). Among peacers, it is considered second only to the Pour le Mérite (PLM). Some have placed it higher, because so few PLMs are awarded to living persons. Despite this, the Valor Star, like the Peacers' Stars in general, is unofficial. It is not recognized as a decoration by the Solar Council (see WAR OF THE STARS). Consequently, no official records of the award or the reasons for it are kept, although sometimes notations are appended to a peacer's record.

Saoirse read it over three times. What had S done? Why wasn't he interested in talking about it? She thought about trying to hack into the peacer personnel records. She could probably do it, but it would not be quick, and she didn't have the time. Worse, if she hacked into S's record and he found out, she understood him well enough to know that he would react very badly. It wasn't worth it. It would be easier to keep working out, enjoy their time together, and tell herself that, sooner or later, she would find a way to pull the answers out of him.

That night, however, after the workout and after he pulled on his shoes and socks, S did not walk to the refreshment area to get a pair of smoothies. He did not even pull a towel from the dispenser to wipe the sweat off his face. Instead, he stood a little past the edge of the mat and stared at her. It was unsettling.

"I think I need to speak with you," he said at last. "Privately."

"Privately?" Maybe he was reconsidering the elbow bump.

"Yes. In my quarters." He waved his hand around, taking in the ceiling and the walls. "That's one place I can be sure no one is listening or watching."

And there it was, Saoirse thought. Back to his quarters. Would she have said yes after dinner the previous night? Did she want to say yes now? No. This was a bad idea. She should say no. She was going to say no.

"Sure," she said.

They walked in silence, S in the lead and Saoirse a yard behind. He led her to D-Ring, to a door in an undistinguished residential area. Saoirse was not sure what she had expected—the image of a sentry behind sandbags in the depths of StatSec popped into her mind. She had sure not expected a regular door, just like anyone else's door.

S looked into the faceplate with his thumb on the pad, and the door opened, as any door would. He went inside.

Saoirse hesitated, telling herself that she did not need to go in. She could turn around and leave, either with an excuse or in silence.

But she went in anyway.

The interior was spartan, as bare as his office. The chairs and couch in the front room were standard station issue, nothing customized, no personal touch. S had been on Titan Station for two years; his couch did not seem to have been sat on at any time in that period. She scanned the walls and shelves quickly, saw no pictures of S or anyone who might have been his family. No pictures of people at all. The only wall hanging was a large print of orange Titan in front of Saturn that might have come with the rooms when S moved in. While Saoirse was conducting her inventory, S went into the tiny kitchen area and busied himself at the refrigerator.

"We didn't get our usual smoothies," he said over his shoulder. "Would you like something to drink?"

You know what's coming, Saoirse told herself. *You should say you're fine. You are fine. Just say no.*

"Sure," said Saoirse.

S turned around and held out a flextainer to her. It was an avocado and açai smoothie, the same Smooth as Silk brand they had at the gym. She was so surprised that it wasn't a *drink* drink that her hand failed to close on the container, which dropped through her fingers and hit the floor. Her mouth was as open as her hand.

S looked down at the still-sealed flextainer, then back up at Saoirse. He grinned, a tight little twist of his lips, then picked it up and handed it to her. Their fingers brushed as she took the flextainer—and she felt a jolt, as though she had touched a high-voltage line.

"Jesus fucking Christ, S!"

She looked at S. He did not appear to have been electrocuted even if she felt that way. He didn't seem to have felt a thing.

"Sorry," he said. "I shouldn't have done that. I mean, not telling you I was getting smoothies, because you probably thought, even though I wouldn't . . ." He shook his head. "It takes one to know one."

"What?"

"Yeah." He hesitated. "Seven and a half years for me now, I haven't had a drink, and my thanks again to Sergeant James Andrew Baker, although I failed to appreciate it at the time. I used to be in the same place as you. Out-of-control drunk when I was in my teens." He let out a sigh. "That's part of why I offered to help."

"Part of?"

"One part." His voice was soft.

Saoirse said nothing and kept her expression blank. She turned the flextainer over and over in her hands without looking at it.

"Sorry," he said again. "This isn't something I advertise—not here, not in my position. But I need you to trust me on some things, and that means you need to know that I understand where you are at."

She nodded slowly without saying anything. That was the story he hadn't wanted to tell. She knew what was coming next.

He continued, "I said I needed to talk to you privately, and I do. It's about that business with the *Bay of Fundy*."

"Wait," Saoirse said. "Wait, wait, wait. You asked me to come to your room to talk about the *Bay of Fundy*?"

S leaned against the fridge and stuck his hands in his pockets, his face rueful. "Yeah, I get it. Look, there're some things I'm not good at. There are reasons, but . . . not for now. I'm sorry I gave you the wrong signals. I *need* to talk to you about what happened."

Saoirse took a breath. Then she took another one. "Okay," she said, "before I kick you in the balls and leave, what is so fuckin' important about that ship?"

He smiled wryly. "Okay. The issue isn't the *Bay of Fundy*. The issue is the ship that came through that wormhole."

Saoirse gestured for him to continue.

"You found a problem with the computer," S said. "That somehow, the gravimetric information for that region of space was directed away from Space Traffic Control to another folder, so we didn't see the wormhole forming before the ship appeared."

Saoirse nodded.

"I started digging through our records. Over a nine-month period before this event, there were three other times an interstellar appeared in Titan space without the wormhole formation being detected in Space Traffic Control. Different people on duty all those times. All three written off as glitches in the system—and, hey, we've had a lot of those with all the staffing issues. Of course, before the *Bay of Fundy*, there was never a ship in the vicinity of a wormhole to cause a fuss. What do you think, Irish? Was this a glitch?"

Saoirse wanted to tell him that she hadn't given him permission to use that stupid nickname, but she had something more important to say first. "That's bullshit. The data path had to be programmed. Programming doesn't just happen. Not on any modern anti-AI compliant system, and this has to be."

"Yeah, that's what I thought," he said. "And if I told you that all four of these interstellars had stopped at a world called Daleko Bałtyckie, what would you say to that?"

She raised her eyebrows. "I'd say it's odd."

"Too odd for a coincidence, wouldn't you say?"

Saoirse nodded. Her anger had faded. This was a puzzle, and she couldn't resist.

"And if you don't know a wormhole is forming," S went on, "a ship will appear at that point in space-time before you can detect it with standard instruments. Right?"

"Sure. Seeing a ship—seeing anything, whether it's telescope or radar or whatever—it's limited by the speed of light."

"Okay. You're the math genius. How long would that ship coming in through the wormhole be there before we saw it?"

"I'm not a fuckin' genius," she groused, but there was no heat in it. "Anyway, it's simple arithmetic." She did not reach for her comm. She just looked up at the ceiling. "Ships set the wormhole formation one to two million miles out from the station. Call it one and a half. That's far enough to be safe, and no need to go farther. Am I right?"

"Yes."

She shrugged. "Speed of light in a vacuum is 186,282 miles per second, so at that distance, the ship will be there about eight seconds before we see it here. The exact time depends on exactly where the wormhole forms, but that's about what you can expect."

S looked at her, intensity rising in his voice when he spoke. "Good enough. What can you do in eight seconds?"

Saoirse threw her hands up. This wasn't part of a puzzle. "I don't know. Have sex with my boyfriend before my father gets up the stairs. That's assuming, of course, I had a boyfriend who *wanted* to have sex in the first place. What can *you* do in eight seconds? Jerk off?"

S grinned. "You have a one-sidetrack mind." The grin vanished and his face was grim again. "Somebody went to an awful lot of trouble to have eight seconds, and I've been trying to find out why. Yesterday night, I got a message from a guy at the research base on Titan who claims to know. He won't talk to me, though—which I can understand. He said he would talk to you."

"Why me? I don't know anyone at the research base."

"He wouldn't say why, but he was clear he would only talk to you. And only in person. Will you do it?"

Saoirse thought about it. Nothing good could come of it; she was sure of that. But she liked the way those blue eyes twinkled when they looked at her. She liked S. Should she do it for him?

She took so long thinking that S said, "What's wrong, Irish?"

"Do you have to call me that?"

He almost laughed. "You're weird, Kenneally."

"So I'm told. And you're weirder, in case you hadn't noticed."

He kept his eyes locked on hers without speaking. Finally, she sighed. "Fuck, I'll do it. Is it going to be another *private* conversation?" She looked around the room to emphasize her point.

"Private, yes. But not here. For the same reason he won't talk to me. He's coming up from the surface in two days. Name is Bill Moore. His file is in the research base system, but I can make it available to you. He said he'd meet you at the Harp. That wouldn't be my choice, by the way. I'll have Gray assigned to cover you in case you need help."

She gave him a sharp look. Did he think she was worried about going back there? "The Harp is fine. No sweat."

SIXTEEN

Saoirse stopped outside Brian Boru's Harp. She did not want to go through the doors. She told herself that she was being a child, that she was being a coward, that she had to do this. Then she disagreed with that last one. She didn't have to do anything. She could leave right now.

"Saoirse, what are you waiting for?" Gusty's voice sounded in her ear.

What are you waiting for? Judgment Day, that's what. Then you can go to hell and get it over with. Oh, Saoirse, will you shut up!

Saoirse ignored the couple that bumped into her in their haste to get through the doors. Then she sighed. Covering Saoirse on this meet-up with Bill Moore had resulted in Gusty's being transferred to the peacers, an event that had nearly blown out the speakers in Saoirse's comm. Gusty was now the most gung ho peacer on Titan Station, if not in the entire solar system. If Saoirse didn't get moving—boy, would Gusty nag. She'd never hear the end of it.

The doors slid open for her as she passed through the sparkling green harp. Music and babble assaulted her ears as soon as she stepped inside. The Harp was as full as it had been the last time she was there. She scanned the crowd quickly, looking for the Bill Moore whose image she had memorized from the file S sent her. He was a short man, five six at the most, hard to spot in a crowd. He had a pink face, chubby cheeks, and light-brown hair that, in some images, had a green fringe. He had no features that would stand out in a packed bar with dim lighting: just a nondescript man with a nondescript name.

Saoirse pushed through the people who stood and talked and took up space she wanted to walk through. She willed herself to ignore what they held in their hands, what they put to their lips, the way it smelled, and the way she wanted it. She could call Gusty to come get her, but needing to be rescued from her own cravings was not why she had come to the Harp. She came because S had asked her. Under her breath, she cursed the attraction that had led her to do it.

No one she saw resembled this Bill Moore. She pushed her way through a screen of people in front of the bar and found herself face-to-face with Bulkhead Bob. His face was flushed, but even on that background, angry red lines stood out plainly where the docs had reanchored the nose she nearly bit off.

"Well, well, little scoppy," said Bob, "we meet again. You looking for someone?"

"Not you," Saoirse said.

"Ah, but it's me you found," Bob said, wiping his mouth with the back of his hand. "That other guy, he's not here."

"What are you talking about?"

"Guy you're looking for. It seems like he decided he didn't want to talk to you. That's good information for you, isn't it? I think you should be grateful. You know, the last time you were here, you didn't want to give me a kiss. Maybe for that information, you'll give me a kiss now. What do you say, little scoppy?" He took a step closer.

"I would rather kiss a prick dripping with pus from the clap and from superinfected herpetic sores. It would look a whole lot better than your face."

Bob's eyes went hard. "Kiss this, you fuckin' Irish bitch!" He swung his right hand at her head. There was a knife in it.

Saoirse reacted. Her right leg arced up, and the bottom of her foot met his forearm as the knife slashed toward her face. Bob howled at the impact; his fist opened and the weapon flew away. A group of people clustered at the end of the bar ducked and the knife clattered off the wall behind them. Saoirse brought her foot down, planted it, spun, and kicked out with her left leg. She buried her heel deep into Bob's gut, above his bladder. His body jackknifed and molded itself around her foot. That kick drove him up and back so hard that both his feet came off the floor. He flew backward, hit the bar, and collapsed in a heap.

The crowd went silent enough that she could hear him struggling to breathe. Then he shuddered and coughed up vomit. A splashing noise accompanied a dark stain growing on his pants, and a puddle spreading out on the floor around him.

"*Póg mo thóin*," said Saoirse Kenneally.

* * *

Olga's Eats was famous, at least within the confines of Titan Station, for its twenty-four-hour breakfast service. If you wanted pancakes, scrambled eggs, sausage links, or even pickled herring, Olga's would serve it along with a gallon of guaranteed high-caffeine coffee. Truth was, Olga's fame was more due to lack of competition in its niche than culinary art, but nearly everyone on the station ate there at one time or another. It was jam-packed during the official station morning, with every table filled and a line at the door. That was when customers were expected to "eat it and beat it," the exact words of the holosign that glowed over the front door. In the station evening, however, the traffic was much thinner, the sign was off, and the manager didn't care if you lingered at your table.

That was, in fact, what Saoirse and Gusty were doing. After Saoirse walked out of the Harp, leaving Bulkhead Bob on the floor and a pair of bots cleaning up the mess, Gusty's voice in her ear had said to meet at Olga's.

They met, and had been there long enough that Gusty's coffee was refilled three times. Saoirse played with her sausage and cheese scramble. She hated powdered eggs, but if she ordered the scramble with cheese, that would make the whole mass sticky enough that she could pretend it was real. Rumor had it that Olga's had managed to secrete a small chicken coop in a cargo storage area in A-Ring and, for enough money, would produce real eggs, sunny-side up. Saoirse hadn't seen any. The yellow flakes that clung to the filaments of cheese she was swirling around her fork were a long way from real eggs.

"He snowflaked," Saoirse said for the fourth time. "Plain and simple, and that's the end of it. He changed his mind."

"He did not change his mind," Gusty replied, as she had on the previous three occasions. "Bob intimidated him. You know that. This guy Moore knows something that we need to know, and we need to find out what it is. That's what is plain and simple."

"Whatever it is, it's back down on Titan with him."

"Your motor's running."

Saoirse's cheeks flushed red, and with an effort, she stopped her leg from oscillating up and down under the table. That was another one of her stupid, useless, and annoying habits. "No, it's not," she said, "and don't tell me that I'm playing with my eggs again."

"I wasn't going to," Gusty said. "What I was going to say is that we need to go down there and see him."

Saoirse stared across the table. "Go to Titan? Fuck that shit."

"Captain S would expect us to."

"Maybe we should tell Captain S to stick it in his S. I was supposed to listen to what this guy was going to tell me, not have Bulkhead Bob try to knife me. For which the most they'll do is fine him, probably."

Gusty drained her coffee mug and signaled for another. "I wish I could have seen it when you dropped him. He didn't intimidate you, did he? What was that you said when you left him on the floor?"

"*Póg mo thóin.* 'Kiss my ass' in Irish." Saoirse's lips twitched in what did not become a grin. "An educational benefit of being sent to school in Dublin, if not the one my parents intended." She sighed. "Forget it. It's done. Doesn't mean anything. Maybe you can see a replay from one of the security cameras."

"I'm not forgetting it." Gusty's voice rose, and she looked around to be sure no one in Olga's was paying attention. "I want you to get feeling heroic so you'll go with me. Moore said he would talk to *you*. Not to anyone else."

"I'm nobody's idea of a hero," Saoirse said. "Just give it up, Gusty. Whatever's going on, we're better off out of it."

"Damn it, Saoirse. Look what I'm wearing."

"Peacer uniform. I said congratulations when you called and deafened me."

Gusty plucked at the light-blue shirt. "I have worked my ass off to get this transfer. I am *not* going back to S and telling him that I can't do my job. And you owe me."

That led to a rueful grin on Saoirse's face. "Maybe that's why I want you to give it up. Okay. There was a time it wouldn't have mattered what I owed you, but I'm done with being like that." She played a little more with her scramble. "If you're going, I'm with you. But tell me, how do you propose to get from Titan Station to the research base down on the surface? Are you just going to stomp over to the flier docks, tell 'em you're a Big Bad Peacer Girl and you want a special ride down?"

"Basically, yeah," Gusty said. "I think a peacer can commandeer transport. Let's go do it."

· · ·

Titan Station had four Titan fliers—small, winged spaceplanes whose sole job was to fly people and materials back and forth between the station and the research base on Titan's surface. In addition to regularly scheduled flights, one of the six pilots was always on call in the event of an urgent need. Gusty pulled up the on-call roster on her comm. For that night, the name shown was Eleanor Reyes. She lived in B-Ring, one stop on the Chute and then a short walk from the station.

Gusty stood in front of Eleanor Reyes' door and said, "Augusta Gray, peacers. Can we see you? It's urgent."

A click announced that the door had been unlocked. Gusty looked at Saoirse. They both shrugged. Gusty put her hand on the door and it slid open. From the doorway, they could see and hear a show playing on the vid screen in the front room and also see a pair of feet in bunny slippers propped on an ottoman.

"Hello?" Gusty asked.

"Well, you made a fuss about coming in," a woman's gravelly voice answered. "Why don't you do it?"

As Gusty and Saoirse stepped forward, the screen froze and the occupant swiveled around in a chair to regard them. Eleanor Reyes was lean in the baggy clothes she wore. She had a broad face with high cheekbones and gray hair that retained only a few strands of brown cut off at her shoulders.

"I was watching *Casablanca* and you've interrupted it," Reyes said. "It's a classic, even older than I am." She laughed at that. "Somehow, I don't think you came to watch movies with me. What's the urgent peacer business?"

A silence followed until Gusty remembered she was the peacer and spoke up. "We need transport down to Titan Research Base," she said. "Immediately."

"Immediate, is it?" Reyes asked. "You could have messaged me so I wasn't sitting here in jammies and slippers. Anyway, they're about to arrest the usual suspects. Don't you have any respect for classic film?"

Gusty and Saoirse looked at each other. "Coming here seemed like a better idea," Saoirse said. "Messages can be seen by others." It might be paranoid to think anyone would be looking for a message, but it was possible. If she had been sitting in the sysadmin chair, she could have plucked out a message between anyone and anyone else on the station. "It wouldn't be the first time I've been called paranoid."

"So, straight to old Eleanor, and straight down to the surface, and you being paranoid is supposed to reassure me that everything is in order?" Reyes steepled her fingers in front of her chest. "You have authorization? For an unscheduled trip, I need an e-sig from either StatEx or head of StatSec. You don't have that, do you?"

Saoirse glanced over at Gusty. This was when Gusty needed to pull her important-and-urgent-peacer-business act, but Gusty was frozen, staring at the pilot. *Some people don't have enough experience in fabrication*, Saoirse thought.

"I can call Szczechowicz's private comm." Saoirse held up her comm unit.

"I have that number too." Reyes pulled a small comm out of a pocket in her top, her eyes never leaving Saoirse's. "I could send a quick message." She didn't do anything, however. "You don't really want me to do that, do you?"

"No, but not for the reason you're thinking." Her first bluff called, Saoirse switched smoothly to another tack. She had done the same in many situations in the past. "We could call and he would say yes, but calls go through the station system, just like messages. And right now, I don't want to bet against someone looking for either." Reyes said nothing, and Saoirse took the silence as meaning she should keep talking. Part of her wondered why she didn't just let Reyes turn them down. Then she could look at Gusty and say that they had tried.

Instead, she mustered the same sincerity she had used—to varying effect—with police in the past, and told Reyes about the eight-second issue that Moore knew something about. Of course, on this occasion, everything she said was true.

"Interesting," Reyes said. "Yes, Bill Moore came up on the scheduled flier earlier today. He said he had a meeting with someone and would need to return to the surface after that. He had authorization from the chief at the research base for the unscheduled return trip. He went back to base fast. The on-call for the day had to take him down, and that's two fliers already used in one day."

"Bulkhead Bob scared him off," Saoirse said. "Somehow Bob knew he was coming and got to him first. He never had the meeting he was coming for."

"Bob scares a lot of people," Reyes said. "He's been out here seven years, no trouble until about three years ago, but now, yeah, he scares people. And sometimes more than that. Nothing ever comes of it, you know."

Gusty pointed at Saoirse. "She kicked him so hard that he pissed himself on the floor of Brian Boru's Harp."

"Did you now?" Reyes' face crinkled into a smile. "That tells me you've done your good deed for the day. Also tells me I should be polite to you."

Saoirse felt heat in her cheeks. She should close the deal, get Reyes to agree. They almost had it. But suddenly, she couldn't think. Part of her mind wanted to know why she was doing this. Didn't she want Reyes to say no?

While she dithered, Reyes finished it for her. "So Szczechowicz sent you two to do this, and something is wrong enough for someone to eavesdrop and have Bob scare your man away. What you haven't said, but I will, is that whoever did this is in StatEx. High up in StatEx." She tapped her fingertips together and let out a sigh. "Okay. When this comes back to me, I'm going to say that you claimed it was an active peacer investigation and time was critical and I simply cooperated like the good pilot I am. No time to chase authorization. That will be enough to cover me as long as you understand you kids are taking all the responsibility."

"I am not a fuckin' kid!" Saoirse's temper flared from nowhere.

"Saoirse! Chill it," Gusty said.

Reyes only shrugged. "From my vantage point, you're a kid, but so are most of the people up here. Whether you're fucking or not is your business."

Saoirse tensed, and Gusty put a hand on her arm.

Reyes ignored the byplay. "You two have suits?"

Both of them shook their heads.

"Okay. I'd actually be surprised if you did. Give me a minute to get dressed, and we'll get going. I'm afraid *Casablanca* will have to wait. It's really sad about her and Rick, you know." She pointed at the grayscale image of some long-dead actress on the vid screen.

It took no more than five minutes for Reyes to emerge from her inner room, now wearing her pilot's uniform and station shoes. They made their way from her quarters through uncrowded corridors and another Chute stop to the Titan flier dock on A-Ring. Reyes stopped at a door labeled TITANSUIT LOCKER. Inside, multiple racks of helmeted suits packed the space. Each of them looked like a thick wet suit with a helmet and a backpack. Large boots with deep lugs were there too. Saoirse put her hand on one of the suits. It had a waxy, rubbery feel.

"These are Titansuits; their only use is down there," Reyes said. "You don't need a pressure suit, so the fit doesn't need to be precise. Atmospheric pressure is about one and a half times Earth, so it's really no different from being in a hyperbaric chamber. You don't need a suit at all for that. What you need is heat and thermal insulation. Titan is *cold*, kids, minus one hundred seventy-nine Celsius, so we want to keep warm. By the same token, most of what looks like rock is ice, and your bodies are red-hot by comparison, so we are careful about how we vent heat. Atmosphere is almost all nitrogen, so we need oxy."

"I know what the surface is like," Saoirse said.

"No, you don't," Reyes replied. "You may know numbers, but you don't know what it's like. It's beautiful but it's dangerous, and I'm not going to end up dragging a scoppsicle over to StatEx and explaining what happened. Hear me?"

Saoirse nodded.

"Now, you're a bit tall for a woman," she indicated Saoirse, "but not extreme. This shouldn't be too hard."

It took only an hour for them to select suits and practice with them and the airflow. Saoirse made a point of showing how carefully she was following directions. Reyes authorized the checkout and then had a bot pick up the suits and take them to the dock.

SEVENTEEN

In front of the *Dragonfly* loomed Titan, an orange ball fuzzy at the edges, growing larger as the flier fell toward it.

"We're already into the atmosphere," Reyes said. "Titan's air goes up seven times higher than Earth's. Low gravity and a dense atmosphere make for a real easy glide."

Saoirse and Gusty occupied the two seats alongside Reyes in the cockpit of the flier. The rest of the flier was empty, so Reyes had invited them to join her. From the moment *Dragonfly* broke away from Titan Station, Reyes had been narrating the trip like a tour guide.

Saoirse broke into the monologue. "The research station knows we're coming to see Moore?"

"Of course," said Reyes. "I had to tell them that we're bringing an unscheduled flight down."

"Okay," said Gusty. "How long until we're down?"

"Not long. Fifteen minutes. Unless you want to tour. I could take you across the lake region in the Arctic, and Kraken Mare. We can skim the flier right over the surface. It's gorgeous. I came out here twenty-two years ago, and it still amazes me every time I go down."

"Thank you, but no thank you," Saoirse said. "The sooner we can get done and get back to the station, the better." To her annoyance, her right leg was bouncing up and down. Although Gusty was sitting on the other side of Reyes, she would probably notice. Saoirse fought to keep her leg still.

An orange-brown murk replaced the black of space outside the *Dragonfly*'s windows as they glided farther into the atmosphere. Then it thinned to a haze that revealed mountains, valleys, and lakes below. The flier rocked and bounced from turbulence as the sky cleared briefly. Then more clouds and haze closed in, and large drops of brownish liquid spattered the windows. Wipers turned on.

"A lot of organics in the rain," Reyes said. "Mostly ethane. Kind of greasy."

Saoirse sat rigid, eyes straight ahead as if willing herself to see through the rain and the haze. She bit her lip.

As suddenly as the rain and turbulence had developed, they were gone. The *Dragonfly* was in the clear no more than two hundred feet from the ground, flying along a broad, U-shaped valley with high ridges rising on both sides. Much of the flat ground below them was orange to brown in color, but they also saw white patches, and the upthrust slopes were mostly white. Lights flashed ahead of them to mark the landing field, a gray-white rectangle set on large piers that held it above the surface. Beyond the landing field, they could see the white domes of the research station.

The *Dragonfly* slowed to what seemed like a crawl. The ground below looked like beach sand or, in places, orange mud. Then they were over the landing field itself. The *Dragonfly* touched down with little more than a hiss, critical because in Titan's gravity, a bounce could take them high and far. Then the forward thrusters and brakes brought them to a stop.

"Okay," Reyes said, "helmets on, and go on suit systems. No flier can be left empty; it's mandatory to keep a pilot on board in case the weather gets problematic. Since we're unscheduled and don't have a copilot, I'll be staying here. So once you're out the air lock and down the ramp, take the elevated walkway to the main lock for the research base. Don't leave the walkway and try to go bouncing cross-country through the sludge. You've got slippery organic sludge on top of uneven rock that's mostly ice. Low gravity or no, you can break an ankle. Understand?"

They both nodded.

Once outside and down the ramp, they saw the landing field stretch away in front of them, a uniformly flat surface, gray with white borders and lanes except where orange-brown precipitation covered it. Blinking lights, white and red on all sides, marked the perimeter of the field. Glow-strips set onto the gray field marked a path to the elevated walkway to the base.

"Okay," Saoirse said. "Let's do this."

It was an effort to stay on the landing field. When they pushed off to step forward, the step turned into a jump, with a slow drop back to the surface. They hopped and bounced across the field. The walkway, no more than fifty yards distant, was brightly lit, a white glow against the surroundings. Squat round piers set into the sludge below held the walkway above the surface.

Saoirse's breath sounded loud in her ears, as though she had just run a mile. Gusts of wind batted at her suit but were not enough to move her. Despite the insulated suit, that wind made her feel cold, but the chill was only in her mind. She turned around to look back at the field and gasped. The *Dragonfly* sat there, incongruous against the wild valley and cliffs beyond it. And right behind the *Dragonfly*, indistinct in the haze but still recognizable, was a giant, banded, glowing ball. Saturn. Its rings were almost edge on and projecting sharply up into the sky, even though they were mostly obscured by the haze. For a moment, Saoirse forgot to breathe.

"Oh wow."

At the words, Gusty turned to look as well. They both stood there silently for a couple of minutes.

"Well, standing and staring never got the work done," Gusty said at last.

With that, they turned again and headed up the walkway, being careful not to bounce too far and end up in the sludge.

. . .

Within a few minutes, they were at the brightly lit entrance to the base. A large sign with glowing letters in multiple languages instructed them to TOUCH ANYWHERE ON THE BLUE SURFACE TO GAIN ACCESS. The blue surface was a portion of the wall in front of them about the size of a garage door. Saoirse followed the instructions and pressed with her gloved hand. Immediately, the section of wall slid aside to reveal a lighted room beyond. As soon as they stepped in, the lock door closed behind them. In front of them was another door with a red light over it.

"Attention," said a voice through their comms. "When the light over the inner door turns green, you may remove your helmets and discontinue suit systems. The inner door will open at that time."

When the green light came on, Saoirse was glad to unfasten her helmet, although the air in the lock proved to be frigid. Then the inner door slid open and they saw a small wheeled bot on the other side.

"Please follow the bot," said the voice in their comms.

The bot led them to a door marked BASE ADMIN CENTER. At Saoirse's touch, that door slid open and they saw a large room with multiple vacant workstations. A man and a woman were the only occupants.

The man stood up and walked over to greet them. He was slim and two inches shorter than Saoirse. His hair was entirely gray. "I'm Dr. Cixin Wang," he said. "Station head of Titan Research Base. Please call me Steve. This is a rather unusual visit, and the transmission from the station gave us little more than your names and ranks. Perhaps you could fill me in on what you are doing here and what you need from us?"

Saoirse took that as her cue. She could always spin a good yarn even with no time to prepare, and even if listeners realized later on, after they thought about it, that it made no sense. Luckily, she'd had time to prepare a story. This time, she left out the matter of the eight seconds. It was only a peacer investigation, she said, one she was not at liberty to speak about, but Moore had important information to give them. She delivered her latest version without any hesitation.

Wang shook his head. "So this is all about having a conversation with Bill Moore. And not one that you can do on a comm. Interesting." A smile touched his lips but not his eyes. "It might have been better if you had let us know that before you came down. Unfortunately, Bill has gone to one of the outlying stations to check an experiment. We'll call him back for you, of course, but it will take a few hours at least, depending on how long it takes him to finish what he is doing."

"If that's what it takes, we'll wait," Gusty said. "This is important."

"Of course," said Wang. "We can give you a private room for your use until he gets back. No problem at all. There are quite a few empty rooms at the base these days. You can leave your suits in the locker in the Admin Center."

Saoirse shook her head at the last. She didn't want to be fumbling her way out of the suit with Wang and his colleague watching. Further,

Gusty's weapons were clipped to her suit harness, and Saoirse didn't want any fuss around the weapons. Silly, she told herself, but she had insisted on sillier things.

Wang did not make an issue out of it, but instead turned to his colleague, a nondescript woman with her hair pulled into a ragged ponytail. "This is Rebecca Amesbury. She's our comm and computer head. You may be more comfortable on an isolated base with a woman showing you to your quarters. Mouse," he said, "I'll leave our guests to you."

With that, Wang left the office. Saoirse turned to inspect the woman. She was small, no more than five feet tall. Brown eyes with heavy lids accompanied a sallow complexion. Her eyes flicked back and forth between Gusty and Saoirse.

"They call you Mouse?" Saoirse asked.

"My nickname." The woman grinned tightly, her lips pressed together. "I've had it since I was a kid."

"If that had been my nickname, I'd have gotten rid of it," Saoirse said.

Mouse looked down and laughed, showing uneven teeth, then pressed her lips together again. "It's fine," she said. "Even my family uses it."

Saoirse didn't think that was much of a recommendation. Suddenly, she didn't want to talk about nicknames. "If we're going to have several hours to wait, can we have computer access?" She aimed a finger at Gusty. "I'm beating her in *Star Conquest*, and I've got a bet to win. Our station access doesn't seem to work here."

"It doesn't," said Mouse. "I mean, it's the same underlying computer system, but it's a separate environment. The research base is older than the station, so the environment for the station system was added after. That's the only reason. I can give you access."

Mouse led them out the back of the Admin Center into another corridor. Windows along this one showed more details of the base complex's domed buildings than they had seen on their approach to the landing field. They could also see other corridors like the one they followed Mouse through, linking the other buildings. All the buildings and corridors rested on the same type of piers supporting them above the rock ice that was Titan's solid ground.

After the corridor snaked up and down a low ridge, it reached a four-way intersection. Mouse turned left and waved for them to follow her.

"Straight ahead takes you to the laboratories," she said. "To the right is the East Wing, personnel quarters where we live. That's full up, so I'm taking you to the West Wing. That's also personnel quarters, but with all the staff reductions, we've all moved into the East Wing and the West is empty."

The corridor passed through an open lock where a sign proclaimed, WELCOME TO THE WEST WING. Mouse took them the length of a corridor marked by closed doors lacking nameplates, and stopped at the last one.

"This was the wing chief's residence, when we still had enough people to use both wings," she said. "It's really nice and I hope you're comfortable while you wait, although I'm afraid that the fridge and pantry haven't been stocked for a long time. We'll send a bot down from the caf if you're hungry, or you can join us there at mealtimes if it takes that long." She pulled her comm out and tapped it. "I've sent you the guest login for the system."

With that, and still looking at the floor, Mouse stepped back into the corridor and left.

"Nice place," Gusty said.

They were in a large room with a couch, two armchairs, and a desk with computer screen, comm port, and keypad. One wall was dominated by a vid screen, while on the wall near the computer desk, a vid of a blazing fireplace added an Earthlike touch, if no heat. Wide windows behind the couch looked out on icy ridges that jutted up against a glowing ocher sky. Interior doors proved to lead to a kitchen, which was empty, and a bedroom. With relief, they pulled off the suits and left them on the couch.

Saoirse planted herself at the computer and left further exploration of the rooms to Gusty. She entered the information Mouse had sent and had the system register her face and thumb. The screen rippled and displayed an aerial view of the base. Saoirse bent over the keypad and bit at her fingernails. After a few minutes of rapid-fire typing and tapping, the wallpaper was replaced by a screen full of code.

"Great access, my ass," Saoirse said.

Gusty walked over to stand behind her and stared at the screen. "What are you doing?" she asked. "And how did you do it?"

"I'm seeing what's there," Saoirse said. "Like when I went through my mom's closet when nobody was around. 'Going shopping,' I called it." She stopped then. There was too much she was ashamed of, and did not want to say. "As to how, I told you about how my father set up hacking tests. If I set up the scheme right, or cracked into his setup successfully, there would be a link for a bracelet or a concert ticket or money. I've been hacking all kinds of shit all my life, and this system is no different from the station. Nothing special."

"And you think whatever deep, dark secret Bill Moore knows is lying around their system waiting for you to find it? Like Mouse gave you access so you could go in and see the file name SaoirseLookHere?"

"Stop with the sarcasm, Gusty. I don't need it." Saoirse's right leg was bouncing again. She was getting annoyed—that happened so easily—and she didn't want to be annoyed with Gusty.

Fortunately, something on the screen caught her eye. "Well, hello."

"What?"

"Remember when I said the gravimetric data that showed the wormhole formation was sent to a folder I couldn't access? Well, I still can't access the folder, but I've found it here. And guess who has the access rights?"

"Who?"

"Mouse." Saoirse pushed her chair away from the computer desk and turned to face Gusty. "I vote that if Moore doesn't show up fast enough, we go and pay little Mousey a visit. That girl knows what we want to know, and I doubt it would take much to . . . persuade her to talk."

"Jesus, Saoirse." Gusty put her hands on Saoirse's shoulders, and the muscles tensed under them. "As I remember, you didn't want to come. Now you're ready to kidnap one of the researchers and beat the answers out of her."

"You're right. I wasn't happy about coming," Saoirse said. "And I'm not happy being here. And whatever gets me out of here and back to the station is what I want to do. And, anyway, the bags under her eyes are so heavy, who would notice a shiner?" When Gusty didn't protest, she added, "Mouse said she lives in the East Wing. I'm going to see her."

Saoirse turned back to the computer. It took seconds to have the map of the research base, the location of all assigned rooms, and the security protocols for accessing air locks, corridor doors, and room doors. When she scanned through the list of the locks and doors, something looked wrong.

"Gusty, that corridor we took into this place, what they call the West Wing. There was an air lock in the corridor between the wing and where the corridor intersection was. Right?"

Gusty nodded, then said, "Yes."

"Why would there be a lock there?"

"I don't know," Gusty said. "I guess so you can seal off part of the base if there's a breach. Probably there's one leading to all the buildings."

"Yeah. Well, it was open when we walked through it. Now it's closed, and it shows it will open only for the face and thumb of the chief admin. We're locked in."

"What!" Gusty grabbed Saoirse's shoulder again and spun her around in the chair. "What's the point of that? Keep us from wandering around? What are they afraid we might find?"

Saoirse turned back to the computer. "Let me look around. Maybe it's not wandering that's on their minds." Her fingers flew over the keypad. The screen flashed different posts just as fast. "Oh my fucking God!" She bolted from her seat. "Gusty! Suits on! Suit systems and helmets on! They're going to vent the wing!"

EIGHTEEN

Saoirse and Gusty grabbed the Titansuits they had dropped on the couch and scrambled to pull them on with limbs suddenly spastic with urgency. Fingers turned to thumbs. Feet stuck in suit legs and would not fit into boots. Helmets were pulled into place and seated, but no airflow followed, not until panicked minds remembered that the clamps needed to be set before the airflow would start, and forced numb fingers to do their jobs. It seemed that an eternity passed before they faced each other, sweaty and breathing hard in their suits.

"Now what?" Gusty asked. "Is this really happening?"

In response, Saoirse pointed at the computer screen. LOW TEMPERATURE EMERGENCY SHUTDOWN, it read.

"Jesus!" Gusty said. "Damn good thing we didn't let them store our suits in the Admin Center. Why would they even have a vent process?"

Saoirse shrugged. "Atmosphere here is almost all nitrogen and pretty damn frigid. Maybe if there's a bad fire, you can snuff it out. Or you can snuff out two unwanted visitors. But they know we still had our suits. Doesn't make sense."

"Sure it does," Gusty said. "Sure we have our suits, but if you weren't being supervillain hacker in the system, would we have gotten them on? Barely made it as it was. And we're still locked in. All they'd have to do is wait for our oxy to run out." She pulled out her comm and checked it. "The network is down in here, and I can't get a signal. I can't call Reyes."

Saoirse pointed at Gusty's equipment harness. "Does that pistol shoot bullets, or do you carry it for show?"

"It's real," Gusty said. "Shoots bullets, I mean. They're the azide loads, explode on contact. Bad for people but station-safe. They won't penetrate the walls."

"Hmmm." Saoirse pointed to one of the large windows. "That's got to be heavy-duty because of the pressure differential, but it can't be the same rating as the station wall, which is in a vacuum. For this, maybe a bullet is a bullet. Blow the window."

Gusty drew her pistol. Five shots flashed from the muzzle in quick succession, followed by explosions as the bullets hit the window. A spiderweb of cracks appeared across the window; then it shattered and fell out of the frame in chunks.

"Nice," Gusty said. "First time I got to carry it, much less fire it for real. I'm thinking I wasted a lot of years as a pacifist."

Saoirse busied herself knocking the remaining pieces of window out of the frame so that they wouldn't risk tearing their suits going through. Then she stuck her head through the space and leaned out.

"Maybe eight feet down," she said. "Piece of cake in this gravity."

"Unless you land wrong and break a leg."

"That's why we each have two," Saoirse said. "Let's go."

"And where do we go when we get outside?"

"East Wing," Saoirse said. "We are going to pay a visit. I think our Mouse is really a rat."

The drop from the window was eerie. A brain that had lived on Earth gauged the distance and expected a quick drop, not the sensation of slow motion. The ground, when they hit it, felt like wet sand. It was mostly brownish with some patches of dark brown and others of orange. It was granular, almost pebbly, to the eye, but their boots sank into it—and it squished. Picking a foot up was like pulling a boot from soft mud. The ground sucked at their boots where they crushed the surface pebbles and left an oily slick behind. Saturn-glow and the sun lit the sky above.

Saoirse looked up at the wall of the dome and the opening where the window had been. To her right she could see the part of the main dome where they had entered the base. "I guess we follow the outside of the dome to the left," she said.

They stepped and hopped around a quarter of the West Wing dome before they came to a stop. An air lock door stood open in the side of the dome. From the lights they could see inside, both the outer and inner doors were open. A flight of mesh stairs descended from the open lock to within a foot of the ground.

"Locked in?" Gusty said. "Looks like the dome had a separate exit, which I guess makes sense as an emergency escape hatch, but all we had to do once we had the suits on was walk out the lock. They must have opened it as part of venting the dome."

"I was a bit rushed," Saoirse said. "I didn't have time to go looking for this. Pretty dumb, though, if you ask me, leaving us an escape route like that."

"Maybe," Gusty replied. "Maybe they never figured we'd get into our suits. Or maybe it only means that researchers aren't used to planning murder and aren't very good at it."

"We're not used to this either, and I can't say we're very good at it," Saoirse said. "I mean, we're outside on Titan, standing in organic slush at minus two hundred ninety degrees Fahrenheit."

Gusty cleared her throat, a harsh sound in the Titansuit helmet. "It could be worse, I suppose. However, if there's a lock like this coming out of the West Wing dome, then it's a good bet each of the domes has one. That's our way in."

They agreed on that and headed for the East Wing dome by following the outside of the connecting corridor they had walked through with Mouse. Their hike ended at a dome that looked identical to the one they had left. Halfway around it, they came to a similar set of stairs to the ones they had seen at the West Wing. The exterior door to the lock was closed, and a path in the slush led away from the dome. Saoirse looked at it, wondered, and turned back to the dome. The path wasn't important.

"Any ideas?" Gusty asked.

"Yeah," Saoirse said. "This isn't going to be a problem."

They mounted the stairs and stood on the platform in front of the lock. A larger-than-life-sized image of a hand glowed on each side of the door. Saoirse put her hand inside the glowing image and pushed. The door slid open and they stepped inside.

While they waited for the lock to exchange Titan's atmosphere for Earth's, Saoirse said, "People lock their doors to keep thieves out. Spies, too, I guess, but I've stolen stuff, so I'm thinking: thief. But this is Titan. Who could possibly want to get through the door from the outside? Only someone who really needs to get in, so it's going to be as easy as possible. Same reason I'm not going to worry about security. Never mind the AI laws, there's not going to be *any* security. There's nobody here but the researchers."

The green light over the interior door flashed, then held steady, and the door slid open. Saoirse unclamped her helmet and stepped through, Gusty following suit. She checked her comm and grimaced. Then she powered it down.

"We're back on the network in here, but I would shut it off. I'm guessing the only way anyone in here can know where we are is by picking up our comm location."

Gusty shut hers down as well, then asked, "What do we do if we run into someone?"

Saoirse hesitated. "I don't think we can just shoot them."

"No!" Gusty strangled what started as a shout. "I can't shoot an unarmed person who has the bad luck to step into the hall when we're there. I can't go that far."

"I don't think I can do that either. You have a nerve tangler, right?"

"Yes."

"Then stun 'em. They'll get over that."

"But . . . no warning . . . minding their own business. They could have epilepsy, heart disease if they're older. Nerve tanglers aren't totally benign."

"Are you a peacer or a New Anabaptist?" Saoirse slapped her hands against the sides of her suit. "I've been stunned, most recently in the Harp, if you remember, and before that on Earth. Give me the nerve tangler. Somebody was willing to kill us a little while ago. If I stun someone and he has a heart attack, well, too bad."

The hallway from the air lock led to a T-intersection with another corridor. They went around the corner and found themselves face-to-face with a large man wearing a gray and black uniform, a Titan Research Base patch over his left breast. He was an older man with gray hair and a heavily lined face. His mouth opened. Whether he was going to yell in surprise or only ask who they were, the words never got out. Saoirse's finger closed on the firing stud. He convulsed, his back arched and rigid, then collapsed.

"Shit," she said. "Shit, shit, shit." He was probably someone's father or husband. Probably a decent guy. A shudder ran through her. "Sorry," she said. "He'll be fine. But we've got to move quick before someone finds him."

It was a short walk from where the man lay to the end of the corridor. The doors along the corridor all had nameplate holders. Some of them had nameplates, but most were empty. At the end they turned, at random, right rather than left, and found a door with the nameplate AMESBURY, REBECCA, PHD.

Gusty stood to one side of the door while Saoirse stood on the other. Saoirse thought they looked ridiculous, then decided she didn't have time to care. She reached out and rapped on the door with her knuckles.

At first, there was no answer. Saoirse knocked again. This time, they heard someone inside say, "Who's that? Why can't you message me?"

It was Mouse's voice. Saoirse grinned. Knocked again.

They heard footsteps come to the door. It slid open, and after a second, Mouse stuck her head out to look around. Gusty jumped in front of her, grabbed her by the shoulders, and shoved her back into the room. Saoirse crowded in behind her. The door slid closed behind them.

"Don't touch me!" Mouse shrieked. "No!" She wrenched free of Gusty's grasp, flung herself backward, and landed on the room's sofa, where she curled into a ball, shivering, her hands up over her face.

Saoirse pushed past Gusty and stood over Mouse. "I'm not going to *touch* you," she said. "I'm going to punch you, kick you, and strangle you. Why did you try to kill us?"

"Wha . . . What? I didn't do . . . Nobody did anything like that."

"Oh really?" Saoirse felt her anger rise. Her view of the room constricted to Mouse on the couch of fake white leather. "You put us in a room in the West Wing dome, sealed the air lock to the corridor going into the dome, and vented the dome. What do you call that, other than trying to kill us?"

"No!" Mouse struggled to push herself upright; tears stained her face. "That must have been an accident. Maybe it was scheduled and we lost track of it. Nobody's lived in that dome in a long time."

"Bullshit!" Saoirse said. "I've told more lies in my life than any number you can count to, and I know what a bad lie sounds like. You're lying." She took a deep breath to stop herself from punching Mouse's face bloody. "The station computer was rigged so that, when the *Bay of Fundy* business happened, the grav data didn't go to Space Traffic Control. It went to a folder you have access rights to. That programming created an eight-second gap before Space Traffic knew the ship was here, and it's happened before. What did you do with the eight seconds that you were willing to kill us over? That's what Moore was going to tell us about."

"Did you already kill Moore?" Gusty asked. "Is that why he's not here? You'd better start talking. We've already got enough to have you shipped back to Earth with a charge of attempted murder. And then we will find out what happened to Moore."

"No, no, no." Mouse was whimpering. Her eyes flicked back and forth from Gusty to Saoirse as if gauging which one of them was more dangerous. "I'd never hurt Billy. And I didn't try to hurt you. Billy is away for a while. Steve said you'd get called back to the station eventually. We'd just wait for that. And I can't go back to Earth. I can't."

"Then what did you do with the eight seconds?" Saoirse asked. "I *know* you got those data. Last chance, Mousey. This cat has claws." Suddenly, she smiled, and that smile might have been more frightening than anything she had done to that point.

Mouse shuddered as though she saw fangs. "The ship launched a drone," she said in a toneless voice. "Dropped it, really. No rocket, no thruster at first. That's what happens in eight seconds. When the grav data feed hits that folder, I have our computer set to send course and landing coordinates on Titan. I get an alert and I tell Steve and Billy."

Saoirse and Gusty looked at each other. A secret drone?

"What was the drone carrying?" Gusty asked.

Mouse shook her head. "I don't know. I only set up the course and the computer response. Billy said it was better for me that way."

"And now Billy decided to tell us about all of this. Why?" Gusty sounded skeptical.

Mouse sniffled. "I don't know, really. He said it would protect me, and he cares about me."

"How truly sweet," Saoirse said, sarcasm dripping from each syllable. "I think we'd better have our talk with Billy. Otherwise, you are going to discover that you are not protected at all. Where is he hiding?"

"He's at the hotel," Mouse said.

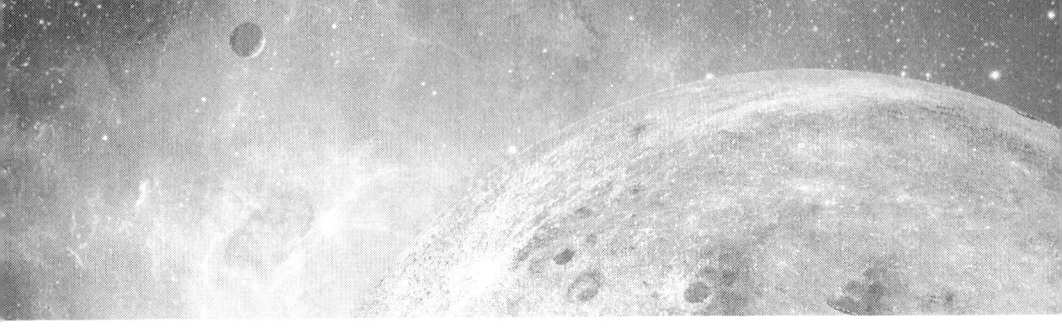

NINETEEN

"The hotel?" Saoirse asked. "We're on fuckin' Titan. What hotel can you be talking about?"

Mouse only nodded.

Gusty and Saoirse glanced at each other, then shrugged. "Fine, whatever and wherever," Saoirse said. "You take us there. And remember: if you think you can be the hero and get rid of us somehow, I'll get a comm out even if it's the last thing I do, and they'll come for you and Billy anyway. His best bet, and yours, is to talk to us. That's probably why he was going to talk to me in the first place. Now, do you think anybody here heard all the shouting in this room?"

Mouse shook her head. "The rooms on either side are empty. Most of the rooms are." She stood up from the couch and stood straight but still wouldn't meet their eyes. "I'll take you to Billy. I guess I always knew this was going to end badly."

Mouse's Titansuit was in a small locker in her bedroom. All the staff at the base kept their suits in their rooms "just in case," she said. Saoirse and Gusty exchanged looks over Mouse's head, but neither one said anything.

Mouse led them back to the East Wing lock they had come in through. The man Saoirse had stunned was still on the floor, but it was evident that he was still breathing. Mouse stopped, bending over him, but when Saoirse reached out to push her, she sidestepped away and walked on. After the last long step down from the mesh stairs to the surface,

Saoirse looked at the boot prints she and Gusty had left on their way into the East Wing. It had been less than an hour ago, but it already felt as though an age had passed.

"Follow me," Mouse said. Helmeted and suited and out the lock onto Titan, Mouse seemed to stand taller and stride longer. Her voice was confident and forceful.

She led the way along the path Saoirse had seen when they went to the lock, trodden into the slushy ground by many boots coming and going. Some looked fresh, like the ones Saoirse and Gusty had left. Others had been partially or mostly filled in by granules of the surface material in all shades from orange to dark brown. It took them up a gentle slope and away from the buildings of the base. Saoirse expected to see another dome come into view as they crested the ridge, but instead they found a flat, gray square filled with ranks of machines that resembled snowmobiles. The square was a parking lot for the base.

"Have you ever driven a snowmobile?" Mouse asked.

She received a yes from Saoirse and a no from Gusty.

"It's not hard." Mouse pointed at the nearest machine. TITANCAT was spelled out in script on its side. "Two skis in front; steer it by turning the handlebar, like you would a bike on Earth. A sealed electric engine behind the seat powers the rear treads. Heat dissipaters at the rear, just like on the suits. Pressure on the right grip powers up and makes it go. Brake by squeezing the left grip. We're not going to go too fast; it's important to stay in control. Don't brake too sharply. Flipping one of these is a bad thing. You do not want to fall off and land on your back. Those heat-exchange fins on the back of your suit will sink into this methane-ethane slush, and the slush will turn to gas real fast. Like bang fast. You could fly."

"You'd love that, wouldn't you?" Saoirse said. "If it really goes bang, maybe you're rid of us that way."

"Even if I could make that happen, I wouldn't," Mouse said. "They'll just send a couple of real peacers, and the people here will get hurt."

"What do you mean 'real'?" Gusty demanded. "I'm pretty damn real, and she's working with me."

"You're just girls."

"Excuse me?" they demanded at the same time.

Mouse completely missed their inflection. "Girls," she said. "Young. I don't think you're out to hurt anyone. If they send some other peacers . . . I know that captain's a combat peacer. I don't want to see it."

The helmets concealed their expressions. Neither found words for a reply, and Mouse took the momentary silence as a signal to continue briefing them on the Titancats.

"Spare battery and spare tread in the compartment behind the engine. Just in case. These cats are old, some of them older than me. The seat covering, the grips, anything you need to manipulate, are a derivative of polychlorofluoroethylene. Flexible even out here, and inert to all the organics. Follow me and stay on the brown sludge. Don't steer onto white ice, especially where it's poking up. Any questions?"

. . .

The Titancats moved off the paved surface of the parking lot and onto the organic slush. A track, almost a dirt road in appearance, ran away from the domes of the base toward a low saddle in the surrounding hills. Mouse steered her Titancat onto it, Gusty behind her and Saoirse bringing up the rear.

The Titancat was easy to steer, and save for not getting too close to Gusty, it took very little thought to drive it. Saoirse found her mind wandering. She daydreamed she was back on vacation with her parents when she was twelve, when they had gone snowmobiling in the Upper Peninsula of Michigan. They were the first group out from the hotel in the morning after an overnight snowfall, so the snow had been smooth in front of them, no other tracks. That snow was blinding white under a brilliant sun; the deep blue sky cloudless. On either side of the snowfield, ranks of tall pines formed a boundary. Her snowmobile had growled and vibrated, and she remembered fighting with the steering to keep in a straight line behind her parents and siblings so they wouldn't think her a fool or incompetent. Bored, she'd concocted a fantasy that it was a parade to the Homecoming party, where she would be crowned queen. *Stupid child*, she thought. *Too many vids.*

This was . . . different. The Titancat purred along, its engine silent and without vibration, the skis and treads cutting through the slush. The open ground they were traversing was mottled browns and oranges, the sky shaded tan to yellow where giant Saturn hid in the omnipresent haze.

No trees broke the barrenness of the landscape; only the sharp cliffs in front gleamed white where the underlying ice thrust through the slush. Saoirse knew that this time a real man, Moore, was waiting for her, not an imaginary Homecoming King. What would he have to say? She wished Mouse would drive faster.

The track they followed—she mentally labeled it Titan Highway 1—climbed into the saddle she had seen from the parking area at the base and then into a narrow pass. White cliffs of ice rose on each side. The ground was rougher there, not a smooth covering of slush. Large drops of methane made a brief shower that splashed on them as they went through the pass. Where the drops hit the heat-exchange fins on the suits or the Titancats, they puffed into gas, then quickly recondensed into a methane fog that the three of them drove through. Mouse slowed her Titancat and told them to leave more space between the vehicles. This was no place for a traffic accident.

Then they came around a turn and were through the pass. Before them was a moderate slope, and at the bottom of it they saw a cluster of domes shaped like a four-leaf clover, with a short stem that was the entrance air lock. A Titancat was parked by the air lock. Beyond the domes, a black lake filled a steep-walled crater.

"We have arrived at the hotel," Mouse said over the comm as her Titancat swept down the slope. "Billy will meet us in what was planned as the dining room. We use it as a work area. I'll take you there."

They parked the Titancats on the slush in front of the lock, next to the one already there. Over the door, a large sign read, WELCOME TO HOTEL TITAN. Gusty and Saoirse looked at the sign, then at each other, and shook their heads. Ignoring them, Mouse dismounted and opened the outer door with a simple press of her suited hand.

Once past the inner door of the lock, Mouse vented her suit and removed her helmet. Gusty and Saoirse copied her. Then Mouse led them through a short series of halls, following signs that indicated the way to the dining room. This proved to be a large room at the outer wall of one of the domes. A dozen tables had been pushed to one side of the room, chairs piled atop them. Workbenches, each with a few chairs, took up the space at the end of the room in front of a wall of floor-to-ceiling windows.

Saoirse and Gusty walked over to one of the workbenches and stared out the windows. The view looked out over the lake they had seen when they rode through the pass. Its surface was black and smooth, with no wave or ripple to mar it. Reflected in the black methane lake was ringed Saturn, shining through the haze and rising out of the thicker murk at the horizon. A little under Saturn's leading ring, and also caught in the lake's reflection, was a single hazy but bright point of light. The sun. Saoirse realized, suddenly, that she was holding her breath.

"It's beautiful, isn't it?" said a voice behind them. "The haze is thinner in this latitude than it was when the first probes came in the twenty-first century, so we can really see Saturn sometimes."

Saoirse and Gusty turned. Saoirse said, "Dr. Moore, I presume."

Moore did not cut an impressive figure. He was average in height, with unkempt brown hair, a pasty complexion, and a pudgy build that baggy work clothes did not hide. Mouse moved away from the other two women to stand next to him.

"Yes, I'm Bill Moore. Welcome to Hotel Titan, also known as the hotel at the end of the universe."

"It is beautiful," Gusty said, "but what is all this about a hotel? I didn't see any of this in the information on the base. If it's some new project, I would think everybody would know."

Moore's laugh was mirthless. "That's because it's the opposite of new. It's so old everyone has forgotten about it. You can find it in the database files, but you have to search. It was built when Titan was the end of man's universe. A twelve-room hotel for guests who wanted luxury—who wanted an incomparable experience—and were willing to pay for it."

"What happened?" Saoirse asked. "Somebody died?"

"No." Moore shook his head. "It never opened. It was almost finished when the wormhole experiment succeeded. Just like that," he snapped his fingers, "this was no longer the end of the universe—it was only a blind alley. The interest and the funding disappeared."

"Okay," Saoirse said. "Old story. Sad story. It's over." She felt her anxiety rising and tried to force it down. "What does that have to do with the eight seconds for an interstellar to drop off a drone? You smuggling supplies to finish the project?"

"No," Moore said. "The hotel is dead. It just makes a convenient location for a research station, so we work out here. Those drones are about survival."

"Fine." Jitters were still rising, despite her effort to suppress them. Now that Moore was in front of her, she wanted the answer—whatever information she was supposed to get—and then she wanted to get back to the station. Immediately. She also wanted a cigarette, which couldn't happen, obviously.

"You know, Saturn rising over a methane lake," Saoirse pointed out the window, "would be a great picture if it were hanging on my apartment wall, but standing here in front of it creeps me out. So, what is the story? Mouse told us about drones and trajectories, but she says *she* doesn't know what's in the drones." She stepped closer to Moore. "So you'd better start talking. What . . . the . . . fuck . . . is . . . going on?"

"Mouse doesn't know," Moore said. "Steve and I needed help on the comm and computer end, but I didn't want her involved any more than that. Safer for her." He looked down at the floor and sighed. "Look, I told you this is about survival, and it is. Titan is dying, Scopp, it's dying. Oh, the base functions fine, we can live here, work here, no problem. But Titan is dying of disinterest and neglect. A century ago, when they built this hotel, the base was full, a hundred and fifty people. Titan was growing; the hotel was coming, the base was going to expand more. It could have been a real colony. Humans can live here. Titan has more hydrocarbon resources than all of Earth's reserves. But then humanity created wormholes. That's what's killing Titan: the wormholes and the stars. What we can do isn't grand or valuable enough in comparison. Why come to Titan when for almost the same trip, you can go to the stars? And that's where people have gone. The money we need to run the base has gone with them. When I came, twenty-one years ago, fifteen years for Mouse, we still had a hundred people, but the decline is accelerating. Down to forty-six now. Not enough funding to keep everything going. For those of us still here, though, it's not only where we do our research. This is our home. We only go up to the station for the mandatory one gee time the body needs." He took a breath, steadying his voice. "We live *here*. We have reasons why we can't, or won't, live anywhere else. None of us could handle living on Earth—and the Reach," he shuddered, "the Reach would be worse. This is our safe place. We have to keep Titan alive! Whatever it takes." He put an arm around Mouse's shoulders and hugged her to him.

"Nice speech," Saoirse said. "But you still haven't told me anything."

"You know, after you spotted the routing of the grav data, and what almost happened with that ship, and then that damned Captain Szczechowicz started looking for information, I knew I had to talk to someone. I thought I should talk to you. People have talked about you; I've looked in the public files. I thought you would understand, might even help. Maybe that wasn't such a good idea. For sure, I wasn't going to do it like this. With Mouse here. And her." He pointed at Gusty. "A peacer."

"Fuck," said Saoirse. "Fuck and fuck again." She looked for a way to relieve the tension building in her muscles, saw a chair next to her, pushed her leg under it and kicked up. Pain blossomed in her shin; low gravity did not change the mass of the chair. It flew up, though, caromed off the ceiling, bounced back up from the floor, hit a wall, and smashed a lighting fixture. "Listen up, fucktard, I am an impatient woman," she said, "and I have poor self-control. You talk to me right now or I'm going to pull you outside and stick your cock in that methane lake so it freezes solid. Hardest you'll ever get. And then I'm going to snap it off and feed it to you like a popsicle. I won't care that you're already dead." She grabbed a pair of long-handled pliers from the workbench and tapped it against her open palm. "Now, fucktard!"

"Her self-control is lousy," Gusty said. "You should see her personnel file. I can't even guess what's going to happen."

"Billy?" Mouse's voice was faint, pleading. Gone was the confident woman who had led them across Titan from the domes of the base. In her place was the frightened almost-child they had seen in her quarters.

Saoirse bluffed a move at Moore and watched him flinch. "Okay," she said. "Last chance. Those eight seconds were what it took for an interstellar to drop a cargo drone and for it to signal the base here. What happened after your computer sent the instructions to come here?"

Moore looked away. She thought he was going to balk again, but then he looked back at Saoirse and cleared his throat. "We signal the drone to fly to Titan once the interstellar has moved on to Titan Station. No one is looking in the region the ship came from at that time, and the drone is small, damn near invisible. It's easy to bring a glider down on Titan with the atmosphere here. Once we have it down, we unload the cargo, split it up, and send it on its way in portions."

"Sure," Gusty said. "That's a good smuggling plan. Any cargo coming in on an interstellar goes through customs on Titan Station, and the ship is inspected too. Any ship coming through a wormhole and *not* coming to Titan Station—hell, that's screaming for the peacers and the national militaries to go for it, and they will. But stuff that comes up from the research base *doesn't* go through customs; it can go straight to a ship going in-system. Right?"

Moore nodded.

"So it will work," Gusty said, "and if the *Bay of Fundy* hadn't been in the wrong place at the wrong time, it would have kept working, but what could possibly be worth enough for a scheme like this and all the people who have to be paid off?"

Moore looked like he was going to cry. In a barely audible voice, he said, "Zombipterisin."

"Zombie!?" The word burst out of Saoirse like a shot and bounced around her brain. Caitlyn's face blossomed in her mind's eye. "You're smuggling zombie. You assholes! You fucking assholes!"

"We had to!" Moore screamed back. "We needed money from somewhere for Titan to survive. If people want to take this drug, well, that's what they're going to do. It lets us survive."

"Idiot," Saoirse said. "An addict doesn't *choose* anything. All they know is that they need to get high or drunk to feel okay. All they can remember is that first time they drank or used and how they felt so good, and all they want is to have that feeling back. There is no 'choice.' They'll do anything. They'll lie, cheat, steal, sell anything, including themselves, to get it. That's the price of your precious research base." *I know*, she added silently to herself.

Images flashed through her mind—of funeral services at rehabs for people she knew who had run away and been found dead, of human wreckage slumped in shelters and begging on streets. Of Caitlyn's slashed throat, the clotted blood on her neck and T-shirt. She tried to clear them, but couldn't. Her mouth closed.

"I'm sorry about them," Moore whispered. "But all of us here, there are reasons we came here and stay. Mouse had a hard life before she got here."

"You don't know what a hard life is," Gusty said. Her hand moved to the pistol holstered at her belt. Mouse shrank back against Moore, her eyes fixed on the weapon.

Gusty did not draw it. "I don't believe you are running this operation," she said. "It needs people on Titan Station and on Earth. You're working for someone else. Who's paying you up on Titan Station?"

"I don't know," Moore said. "Steve is the one with that connection. He's the only one who deals with Titan Station."

"Then I think, Dr. Moore, you'd better get your suit on. The four of us need to take a ride back to the base and have a conversation with Dr. Wang," Gusty said.

Moore and Mouse nodded, their eyes now fixed on the floor.

"Don't think you can pull something fancy with those Titancats and dump us in the slush and leave us out here," Saoirse said. "I actually would like to kill you, and I really do have poor self-control."

TWENTY

After they stepped through the lock from Hotel Titan, Saoirse turned to have a last look. She tried to imagine it all lit up, guests headed inside to their rooms, a party in the dining hall watched over by Saturn. She smiled at the thought of a valet parking the Titancats. None of that was real, and it never had been. Maybe in a different universe with different laws of physics, or maybe not even then. Some ideas, no matter how grand, were not meant to be. She turned her back on the forlorn hotel and walked to her Titancat.

The haze had thickened just in the short time since they left the dining hall. Saturn was hidden in the sky, only a glow in the haze giving away its location. The sun had dipped close to the horizon—Titan was tidal locked to Saturn, not to the sun—and looked like a bright blob through the thick atmosphere. With the increasing haze and lowering sun, the light had dimmed considerably. Saoirse shivered as if she had stepped into a chill evening, even though the temperature in her suit was unchanged.

They drove the Titancats toward the pass they had come through. Even the pass was disappearing into the growing murk. As they climbed away from the hotel, they drove into a layer of fog and cloud. Rain started, large drops that splattered on faceplates and sizzled off heat-exchange fins. Visibility dropped. They could only dimly perceive one another and the Titancats as vague shapes marked by running lights and headlamps. Those headlamps were of little use except as markers, the beams vanishing into a wall of brown sleet only a foot or two in front of the Titancats.

Saoirse was driving next to Moore's Titancat, as close to knee to knee as she could manage—when his lights went out. No headlamp, no running lights. She sensed, more from a change in the sound of his Titancat as it pushed through the slush and sleet than from anything she could see, that he had turned away from her, away from the direction they had been traveling.

What did he intend? This was Titan. They had nowhere to go except for the research base or back to the hotel. Suicide? No, that would be too easy. Plus, she didn't think Moore was the type. He and Mouse wanted to lose them in the storm. That was the answer.

Saoirse spent no more time thinking about it. To go away from her, Moore must have turned to the left. She turned her Titancat that way and strained to hear. The damned electric engines were so quiet. The comm was useless. She couldn't see the screen well enough in the slop to use it to guide her to him. She gripped the accelerator as hard as she could. Methane rain smeared oily streaks across her faceplate, making bad visibility even worse.

The Titancat tipped as one side ran over an ice rock outcrop she could not see. There! Dim but close at hand on her left side, she could make out Moore on his Titancat. Heedless of more ice rock projecting through the slush, she gripped the throttle tightly to squeeze out every possible erg the engine would give her. She pulled ahead of Moore, then swerved left to cut him off. The Titancat hit something, bounced unnaturally high—Titan-gravity high—and came down across the skis and front of Moore's Titancat. As if in slow motion, she felt her Titancat flip up toward Moore. Frantic, she grabbed for his handlebars, for him, for anything that would anchor her. Both Titancats bounced off ice rock; hers went into the air and flipped over. That drove the hot heat-exchange fins deep into the frozen methane-ethane slush. A bang and a flash followed almost immediately, and the Titancat flew into the air again. Saoirse gripped Moore's handlebars for dear life. He'd stopped his Titancat and was trying to pry her hands away, screaming, looking up for her Titancat, which was now falling back down to the surface. Both of them ducked by instinct, their hands covering their heads—as if that would do any good if the Titancat landed on them.

To her relief, it landed with a crash a few feet ahead of Moore's Titancat. They heard a loud clatter as it tumbled down an unseen cliff that proved to be scant feet in front of them.

Moore sat as frozen as the landscape, his eyes fixed on the point in the gloaming where the Titancat had gone over the cliff. Saoirse did not hesitate. They were in suits and she had no weapon, but she battered him with her forearms, one after the other against the helmet of his suit, knocking his head from side to side.

"Enough! Enough!" Moore screamed.

"Why should it be enough?" Saoirse screamed back. "What the fuck were you doing, asshole?"

"I hate you! I wanted you to die! I want to die!" Moore was sobbing now. "I wish you would die now!"

"Guess what? You're not the first," Saoirse said. "Not even close." She grabbed him by the shoulders and shook him. "Listen, motherfucker, if I didn't think we needed you, you would die. Pretty horribly, I think. But I do think we need you. So this is what we are going to do: I'm going to ride behind you on the Titancat, and I'll have one arm around you, with one hand on your helmet clamp. My other hand is going to be on your life support pack. Try something, and I will kill you. Then I will find the other Titancat and kill Mouse. Got it?"

Moore slumped in his suit. "Don't hurt Mouse. Please."

Whether his last reserve of fight was gone or the threat was effective, he proved meek and compliant. Using comm signals from Gusty and Mouse to home in on, he drove back slowly to their location. When they came up to them, they could see Gusty covering Mouse with a weapon. It was the pistol, not the nerve tangler.

"I'm sorry, Billy," Mouse said. "I didn't have the nerve to follow your lead. Even though I saw the weather when we came out, I can't do things like that if I don't set my mind in advance."

"It's okay, Mouse," he said. "It didn't work anyway. This scopp is crazy. But we lost a Titancat. I don't know how we can replace that."

"You're on an open comm," Gusty said. "What did you mean, you 'saw the weather when we came out'? Out of the hotel? You knew this was going to happen?"

"We both did," Moore said. "We know the weather in the pass when the haze thickens. It's possible to drive through it, of course, but it's tricky. Normally, we would have gone back. But . . ."

"It seemed like too good a chance to get rid of us," Saoirse said. "But you are a fuckup and Mouse lost her nerve and here we are. Now, we are going to make the rest of this tricky drive carefully. Or else."

Saoirse and Gusty collected the comms from Moore and Mouse before they set out. Whether or not that helped to prevent mischief, the remainder of the ride back to the base was uneventful. When they reentered the Admin Center through the main lock, they found a dozen people waiting for them. Gusty's hand went immediately to her pistol, but there was no fight in this group.

Steve Wang was not among them. When Moore asked if anyone could tell them where he was, there was an awkward silence. One of the group tried to speak, then another, each failing to get past a word or two. Finally, one of the women stepped forward and answered.

Cixin "Steve" Wang had left the research base, going out through the lock in the East Wing.

Without a suit.

TWENTY-ONE

The only thing to do was to go to the East Wing's air lock and extract Steve Wang's frozen corpse. Gusty and Saoirse had Moore and Mouse come with them and bring a cargo bag for the body. Then they told the rest of the assembled base personnel to go back to their rooms. After they cycled the air lock and opened the inner hatch, they found Wang on the floor, covered in a rind of frost that had deposited on the Titan-cold body from the Earth air pumped into the lock.

Moore said only, "His blood is on your hands," to Saoirse and Gusty, but he at least helped put the body in the bag for shipment. That was a difficult job, as Wang had frozen with his legs and arms outstretched. When Saoirse muttered that he'd done that to make it difficult for them, Moore glared at her but said nothing.

Mouse buried her face in her hands the moment the lock opened and did not uncover her eyes until Wang was in the bag. She did not say a word after that and moved only when someone told her to. For all the life she showed, she might have been a second corpse.

Once the bag with Steve Wang in it was loaded onto a cargo bot for the trip to the flier, Saoirse and Gusty busied themselves with gathering whatever information about Steve Wang the research base had. The other personnel were eager to hand it over; they would do anything, it seemed, to speed the departure of Saoirse, Gusty, and their former chief's corpse from the moon. While this went on, Mouse and Moore sat in silence in the Admin Center. They seemed to carry their stress like weights strapped to their backs and appeared at risk of having it pull them from the chairs to the floor, low gravity or not.

When they reached the flier, Reyes took charge of the body bag and stowed it in the cargo hold as though she handled frozen corpses on every trip. She said nothing, though, until they had Mouse and Moore belted into seats in the passenger compartment and she was in the cockpit along with Gusty and Saoirse.

"Zombipterisin," Reyes said quietly. "Well, these certainly aren't the usual suspects. The people here, I'd say they've all got their own kind of weirdness, but I'd also have said they're about as harmless as any group of humans could be. Until today. Any idea why Wang snuffed himself? Not that being tried for zombie smuggling would be fun, but that still seems drastic."

"Actually, we do," Gusty said. In response to the quizzical expression on Reyes' face, she continued. "The people here gave us Wang's access codes. He triggered the emergency vent. Seems he just made a snap decision—a bad one—and I guess he told some people here they had to support a cover story for him or they would go down with him. They're scared shitless now. They gave us everything he had."

Saoirse continued the story. "Anyway, once we got his codes, I looked. I can't find who he dealt with on the station; my guess is that he left coded files in certain directories on the base system, and somebody with the correct access rights to down here could go in, pick them up, and then erase their trail. But I can tell what he was doing. Moore," she pointed back to the passenger compartment, "thought he was a hero, doing the dirty work to get the money to save his precious base, at least until the *Bay of Fundy* scared him enough that he wanted to find a way out of the scheme. Wang, however, was siphoning most of the money into his own accounts. Not only that, I think he was also skimming some money that was supposed to go elsewhere. How he ever figured he would get away with it, I have no idea. Getting caught, though, and having all this come out—yeah, I can believe dying looked like a good idea."

"So, no honor among thieves," Reyes said. "That's a very old story. Well, let's get this bird back to the nest and hand the mess over to Captain S. Maybe you'll come watch an old movie with me sometime and we'll talk about more pleasant things."

· · ·

A squad of peacers met them at the Titan Station dock, with S at their head. He made a point of congratulating them on a mission well done, assuring them that formal commendations would go in their files. Then he and his squad took charge of Moore, Mouse, and the cargo bag containing Wang. S did turn to Saoirse and say that he would see her in the gym, and he did wink—she was sure of that—but that was it. He left with the peacers.

That bothered her. Okay, he was on the job and had a squad with him and they were in public so it all had to be formal, but he could have done more than that. She liked him; she more than liked him. She *knew* he liked her. So maybe this was not the setting where he could have hugged her and told her how glad he was that she had not *died*, for Chrissakes, but he could have done *something*. Or said something.

She kept her sigh to herself. Damned if she would let anyone else see that she was upset.

It was much better when Mom showed up. She arrived right on the heels of the peacers, went straight to Saoirse, and took her hand. She told Saoirse that they must get away from the dock—she would take her to her favorite restaurant for a cup of chai. Saoirse would have preferred Olga's, but Olga's didn't serve chai. Mom took her to the Vegan Orbit, a much fancier place in the Mall that catered to vegetarians with an ample budget. The bot brought the pot and Mom filled their cups with chai, just as she did in her office.

Over a steaming cup of chai, Saoirse poured out her story of the adventure on Titan, and all the thoughts that had ricocheted around inside her head. Mom cradled a cup in one hand and sat with the other stretched across the table, laying it gently on one of Saoirse's.

"When I learned where you had gone, I feared for you, child," Mom said. "I truly did. It is not wise, not safe, to get mixed up in these sorts of things."

"I know how to take care of myself, Mom."

"No, child, you do not," Mom said firmly. "I believe there was a plan that you would not return. I do believe this."

"Oh, Mom!" Saoirse laughed. "You are such a worrywart. How could there be such a plan? I was never going to go down to Titan, so how could anyone plan this? I only went because Gusty sort of argued me into it."

Mom sipped her chai and said nothing for a minute. Then she said, "Hmm," and sat up straight, a light in her eyes.

Saoirse stared at her. "Gusty? No, no, and no. Gusty is my friend. There's no way she would be . . . I mean do . . ."

"Not intentionally," Mom said as Saoirse trailed off. "She would not want to hurt you. But whom does she report to in the organization on Titan Station? S. And she is a peacer now, which is what she always wanted more than anything else. So you have told me. And who gave that to her?"

Saoirse shrugged. "S, I guess. I mean, he didn't just *give* it to her."

"Hush, child." Mom waved her hand in the air between them. "Captain S did it for her. If he said she should go down to Titan and take you with her, she would do it. She is a pretty girl, but scarcely two brain cells in her head to click together. I do not understand why you associate with this type of people. Now, have a piece of chocolate with your chai." She unwrapped a small square from a dish on the table and held it out to Saoirse. "Now, tell me what you think of Avish, our new programmer. Surely you have noticed him. He has noticed you, I will tell you, and I think there is a possibility."

In spite of herself, Saoirse giggled. Mom could have been commenting on a boy at a middle school social. Saoirse wondered how she would have felt if Mom had been there to do that when Saoirse was that age.

·   ·   ·

The next time she saw S was the following day, when she was invited to StatSec for what they were pleased to call a debriefing. He was not there alone, however. Two other peacers were with him, and it was a sergeant, a sour-faced woman whose natural disposition seemed to have been distilled from a lemon, who asked most of the questions. Despite spending three hours with them, reviewing every detail of what had happened on Titan and what she had done, Saoirse had no chance for a private word with S. He did give her a smile at the end and made another comment about the gym, but nothing else.

Saoirse did not go to the gym for two weeks, and she did not see S. On her side, this was not by accident. If he thought he would see her because she would show up at the gym as usual and they would work out and share smoothies, then he was a goddamn fool. He needed to *ask* her.

Except he didn't. Which annoyed her. And she still didn't go to the gym.

She did see Gusty every few days for eggs at Olga's. Gusty came bubbling and happy, a sharp contrast to Saoirse's increasingly dour mien, but that was understandable because Gusty had been promoted to corporal. Even the fact that the investigation was not making progress was not enough to dampen her enthusiasm. Saoirse considered that she could do with less bubble and claimed that she didn't care about the investigation and couldn't be bothered with checking up on it from StatOps. If Gusty found Saoirse's lack of interest odd, she didn't say. She did tell Saoirse that S asked about her every time he saw Gusty. Saoirse thought that was ridiculous. If S wanted to know about her, there were simpler and more obvious ways to do it. After all, they were not schoolchildren.

Saoirse did see Mom every day for chai, and three times Mom took her to the Veg, as the restaurant was commonly known. Most of their talk was, as it always had been, about what Saoirse was doing on the boards when she was sitting as sysadmin. Still, Mom was careful to ask about her feelings and provide sympathetic words, even if there was nothing she could do. Mom's opinions about S were, of course, predictable. Saoirse began to wonder if Mom was right.

Then, two weeks to the day after the *Dragonfly* had returned to Titan Station, Saoirse's routine was upended. She signed off late after a boring double shift. No ships had come in or gone out. Most of the activity on the station revolved around the construction to expand the Spacedock, which was so continuous as to be routine. Once one expansion was complete, another was needed. Saoirse did not care about graphene supercoil panels or wiring diagrams. No interesting (juicy) communications crossed the station channels. She was going to go to the Veg with Mom for chai, but Mom canceled as Saoirse was getting out of her chair. Gusty was nowhere to be found. Saoirse was damned if she would go to the gym. She went back to her room, pretended to read for two hours, and then changed for bed. That was when a message hit her comm. URGENT. PRIVATE. FROM S.

Saoirse looked at the screen and considered throwing the comm to see how many walls it would bounce off before it hit the floor. Instead, she tapped on the message and read, WE NEED TO WORK OUT. MEET ME AT THE GYM. NOW.

What idiocy was this? Again, Saoirse thought about hurling the comm. Then she thought about going to the gym in pajamas and slippers. She liked that image, but finally pulled her SCOPP dark blues back on and went out in uniform. The whole situation, she muttered to herself, was ridiculous.

When she reached the gym, however, S wasn't on the mat and he wasn't in workout clothes. He was at one of the little tables in full uniform. The red and gold stars on his chest glittered in the overhead lighting.

"Irish, where the hell have you been? I haven't seen you in two weeks."

"What the fuck do you mean, where the hell have *I* been? I'm on Titan Station! You know, a space station in orbit around Titan, one of Saturn's moons. You'd know if I left. And, oh, by the way, S, this is the twenty-third century. There are ways to send a gi—someone a message, as you seem to have figured out. God knows, some guys worked it out two hundred years ago. Or you could have gone to StatCent on your own two little legs. Or my quarters. I am listed in the station files. Sometimes I have no idea what you want."

S put his hands in the air as if surrendering at gunpoint. "Please. Can we not go to Saoirse DefCon infinity? I don't trust messages in this station. Never really did, and definitely not now. Anything can be read if someone wants to do it bad enough. Someone like a sysadmin, even an assistant sysop."

Saoirse was forced to nod.

"We always meet here without discussing it, so I don't need messages, and this is a place where I have an innocuous reason for having the peacers make sure there are no bugs. I don't even trust my own quarters right now."

Saoirse felt her anger drain away. Part of her wanted to stay mad, but she couldn't do it. She moved her focus from the red and gold stars and actually looked at him for the first time since she had entered the gym. Saw stress. His face was drawn and tight. It spoke of many skipped meals and little sleep. Saoirse walked over to the refreshment bar, keyed for Smooth as Silk avocado and açai, and waited for the mug to fill. Then she brought it back to the table, placed it in front of him, and sat down.

"This is about the zombie." She made it a statement, not a question.

"Probably." He shook his head. "No, certainly." He tapped his knuckles on the table. "You shouldn't know any of this, although maybe you already do if you've cracked the StatSec secure files without triggering our alarms. I hear you could be that good." He peered at her, and Saoirse shook her head. She probably could have done it, but she hadn't tried, hadn't wanted to take the chance that he would know. "Doesn't matter," S said. "I'm telling you anyway because you are involved and I think you'll be safer if I do."

Safer? That didn't sound good. She motioned for him to continue.

"We've gone through the systems at the research base with a fine-tooth comb. Had Mom lead it herself. Couldn't find anything to tell us who Cixin Wang was communicating with. Mom was very complimentary, by the way, about your idea with the file pickup, but there was no indication of who might have been doing it. We had Moore probed under drugs. Took me a week to get that warrant, but I got it. Nothing. He really doesn't know. Amesbury has been catatonic since we brought her on station. She's got a medical file from Earth big enough to fill a hard drive by itself. Sealed. No way I can get a warrant to probe her, but I don't think it matters. If Moore doesn't know, I'll bet she doesn't either. We wanted to interview your old friend Bulkhead Bob Deroach. Kept being put off. He was working on the Spacedock expansion, in-suit construction work and away from the station. Couldn't get agreement to have him brought back until today. We were going to question him tomorrow and I had the warrant for a probe under drugs. He didn't know about the probe part. What time did you come off the boards today?"

Saoirse looked at her comm. "Two and a half, three hours ago now."

S nodded. "So you missed the excitement. Bulkhead Bob Deroach had a suit failure."

Saoirse stared at him.

"He's dead. Convenient, wouldn't you say? And I've been relieved."

"What!?"

"I see I have your attention." S drained his smoothie and looked at her for a moment. "That's not the way it's phrased officially, of course. I have been congratulated for disrupting a huge zombie-smuggling operation; with the potency of that drug, those drones could bring in tens of millions of doses each. Written commendations in my file. Promotion to major and my pick among a group of plum assignments. All combat units way out in the Reach, of course." He slammed the mug down on the table with a bang that made her jump. "I'm not taking any of them."

Did that mean he was refusing the promotion, so he could stay on Titan Station with her? She could feel her face breaking into a smile. "Wait. You mean you're turning down the promotion and staying here?"

"No."

She tried not to react, tried to ignore inner Saoirse telling her that she was a fool to think a man would give up a promotion, would give up anything, to stay with her. But she knew the idea was a delusion.

"That's not a choice I have," he said. "I do have some friends, though. Maybe not friends—let's say people up the peacer chain of command, who know my record and respect me." He smiled a rueful smile, and her eyes flashed to his gold Valor Star, the one he wouldn't talk about.

"Colonel Jacob Fromm at HQ on Earth is one of those people. He got me the assignment here back when the argument was about whether I should be required to take medical retirement." He smiled again, a twitch of his lips. "Anyway, Fromm now signs off on all officer positions and system transfers. He let me know about a position in the Reach, with a local militia. Bunch of towns on a world are trying to upgrade their militia because they're being pressed by a wannabe dictator who's building an armed force of his own. They want a retired peacer who knows how to train people in the Reach, which is why Fromm knows about it, and they're offering the rank of colonel."

"Sounds great," she said woodenly.

He examined her face. "The world is called Daleko Bałtyckie. Ever hear of it?"

"No." Saoirse shook her head. Too many worlds out in the Reach, and most of them too poor, too undistinguished to bother with even if you spent your time trying to keep up.

"It means Far Baltic in English. The name is from Polish. If you remember, I told you the ship that came through the wormhole when you saved *Bay of Fundy*, that ship came from Daleko Bałtyckie. Zombipterisin comes from Daleko Bałtyckie. Yes, they make it in pharmaceutical labs to make the schizophrenia drug, but that's tiny amounts. It's too hard, too expensive to make large quantities in the labs. What's on the street, one way or another, comes from Daleko Bałtyckie."

"And?" She let the word hang. At a different time, she would have been interested in where zombie came from, but not now.

"And that's where I come from," S said. "That's where I was born. When I left eight years ago, I swore I would never go back." His eyes darkened. "But I guess my world is an even bigger mess than when I left. I'm going back to see if they'll take me as colonel of the militia for the coastal and lowland towns. Maybe I can set things right."

Saoirse thought the room had started to spin, or maybe it was her head that was spinning. "What? Wait! You are going out there, alone? When?"

"My replacement is already headed out from Earth," S said. "He'll be here in three weeks. I don't need to wait, though, and I'm not. The interstellar *Qui Shi Huang* is headed out tomorrow. Not direct to Daleko Bałtyckie, but the sooner I leave here, the better. You should think about leaving too. Somebody way up the chain is looking to tie up loose ends."

"Somebody?" Saoirse was nearly shouting. Listening devices would not have been necessary, only another pair of ears anywhere in the gym. "It has to be Concannon. You know that! Unless you really do work for him—and I don't, won't believe it—you need to arrest him, or whatever you call what peacers do!"

S lowered his voice, as though compensating for her volume. "I can't, Saoirse. He's on Earth and has powerful political protection. And I've got nothing to directly tie him to it. It's not like one of the vids where we figure out who the bad guy is and, even if we can't prove it, we walk in and shoot him and everyone lives happily ever after. Doesn't work like that. Even if it did, someone would replace him. Zombie still comes in. Maybe I can do something about that. At the source. And think about what I said for you, about leaving here. You make good decisions in crisis situations, so I know you'll do well wherever you go."

The lid on Saoirse's temper blew. "I'm so glad I make good decisions in crisis, because I seem to make shitty decisions the rest of the time. Like having feelings for you!"

S smiled a sad smile. "I'm sorry, Irish. I told you there are some things I'm not good at. Let's just say there are reasons. Maybe someday you'll come to Daleko Bałtyckie and call me. Maybe I can talk to you then."

"Call you? I'm not going to call you anything! Except asshole!"

The shouts should have killed S, or at least left him badly wounded, but there were no bloodstains on the table. His face still wore that sad smile. "I'm sorry. I know I already said it, but I am. I like you, Irish. That's why I had to see you before I left. You're going to be fine."

S stood up. He bent over and placed a light, very light, kiss that touched only the hair on the top of her head. Then he walked out of the gym.

Saoirse sat rooted at the table. With a convulsive sweep of her arm, she sent the smoothie mug flying. Then she cried.

TWENTY-TWO

Over chai with Mom at the Veg, Saoirse poured out her feelings about S's sudden departure. Maybe it was whining. She went on for nearly fifteen minutes, with scarcely room for a breath.

At long last, Mom held up a hand. Her usually calm face looked worried, with furrows across her brow and tightly pursed lips. Startled, Saoirse stopped talking. Mom spoke into the silence.

"He was relieved of his command, he told you."

Saoirse nodded.

"And he has magically found a new command back on his home world, which happens to be where all the zombipterisin comes from. That is correct?"

Saoirse nodded again.

Mom paused, as though organizing her thoughts. "This is not good, child," she said at last. "I told you he is Concannon's man. Concannon is getting him out of here before his true role can come to light. And of course he is going back to Daleko Bałtyckie, where he will have another role to play. He is a bad man, this Captain S, and I fear for what he will do on his home world. But I am not there. My job is here, and I must protect you."

"He can't be that bad," Saoirse said. "I can't believe it. He is nice when we are . . . when we talk."

"You are listening to your foolish child's heart," Mom said. "He is like a bad apple. Shiny on the outside, rotten at the core. I told you that I believe it was planned that you would not come back from Titan."

Saoirse considered that she had a history of choosing bad men. Almost every boy or man she could remember being involved with, in fact. And she had never seen it, even if others had. She remembered her father saying . . . But, no, her father would have said that sort of thing anyway, and it had really been all about sex—and that wasn't any of his business, or it shouldn't have been.

She pulled her careening thoughts to a halt. Mom's gaze was intent on her face.

"How do you know all these things?" Saoirse asked. "How can you be so sure?"

Mom pursed her lips, then took another sip of chai. "I cannot be certain," she said finally. "I do not have proof, like in a court. We are dealing with smart and dangerous people. They do not leave trails for others to find. You can be sure that there are links, communications, between our Captain S and Mx. Concannon that even Mom cannot see. I have been here a long time, however, and I have seen many things. Enough that I can tell what is going on."

This was the first time she had heard Mom say that parts of the station computer system were beyond even her access. "I can hack it," Saoirse blurted out. "I can get in. The only reason I couldn't access Mouse's files on the grav data is that they weren't really on the station system. If Concannon thinks he's got a totally secret storage area on this system, well, he doesn't really know me. I'll get it, and I'll show you what's in there."

Mom's eyes opened wide. For an instant she looked startled; then her face settled into an even more worried expression. "I would not do that, child. I would fear for your safety. You could get into things you cannot get out of. You could go where even Mom cannot protect you. Now, have one more cup of chai and let us not talk of things that are not safe. You should find a good man to set your heart on. I have mentioned a couple, you know. We should talk about them."

Mom poured out what was left in the pot and turned the conversation to the virtues of other men in StatOps. Saoirse listened, but her mind kept going back to S. Back to S, and to whether there was a secret section of the computer that she had not seen. Yet.

* * *

"I ordered for both of us," Gusty said as Saoirse slid into a chair opposite her at Olga's. "I'm having shakshuka. I got you your usual."

"Thanks," Saoirse said. "Are you going to tell me you made your stars for what we did on Titan?"

"Made my stars?" Gusty sounded surprised. "No, no, I won't make stars for that."

"Well, you should," Saoirse said. "You're a peacer and they tried to kill us, unless you've forgotten. It's not fair if you don't."

Gusty raised her eyebrows, her face cynical. "Life's not fair. As you know. Stars are for real combat, and I'll be quite happy to never be in a situation where I could make them, thank you very much. No, I messaged that we needed to meet because we need to talk about you."

The conversation paused as a bot rolled up with their food.

"Gusty, not even Olga's can make shakshuka with powdered eggs."

Gusty scooped up a forkful of yellow reconstituted eggs with tomato and onion. "You should try it," she said. "These eggballs are quite tasty with the mixture."

"My family used to take me to restaurants that made shakshuka when I was a kid. It doesn't have eggballs."

"Well, my family didn't, and this tastes just fine. And we're here because of you, not my shakshuka. Saoirse, we need to talk."

Saoirse stuck her tongue out at Gusty. "I miss S."

"Again?" Gusty put down her egg and tomato. "We're not going to do this again. That's not what we need to talk about."

"Maybe I do," Saoirse said. She picked up a piece of toast and rotated it in her hand. "I miss him."

"Jesus, you miss S," Gusty said. "Okay, let's take a minute. This is not what we need to discuss, but I can see if we don't, you won't listen to anything else. The man has been gone three days, and that's all I've heard from you. You're mooning over him like he was the love of your life. I mean, seems to me what the two of you did was fight. Literally. Did you ever do anything else?"

"What do you mean, 'anything else'?"

Gusty put her fork down. "What do you think I mean? For starters, did he kiss you? Did *you* kiss him? For starters."

"What the fuck is that supposed to mean?" She could feel her temper rising.

"Jesus Christ, Saoirse, you're not ten years old. What do you think it means? I asked a simple question, but don't bother answering, because I know the answer is no. And I know the answer is no because if it were yes, you would have told me about it. Not only would you have told me about it, you would have told Mom and then you would have told me about telling Mom, and you would have told me everything she said about why S is a bad man. Right? And don't start using *fuck* every third word, which is what you do when you get riled up."

As Gusty returned her attention to the ersatz shakshuka, Saoirse felt her face flood with heat. "I liked the fuckin' guy. Is that a fuckin' crime? And I would have liked it to be more than it was. Is that a fuckin' crime?"

"No crime." Gusty took another mouthful of egg, then spoke around it. "For the record, I think he is one of the good guys. And not just because he got me into the peacers. Not bad looking, either, if your taste runs to white guys—which in your case makes sense. But that's enough about the departed Captain S." Heat built in her voice. "I have been listening nonstop to you going on and on and on about a love life that exists only in your head. If you need a solution to your love life, I'll give you one you can implement all by yourself."

"Fuck you, Gusty."

"That was not the solution I had in mind. Now, will you stop spinning your toast around and listen to me before I start using words that my religious upbringing would frown on?"

"Shit." Saoirse put the toast down on her plate. "Okay. What is the big fucking deal that is so important?"

"We caught a guy. No, wait." Gusty stopped herself. "Let me back up. You make coffee for yourself in your own room, right?"

"Yeah." Saoirse looked puzzled. "What's the big deal? Didn't I pay for it?"

"Shut up, Saoirse. The water comes from a line to the station system. You just pop a pod in the machine." Saoirse nodded. "Well, we caught a guy, name of Pavel Brennikov—rings no bells, I'm sure." Saoirse shook her head. "He's in systems maintenance. Was paid to install a little reservoir in the line right behind the panel where it comes out to connect to your coffee maker. That would have squirted quite a dose of drug—I forgot the name the doc said—into your coffee." Gusty snapped her fingers. "Just like that. Dead Saoirse. Doc says it would have looked like a drug overdose. With your history, I don't know how hard anyone would have investigated."

Saoirse sat, her toast forgotten. Then she leaned across the table until she was practically in Gusty's face. "You're saying somebody tried to have me assassinated? Who? Why?"

"Don't know," Gusty said. "You're not the only one who wishes S were still here. Probably something to do with what happened on Titan. People get killed over zombie. You know that. Timing fits with S gone and the new head of StatSec not here yet. But who?" She shrugged. "Dear Pavel won't, probably can't, tell us. He finds a physical packet in his room. It had the reservoir and instructions on a chip, but he doesn't know what's in it. He just does a job. The drug the doc has, the chip and packet Pavel has already turned to dust. Pavel gets little jobs like this from time to time. He does them and credit shows up in his account. He hasn't been paid for this one yet, though, so there's nothing to trace and probably won't be. We'll probe him under drugs—we're getting the warrant for that—but I doubt we'll learn anything more."

Saoirse let out the breath she had been holding. "What the fuck am I supposed to do, Gusty? We're on a space station. It's not like I can go hide in the woods."

"Yeah." Gusty nodded. "For starters, I'd say you change around where you eat. Randomly. Don't trust anything in your room; watch your back. But there's more news—both good and bad. The good news is that I don't think anything will happen right away. Bad news is that right after we caught Pavel, a message went to Earth from StatEx. Can't tell from whom or to whom, can't tell what's in it. What I can tell you is that StatSec got an alert not long after, about two Americans with, shall we say, very bad connections, who booked on the *Vandenberg*. That's an in-system ship coming here. Allow for the time for that first message to get to Earth from here, and the alert to get back to us, it seems they booked their flight here immediately after they got the message."

"Fucking-A," Saoirse said. "You're telling me somebody decided to quit fucking around with locals here and send someone who knows what they're doing to get me."

"Yeah." Gusty nodded.

"I have to talk to Mom. I'll bet she's got access in StatEx to find out what this is about."

"Don't," Gusty said quickly. "Look, no disrespect here, but everybody knows you're Mom's pet. Get her any more involved, and you make a target out of her. And it doesn't solve your problem, which is these two guys when they get here."

Saoirse chewed at a fingernail. "Come on, Gusty, you know they're coming. Can't you get them at the dock?"

"And do what?" Gusty asked. "Say, 'Hi, welcome to Titan Station,' and shoot them? We can't do that. Sure, we can shadow you, and once they go for you, then we can take them, but that's taking quite a chance. I'll tell you there is an opinion in StatSec that we should do exactly that. Use you for bait. Of course, that assumes that no one in StatSec is in on this. Which I wouldn't bet my life on. Which is why I had to talk to you. The safest thing is for you to get off Titan Station."

"Oh wonderful. Just fucking wonderful." Saoirse slumped down in her seat. "Where am I supposed to go? If someone is taking the trouble to send two men from Earth to Titan Station to get me, where in the solar system am I supposed to disappear to?"

"You can resign from SCOPP, take an in-system back to Earth. Billions of people to vanish into."

"Sure, and people get found all the time. And the prosecutor dropped the charges only because I joined SCOPP. I don't serve my term, the law is looking for me too."

"Then go into the Reach," Gusty said. "Do you have enough money? I can help some."

"I'm not taking your money." Saoirse was silent for a moment. "I'll check the schedule for the upcoming interstellars. I can't do one of these luxury boats—and, no, I won't take your money." She said it twice because she knew how many times in the past she would have taken someone's money, and for much less reason. But she had changed. She refused to do it now. "Maybe there will be a cargo ship that takes passengers. I'll see."

"Then those are the options," Gusty said. "Try to vanish on Earth, or into the Reach. Like I said, I don't think anything happens until *Vandenberg* gets here. But whatever you choose, you better be off Titan Station in three weeks."

TWENTY-THREE

StatOps was quiet during the evening shift. Everyone was looking at Saoirse to see what she would do. Actually, no one was looking at Saoirse. She only felt as though they were. "The wicked flee though none pursue." The old line from the Bible ran through her head. She was wicked, that was true enough; she'd known that for many years. In this case, however, she had real pursuers.

Gusty had said she needed to be off Titan Station before they arrived, and she was inclined to believe Gusty. The three weeks were now down to three days, and still she sat her usual shifts in StatOps, drinking chai with Mom and not fleeing. What was she going to do?

The problem was that she liked where she was. Her sysadmin seat, bathed in the glow of all her screens and the windows within her screens, was comforting. From here, she could be part of anything and everything on Titan Station, from the planning of a surprise party in B-Ring to the updating of the bot programming for Olga's. Walking back to Mom's office for chai was part of her comfortable routine, and she hated the thought of leaving it.

You should have been a nerd. You should have been a lot of things, but you always got in your own way because you're such miserable fuckup that you don't deserve to have anything work out, and why would anyone really want to have someone like you around, which is probably why S didn't fight to stay and— Shut up, Saoirse!

Letting her mind wander wasn't useful, because it always came back to the same old things. She couldn't keep sitting in the sysadmin seat. She couldn't open a file labeled Escape Route. But what was she going to do?

She was not going back to Earth. She had said as much to Gusty, and that was the right decision. Anyone who would bother sending hit men from Earth out to Titan Station would find her on Earth no matter where she went. Saoirse knew that, even if Gusty did not. Earth was a dead end. Emphasis on *dead*.

That left the Reach. How many stars in the Reach? She ran some quick calculations and came up with half a million to a million. How many had planets of one sort or another? Probably 20 percent. How many of those had humanity planted a settlement on? Who knew anymore? She remembered what S had said about the Reach being chaos. Did it matter? She bit at a fingernail that was already down to the quick.

Four interstellars had already left in the time since she spoke to Gusty. Two were the luxury liner type that took well-heeled tourists to places like Lincoln or Tokugawa. She could not afford a ticket like that, and she had paid no attention as they left. The other two were cargo ships with passenger berths, but the worlds they were headed for meant nothing to her, and she did not want to end up on some end-of-the-line planet that saw a ship every two years. Two more luxury interstellars, the *Viking* and the *Volga*, were in the Spacedock now. Could she fake a ticket? Maybe, but as she looked at the idea, she found too many other documents that would need to be faked. The lie would unravel too fast. They paid too much attention to the passengers on those ships. Being found out while on board a ship like that was probably nothing more than a long trip back to jail. She needed a lie that would last until she got off the ship.

There was a third interstellar in the Spacedock: the *Long Haul*. It was a cargo ship, but it would take a limited number of passengers. She pulled up the schedule. It was scheduled to leave the day before the *Vandenberg* arrived, and its second port of call was Daleko Bałtyckie!

The latter fact riveted her attention. If she could somehow get to Daleko Bałtyckie, S would be there. He'd extended an open invitation, at least before she had called him an asshole. Most likely, he would be able to fix whatever mess she made in getting there.

She bent to the task. How could she get on the *Long Haul*? She could afford the ticket, but right after checking the cost, she hesitated. Scopps did not buy tickets on interstellars. Would that set a flag in the system and alert someone? Could she get on that ship a different way? What did she need to fake? She thought back to what S had said, and an idea started to grow in her mind. A crazy, fucked-up, impossible, and stupid scheme. So like her!

Her fingers played across the boards almost of their own accord. She wanted the peacer folders and the files inside them. The secure ones. That took a little while, but in the end, their security was no match for someone with her level of access, who knew the system inside and out. What took most of her time was not hacking into the files but making sure that her activity did not send out any alerts and that all evidence of her access would be erased after she exited.

Once she was in, she thought about finding S's personnel file and having a look, but she didn't do it. Maybe it was time for her to behave. What she did go for were the files on the Peacemaker organization. She found a folder that seemed promising, with the notation, "Head StatSec access only."

"Yeah. Head StatSec and me," she said to herself.

She opened it and scanned through files. One showed outstanding personnel requests from peacer units in the Reach. It was a monthly report, now a month out of date. Current status reports from the Reach did not exist. A month out of date and God knew how far behind the actuality was the best she could do.

"Work with what you've got," she muttered.

She found Daleko Bałtyckie. They were understaffed, and looking at the volume of files, they weren't the only ones. The Thirty-second Battalion was on Daleko Bałtyckie, commanded by Lieutenant Colonel Dimitris Venezelos. The battalion had three companies and a headquarters company, all short of troops. This Venezelos had been complaining about it for a long time; a lengthy list of messages from him was attached. She skimmed the messages.

Company C lacked a lieutenant for its third platoon.

Saoirse smiled what she was sure was a wicked smile and pulled up her own file. There she was: a uniformed SCOPP with the rank of specialist, IT. Further detail showed her as administrative personnel, unarmed, with the assignment as assistant sysop. She found her rating as temporary sysadmin. *Thank you, Mom.* Then she found commendations for the *Bay of Fundy* and Titan incidents. *Thank you, S.* She pulled up her marksmanship scores and spent a moment admiring them. Red lettering below the scores proclaimed that her marksmanship met standards as expert for all Peacemaker units, including combat units. Now it was time to work.

It was a quiet shift. No one paid attention to what she was doing on her boards. She pulled up transmittal forms. *Do it, Saoirse*, she told herself. She modified her file. Specialist Saoirse Kenneally was transferred to the Off-Earth Armed Peacemakers and promoted to first lieutenant. She typed out orders that assigned her to fill the long-vacant position in Third Platoon, Company C, Thirty-second Battalion on Daleko Bałtyckie. She cross-checked with the *Long Haul* to verify the price of a passenger berth. Then she input the orders for her to reach her new position by any available transport, with a maximum cost set slightly above the price of that berth on the *Long Haul*. Finally, she set the notification to her unit—to StatOps—to be sent only to one temporary sysadmin—her—and made the transfer effective on her arrival at Daleko Bałtyckie.

She sat back and admired her handiwork for a few minutes. There she was on the screen, First Lieutenant Saoirse Kenneally, Off-Earth Armed Peacemaker Force. She had a few more items to fix. She checked the files of a few other lieutenants, then went back to hers and added Officer Candidate School to her record. Then she stole an e-sig from the Colonel Fromm that S had mentioned and affixed that to her file and her orders. It was a magnificent fraud, the best she had ever done. Saoirse tapped first Verify, then Sync and Send. The system on Titan Station updated immediately. In a little over an hour, the files at HQ on Earth would synchronize.

Her comm pinged as orders came in with her transfer, promotion, assignment, and transport authorization. Another ping heralded a message from the *Long Haul*. Pursuant to peacer orders, they had assigned her a berth.

That last ping from the *Long Haul* pulled her out of her fantasy and back to StatOps on Titan Station. God in heaven, what had she done? This would never stand up to any kind of inspection. She was doomed. She wanted to cry. She wanted not to have feelings.

Slowly, with deep breaths that she hoped no one else saw, she steadied herself. It might not stand up to inspection, but if she could get to Daleko Bałtyckie, who would inspect it? This Lieutenant Colonel Venezelos might throw her in whatever he used for a jail. More logically, he would throw her out, with or without putting her in jail first. He wouldn't waste an interstellar berth transporting her back to Earth. She would be free to go and find S.

Anyway, her personnel file and her orders were, in fact, authentic. The only people who could know otherwise were in the solar system, and no message could travel between stars faster than a ship dropping through a wormhole. By the time anyone could let Lieutenant Colonel Venezelos know there was a problem in the file of a certain first lieutenant, she would be able to find S and figure out her next step.

That was when another ping hit her comm. It was from the *Long Haul*. Her breath quickened and her pulse raced. Her magnificent plan could not have fallen apart that fast. The information hadn't even reached HQ on Earth yet! Not daring to breathe, she opened the message. *Long Haul* was notifying crew and passengers that a maintenance issue was going to delay the departure by one day. They were sorry for the inconvenience.

Saoirse stared at the message. The departure time for the *Long Haul* was now three hours after the *Vandenberg* docked. And they were sorry for the inconvenience!

There was one more trick she could play. She invaded the StatSec system again and removed her face from the computer's recognition file. That meant she had to reset the door of her room to open to thumb only, rather than thumb and face, but that was a minor point. She would be fine. She had to tell Gusty.

· · ·

"You little shit," said Gusty Gray from across the table in Olga's. "You are such a little shit. No, you're not little. You're just a shit." Her face was furious.

"What?" Saoirse gaped back at her. "What is the problem here? I did what you said. I *listened* to you. I worked out a way off Titan Station."

"Oh, I don't deny you did that," Gusty said. "It's just that . . . Crap." She shook her head. "I busted my ass to get transferred to the peacers. I went down to Titan, dragged you down to Titan, and damned near got myself killed on Titan to get my promotion. To corporal. But you—you go into the computer system and hack around and, hey presto, you're a peacer and an officer, with a free ticket to the Reach on top of it."

Saoirse was quiet for a while, and Gusty didn't say anything either. The wait bot rolled over, and Saoirse keyed in shakshuka for Gusty and toast and coffee for herself without either one speaking. When she looked away from the bot, she realized that Gusty's eyes were still fixed on her.

"I'm sorry, Gusty. I guess it never occurred to me how you would feel or how it would look. I was just thinking of myself, of how clever I was." She searched for a fingernail to bite, but didn't find much. "I guess that's what I do. I am sorry."

Gusty's eyes softened. "It's okay," she said. "Well, maybe it's not right now, but it will be. You're my friend and I still love you, even if I hate you a little bit right now." She held up her thumb and forefinger close together. "But you're cutting it a bit close, aren't you? I've seen the schedule for Spacedock. That ship doesn't leave until the day before those two get here."

"Actually, it's a bit closer than that," Saoirse said. "*Long Haul* has a maintenance issue. They won't leave until the next day. It'll be a few hours after the *Vandenberg* docks."

Gusty stared at her. "Crap, Saoirse, I've heard of living dangerously, but this is ridiculous. You need to find a good hidey-hole once the *Vandenberg* docks until you can get on the *Long Haul*. Maybe use the damn computer system to find Olga's fabled chicken coop and hide out with the chickens."

Saoirse laughed. "If I do, I'll get you a real shakshuka."

"I'll hold you to that. And one more thing." Gusty pointed her fork across the table at Saoirse. "You don't tell Mom what you did. I don't care how much of her pet you are, you've broken about every rule of computer systems that exists."

"I won't," Saoirse said. "I'm not a total idiot."

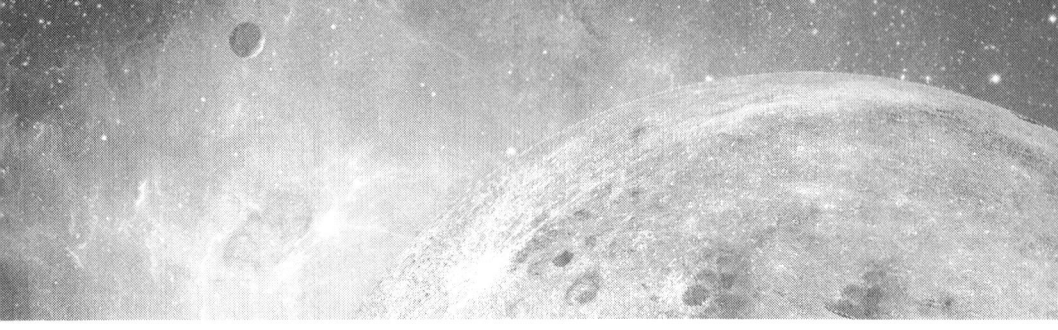

TWENTY-FOUR

The day of departure arrived with a suddenness that made Saoirse feel no time had elapsed since she set up her escape. She woke early in the morning and began her preparations. First, she left a message for Mom that she felt ill and would not come to StatOps that day. Perhaps, she suggested, it had been a late-night snack at Olga's that was wreaking havoc on her gut. She knew that would attract attention, since she had never missed a day's work since arriving on Titan Station, but there was nothing she could do about that. She had plans that did not include sitting in StatOps until the *Long Haul* opened for boarding.

Packing was quick. She had only three changes of civilian clothes; those were stuffed into a small backpack. She left her SCOPP dark blues hanging in her closet. She didn't have a peacer uniform, but probably by luck, when she faked all those files, she had made her assignment effective on arrival on Daleko Bałtyckie. She figured that she could talk her way through a need to travel in civilian clothes if anyone brought it up. In the closet, next to the SCOPP uniforms, she left the old shirt and jeans she had worn when she left Earth. She was glad to close the closet door on them. Nothing but a bad and soon-to-be-forgotten memory, she promised herself.

Preparations made, she checked her comm for the time. She had six hours until the *Long Haul* would be open for boarding by passengers. The *Vandenberg* was in contact with Titan Station and would dock in three hours. She needed to disappear for a while, and she had the perfect plan.

Titanic Ink was a small shop in the Mall a few doors down from Olga's. Saoirse had passed it almost every time she went to Olga's, and she had stopped in front of the displays on many occasions to look at designs and daydream. This day was perfect for turning a daydream into reality, and Saoirse intended to do it. She walked through the holo of ever-changing ink designs and stepped inside.

Titanic Ink was actually tiny, a narrow space in front of a desk with a screen. Behind the desk sat a beefy woman wearing only shorts and a halter top, as if to emphasize that nearly every square inch of her skin was inked. Saoirse explained what she wanted and showed the woman a page in her journal where she had sweated over drawing it with her very limited artistic skills.

The woman leaned back in her chair with her hands behind her head, showing off ink even in her armpits. Her face was skeptical. "You've never had one before, have you?"

Saoirse shook her head.

The woman sighed. "Look, this is a fair-sized job, even with the fast needle guns we use today. And you want those colors? You'll have to come back at least once. No way it's getting done in one sitting."

Saoirse was horrified. She had no way to come back on another day. Literally. "Skip the different colors, then," she said. "Just do the design, all one color. I have to have it all done today."

"Afraid you'll lose your nerve in the middle, huh?" Now the woman was shaking her head. "Even without colors—and it will work without them—this is still six hours. Maybe a little more. It will hurt, kiddo. It's needles in your skin; we're not painting you like some kid school thing. How do you do with pain?"

"Pain is my specialty," Saoirse said. "Look, it's my money and my skin. I want it."

"Okay." The woman stood up and ushered Saoirse through a curtain to the back of the shop, where a tattoo chair, workstation, and other equipment were set up. "Three rules. One, you don't wiggle. If you move and I haven't said you can move, it's your problem. Two, I don't listen to screaming. I'll give you a towel to bite on if you need it. And three, turn off your damn comm. I'm not going to listen to pings and dings, and I'm not going to have you begging to look at it."

. ○ .

True to her estimate, it was six and a half hours before the woman was finished. Saoirse stood up shakily. Sweat stood out on her face, and the back of her shirt was soaked where she had pressed against the chair. She had not let out a peep the entire time, though, and she was proud of that.

"It's beautiful," the woman said. "You damn well better like it. It's not coming off."

Saoirse looked down at her left arm. Starting with its tail at her wrist, a massive rattlesnake coiled around her forearm and her elbow, ending with its open mouth baring fangs on her lower biceps. Above, on her deltoid, were the words DON'T TREAD ON ME.

"I like it," Saoirse said.

The woman grunted and sprayed a mist over the tattoo. "This will prevent infection," she said. "Keep it covered for a few days, and don't do anything rough. Those are all punctures in your skin, you know."

Saoirse nodded without really listening. She was admiring her snake. With reluctance, she pulled on a long-sleeved shirt, at least heeding the instruction to keep it covered. She did not like the snake—she *loved* it. Even though she knew Mom and Dad and her brothers and sister would have hated it.

. ○ .

Saoirse stepped out of Titanic Ink and tried to focus her mind. She had spent the day trying not to wiggle and refusing to moan, with her mind fixed on what the snake would look like when it was finished. Now the *Long Haul* should be open for boarding. She needed to regroup, get the rest of her meager possessions, and go to the dock. She pulled out her comm to check the time and remembered she had turned it off before the tattoo procedure. The moment she turned it on, the screen lit up with a string of messages from Gusty. Ten of them. All in the last hour. They started with a simple, CALL ME, and ended with, SAOIRSE, WHERE ARE YOU, YOU IDIOT?! Saoirse hit Callback.

"Goddamn it, Saoirse," Gusty's voice exploded in Saoirse's ear as soon as the connection was made, "what fool thing have you been doing?"

"I had something important to take care of," Saoirse said defensively. "I'm headed to the dock. I just have to get my things from my room and say goodbye to Mom."

"No! You're not doing either of those things." Gusty's voice was sharp, an order. "While you were doing something important, the *Vandenberg* docked. An hour and forty minutes ago. Those two guys are on the station. One of them is on D-Ring, by your room. I'm watching the camera feeds. The other went up to StatCent. I'm not sure where he is; I don't have a camera in there."

"Shit." Had she been stupid? Probably. Almost certainly. Her mind snapped into focus. Whatever was packed in her room could be forgotten. It wasn't all that much, and she had survived with much less in the past. As for Mom, leaving without a goodbye hurt, but this wouldn't be the first time she had ghosted on someone who had been close. "Okay, Gusty, thanks for the heads-up. I'll go straight to the dock. I'm not in uniform, and even if they've got a hack for your camera feeds, I took myself out of the recognition system. No sweat, I'm a ghost."

She clicked off and pushed her way through the early-afternoon crowds in the Mall corridor. This would be simple. All she had to do was take the Chute down to the dock and leave the two Americans on Rings D and E. She had planned well.

Five minutes later, her comm pinged. It was Gusty.

"Saoirse, what are you doing?"

"Taking the Chute to the dock."

"Bad news. When you started moving, so did they. Cameras are picking up both, and they are headed to the Chute. The one on D-Ring will get there before you will."

Fear and anger welled up inside her. "Gusty, that's not possible. Even if they have a hack, even if one of the peacers was bought and is watching the system like you are, I'm not in the system."

"I don't care what you think is possible. They're reacting to you. You're a ghost that got sprinkled with fairy dust. Don't take the Chute."

"Fine. I'll use corridors and the inter-ring hatches. I'll still get past them."

Saoirse started to run, then forced herself to slow to a walk. Running in a panic through the Mall corridors, bouncing off people and knocking them over, was the surest possible way to attract attention. *Cool it down,* she told herself. *A quick walk is okay, like you're late for something. Don't breathe so hard.*

Gusty was back on the comm. "One asshole took the Chute. He's getting off on B-Ring. I'd bet that he's headed for the inter-ring hatch you're going to use. The other one is at the E-Ring Chute stop. My bet is he goes to the dock. I'll try to get a couple of peacers I'm sure of to go down there."

"Fuck! How are they doing this? Can they listen to our calls?"

"I don't know how they're doing it." Saoirse thought she could hear alarm in Gusty's voice, although that could have been her own fears. "I mean, yes, StatSec can tap the comms, but you have to go into the system to do it. There are two levels of authorization, and an internal notice comes up on our system. It's not like checking cameras, which is passive."

Saoirse forced herself to stop scrutinizing every face in the Mall corridor. The two chasing her weren't in the Mall. They seemed to know she was headed for the dock. She needed another way to get there, one where they couldn't track her or get ahead of her. An idea came to her.

"Gusty," she said, "assume one of your peacers is in on this and they're listening to the comms. I don't care what the security is. That's the only explanation. I've got another idea."

With that, she clicked off the conversation. She started off as though she were still making for the nearest C-to-B-Ring connecting hatch. After three minutes of that route, she shut off her comm, took a deep breath, and changed direction.

Her new route took her to the Number Two cargo elevator for the Mall. This was a pair of closed doors twenty feet wide marked STATCARGO ONLY: NO UNAUTHORIZED PERSONNEL. The cargo elevator traveled up a spoke to Titan Station's central shaft. That was how goods came from the dock to the shops and food places in the Mall. Bots took the loads from the dockside to the A-Ring spoke, went up to the central shaft, and from there to the C-Ring spoke. Personnel from StatCargo went into the cargo elevators or the shaft for maintenance or to fix problems, but otherwise it was bot-only. The doors would not open for her.

She took out her comm and looked at it, debating with herself. The doors would not open. No delivery arrived for them to open by themselves. She turned the comm on.

"Gusty, open C-Ring Spoke Elevator Two and authorize me to use the shaft."

"Saoirse, what? How do I do that?"

"Figure it out!" She shut off her comm.

Two minutes later, the doors opened. The interior was a huge empty box, fifteen feet high. A faceplate and thumb pad were placed on the wall near the door. The faceplate would be useless; she had cleverly removed herself from the recognition system. But the thumb . . . she had kept the thumb to allow her to go in and out of her room. She pressed the pad and the doors slid closed. *Thank you, Gusty.*

A row of webbing descended from the ceiling with a whir. It stopped at the floor of the elevator and the webbing reached to a little above her head.

"Human personnel should take hold of the webbing," a synthetic voice said. She felt the elevator begin to rise. "At the top of the shaft, the environment will be zero gee."

Right. Zero gee. Of course the central shaft of Titan Station was zero gee. She knew that, but she'd forgotten about it in the urgency to find a route to the dock.

Even before the elevator's rear doors opened onto the central shaft, her stomach was queasy. Gingerly, she moved hand over hand and foot over foot along the webbing to reach the rear doors. She was acutely aware of the fact that when she picked up a foot to move it along the webbing, it hung in the air until she hooked it into the next row. Once she reached the doors, she looked out into the shaft. The other side looked a mile away. It wasn't, of course, but it felt like it. Painted letters and arrows showed that A- and B-Rings were to her left, D and E to the right. She stuck her head past the door and looked left. Saoirse was at the edge of a cliff, looking down. And down. Endlessly.

Her stomach tried to retch, and she suppressed it. Barely. She closed her eyes and tried to tell herself that the shaft was level, that it was nothing more difficult than walking down a corridor. But when she opened her eyes and edged out into the shaft, her feet came off the surface and floated. Frantically, she grabbed for a nearby handhold on the wall and anchored herself, gripping for dear life, her breath coming in shudders. She was going to have to push off and float along the shaft to A-Ring. Her stomach said that she was going to *fall* all the way to A-Ring. She looked down at the floor of the shaft and saw the track that the cargo tram took when the bots brought supplies up from the dock. She could follow that.

The same synthetic voice announced, "Human personnel must remain clear of the cargo track. If you are unattached when a tram comes, you will be hit."

Great, she thought. *Stay away from the track. Any other suggestions?*

She found a line on the shaft floor that showed how wide a tram was and, making sure of her handholds, climbed to a point where she would be clear of any trams that came along. She didn't feel as if she had climbed, though. She still felt as though she were falling. The only difference now was that the track was partway up the wall and the elevator doors seemed part of the floor.

"Do it, Saoirse. Do it," she said aloud.

So she pushed off and drifted along the shaft. Her stomach convinced her brain that she was falling down the shaft. Falling forever. She clamped her jaws and told herself not to vomit. At least she didn't feel like she had diarrhea. That would have been intolerable.

Soon enough, she saw the end of the shaft coming up in front of her. Thoughts flashed through her mind: How was she going to stop? She would hit the end of the shaft and bounce right back up to C-Ring. Or if she didn't bounce straight, she would ricochet off the walls, becoming a Saoirse pinball, bouncing forever in the central shaft until a cargo tram finally hit her.

Ahead of her, a frame slid out of the shaft wall, filled with netting. "Human personnel not using handholds should grasp the netting when you reach it," said the synthetic voice.

Handholds? Saoirse looked at the walls of the shaft and saw lines of handholds all along the shaft. She had not noticed those before, only the ones right by the elevator door. There had been no reason to launch herself into the air. *You are so stupid!* She hit the net and clutched the strands to her. A bubble formed in her stomach and forced its way up and out in a wet burp. She watched the globule float away from her and hoped that bots handled cleanup in the shaft. Then she worked her way along the netting to doors lettered A-RING SPOKE ELEVATOR TWO.

They slid open at the touch of her thumb and she climbed inside, panting as the elevator brought her back to blessed one gee.

When the elevator doors opened again, ahead of her was the dock of Titan Station. She had arrived in a cargo area, so there were not many people around. None of them looked menacing or paid any attention to her. She took a deep breath, wiped her mouth in case any liquid was still there, and swore that she would never, ever complain about having gained a few pounds.

She hurried toward the gate that divided the cargo area from the passenger concourse and was waved through by the peacers. Their job was to stop passengers from going into the cargo area, not from leaving it.

People thronged the passenger concourse. She checked a screen and saw that the *Long Haul* was taking passengers and crew from pusher gate A-3. Between her and A-3 milled a disorderly crowd. Families, either migrating or touristing, stood in bunches, with parents desperately trying to control young children who wanted to play hide-and-seek in the crowd. A passenger interstellar was boarding as well as an in-system ship, and lines stretched out from those kiosks. Here and there, men tried to cut into the queues simply because men wanted to be first, and never mind that everyone would arrive at the same time regardless of where they stood in line. Bots hauling bags formed a longer but more orderly line at the outbound customs station that led to the cargo pusher ports. People from the *Vandenberg* were still in the concourse as well, collecting their things and trying to orient themselves. She looked for peacers but didn't see any. On the bright side, she also didn't see anyone who looked like a hit man.

She found the queue for an outbound control kiosk and fingered the comm in her pocket. She would have to turn it on in order to show her orders and her transport voucher. She didn't want to fumble with it at the kiosk and draw attention. So she clicked it on. The queue moved forward, slowly.

It was almost her turn when a thickset man shoved into the line in front of her, ignoring the protests of the other passengers. He faced Saoirse, his hard eyes locked on to her face. His right hand slid beneath his jacket, open down the middle over an untucked tunic.

"There are people who want to talk to you." His voice was so soft that nobody else heard him.

Saoirse froze, knew what he'd said was a lie. If Pavel Brennikov had been hired to leave her poisoned and dead in her room, no one was looking to talk to her. This man just wanted her to go with him without making a fuss. She could not find words, doubted any would matter. The only movement she managed was a shake of her head.

"Make it easy on yourself." His free hand patted the jacket where it hid his other hand. "You don't want to go all spastic in front of everybody here, but I'll do it if I need to and pay you back for the trouble later."

Spastic . . . did that mean it was a nerve tangler, and not a real gun that would blow a hole in her? She didn't care. If she went along with him, no one would ever see her again. She'd have an "accident," like Bulkhead Bob. She should at least make him work for it—if he had to fire whatever was under his jacket in the middle of a crowded concourse, it would make a mess. Plus, she might survive.

From training with S, she knew what she should do up close against an enemy with a holstered weapon. She had never done it for real, of course. She readied herself for the leap to get a hand on his hand and block the draw.

"Fuck you," she said with a smile.

Before the man could draw, before Saoirse could make her desperate move, his face spasmed. His eyes went wide, his mouth stretched as far as it could in a gross rictus imitation of a smile, and his back arched. Then he collapsed on the deck, all four limbs twitching uncontrollably. Everyone nearby backed away, leaving a clear circle around the convulsing man.

Behind him stood Gusty Gray, a nerve tangler in her left hand and a pistol in her right. "You, get your hands on the top of your head," she said.

Saoirse almost put up her hands, then realized the pistol was pointed past her. She turned to see another man there, his eyes calculating. When he didn't move immediately, Gusty repeated, "Hands on your head, now. I've got ship-safe exploding azide rounds in this, and I will turn you into mincemeat if you don't. Peacers are here."

The man decided to do as he was told. Two more peacers pushed through the ring of people and took him in hand.

Saoirse felt the adrenaline begin to ebb. "Oh my God, Gusty! Thank you, thank you so much!"

Gusty didn't smile at first. "You can go easy on the gratitude, Saoirse. I know it doesn't come naturally." Then she gave a big grin. "I think you can board your ship now, Lieutenant. Maybe I'll see you here when you come back from the Reach."

Saoirse grabbed her in a bear hug. "When I come back, I bet you'll be running this place."

PART III
THE REACH

Blessed are the peacemakers, for they will be called children of God.
MATTHEW 5:9

Nothing in life is so exhilarating as to be shot at without result.
WINSTON CHURCHILL

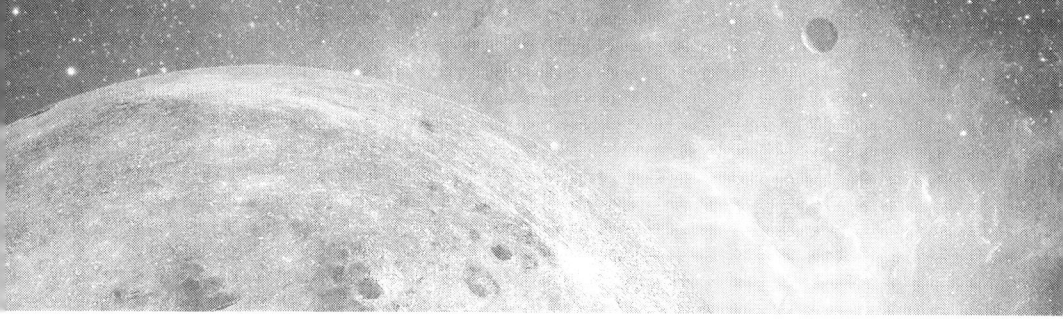

TWENTY-FIVE

The problem with starflight, Saoirse reflected, had nothing to do with going from one star to another. That was the easy part. The engineering crew on an interstellar fired up the generators in the ring that encircled the ship like a mini Saturn. The fields they generated unmasked negative mass, the captain pressed a control, or probably more than one, and voilà, a wormhole opened with the ship in the middle of it. Exactly how that happened, Saoirse didn't know, and she didn't know anyone who did, but that didn't matter. After all, she didn't know how tapping a button on her comm screen in Chicago sent a message to someone on the other side of Earth, but that also didn't matter. The comms worked and people took them for granted. Same for starflight. The wormhole opened and the ship dropped, or fell, or flew, or whatever, through it, and—snap!—you were in another star system in the time it took to eat a chocolate bar. Maybe faster. Saoirse was into savoring her chocolate bars.

No, the problem with starflight lay in getting to the point in space where the Riemann-Christoffel tensor said space-time was both flat enough to form a wormhole, and where it was possible to predict where you would come out on the other side. In the solar system, as in the system of any star around the size of the sun, that meant you had to go approximately as far out as the orbit of Saturn, which was why Titan Station was important.

The same issue with distance existed on the other side of the wormhole too. When you got through the wormhole, it wasn't as if habitable planets orbiting stars similar to the sun were right there, waiting. They would be in the Goldilocks zone, not too hot and not too cold, where water was liquid and humans could live on the surface under a sky. To get from a wormhole to the Goldilocks zone in a ship that could accelerate at only one gee took weeks.

Worse than that, when a ship came out of a wormhole, its velocity vector was whatever it had been when it went in—conservation of momentum, after all. But star systems move in the galaxy, and are in orbit around the galactic center. The velocity vector of whatever system a ship transited to might not match the system it left—it could be very different, and that would affect the relative velocity vector of the ship.

Ships emerging from wormholes needed to correct for that difference in order to reach their target planet. And again, that correction had to be made at a paltry one gee. It wasn't that a ship with a Mach effect drive couldn't manage more than one gee acceleration. The ship could do that, but the humans inside wouldn't be happy with it. So, one gee was what it was, and weeks was what it took for the *Long Haul* to go first to New Shanghai, then from there to Daleko Bałtyckie.

At least on the trip to Titan Station from Earth, Saoirse had had Gusty. They'd talked and giggled and played at being school-age girls again, and had managed to kill the time. The *Long Haul* was different. The ship was registered by the Church of Latter-Day Saints, which meant there was no bar and no alcohol on board. That was good for Saoirse in one key respect. There were also no passengers other than Saoirse, the former condition quite possibly accounting for the latter. Saoirse had not noticed the lack of a bar when she booked her berth, and in the chaos of reaching the *Long Haul* at the dock, she did not pay attention then either.

The ship's gym was small and cramped, and none of the crew would work out with her after the first couple of days. Saoirse's idea of a workout came from S, and after she left two crew members with a set of bruises, she found the gym vacant whenever she went there. That left her to hide in her cabin most of the time. Unfortunately, she was as bad at meditation as she had been when she tried it with Gusty. She spent hours detailing the mistakes of her life in her bound journal and then ran out of paper.

She tried using the ship's computer to read up on her destination and found out firsthand what S had said about the Reach. As soon as she brought up Daleko Bałtyckie, a warning popped up on the screen: "Information on this topic was last updated two years and three months ago (Standard Earth). Political, business, and social information is out of date and should not be relied upon." That was very useful. What was the point of studying useless information? That had been her motto through high school, and having it triggered by the computer sent her scurrying back to her journal to find space to write about that.

The computer did have some reliable information about Daleko Bałtyckie, though. The star was a G5, similar to Earth's sun but believed to be a couple of hundred million years younger. There were links to papers on why that was important, but it didn't seem important to Saoirse. She did not click on them. Daleko Bałtyckie was a near twin for Earth in size. Part of one continent had been settled, an area with a subtropical climate. The computer warned that the description of the settled area was two years and three months out of date. There were links to papers detailing the interesting geology of Daleko Bałtyckie, if she cared to read them. No, she did not. There were also links to a treatise on the flora and fauna of Daleko Bałtyckie, if she cared to read that. No, and no again. Anything interesting was either missing or out of date, and what was there was the type of boring stuff she had ignored in school. Ugh.

S had downloaded to her comm all his books as a parting gift. On Titan Station, she had been too pissed at him even to look at what was in there, but now, with four sterile walls around her, she decided to peek. She did not expect romance novels—she knew her S too well even to dream of that—but she hoped for some decent fiction. Even classics would have been fine. What she found was *The Art of War* by Sun Tzu, *Strategy* by B. H. Liddell Hart, *On War* by Karl von Clausewitz, *Anabasis* by Xenophon . . . and on and on in the same vein. She sighed, looked at the walls around her, and read. Maybe she would surprise S by quoting from them when she found him. Beyond her reading and her solo workouts in the gym, as the *Long Haul* made its way to Daleko Bałtyckie, Saoirse emerged from her cabin only to eat quickly and launder her few clothes.

. . .

Lieutenant Colonel Dimitris Venezelos of the Off-Earth Armed Peacemakers was a frustrated man. He had managed to wall off his frustration, to ignore it, for the almost four weeks since the *Long Haul* had dropped into the Daleko Bałtyckie system and transmitted its cargo manifest, a manifest that made clear that it carried nothing of what he had requested.

Of course, the reality of interstellar communications was that any message he sent to HQ had to go on a ship, which meant it would take a month, or two, or three, depending on the ship's route, before the message arrived in the solar system. Then it would take another month or two or three before the response came back.

However, he had been sending off supply requests for nearly a year with each ship that left, and the meager supplies he'd received were far from what he needed. If anything, ships had been more likely to bring orders transferring out his good personnel, and not just the fuckups he wanted to get rid of.

On this day, however, the interstellar had shuttled its cargo down to Daleko Bałtyckie's sole spaceport and transformed his aggravation with the message and the manifest into reality. None of what had landed was going to meet the needs of the Thirty-second Peacemaker Battalion. The men and women of his battalion depended on him for what they needed, and he would have to say that he had failed. Again. All he could do was send the request that he had sent before, different only in that the list would be longer, the quantities greater, and the need more urgent. It would be typical if someone at HQ finally woke up and organized all the resupply only to have it arrive months after a crisis had come and gone.

So Venezelos sat at his desk in battalion HQ and stared at the needs on his physical computer screen, which he preferred to a projection when it came to small fonts and numbers. The screen reflected his visage: a hatchet face with close-set intense eyes and a large aquiline nose, a prominent widow's peak in his thinning brown hair. The numbers on that screen represented the resources he lacked to carry out a mission that was only vaguely defined by an HQ far removed in time and space from reality on the ground. That, too, was typical.

He remembered Augustine, a miserable mudball of a planet that had been settled, if you could call it that, by the Church of All Humble Saints, a religious order off to found God's Kingdom, utopia in the stars. How old and common a story was that? Huts and falling-down shacks and neighbor on neighbor; theft, brutality, and rape had been the reality. Scopps had been sent in to build schools and clinics and take care of the people. Then the *óchlos*, the mob, set on them. When word finally got back to Earth about the chaos, the SC had sent the peacers to create order where there was none. But the peacers were not police and were poorly equipped and trained for that.

He remembered Eden—a sweet world, a beautiful world, so much better than simply a new Earth. It was such a wonderful world that the Americans and the Russians and the Chinese had planted colonies. And then they brought their soldiers. Not even a million people on a whole wide world, but they were ready to go to war. Whereupon the SC sent in the peacers to keep a peace no one seemed to want, with no clarity on the mission beyond taking casualties. But the peacers were not an army and lacked the resources for a full-scale war.

Oh, they were organized like an army, the peacers were. Venezelos' battalion, short of everything as it was, was still proof of that. They fought like an army and died like an army. But Venezelos wondered, and not for the first time, about the missions they fought and died for. Men and women did not willingly offer up their lives for the sake of SC bureaucrats on Earth Station who, when they knew anything at all about what was happening in the Reach, were behind the times. That was for sure.

Peacers came from dozens of countries on Earth, and more dozens of planets in the Reach. They scorned the SC Commendations as nothing more than lines in a file, cherished their stars, which the SC refused to recognize, and had been forced to beg Germany to take over and revive the PLM, the Pour le Mérite military order that had been extinct since the end of the First World War in 1918.

Venezelos sighed, his eyes no longer focused on the mundane problems in his screen. The peacers had been good to a poor Greek boy from the outskirts of Sparta who wanted to be a soldier. That mess on Eden had given him a wound that made the stars he wore red, and a promotion that led him to the mess that was Daleko Bałtyckie.

The planet was, at least, decent real estate, and had been taken by a colony of Poles, Lithuanians, and Latvians after the Eastern European economic meltdown eighty-odd years ago. The settlements had grown and prospered, with the population now near two hundred thousand, 40 percent of whom lived in and around the city of Sobieski in the highlands. The SC had appointed a legate, sent out the usual SCOPP help, and dropped in a peacer unit, now grown to a battalion, with a mission that was . . . what? What was the mission, truly, and what were they expected to do? Stop the flow of zombie? Certainly.

Zombipterisin was a wildly complex molecule, found only in a lowland plant. One simple chemical tweak of zombipterisin, and it was the best drug ever seen for treating schizophrenia. An equally simple but different tweak, and you had zombie, the worst addictive euphoric in the long and sorry history of human drug abuse. Yes, the peacers were on Daleko Bałtyckie to stop the flow of zombie. Were they there to keep the peace and help the colony meet the three benchmarks of a planetary government, power generation, and sufficient gross domestic product, which would allow Daleko Bałtyckie to join the Assembly of Worlds as an independent world? Probably, even if too much of that GDP secretly came from the zombie trade.

Venezelos figured that he could choke off the zombie trade with one company. Just take over the spaceport. Going from a planet to an orbiting interstellar was not a simple matter, and there was only one spaceport on the planet. Of course, another landing and takeoff area could be prepared, but it was hard to hide a spaceplane landing. One mobile platoon with drones and a simple satellite would have taken care of that additional risk, although the SC had not seen fit to put even one satellite in orbit around Daleko Bałtyckie. Keeping the peace between the city and highlands on one hand and the coast and the lowlands on the other was a different matter. The enmity and the exchange of accusations about trading zombie had been escalating for years, and any fool could see where they were headed. Still, with a full-strength battalion, he could suppress it. If he acted soon.

However, the SC legate, Liu Honghui, who represented the authority of the Solar Council and was Venezelos' superior, had other ideas. He was convinced that talk—negotiation—was the way to settle both the zombipterisin trade and the growing community tension. Venezelos thought that a fool's errand, but the legate was in charge, so the battalion sat in its base. Venezelos could guess the real reason. Getting Daleko Bałtyckie admitted to the Assembly as an independent world was the surest route to promotion for a legate, and to a posting back to Earth. Having peacers in charge of the spaceport and occupying villages and key points in the city, to say nothing of fighting with the locals, would ruin any such scheme. Of course, if—when—talks failed and the witches' brew boiled over and everyone screamed for the soldiers to bring law and order and peace, it would fall back in Venezelos' lap.

That brought him back to the problems on his computer screen. He leaned forward to scrutinize the lines again, even though he knew them by heart. All the *Long Haul* had brought him was a single first lieutenant to take command of Third Platoon, Company C. Venezelos needed a captain, he needed two lieutenants, he needed troopers in all three rifle companies, he needed drones, and a list of supplies that ran from the top of the screen to the bottom and kept scrolling. But what he had was a notice that came with the *Long Haul* stating that, "it has been determined that your resources are adequate for your mission." That was what he had gotten . . . and a first lieutenant. *Might as well meet your new officer*, he thought.

"Send Lieutenant Kenneally in," he said into his comm.

Venezelos studied the young woman as she walked to the front of his desk and saluted. She looked fit, which was something, although the ill-fitting civilian clothes she wore could have concealed much. Those clothes! The colors had faded away, and calling them threadbare was generous. He returned the salute, gestured to a chair, and told her to sit down.

"Peacers travel in uniform." It was another way of building a common bond, for whatever value it had.

"Titan Station did not have a woman's uniform in my size," she said. "It was unreasonable to wait for resupply, and I thought that SCOPP dark blue would be equally wrong."

Her words sounded practiced, but what difference did it make? "We do not have any officer uniforms for women in our supply."

He turned to the computer screen and brought up the file of First Lieutenant Saoirse Kenneally. It made as little sense as it had the first time he reviewed it.

"How did you get this position? Did you do someone a favor, or did you really piss someone off?"

"Sir?"

At least she had the grace to look surprised. "Please spare me the story," he said, "about how you worked tirelessly for this transfer and the promotion and how you chose to come here to risk yourself in service to humanity and to bring peace to the Reach. My guess is that you pissed someone off in a major way. Because if you did favors to get here, you need both your intelligence and your sanity checked."

"I may have some people angry at me, sir."

"Right." Venezelos steepled his fingers and looked at her. Black hair, pale skin, something twitchy in her manner. But he'd seen worse. "You understand that a Peacemaker officer is required to have a college degree?"

Was there a hint of alarm in her eyes?

"No one told me that, sir."

"Look it up," he grunted. The peacers had been organized along the lines of the American military, and they required it. Of course, the peacers gave plenty of waivers. Too many peacers came from places where college didn't exist, or was a joke, and the shortage of officers was even greater than all the other shortages. But her file should have had a waiver.

When she remained silent, he shrugged. "Never mind. You will either perform your role or not. I've never been convinced that a degree in Art History fits a man or woman to be an officer. Certainly, going to college won't make you brave."

She looked so relieved that his antennae rose. Maybe he should send an additional message back with the *Long Haul*, asking HQ for more information on this Lieutenant Kenneally and her transfer. What was the point, though? The file was the file, and that was likely all anyone would tell him. He did not have the kind of connections that would yield gossip about score-settling, and besides, she wasn't that important. Kenneally was a lieutenant, not a major. By the time any response got back to him, she would have proved herself adequate or a failure. Or she'd be dead and he would be asking for another replacement. Maybe there was something in that file he could make use of.

"When you served at Titan Station, you weren't a peacer," he pointed out. "You were a scopp reporting to the civilian side of SCOPP." When she let that pass without offering any comment, he continued, "The coastal and lowland villages have brought in a former peacer from Titan Station named Tomasz Szczechowicz to expand and improve their militia. How well do you know him?"

Again, she startled, followed by a quick recovery.

"We, ah . . . sparred. From time to time."

He wasn't sure what to make of that comment, then decided he didn't care. "I don't suppose I should expect you to tell me if he is a modern Gylippus."

"A what, sir?"

"Who, not what." Venezelos grinned. "You have a Greek battalion commander." He pointed at the wall behind his desk, where he had pictures of the Parthenon ruins and the statue of Leonidas at Thermopylae. "You may find it useful to read some Greek history and mythology. The base computer has a few works. During the Peloponnesian War, Syracuse asked for help against the Athenians who were besieging their city. Sparta sent one man, a general named Gylippus, who organized the Syracusans, defeated the Athenians, and changed the course of the war."

She stared at him. "Yes, sir."

"Is that Szczechowicz here? I want you to meet with him, develop a rapport, a relationship, and bring me some intel. See Cyber once you settle in. She'll brief you on what we know about him."

She nodded and said, "I can do that, sir."

"Good. The political situation here is, shall we say, complicated. You can access a detailed briefing in the computer once you interface your comm." He hesitated. "When you were briefed on this post, did they tell you about nail-joint syndrome?"

Kenneally shook her head. "No, sir."

"Figures. We don't know what causes it. Three percent, approximately, of humans who come here get it. Fevers, joints swell and stiffen, your nails turn black and fall out. Sometimes your hair too. Most recover, but not everyone. Humans born here don't get it at all. Make sure you have the doc tell you the early signs to look for. All right, Kenneally, your orders are to have your platoon ready for action, whether or not we have any. Captain Gelashvilli of Company C is in Sobieski today. You can report to him when he returns. In the meantime, First Sergeant Jeremiah Mwesigye of your platoon will take you to supply so that you have something appropriate to wear. He will introduce you to your platoon. One final thing, Kenneally. I've got no use for a drunk officer. There are no second chances in the Reach."

"Yes, sir," she said. "Thank you."

Venezelos' eyes went back to the screen, then back to the chair. She was still sitting there.

"Dismissed, Kenneally."

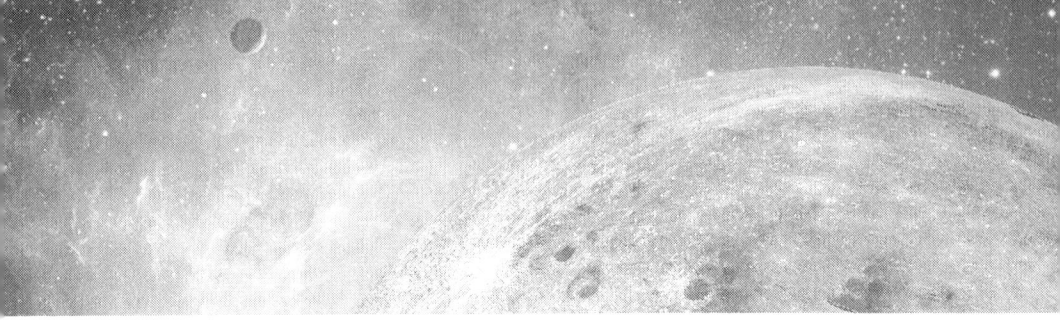

TWENTY-SIX

Saoirse left Venezelos' office and walked down the hallway to the exit, her mind in a whirl. How had she missed the requirement for college? Venezelos must have known her records were faked, but he hadn't said anything. Hadn't thrown her in jail or out the front gate. All he had said was she could do her job or she couldn't, as though this sort of stuff happened all the time. Then he had as much as told her to find S and get close to him! She wondered if Alice felt this way when she went down the rabbit hole.

She walked through the exit from the HQ into the blindingly bright Daleko Bałtyckie afternoon and, between the sun and the thoughts racing through her mind, almost walked directly into the man standing there. He snapped to attention and saluted. She thought he looked like an African war god, six foot four without counting the beret on his head, and broad through the shoulders and chest even for that height. This could only be First Sergeant Jeremiah Mwesigye.

It took several heartbeats before she realized *he* was saluting *her* and she needed to return it. She made a hasty salute, all the while aware of dark eyes that looked down at her with a stare that told her she had already been weighed and found wanting. She tried to tell herself that it was only her clothes that Mwesigye was judging, but she didn't believe it.

Mwesigye introduced himself, then said, "May I suggest, Lieutenant, that I take you to Base Supply first so you can draw uniforms? Then, after you change, I can take you to the platoon."

It was easy to agree to that, but the moment they left the headquarters building, Mwesigye started to fill her in on her responsibilities. It was one acronym after another and a ton of computer pixel work. The acronyms meant nothing to her, but she was afraid to ask, while being equally afraid of what would happen if she didn't. She stole a look at the sergeant as they walked across the compound and read disapproval in his expression. With each step they took, her brilliant plan for escaping Titan Station and coming to Daleko Bałtyckie felt progressively more stupid. How had she ever thought she could pull this off? Had she really thought it through before she hit Send on the file and orders? Why was she thinking about it only now? Why hadn't she talked to Mom? She was sure Mwesigye's expression had turned into a scowl.

Halfway across the field, Mwesigye stopped to kick at an ankle-high chartreuse stalk with four tiny leaves that stuck up from the packed dirt. "Damn fern-clovers," he said. "Some things you need to know, sir, that are not in briefings. Like oxy. You know that oxygen is twenty-eight percent in the air here, sir?"

Saoirse nodded. "I read that," she said, even though she hadn't.

"Well, it's not just a number, sir. It's fine for us. We'll run better and longer here than anywhere else. Some people swear this place is the best cure for a hangover going. Drink all night and wake up the next morning fresh as done laundry."

"I don't drink," Saoirse said. "Not ever."

"Hnnh." Mwesigye's face said that he found her statement dubious at best. "As may be," he said. "What you need to know is that all that oxy comes from plants, and the plants are all over the planet. Grow crazy fast. No grass here, but these little fern-clovers," he scuffed again at the low four-leaved ground cover, "they'll grow on any open dirt. Seems like overnight. The big ferns grow fast too. We keep goats on the base to help keep it down. Nasty animals, but they'll eat anything and they like the fern-clovers. Platoons swap off each week being responsible for keeping the base clear."

"I work that out with the other platoon leaders?"

"Yes, sir," Mwesigye said. "The real downside to the oxy, though, is fire. Catches easy, burns hot. You'll see our rifles have little fire-caps to capture the muzzle flash. All vehicles and equipment have built-in flame retardant and spew foam on impact. If you smoke, don't smoke outside."

Saoirse nodded again.

"It's strange to think of oxygen as your enemy, but that's what it is here," Mwesigye said.

"That is weird," Saoirse said. "Especially after being on Titan Station or Titan, where making sure you had oxygen was critical."

"I was told you were off Titan Station, that's why I brought it up, sir. It's a different set of reflexes here." He chuckled. "No intelligent life here, and I bet there can't ever be. The moment an intelligent creature invents fire, they'll burn themselves to a crisp."

Saoirse wondered if he was including her with those hypothetical creatures.

"Also, be aware of the situation with the comms, sir. Here, and in or around Sobieski, you can use them like you would anywhere, except there's no database outside of the base to connect to. Once you get away from here, though, the signal is poor to nonexistent—unless you can connect to one of the relay towers, and almost all of those are in the highlands. This place isn't really computerized. We'd do better with old-style radios, but we don't have them." He paused. "Motor pool is to the left of Supply." He pointed. "I can show you the vehicle mix we have. So you know the issue."

"What issue?" The moment she said it, she was sure it was a mistake. Another mistake.

His face did not react to the question. "We've got only a few ground effect vehicles or electric wheeled vehicles. Mostly alcohol-based internal combustion engines, which need a lot of maintenance and can't haul that much of a load."

"Why?"

Again, he studied her face.

"All the electricity here comes from the nuke plant. There are solar panels in some of the villages, but we don't have them. The prezydent of Sobieski controls the plant, and the lieutenant colonel doesn't want to be dependent on him. Same time, there's no oil or gasoline, so combustion engines have to be alcohol, and maintenance is its own problem. It's in the briefing."

Saoirse hoped he meant the briefing that Venezelos had told her was in the computer here, not something she was expected to have read beforehand. Again, she would not ask. "I'll go to the motor pool later,

Sergeant. I want to get out of these clothes and meet the platoon first." She hoped that was a reasonable position, one a real lieutenant would take. Was everything this Sergeant Mwesigye said a test of some sort? Would he report the result to Venezelos later? She was failing badly, she was sure. Maybe had a zero. Every move she made, every word she said, felt awkward.

Mwesigye said only, "Yes, sir," and led the way to the Base Supply building.

· · ·

The corporal in charge of the Base Supply was not happy to see her. As Venezelos had said, they had no uniforms for female officers. That meant the corporal had to pull out multiple sizes, and then had to go back and find a duffel when Mwesigye made it clear that neither he nor the lieutenant would carry a stack of uniforms.

Then Mwesigye walked Saoirse over to officers' quarters and pulled a two-inch-long piece of metal out of a pocket. "This is your key, sir."

"Key?" She looked at the metal: smooth on one edge, jagged on the other.

"Locals put this building up. Doors are metal—fairly thin metal usually, but at least it doesn't burn. They don't have the plastics that go into our recognition plates and locks, so this is an old-style key. You stick it in the lock," he pointed at a round metal button on the door, "and turn it to the left to open and right to lock."

"I think I can manage that." Saoirse inserted the key, turned it to the left, and smiled as the door unlocked and swung open. Then she couldn't get the key out and yanked on it several times before she realized that she had to turn it back to vertical to withdraw it. She was red in the face by the time she figured it out, certain that Mwesigye was laughing at her despite his impassive face.

Trying to find a uniform that fit went no better. She had always regarded herself as narrow-hipped and had been laughed at in school for having no butt. However, the men's pants were cut all wrong—the ones that fit her in the hips were far too wide at the waist, and the waistband folded and crumpled when she cinched the belt. The shirts were just as bad—either stretched tight over her breasts or draped like a tent over her lower torso. She settled for tight.

Matters did not improve when Mwesigye took her to meet the platoon. She knew she fumbled the return of their salutes and said the wrong things to the men and women standing in front of her. She knew that from the way they looked at her. All of them. No sympathy there. About a third of them wore Peacers' Stars. She thought their eyes lingered on the single bar on her collar that was her emblem of rank. The rank was real; it was she who was fake. And awkward. With their stares on her, again she wondered why she had thought she could do this.

Because you never think about the consequences of what you do. Nothing new about that. You remember the time— Stop it, Saoirse!

All through the fiasco, Mwesigye stood next to her. Finally it was over and he accompanied her outside. It was a relief to escape. She couldn't wait to get back to her quarters, where she could cry by herself. But just as she thought her nightmare of a day was ending, Mwesigye said, "Lieutenant, may I speak to you for a moment? In private?" His posture and tone were tense. Clearly, there was only one right answer to the question.

"Certainly, Sergeant," she said. "Shall we go back to the offices?"

"Yes, sir," he said, and they walked back across the compound in silence.

The office she was to share with the other junior officers was empty. Only when they were inside with the door closed to afford them a modicum of privacy did Mwesigye speak again.

"May I have permission to speak openly and candidly, sir?"

Saoirse didn't like the sound of that but saw no way to refuse. "Permission granted, Sergeant."

"You don't know what you're doing, sir," Mwesigye said. "You don't have a clue." It was a statement, not a question.

A ready lie rose to her lips. No matter the situation, she'd always been able to come up with one. This time, though, she stifled it. Instead, she gave him a rueful smile. "You are correct, Sergeant. I don't have a clue. Not the slightest."

She was surprised to see the big man relax. The tension left his face.

"Well, sir," he said, "at least you know what you don't know. That's something." He paused as if weighing his next words. "Since I've been here, and it's a standard year, I don't know what it is, sir, we can't get replacements or, if we get them, they're fuckups somebody else got rid of, or . . ."

"Or they don't have a clue," she finished for him. She took a breath, held it, and decided to take a risk. "Sergeant, can you show me what I am supposed to do?"

A startled expression crossed his face; then it went back to impassive. "I can do that, sir. A lot of it is computer work. I'll go over the reports with you, if you wish, sir. The mission essential task list is in the computer. We train on that. You need to see to the training for the platoon. Company C is a light rifle company, emphasis on the word *light*. Actually, all the companies and platoons are the same. The heaviest weapons we've got are shoulder-launched rockets, some light mortars, and, as you saw, one machine gunner in each of your three squads. I would suggest you learn every piece of equipment the platoon has. Not just learn the inventory, but inspect all of it, make sure you know how it works and that it does work. That's a part of your responsibility. And take an interest in the men and women, sir. Whatever mission we're given, they are the ones who accomplish it, and to do that, they need to become your team."

He paused, and took her continued silence as permission to continue. "We peacers, the troops here and everywhere in the Reach, we don't fight for the glory of the Solar Council. That's a bunch of corrupt assholes at Earth Station. We're not looking to die bringing peace to the Reach. None of us could tell you what that means. Our loyalty is to each other. That's who we fight for, and that's why we fight. That loyalty, that willingness to fight and die, that's what makes the team. We need our officers to lead us and to build the team that will die for each other. That's what you need to do, sir."

Saoirse looked at Mwesigye. "I won't disappoint you."

She was sure it was a lie even as she said it. Saoirse Kenneally had never done anything except disappoint people. But standing there, looking at Jeremiah Mwesigye with his red Peacers' Stars on his breast, she could not think of anything else to say.

"Just remember, sir, when the fighting starts, that's when you will have to have already done everything I just said. If you haven't, it'll be too late. Lieutenant Yee, before he was transferred out, was rather lax." He stopped abruptly.

"I hear you, Sergeant." Saoirse said. "That's why you were hoping for someone with more than just a clue." An idea blossomed in her mind. "You mentioned training, Sergeant. How is marksmanship in the platoon?"

"Could be better, sir."

"I'd like to see for myself. At the target range. Tomorrow morning."

※ ※ ※

The plan for tomorrow got Mwesigye out of the office, and the man looked satisfied when he left, which Saoirse found odd. She had no time to dwell on that, however. She had other things that needed attention. The platoon's equipment, starting with the vehicles, was what Mwesigye had told her to take care of, and she was going to do that. First, though, she was going to find out about S. It was an order, she rationalized, which meant it had precedence over what Mwesigye had suggested she do.

That meant she needed to figure out where and what this Cyber was. Venezelos had said "she," so Cyber would be a person. Venezelos had also said "intel," so maybe headquarters company would be the place to look. That group was housed in the same building as Venezelos' office, a nondescript concrete structure painted white, with a flat roof and the same type of flimsy metal door that had been mounted on the officers' quarters. The corridor that led to the back of the building, past Venezelos' office, ended in a door with HHC, 32ND PEACERS painted on it. The door did not slide open when she stepped in front of it, and neither faceplate nor thumb pad was present. Saoirse pushed it open and walked in.

The room was a large square, with office doors lining the perimeter, all closed. The central area was divided into multiple work areas by seven-foot-high movable screens, each area with a desk, computer screen, and comm port. Most had an occupant. Placards listing function and name were fixed on the partitions like road signs. The inhabitants of the office ignored Saoirse as she walked around. Finally, she found a placard that read CYBER OPERATIONS, A. ALVES. A woman was sitting at the desk, playing a game on her comm.

"You're Cyber?" asked Saoirse.

The woman glanced up, saw an officer, stood and saluted. "Yes, sir. Cyber Ops Specialist Ana Alves."

Saoirse sighed inwardly. She doubted she would ever get used to being called *sir*, especially by a woman. Alves was half a foot shorter than her, with a round face and brown eyes. Hair that matched the eyes was wound into a tight bun at the back of her head. Her uniform did not have stars.

"At ease, please," Saoirse said. "Relax. Whatever. I'm Lieutenant Kenneally." She would need to practice saying that. It didn't sound natural.

"Yes, sir." Alves did relax. "We heard the new officer was going to be a woman."

"Yes, I'm going to be a woman," Saoirse said, "and I always have been. They call you Cyber?"

Alves smiled. "Yes, sir. There should actually be three of us, one each for IT, cybersecurity, and e-warfare, but the legate's office handles most of the IT and I do the rest. If you need any electronic work, come to me. Hence, Cyber."

Girl after my own heart, Saoirse thought, although when she looked at Alves more closely, she realized Alves was older—midtwenties, at least.

"Okay." Saoirse smiled. "Cyber is the cyberwizard who can make our computers dance a jig." Alves' face lost her smile and she put her hands up. She had said something wrong. Again.

"Look, Lieutenant," Alves said, "I didn't intend to sound like I'm boasting. I mean, I'm good at what I do, but if you want the truth, back on Earth I was always just good enough to reach the point in a job screen where they tell you you're not quite good enough."

"Wait a minute," Saoirse said. "This isn't training you got in the peacers. You actually studied computers and electronics in school on Earth? And you joined the peacers, went to a combat peacer unit?"

"Peacers pay more than SCOPP, and combat units were offering bonuses for technical skills. Lieutenant, I've got my mother, my grandmother, and I'm the oldest of five. There's no Guaranteed Benefit in Brazil."

"I'm sorry," Saoirse said, and she was. Alves had taken whatever opportunities she could get. She hadn't thrown them away. "That doesn't sound fair."

Alves laughed. "Life will be fair, sir, the day after there's peace in the Reach."

"What?"

"You haven't heard that one yet?" Her grin was back. "It's a peacer saying, but I didn't hear it until I got out into the Reach either. 'The day after there's peace in the Reach.' It means—never." She met Saoirse's eyes. "I'll bet you didn't come to find me to hear my life story or learn peacer sayings. What can I do for you, sir?"

Saoirse was glad to have the conversation move away from personal matters. "The lieutenant colonel wants me to find the man who came here to run the militia and get to know him. He said I should find you, although I guess I should be finding the intelligence officer."

"That still brings you to me," Alves said. "Captain Bronson is Intelligence," she pointed to one of the perimeter offices, "but he basically makes the nice presentations to the lieutenant colonel and the legate. He is highly thought of by the legate and spends most of his time at the legate's offices in Sobieski. We should have intelligence specialists, but we're shorthanded there, like we are almost everywhere. I handle the electronic surveillance, so I also work with intelligence. We can use Bronson's office for this."

A couple of minutes later, they were both leaning against a desk in an office that did not appear to get much use.

"So you want to know about the man who wears red and gold," Alves said.

Saoirse nodded.

"Tomasz Szczechowicz," Alves said. "Native of Daleko Bałtyckie, joined the peacers at sixteen, last posted as captain on Titan Station, but you obviously know that. Resigned from the peacers and came here for the colonel's position commanding the militia for the coastal and lowland villages. Each village has its own independent unit, all poorly trained and even more poorly led. For all of that, there was a huge stink about having a centralized command and, apparently, about him in particular.

"Don't know what he did in his first sixteen years here, but they obviously didn't welcome him back with open arms." She shook her head. "He's definitely qualified, if not overqualified. Szczechowicz gave the villages all his records from the peacers, so I was able to, ah, obtain them, too, and a lot quicker than it would have been trying to get them from Earth.

"This Szczechowicz has one hell of a combat record. He earned red and gold, and you wear those forever. It's not the kind of record you see often, but I guess people from a bunch of fishing villages on a Class Two world are ignorant about that sort of thing. It took a lot of argument before they gave him the militia command. I'm sure the lieutenant colonel wants to know what's behind all the fussing. It didn't seem to make sense."

"I know he wears red and gold," Saoirse said. "Do you know the story about the Valor Star?"

"Yes, sir, I thought you'd ask about that." Alves looked up at Saoirse. "It's not in the official records, which is no surprise because those often aren't, but the village heads here—I forget the local word for *mayor*—wanted to know, so Szczechowicz gave it to them. That's how I got it. Apparently, there was a rebellion on some godforsaken world. Peacers were sent in to put it down. Szczechowicz was pretty young at the time—seventeen or eighteen. Anyway, the rebels took hostages, a school full of young teens, and threatened to start killing them if the peacers didn't leave. The government took their own hostages and threatened to start killing *them* if the peacers didn't attack. Somehow, Szczechowicz found a way to infiltrate the complex where the rebels held their hostages. His sergeant was the only one who went in with him. They killed the hostage-takers and freed the kids. Szczechowicz was badly wounded; the sergeant was killed."

"That sergeant," Saoirse said, "was his name James Andrew Baker?"

Alves stared at her. "How did you know that, sir?"

"I have some sources of my own." Unbidden, her hands twisted together. She wanted to hold something, preferably a cigarette. "If you learn about where Colonel Szczechowicz is—preferably a time and a place I can just show up, like it's chance and spontaneous—you let me know."

TWENTY-SEVEN

The next morning was foggy and damp when the Third Platoon of Company C assembled at the firing range on the perimeter of the peacer base. The backstop wall that blocked stray bullets hid most of the view of the fern-covered field beyond. Beyond the wall, Saoirse could just see the tops of distant trees that marked the beginning of the slope down to the coast.

The platoon, consisting of twenty-five men and five women, along with their corporals and sergeants, stood by squads in a sullen silence at the firing stations. Saoirse saw hard eyes, all of them fastened on her. She had found a set of dark-green camo that was close enough to her size. It was a vast improvement over yesterday's uniform, even if it covered up her snake. She was pleased to see that she was dressed as they were. Hopefully, they would take that as a sign she knew what she should be doing.

What were they staring at? She didn't have Peacers' Stars, but most of them hadn't made stars either. She wanted to tell herself it wasn't fair, then remembered what Alves had said about fair and pushed the thought away. She looked for Mwesigye and saw him watching her expectantly.

Of course! He was waiting for an order to begin.

"Let's get started, Sergeant," she said in a voice that she hoped betrayed nothing of what she was feeling. "Have the bots set aggressor targets, twenty-five per person."

Had she said more than she needed to? Should she have said only, *Let's get started*? Was that the right choice for targets? Adelayo had used them most of the time at Hammarskjöld. Bots would stream out into the field and pop up man-sized targets in various poses of an attacking enemy. The shooter had a set time to fire at each target, and if a shot had not been fired before the next target popped up, it counted as a miss.

Would the platoon resent being given a basic training exercise for what they would see as a test? She tried to think it through. It would be a test if she were a real officer come to assume command of this platoon. For all any of them knew, she was a real officer. It said so in her very real orders and records in Lieutenant Colonel Venezelos' office. Only she knew the orders and records were as fake as she was. *Bad way to start thinking*, she warned herself.

Mwesigye said only, "Yes, sir," and stepped over to the range control.

The control panel was in a small desk mounted on a stanchion at the center of the firing line. Mwesigye tapped at the controls. In response, a door opened in a small shed off to the left, and a line of low, circular bots headed out onto the range.

"Jacobson, your squad first," Mwesigye said. "One by one."

A corporal pointed at a peacer, and the man stepped to the line. The first target popped up, and his rifle cracked. The shooting continued with no sound other than that of the rifles firing. After each peacer had finished their twenty-five targets, the bots would bring them in, drop them, and replace their target canisters. A panel on the control desk displayed the score for each shooter, but it was also apparent from where each target had been hit—or not hit—how the shooter had performed.

When all of them had finished, Mwesigye turned to her and said, "What do you think, Lieutenant?"

Saoirse glanced at the control panel, where the scores were displayed by individual and by squad. She didn't really need to look; she had seen all the targets as the bots came in. What should she say? What was she supposed to say? She knew what Adelayo would have said. She couldn't say that, though, could she? Would they take that from her? Then she remembered Mwesigye's comment the previous day.

"Could be better." She hoped those words sounded both mild and forceful at the same time.

Now, if only Mwesigye would dismiss the platoon right at that moment, and tell them to go do whatever they should have been doing that morning had it not been for the interruption of a new lieutenant who had to act like an officer. If he did that, she could go to the motor pool and supply depot and figure out what equipment belonged to the platoon and whether it worked. Or she could go to the battalion office building, stare at the computer, and brood.

Not quite.

"Yes, sir. We will improve." That came from Corporal Jacobson, the one Mwesigye had pointed to at the start of the session. His squad had not done well. "Perhaps," he added, "the lieutenant would like to show us how it should be done."

Saoirse was certain the entire platoon held their collective breath, waiting to see how she would react. She tried to smile but was afraid it looked like a smirk. It had been in the back of her mind that something like this would happen. That was why she had picked the firing range. It was a place where she had a skill she actually excelled at and one that should matter to them. But now all she could think about was how long it had been since Hammarskjöld. She had not practiced at all on Titan Station, obviously. What if she forgot how?

You're going to have the shakes, you know, and they're all going to see it. Just like that high school play when you were ready to shit your pants even though you knew your lines. Of course, this time you're sober. That has advantages . . . and disadvantages, you know— Stop it, Saoirse!

"Your weapon, Corporal." Saoirse held out her hand to Jacobson.

He looked surprised, but handed over the rifle promptly. As soon as her hands closed on the weapon, she felt better. She was *not* shaking.

"First, we should clean it, don't you think?" She locked eyes with Jacobson, her fingers automatically starting to disassemble the rifle and lay the pieces on the control desk.

She kept eye contact with him, never looking at the rifle as she took it apart. When it was completely disassembled, she asked, "Anyone have an ultra-cloth?"

Mwesigye produced one, and she wiped off all the contact points and ran it through the barrel. When she was done, she made a point of looking at the light-gray cloth, which was as smooth as silk and as tough as body armor.

"Not bad. Could be cleaner."

Again, she stared at Jacobson, as though daring him to drop his eyes to watch her reassemble the weapon, which she did without a glance at it. At the last, her hand closed on the magazine. A loud click was the only sound at the firing line as it snapped into place. She stepped away from the desk, rifle aimed at the ground.

"Sergeant Mwesigye."

Mwesigye tapped the controls. Saoirse brought the rifle up and fired as the first target presented itself. Target followed target; shot followed shot. It was automatic: sight and fire. Each target filled her eye and her mind. The world disappeared. No need to think, no thought at all. Just shoot. She was sad when the last target had been hit and no more popped up. She would have been happy to shoot all morning.

After that last shot, the bots brought her targets in. Barely suppressed snickers came from the women, while the men stood in openmouthed silence. Of the four aggressor targets that had been largely concealed behind a boulder, a door, a wall or peeking out the corner of a window, all had a bullet hole in the visible portion of the aggressor's head. For every other aggressor target, the bullet had been drilled straight through the center of the groin.

⁂

Saoirse did not sleep well the night after the demonstration. The reason was not entirely her ribs, although they were sore enough. Why, she thought every time she rolled over on the mattress and her ribs responded by waking her from whatever fitful sleep she was managing, why had she not let well enough alone with the morning's marksmanship display? How could she have been so stupid as to announce that they would work on hand-to-hand combat drills before the evening meal? How could she have been even more stupid and chosen Mwesigye as her partner for demonstration? The man was at least seven inches taller than S, and God knew how many pounds heavier.

True, nothing had actually broken. She was merely bruised and battered, and ribs would heal. She remembered saying that at some point and hearing Mwesigye agree with her, but it was cold comfort now, wide awake in the middle of the night. She only wished his skin wasn't so damned dark, so that the shiner she had hung on him would show better.

Of course, the reason she had done it was the rest of the reason she could not sleep. The riflery demonstration had impressed the platoon, she was sure. But for all of that, she could not escape the feeling that she had only bought a little time. She still did not know how to act like an officer;

she had no idea how the peacers of Third Platoon expected an officer to act.

It was, naturally, her own fault—as most things were. She had never dreamed that Venezelos would look at her, review her record, and... shrug. That he would effectively say, *Oh, another HQ fuckup. We'll go ahead anyway.* Or that Sergeant Mwesigye would do, essentially, the same, even after she told him that she had no idea what she was doing. So there she was awake at night, Lieutenant Saoirse Kenneally, girl without a clue.

She sat up, put the light on, and found herself staring at her hands while thinking about the nail-joint syndrome Venezelos had mentioned. She never paid attention to her nails, other than biting them. She'd never done anything with them since high school. But the thought of having them turn black and fall out was, well, gruesome. She needed to talk to the doc. One more item on her to-do list, but it couldn't be the first.

Mwesigye had said that she needed to take an interest in her peacers, as though Third Platoon had magically become her team. Of course, in a way it *had* become her team. Take an interest in the peacers. She should go talk to one of them. Which one? She had reviewed all their files after last night's meal and had seen how little she had in common with any of them. Well, six of them had "known alcohol abuse" flags in their files, but that was not how she planned to start a conversation. Only five of them were women, despite the fact that the peacers claimed to be 38 percent female. Maybe she should try one of the women.

Corporal Juliana Hopkinson—the peacer who laughed the loudest when Saoirse's targets had been brought in the previous day—was alone in the barracks, fixing the closure of one of her boots, when Saoirse walked in after breakfast. Hopkinson rose and saluted, leaving the boot open on her foot. She was taller than Saoirse by a good inch and broad through the shoulders. She wore her auburn hair in a plaited braid that extended halfway down her back—much farther, Saoirse thought, than regulations permitted. She was one of the peacers in the platoon who wore red stars.

Saoirse returned the salute.

"Can I do something for you, sir?" Hopkinson asked after an awkward pause.

"Yes, yes. Relax, please," Saoirse said with the feeling that she was screwing it up already. "I just wanted to talk to you about a couple of things."

"Certainly, sir." Hopkinson sat back down on her bed and finished closing her boot.

Okay, Saoirse thought, *I'm here. What do I want to talk about?* "I was curious about this place." When Hopkinson said nothing, she searched for something to be curious about. "There are only five women in Third Platoon, and that seems to be the most in any unit of the battalion. When I came in, Supply didn't have a uniform for a female officer. Why so few of us?"

Saoirse did not expect Hopkinson to laugh, but that was what she did, every bit as loud as on the firing range. "Daleko Bałtyckie has, the prezydent's office likes to say, a traditional culture based on their roots in the Baltic. Personally, sir," she said, "I don't know where the Baltic is, although I guess it's somewhere on Earth and not another planet in the Reach, and I don't know what their traditional culture was, but what it means in Sobieski is that a woman's place is either in the kitchen or having children. It's not the kind of place a woman peacer wants to serve. If there's a way to transfer out or not come here at all, most will take that."

"You're here," Saoirse said.

"Didn't get a choice," Hopkinson said, "just like, if I may say, rumor has it you didn't get one either." When Saoirse stayed quiet, she continued. "I made my stars on Middle Kingdom, where we were trying to stop a civil war. When I got out of the hospital, the sergeant thought I should celebrate with him. I said no and left him with a pointed reminder." She pushed the fingers of her right hand under her waistband and pulled out a small dagger with a razor edge and a needle-sharp point. "That got me here."

"And the men here?" Saoirse asked.

Hopkinson slipped the blade back into its sheath and shrugged. "As far as the battalion goes, Lieutenant, you're an officer. That matters. Venezelos is a decent man, won't stand for crap, but I can't say the same for all the officers. You'll forgive me, sir, if I don't mention names. If you're interested, there's plenty of men in town. Keep in mind, sir, that there are two classes here. People who live on the coast or in the lowlands, they'll treat women pretty much equal, but the people in Sobieski and the highland towns call the lowland people swampers and look down on them. Men from the city and the highlands, for all they talk about how superior they are, they think women are only good for cooking and fucking. To them—as the phrase here goes—women are worth less than the pig shit on a swamper's bootheel."

She looked quizzically at Saoirse. "Assuming your preference is men, that is."

Saoirse was certain that Hopkinson was opening a door, and she was just as certain that she wasn't going to walk through it.

"Thank you," said Saoirse. "You've cleared up a lot for me."

TWENTY-EIGHT

Sobieski, the capital and indeed only city on Daleko Bałtyckie, was set on the highlands beside a half-mile-wide river, the Nowy Vistula. Eighty years after the founding of the colony, Sobieski was home to upwards of forty thousand souls, more than a fifth of Daleko Bałtyckie's human population. Another thirty-five thousand or so lived in the villages scattered across those highlands, mostly running in a band toward the continental northeast along both sides of the river. If viewed from an orbiting spaceship, the city and those villages with their farms resembled islands carved out of the otherwise omnipresent yellow-green vegetation that carpeted the land.

Keeping that vegetation from growing back over the roads that linked the settlements, the buildings themselves, and indeed, every evidence of human presence, was a ceaseless task. The little fern-clovers covered open ground like a skintight garment. Over them grew bigger ferns, the flexi-ferns, as the settlers called them. Those sprouted multiple waving stems that pushed up from the earth and reached twenty feet into the air. They grew everywhere and they grew fast. Any crack in pavement, any open patch of dirt, was an invitation to the flexis.

It wasn't only the flexis that threatened to sweep over the cities and towns. At least thirty varieties of low, spongy plants that reminded Saoirse of moss, except they were yellow, competed with the flexis for the ground and grew heavily on any surface the flexis did not cover. These ranged from little puffballs, as soft as fur, to spiky plants reminiscent of porcupines. No flowers bloomed on Daleko Bałtyckie to break the yellow-green monotony, and none of the native plants bore fruit. Instead they made spores. When a stiff wind blew, it was as if smoke curled up from the fields.

Its human settlers had built in concrete and brick and painted their structures bright red, or blue, or purple, or even black as retaliation against the sameness of the color of the vegetation. They raked and they scraped in an unceasing war against the hordes of Daleko Bałtyckie plants, and where the battle lines wavered, they turned loose pigs and goats for whom the unending supply of plants was manna from heaven. Overall, the humans of the city and the highland villages held their own. It gave them one more reason to be contemptuous of those men and women who lived on the coast or in the lowlands, either inside the huge forests there or on the narrow open stretches where the plants were forced to yield by solid rock and pounding waves.

Sobieski had begun as a port above the falls on the broad Nowy Vistula, and its docks were still critical to the river traffic that connected many of the highland villages. The river was a useful route, as it was one place that did not need to be kept clear of the flexis. The city had grown inland from the original port area, so City Center Plaza was no longer near the actual center of Sobieski even though it remained the city's heart. Only a few blocks from the port area stood the prezydent's mansion and the offices of the Solar Council's legate.

In the center of the plaza stood the statue of Jan III Sobieski, armored and on horseback, wearing a plumed helmet and holding a mace in his right hand—just as the sculptor had imagined the King of Poland to look in 1683, when he drove the Turks from Vienna. The facts that Vienna was 186 light-years away and that no horses—or indeed, any animal humans could ride—existed on Daleko Bałtyckie did not bother anyone. The statue was where people met, where they sat on benches for an outdoor lunch, and where children played at being the old king and his soldiers. The efforts of the City Guards to keep moss from growing over old King Sobieski were also a continuing source of amusement.

· · ·

Saoirse tried to find a comfortable gait as she walked into Sobieski that evening, but she couldn't. It was as though a Fate conspiring to make her as uncomfortable as possible had decreed that the resourceful Cyber would learn that the ex-peacer known here as Colonel Szczechowicz would spend this very evening at a place called Nowy Zoni. Who had told her that life was what happened while you were making plans? Someone at a rehab, probably.

Scores of buzzing insectoid fliers the locals called tinkerbells filled the air and made a cloud around her head. They ranged from barely visible to four and a half inches long with four, six, or eight gossamer wings. The tinkerbells showed no interest in biting, or even alighting on her, but an open mouth or eye could easily collect one.

She wrapped her arms around her ribs, winced, and wished that she were in an Earth city, where a tap on her comm would summon a ride anytime she wanted. But, no, she had gone out into the Reach, where what passed for a city was small enough and transport limited enough that people walked, and where taking a vehicle from the motor pool with BRINGING PEACE TO THE REACH on its doors could frustrate her purpose.

It wasn't the long walk that bothered her. She had done plenty of that on Earth, when her account was empty or frozen and she'd had no choice. It was the jostling of her ribs while she walked and breathed. They had been recovering from her ill-advised demonstration with Mwesigye, but she'd taken a fall and reinjured them again at a training exercise that afternoon.

You shouldn't show off. That's what you always do, and you always get in trouble. Like that party at O'Brien's senior year, when you had to dance on the bar and you had to be the one up there when the police arrived and then you had to— Shut up, Saoirse!

She ordered herself to stop thinking about the ribs and her school misadventures, and followed that order as well as she had ever followed orders. Then she tried to focus on S. He had been on her mind since the day they last spoke on Titan Station, and she had worked out in great detail how she was going to manage the scene when she saw him again. Now that it was happening, though, her thoughts couldn't settle. She was nervous. Would he be happy to see her? Angry? What if he didn't remember her? That would be the worst. It would be so awkward to sit down and have him stare at her with a vacant *Who are you?* look. She would die. It would be easier if . . . *No, no, no, stop thinking like that.*

Her clothes didn't help. For all the thought she had put into seeing S again, she was wearing field boots with camo pants and the T-shirt from the physical training uniform. At least the shirt fit snugly, and the short sleeves would show off her snake, which she hoped he would like, but the damned shirt had 32ND BATTALION, PEACEMAKERS printed on it, and there wasn't a damned thing she could do about that. She couldn't beg clothes from the women in her platoon, and Cyber was too small.

Where in hell was this Nowy Zoni? Between dwelling on her ribs and her nerves and her clothes, she had walked all the way to the Sobieski statue. Teenagers were clustered around it, drinking and laughing at the foot-long fuzzy worm that had crawled up the horse's rump only to be attacked by a half dozen tinkerbells. The whole city seemed her age or younger. Frontier planets tended toward large families.

She turned her back on the carousing and looked around. There was a restaurant on the plaza, but it looked fancy, and a sign low down on the door said, NO SWAMPERS HERE. That didn't look promising. She studied her comm. Daleko Bałtyckie had no GPS, and the static map on the small screen of her comm was hard to follow. Six streets radiated out from City Center Plaza; all the names were tongue-twisters, and no street signs existed. She made her best guess and started out, ignoring the whisper of tinkerbell wings around her and the occasional touch as they flicked her head.

Perhaps it was luck, but ten minutes' walk down the street she had picked brought her in front of a low concrete building with NOWY ZONI spelled out over the door in bright LEDs. Outside the restaurant were five small tables, all unoccupied, each with a sign that her comm translated as, "No smoking here, inside only." She took a breath, pushed the door open, and stepped in. It was a bar. Of course.

"I can handle this," she said softly, and let the door close behind her.

To her left was the bar with its row of metal stools, all occupied, and then a couple of rows of men and women standing around, all holding drinks. Multiple simultaneous conversations merged into a dull cacophony. Even if she'd understood the language, she couldn't distinguish individual words from where she was standing. Woven wire mats covered the concrete floor beyond the bar. To the right, other guests sat at tables and had food with their drinks. A haze of smoke covered all of them. Two frantic human servers hustled from a door in the back to tables and then back again.

Saoirse scanned the room for S and did not see him. Had the information been wrong, or had he already left? Was she upset or relieved? Then she saw a man come through another door at the back of the room and glimpsed more tables beyond. She swallowed hard, crossed through the crowd to the back door, and walked in.

The back room was similar to the one in front, distinguished primarily by thicker smoke and no mats on the floor. It was also smaller and less noisy. A young couple near the entry held hands across their table. Saoirse did a slow sweep of the room. There, in the back corner, was a larger table with four men and an empty chair. One of the men was S. Her eyes locked on him and she felt her heart hammering in her chest.

S had a steaming cup of some liquid in front of him. The other three had large glass mugs of beer, mostly drained. While she watched, a server bustled by and replaced them with three full mugs. They leaned across the table, heads close, intent on their conversation, breaking only when one of the men paused to chug down half his fresh beer. S sipped from his cup. They gave no sign that they'd seen her.

What should she do? Wait for someone to see her standing there like she was waiting for a bus? Wave? She settled on her customary approach: fuck it all.

Saoirse walked over to the table, pulled out the empty chair, and sat down. "Thanks for saving me a seat."

The three men she didn't know recoiled as if a real rattlesnake had joined them, not the one on her arm.

Surprise flashed across S's face—surprise and then something else. But he shut it down so quickly Saoirse could not be sure what it was.

"A peacer?" sputtered one of the men. He had a short beard of curly brown hair and a high forehead. His face looked as hard as his hands that rested on the glass tabletop. Another man put his hand in the pocket of his heavily stained jacket.

That broke the brief stasis that had gripped S. "Peace, Jan," he said to the one with his hand in his pocket. "She is a friend, although she's not the fifth I had expected tonight."

"She is a peacer," said Jan.

"They are not our enemies," said S. "I used to be a peacer, if you remember."

"That may be true now," Jan said, "but if Strazdins can get himself elected Marshal of the Sejm, you know the peacers will side with him. Even if the Sejm dissolves again, which it probably will, the peacers are likely to side with Strazdins."

"I would not be too sure of that," S said. "I think brief introductions are in order. Irish, these are my associates: Jan and Filip from the southern coast, and Stanislaw from the north shore." He indicated a large man with sloping shoulders as Filip, and the one with the curly beard as Stanislaw. "This is my old friend, Irish Kenneally, although she wasn't a peacer when I knew her, and I certainly never expected to see her here."

"But here she is," Saoirse said. "And a peacer. Lieutenant Irish Kenneally." She found a bit of a thrill in using the nickname S had given her back on Titan Station, and an even bigger thrill from the expression on S's face. She was feeling a little giddy. He was happy to see her. She was sure of that.

"As may be," said Stanislaw, "but I would feel better if we continue our discussions at another time."

Jan and Filip nodded their agreement. As one, they drained their beers, pushed back their chairs, and took their leave.

Saoirse turned to watch them go, and it dawned on her what she had done. She had barged into whatever business S was conducting, had disrupted it, blown it up, ended it. He was going to be furious.

She wasn't sure she could turn back to face him, but somehow, she did. And saw a broad smile on his face, the warmest she had ever seen. She should say something, but her voice might squeak.

"Well, it is good to see you, Irish," said S. "I missed you, and I hadn't realized how much until I saw you sit down and break up my meeting." He paused to look at her, as if wondering whether she was real. "You seem to have ended it earlier than I had planned, but they'll get over it. Anyway, the fifth we needed never showed. Call it good timing."

He looked at the logo on her shirt. "This should be good. Tell me, how are you a peacer, and how are you an officer?"

"It's a bit of a story," she said. "The short version is that I had a chance to come here and I took it. I missed you, too, S."

"Don't call me S. Please. That was Titan Station. My friends, those few I have, call me Tommie."

"Tommie." Saoirse smiled. "You do know that I went to school in Dublin on Earth? Irish and Tommie don't go together."

His eyes widened. "What? That makes no sense at all."

Saoirse smiled again. Definitely, she was pleased with herself. "It makes all the sense in the world, but the world is Earth. Too long a story for now. If you want, we can be Irish and Tommie here."

He smiled back at her, his eyes so intense that she had to look away for an instant. Her gaze was captured by the remnants of foam in the empty beer mugs. She ought to push them away, but she didn't want to touch them. *That's okay*, she thought. *I'm handling this just fine.*

"What are you drinking?" She pointed at his cup.

"This?" Tommie laughed. "We call it coffee, but it isn't." He hesitated, so she gestured for him to continue. "Okay, a *short* story. The big trees here that grow in the lowlands don't have wood. They're just soft pulp on the inside. The only way they can grow as high as they do, and some of them are two hundred feet, is that they have hard bark on the outside. One type, we chop that bark up and brew it. It even has caffeine in it, so we call it coffee. Coffee from the coffee tree. It's brown and it keeps you awake, but it's bitter as hell."

"I'll have one."

He signaled a server, and before long there was a cup of the brown liquid in front of her. She took a sip and fought to swallow it rather than spit it back. A liquid extract of kale might have tasted similar. Actually, the kale might have been sweeter. "It's not that bitter," she said, the aftertaste making her gag. "I like it."

"You're a good liar," Tommie said.

She almost laughed. "Let's not go there!"

"Okay." He relaxed, cradling his cup with both hands. "So, are you going to tell me how a scoppy computer jockey and part-time Titan adventurer has morphed into a peacer officer?"

"I'll tell you. I'll tell you. Just . . . not now."

"But you did say it was so you could come here. Where I am."

She caught her breath. Held it. Knew she had to take a chance and say, "Yes."

Saoirse was prepared for him to laugh, to say she was crazy, to stand up and leave. He did none of those things. He sat silent for a minute, a wry smile on his lips and his eyes on the table.

"I would never have thought I was worth coming after," he said at last, and looked up at her. "I can't believe you really did. I was born here, I think I told you that. It was in a small coastal village on the northern coast; I'm what they call a swamper. Nothing special. I can't say I grew up well. I've told you a little about that. The peacers had their base here then—smaller, but it was here. That's where I ran away to when I was sixteen. I begged them to take me, and by some miracle, they did. Shipped me to training camp on Winston's World, and I made it through. All my schooling is through the peacers. All I've ever done is the peacers. Why am I worth your time, Irish?"

"You taught me how to fight," Saoirse said. "You cared."

"I do care." Tommie's eyes focused on hers, the heat in them surprising her. "I'll warn you, I'm not any good at this."

Somehow, she found herself laughing. "This is the third time you've given me that warning. You don't need to say it, because it's obvious. And I'm not any good at it either, which you should have figured out except you're no good at this. If you promise not to count my mistakes, I won't count yours."

He laughed also. "Agreed. Should we sign in blood?"

"Not necessary." She had that giddy feeling again—he wasn't mad at her, and he cared. Then she remembered her official reason for coming here: Venezelos. She had to come back with something he would want. "You said you came here to run a militia. To clean up a mess and stop the zombipterisin trade. How are you going to do that?"

"I don't know. I'm making it up as I go along." He put his hands to his head for a moment. "Daleko Bałtyckie is close to the point where the SC can certify it as an independent world and grant it membership in the Assembly of Worlds. Then, if the planet is at peace, the peacers will probably leave. Think about what all of that means. To be a member of the Assembly of Worlds, a world needs to meet three requirements: a sufficiently strong economy, a stable power source, and a stable planetary government. That nuclear plant out at Sobieski Point, where the Nowy Vistula goes over the falls, that generates enough power to make the hurdle. But it's the only real source of electricity on the planet, and it's controlled by the city, by Prezydent Strazdins. There's no oil, no coal, no natural gas, and not enough solar. There's no way to have enough electricity except that plant."

"They told me about no oil or gasoline at the base. I don't understand why."

"You know oil, gas, and coal are called fossil fuels?" Saoirse nodded. "Okay. Daleko Bałtyckie is about three hundred million years behind Earth in evolution. All these plants, especially the swamp forests in the lowlands around the planet, they will *become* fossil fuels in three hundred million years. Right now, though, there aren't any, because they haven't formed yet. So power comes from the nuke and that's it. Strazdins controls the spaceport because that's under the control of the city, and in order to keep their nuclear monopoly, they won't allow importation of solar panels or wind turbines. On top of that, Strazdins wants the zombipterisin trade. There is money from the schizophrenia drug, but not enough. It's zombie that puts the economy over the threshold for membership.

"The final point is the planetary government. On-screen, we have one. That's the Sejm, our version of a parliament. The head of state is the Marshal of the Sejm, elected by the Sejm. It's a system the first settlers designed from back in their history on Earth—but it doesn't work here. I doubt it worked there either. Fact is, the Sejm is paralyzed. It rarely meets and hasn't elected a Marshal to do anything since I was a child. Power vacuums aren't stable, and Strazdins is moving to fill it. He is aiming to be Marshal, legally or by other means."

He took a sip of the dark liquid. She was surprised he didn't wince. "That's why the militia is crucial," he continued. "And that's why I'm with them. The coastal and lowlands towns have always had their militias because the city and the highlands have always tried to dominate us, but now we need a single strong militia. We are going to stop the zombie trade, we are going to break this power monopoly, and we are going to stop Strazdins from taking over the government. We'll do it by force of arms, if we need to."

Saoirse looked at his blue eyes, suddenly intense again. She could see men following him into battle. Women too. "I'm surprised they let you have a militia at all."

He nodded. "I know. There are advantages to paralysis, I suppose. The Sejm can't act to outlaw us any more than it can do anything else. Our risk is that Strazdins can build up his City Guards to the point that they can crush us. He's working at it. You know, twenty-five years ago, the City Guards were little more than Sobieski's police. There were fifty-three of them then. Today they number fifteen hundred, and we believe Strazdins will increase them to two thousand this year. So we build the militia to counter them. The militia needs to become a real force, which is why I am here, and it needs to be good soon."

He sighed. "But you can't rush training. It's hard enough anyway. Scant money for equipment, barely enough to provide rifles for everyone. Forget body armor. The time it takes to train, that's time away from the work that needs to be done for the villages to survive."

"So, against fifteen hundred Guards, what do you have? Yourself and your three friends?" Saoirse forced a laugh. "Do you have superhero capes?"

"No. And it's not quite that one-sided." Tommie smiled and sipped his coffee. "I told you there used to be militia units in each village. In the smaller villages, particularly on the north coast, they could be tiny—six or eight people sometimes. We've merged them into three companies. Each of the men you saw tonight commands one of them. We're about four hundred and fifty strong now. I'm happy for the peacers to know this, if they don't already."

"Four hundred and fifty?" Saoirse let out a low whistle. "You're still outnumbered three to one."

"In a practical sense, more than that," Tommie said. "Villages need defenders, so I can't really bring all the militia together in one place. That's why the highland villages are so important. Most of them joined with the Guards two years ago when Strazdins became prezydent of Sobieski, but if we can raise some units in the highlands, it will both add to our strength and make the Guards worry about where they have to defend. That chair you took, that was supposed to be Ivars. He's a highlander, and I have been hoping he will bring support from his village and a few near his. Maybe there is a good reason he didn't come. I'll see."

She thought about the situation he described. Three to one, or worse, and a well-supplied City Guard versus an untrained militia? Trying to get highlanders to work with his swampers? "And you're doing this," she asked, "no matter what? Even at these odds? Even if it's hopeless? Even if your towns didn't seem to want you in the first place? By the way, you didn't tell me that bit when you said you were coming here."

Tommie leaned back and stretched, his smile fading. It was as if a light had gone out in his eyes. His voice hardened. "That stuff, well, it's all personal and from very long ago. Just some old business I had to work through. I have to do this. These are my people." He shook his head. "It's so odd to say that. We're all the same people here, all from the Baltic region on Earth. But we've become divided in eighty years. Almost different people now."

Saoirse felt heat rise in her cheeks. She'd made him uncomfortable, raising the question about his past. Something personal, something he didn't want to talk about. She had to step carefully or she could push him away. *Don't blow it*, she told herself. She should talk about something else, anything else. But she couldn't think of anything to say. She started to feel edgy, as though she were going to blow it and couldn't stop it. She looked away from him, and her eyes lit on the server walking past with a tray holding five large mugs of beer. Foam danced on the top of the beer, spilling over the top of one mug as he walked. A small river of white bubbles ran down the side.

A beer would be cool. And it would lighten the mood, erase the dark place the talk had gone to. Over beers, they could talk about other matters; they could have fun. She knew where her thoughts were going, knew what would happen, knew she had no power to stop it.

"Tommie."

Something in her tone made him look sharply at her. "What's wrong?"

"I need to get out of here."

He was out of his seat fast enough to knock his chair over backward. With one hand around the snake on her arm, he half guided, half pulled her to her feet. He did not let go until they were through the door and into the street. The humid evening had turned into a light drizzle that had chased away the tinkerbells.

"I'm sorry," she said.

"Don't be sorry. It happens. It's important to recognize it when it does." He scuffed at the pavement with his shoe, then pulled a cigarette from his jacket. "Tobacco grows real well here. You're not supposed to smoke outside, because of the fire risk, but I think you need this. It's treated with a flame retardant, so it won't burn down too fast. Won't give you cancer any quicker than smoking plain tobacco will."

"Thanks." She took the cigarette and sucked air through it, then looked quizzically at the tip when it didn't light.

Tommie held out a tube with a glowing end and touched it to the cigarette. "We don't have self-lighting ones here. Again, fire is too easy."

"Thanks again," Saoirse said, drawing in a lungful of smoke.

"What should we do?" Tommie asked. "We're getting wet standing here."

"I'm sure there's someplace we can go." Saoirse said.

Without saying anything else, she slipped her hand into his.

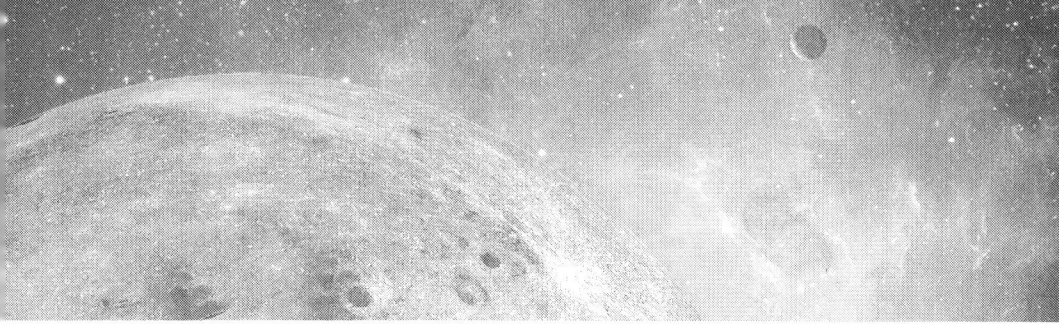

TWENTY-NINE

Lieutenant Colonel Venezelos wanted an eye kept on Colonel Szczechowicz of the militia, and he had selected Saoirse for that task. If he had any concern about how closely she was keeping her eyes on the colonel, he did not mention it. He was happy with her reports on the size and readiness of the militia, and with what Szczechowicz passed along about the doings of the City Guards and his views of the zombie trade. To Saoirse, it seemed that Tommie had no problems with her making those reports. Of course, she omitted mentioning any further nighttime conversation or activity. If she felt that Tommie kept some level of his feelings reserved, that a final rampart remained unscaled—well, she told herself, that was natural. It would take time. She could practice being patient; that would be a good thing.

After a few days, Colonel Szczechowicz sent a message to the battalion in the form of a young messenger to ask that Lieutenant Kenneally be assigned as a liaison to the militia and to request that she observe their training. Venezelos called Saoirse into his office to tell her this, and wondered aloud who was playing whom. Then he smiled and told her that it was fine as long as she kept her eyes on what the militia were doing and not only on their colonel. That comment was enough to make Saoirse wonder what information Cyber might be picking up and feeding to Venezelos, but she decided that she didn't care. It wasn't like she could ask, anyway.

She took a ground effect from the motor pool out to the area south of Sobieski where Tommie ran his training. It couldn't be called a base; no permanent facilities existed. It was a lightly rolling stretch of ground where the militia had hacked down the flexis and, between trampling what was left and having a group of goats, kept it open enough for tents and drilling. To Saoirse's eye, Tommie was as demanding as Adelayo but much more patient. He would first teach his officers and noncoms a technique, be it a leapfrog advance under fire or infiltrating an enemy line, then he would watch as they tried to teach their troops, and then he would correct both and start over again. Saoirse had thought she would have difficulty understanding what was being said, as trying to get translation through a comm with multiple voices in the open was difficult, but all the training was in English. Some villages spoke Polish, some Lithuanian, and others Latvian, but they all understood English.

Tommie managed to be everywhere in that camp, seemingly all at the same time. His attention was entirely on his troops. She told herself that she understood, even if she wished it did not have to take 100 percent of his focus.

She found the militia a curious mix of too old and too young, with too few in between. They were all men. Many were gray haired and gray bearded and told her, when she asked, that they were no longer needed in their village or at home. They were quick to learn, but often lacked the physical flexibility or strength to execute it properly. The rest were teenagers, given leave to join to get the wildness out of their systems somewhere other than in their villages. They had all the physical tools anyone would wish for but needed multiple repetitions to understand what was to be done. To say their attention wandered was being kind.

All the militia called Saoirse Irish, following Tommie's lead, or occasionally Lieutenant Irish, and that was as formal as it got. All of them dressed in ill-fitting dark-blue uniforms that made Saoirse think of SCOPP surplus that had been dropped off in a pile at a shelter. None of them had any badges of rank. Tommie dressed the same as them, with the one exception that he still wore his Peacers' Stars.

The informality extended to everything and everyone. Part of it was that the companies raised by Stanislaw, Jan, and Filip came when it suited them, and never a complete company. Saoirse never saw the highlander, Ivars, who hadn't shown up the night she met Tommie in Sobieski. Nor did she see a company that called themselves his. On her first day at the training ground, she heard Tommie mention something about Ivars to

Stanislaw, but she could not hear exactly what he said. Tommie never mentioned him again.

Stanislaw's company was the one most often at the training ground. Stanislaw had drawn his men from the northern coast, where there was only one large village and a string of small ones. Each of the small villages had sent a tiny contingent, and each of those had their own ideas about what a militia was, so melding them into one unit was taking a major effort and as much practice as Tommie and Stanislaw could get them to agree to. They were similar to the other two companies in having old men on one hand and teens on the other. The teens, as with most groups of teens, had an unofficial leader. His name was Andrzej Abramowicz, seventeen standard years old, whose dark beard and mustache had come in enough to cover his thin face. The other teens followed his lead in horseplay when they were not being directed or otherwise observed, and in showing off when they saw her nearby. She drew plenty of looks from them. When she wore her physical training T-shirt to show off the snake, they gave her even more attention, and their eyes were not on the snake. Maybe she should have thought of that in advance.

Firearms drill and riflery were a critical part of the militia training. They used the same MK32 rifle the peacers did, same as the one Saoirse had trained with on Earth, although the ones the militia had showed evidence of previous hard use that no amount of cleaning could erase. As with her peacer platoon, Saoirse was the ideal person to demonstrate, and she had, she believed, learned how to teach. She enjoyed leading off at target practice, leaving a perfect score for the militia to try to emulate. After she had demonstrated, she would have the militia sergeant select the order in which her trainees would fire. But one day when she had mostly teens, that did not work.

One of the younger teens jumped up before she'd even voiced her instruction to the sergeant, and dashed for the firing line, yelling, "I'll match that today! Watch this!" He tossed his rifle into the air with his left hand, intending to catch it with his right and fire immediately.

However, even with the incorporation of lightweight ceramic and plastic parts, a loaded MK32 weighed a good six and a half pounds. Snatching one cleanly out of the air one-handed was not easy. On top of that, the MK32 had a very light trigger pull. When the boy grabbed his rifle, his finger hit the trigger. With a bang, the rifle fired. The kick knocked it out of his hand, and it fell to the ground and discharged again.

To Saoirse, it all seemed to happen in slow motion. "Down!" she screamed. "Everybody down!" She dropped flat herself, ignored the flexi stems that poked at her face, and clutched the earth as if to pull herself tighter to it. She waited to hear screams. She heard nothing.

So she stood up and walked over to retrieve the errant rifle. The boy who had dropped it was still on his feet, standing almost on top of it, frozen in place and shaking.

"I—I'm sorry," he stammered out as she picked up the weapon.

"That was stupid. Showing off and stupid. You're lucky you didn't kill anyone."

"I know," he whispered.

She opened her mouth to keep going, but suddenly Tommie was next to them, as though he had materialized from the air.

"You are under arrest," he said to the boy. "Wait for me by the command tent." He pointed to a large tent across the open field. Meekly, the boy did as he was told. Then Tommie turned to Saoirse, his eyes cold. "We need to talk about this, but it will have to wait until I take care of other problems." His voice was harsh, his words clipped off. "The lack of discipline in this militia makes the worst SCOPP units look like elite troops. When we first formed these companies, merged the old ones together, Jan, Filip, and Stanislaw appointed the lieutenants, sergeants, and corporals. They took it as their right since they were leading the companies and they knew their men, or so they said.

"The problem was most of the ones they picked were friends or drinking buddies, and didn't know what they were doing. They weren't teachable, either. So, I removed them and had the companies elect men to those positions. It's better, but not by much. You should know how a unit needs to be run, and this is where I need you to set a good example. For now, make sure those shots did no damage and I'll figure out what to do next."

One of the shots had killed a goat, bullet straight through the eye. The other had hit the vehicle she'd driven to the training area. BRINGING PEACE TO THE REACH on the driver's door now had a bullet hole period after the word REACH. She stared at it, thinking that she would need to explain it to Captain Gelashvilli of Company C and then endure the silent look she would get from Mwesigye when she told him to have the motor pool fix it. No, she decided, she would not tell Mwesigye to get it fixed. She would cajole the motor pool into doing it herself.

She was still staring at the bullet hole when Andrzej walked up.

"Uh, Lieutenant?" He did not salute. Those were rare in the militia, even to Tommie.

"What is it, Andrzej?" She found herself adopting the same informality with the teens that the militia used with her.

"Look, Lieutenant Irish . . . I mean, Jerzy is a good guy, he really is. I mean, look, it's just, well, girls here don't . . . I mean pretty girls don't . . . shit." He looked down at the ground. His beard could not hide how red his face had become. "He didn't mean to do that. He just . . ."

"I know what he was doing," Saoirse said. "He was trying to show off in front of me."

Andrzej bobbed his head up and down in agreement. "Can you speak to the colonel? Jerzy doesn't want to be kicked out. This won't happen again. Nothing like this will happen again. I'll be responsible for Jerzy. I promise. I'll see to it."

"No." Saoirse waited until he looked up at her before she continued. "He has to be responsible for what he does. Not you. That's true for all of us—you, me, everyone here."

Great advice, Saoirse, she thought. *I should take it myself.*

Andrzej nodded again. "I understand. Will you speak to the colonel, though?"

"I will," Saoirse said. "I can't promise what the result will be, but I will talk to him."

Were you just the adult in that conversation? she wondered after he walked away. That was a weird sensation. She doubted it had ever happened before.

She had little time for further contemplation, however, because one of the older men took Andrzej's place almost immediately.

"Casimir Nowak." He put his hand out, then pulled it up into a vague salute, and finally offered it again. As Saoirse shook it, he said, "You handled that well." He paused and pulled a waxy package out of his jacket pocket. It contained two brownish bars with flecks of gray in them, each about four inches long. He extracted one, took a bite from one end, then offered the other to Saoirse. "An old man needs some nourishment with all the exertion," he said. "One is plenty, though. You take the other."

Saoirse accepted the bar and took a bite as well. It was creamy and sweet with little crunchy pieces mixed in. It reminded her of a bar of pressed sesame seeds someone had given her back in school. "What is it?" she asked.

"It's made from a paste of crushed tinkerbells with sugar added. High in digestible protein."

Saoirse stopped chewing with her mouth open, fought the impulse to spit it out, and managed to swallow the mouthful.

Nowak grinned. "It's good for you!" He finished his bar. Then he gave her a wink. "You know why the boys are doing that stuff, I assume."

"Yes. Believe me, I get it. They're men." She looked back at the bullet hole in the door of her vehicle. "I don't think it changes with age, either."

Nowak grinned. "I like to think we older folk hide it better."

"Not always so well." Saoirse turned back to him. Nowak's beard and hair were entirely gray; the skin on his forehead and where the beard did not cover his face was seamed and leathery. "How much older are you?" she asked. "You look too old to be playing at soldier."

"I came here with my family as a nine-year-old," he said, "and that was sixty standard years ago. And I am not playing at soldiers. None of us are. We came here to get away from soldiers and police and all the trouble that went with them. Daleko Bałtyckie was young then, and we were all poor. A bunch of poor Eastern Europeans who got a Class Two world on charity, nobody better than anyone else. And look at us today." He shook his head. "In only sixty years, we have the city and the highland folk who look down on those of us from the coast and the lowlands. Call us swampers. Say we are inferior because of genetic drift." He let out a harsh laugh. "It started with the nuke. Do you know how that happened?"

Saoirse shook her head. The way he said it made her curious, and she was there as an observer. If she wanted to take time and listen, she could.

"That nuke up there at the Point, for the cost of that plant, we could have had enough solar cells and generators to give us all the power we needed. Could have had hydroelectric, I suppose. But nothing for nothing. It all costs money and we had none. Raise a fortune for a nuclear plant to power a world—that you can do. Companies, rich people, get their names on reactor rooms, control rooms. Governments give tax breaks.

Great charities. Solar? What are you going to do: 'Send ten credits, it will buy a solar cell for Josef,' and you get a picture of a happy villager? Please. They built the nuke.

"So the prezydent has the nuke and controls the power, and the money flows to the city and the highlands. Now they are building an army. So it is time to become soldiers. What my parents swore would never happen again, and here we have it. I'm glad they are no longer here to see it. The young ones know nothing of this or of what it will bring. So tell the colonel to forgive the young boy. We need the young boys to be soldiers." He turned away and left her by the car.

Saoirse looked at the remainder of the tinkerbell bar in her hand. It wasn't bad, she decided, if she didn't think about where it came from. She was hungry. She finished the bar.

· · ·

It was the end of the training day before Tommie came to find Saoirse. To her surprise, she had no difficulty convincing him to retain Jerzy in the militia. He appeared to have decided that for himself before they spoke.

"We cannot afford to lose any of our men," he said, "and he is far from the worst fuckup we have. I will give him some punishment details that will help him remember not to make such mistakes again, and we will keep him on." He shook his head. "The storm is coming soon. The Sejm will need to meet, or try to, and that will bring it on."

Saoirse was even more surprised to discover that Tommie held her responsible for what had happened. She was the officer present; whatever the men did was ultimately her responsibility. She found that extremely unfair. Even if the officer present were responsible, she was an observer, not one of Tommie's militia. She pointed out all those particulars and found scant sympathy in his face or his words.

"This is not about fairness," Tommie said. "It is not about friendship. It is about discipline and responsibility. They go together, and in combat, they can be the difference between success and disaster. I don't know how you became an officer, but you are one. You need to take the responsibility that goes with it. Please think about this. I have some work to finish up."

Saoirse's drive back to the base was full of turmoil. She tried to think about what Tommie had said, but her emotions got in the way. He was angry at her. Somehow that stupid incident had become her fault, and that hurt. It felt like so many other things she had been blamed for in the past, and being blamed had always made her angry. She could feel the inner boil as she drove. People being angry at her made her angry at them. Tommie was going to have to get un-angry and apologize to her. First. As she stewed about it, she wondered if the militia was simply Tommie's replacement for the peacers. Did nothing else matter to him? Where did Saoirse Kenneally fit in his world? Did she fit anywhere? She was not going to ask those questions.

THIRTY

Saoirse found a reception committee waiting for her when she returned to the base. Captain Gelashvilli, Captain Bronson, and Cyber Alves were all arrayed outside the motor pool where she parked the car. Whatever they had planned to say was put on hold as they focused on the bullet hole in the driver's door.

"I thought the word was that you got on well with the local militia," Bronson said.

Still angry, Saoirse stepped out and slammed the door. "I do."

"Hah." Bronson pointed at the bullet hole. "If that's getting along well, I can only imagine what taking you out on a date is like."

She managed to strangle the comment she wanted to make while it was still in her throat. "You'd find it a lot like playing the game of golf on Earth," she said. "You'd lose your balls."

She found a second to be proud of herself for not having exploded. That would have been typical Saoirse, but somehow, she had avoided it. Then she looked at their faces. Bronson, it was clear, did not like her at all; Alves liked her a lot. Gelashvilli was laughing.

"So, Captain Bronson," Gelashvilli said in his thick Georgian accent, "does this apparent lack of affection change your plans? Should we use someone else?"

"No," Bronson said. "Not unless their next bullet is in her."

Saoirse put Captain Hubert Bronson on the long list of people who would like to see that happen. "Use me for what, sir?"

"Come with us. We need to speak with the lieutenant colonel." Bronson stalked off toward the battalion office building.

A few minutes later, they were gathered around the conference room table with Venezelos. "So far," Bronson began, "we have been able to develop an association between Lieutenant Kenneally and Colonel Szczechowicz of the local village militia, and we have been able to insert her into their training camp as an observer."

Again, Saoirse had to fight with herself, but this time it was to smother her laugh. When Alves caught her eye from across the table and winked, it became that much harder.

"I'm familiar with what has been done," Venezelos said. "Surely the purpose of this evening's meeting is not to expound on that and your role in it?"

"No, not at all." Bronson missed the sarcasm in Venezelos' voice. "I want to bring up another opportunity." He paused to let his words sink in and to make certain everyone's attention was centered on him. "I have picked up, through my contacts at the legate's office, that some of the swamper delegates to the Sejm—I mean, delegates from the coastal and lowland villages—that some of them would like an unofficial conversation with us. I would like to make use of Lieutenant Kenneally for this. I'd like to have her go in civilian clothes, unofficially, and see what they want."

"Why Lieutenant Kenneally?" Venezelos asked sharply. "She is not trained in intelligence work, and she is unfamiliar with local politics. She is involved now only because we have been able to leverage her prior acquaintance with Szczechowicz. You are far more suited to this role."

"Ah no, sir, I am sorry to differ," Bronson said. "I am too well known in Sobieski because of my work at the legate's office."

Venezelos was not ready to accept Bronson's excuse. "Lieutenant Kenneally is no secret either," he said. "I'm sure there are plenty of locals who know she's our observer at the militia training. And since she is the only female officer in this battalion, it would be hard to confuse her with anyone else. At the same time, no interstellar is in orbit, so there are no outsiders on this world now. She can't pretend to be someone else."

"All that's true," Bronson said. "But I'm thinking of more than a casual conversation. There is another opportunity here, perhaps the more important one. As you know, we have had trouble getting access to the delegates' offices at the Sejm, and with a critical session coming up, we should know what they are doing. The swamper delegates, in particular. We can use this conversation as a chance to plant some ears there. If there are difficulties in doing this, however, it would be problematic for us and the legate if I were involved. At the same time, the fact that city officials don't take women seriously could work in our favor if anything goes wrong."

Saoirse translated Bronson's wordy explanation: if the person planting the bug was caught, there was a good probability they would be shot, and he didn't want it to be him. Venezelos looked over at Alves, and the flash of fright on Alves' face confirmed Saoirse's assessment.

So, the bug had to be planted by someone the city officials didn't know, preferably a woman, someone they were not likely to pay close attention to. Bronson wanted her to do it, while Venezelos was thinking about using Alves. Saoirse had come to like Cyber Alves. She knew what she had to do.

"I'm the one to do it, sir," she said. "Nobody else."

Venezelos gave her a hard look, then turned to Gelashvilli. "Any objections, Captain?"

"No, sir."

"How do I do this?" asked Saoirse.

Alves opened a small case and took out what looked like a piece of translucent tape. "I'll give you three of these," she said. "Microfiber transmitter is embedded in the tape. Part of the tape is a lithium polymer battery that powers it. It has enough juice that I can pick it up from anywhere in Sobieski. Peel off the backing, and it sticks just like adhesive tape. Stick it anywhere: under a table, under a chair, wherever you find a convenient spot they won't notice."

"And try not to get caught," Venezelos added. "Now, can you give me your assessment of the militia's current readiness before we break for dinner?"

* * *

Half an hour later, Saoirse was walking back to her quarters, not feeling hungry at all. She spotted one of the motor pool corporals staring at the bullet hole in her car. His hands were on his hips. "Lieutenant," he called out when he caught sight of her. "What am I supposed to do about this?"

"Fix it," she snapped.

· · ·

The building that housed the Sejm was a three-story pile of irregular brick hard by the riverfront and adjoining the Old Port where Pilsudski Road, the route down to the Point, initiated. Most of the other buildings around it and in the port itself were of the same reddish-brown brick that the settlers had used before the concrete plant was built. This cluster of buildings had survived the multiple fires that nearly wiped out Sobieski in those early days. From the street in front of the Sejm, the broad expanse of the Nowy Vistula was visible beyond the fake brick battlements of the top story, and the sound of the falls was audible despite the many miles to the Point.

Saoirse cared little about the architecture or the setting beyond the fact that they told her she was in the right place. She tugged at the waistband of the ankle-length skirt she had been given. She hadn't worn a skirt since she was eleven, and besides being ugly, this one didn't fit. The blouse that went with it wasn't much better: prints of random yellow-green leaves on an itchy white fabric. It had been sewn for a woman much larger in the bust. Charity clothing at the shelters had been of better quality. Plus, it was a hot afternoon. But she'd been ordered to wear it. Neither Bronson nor Venezelos wanted to advertise that the peacers were coming to speak with the swamper delegates. The idea was that this way she would at least look like a young woman of Sobieski. To enhance the disguise, she carried a woven bag with two loaves of bread sticking out the top.

"As long as you keep your mouth shut until you're in the meeting, this should be fine," Bronson had said.

Of course, if you could keep your mouth shut, you wouldn't be wearing this damn costume in the first place, and you wouldn't have gotten the shit kicked out of you in that Streeterville bar, and you wouldn't— Shut up, Saoirse!

Naturally, Bronson had stepped in to make a few "adjustments" to the disguise right before she was ready to go, and she had known exactly where he was going to put his hands. There hadn't been a goddamn thing she could do about it. Well, not quite. When his hands went to her waist, she'd pressed close against him, letting him feel the outline of the pistol under her loose clothing, and whispered, "Accidental discharge." He'd stepped back like a scalded rat. Still, she wanted to take a shower. Or do something more violent. At least the omnipresent cloud of tinkerbells thinned out this close to the river.

She walked up the steps and through the front door of the Sejm building. A pair of City Guards were stationed at the doorway and two more in the hallway beyond, but they paid no attention to her. Indeed, a conservatively dressed woman was nothing more than background scenery in Sobieski. She took some satisfaction at the sheen of sweat on their faces. Those uniforms had to be even less comfortable than her outfit in the heat of Daleko Bałtyckie's afternoon.

According to the plans Bronson had shown her, the ground floor consisted of public areas, rooms where people could wait to talk to delegates or to speak at a session of the Sejm. Those rooms were empty and stifling. The Sejm was not in session. She'd gathered it was almost never in session, so this came as no surprise. The delegates' offices were on the second floor: those from the coastal and lowland villages to the right of the main staircase, the city and highland villages to the left. She climbed the stairs and found two pairs of City Guards stationed at the second-floor hallway. Like the ones below, they ignored her. Silently, she wished them a pleasant heat stroke and took the right-hand hallway.

At the end of the hall, she found a door labeled COASTAL AND LOWLAND VILLAGES. She tried the handle: locked. Through glass panes she could see a dark hallway. No evidence of occupancy. She banged on the door, which achieved nothing except that when she glanced over her shoulder, the City Guards at the stairwell were looking her way. She thought about trying to pick the lock—it was another of the stupid mechanical ones they used on Daleko Bałtyckie—but she had no tools for that. She might be able to kick it open, but that would definitely attract attention. Although come to think of it, so would vanishing from a hallway with a locked door at the end of it.

Anyway, it was moot. The fact was that no one was here to meet with her, and there was no good place even to plant one of Cyber's magic transmitters.

Saoirse cursed under her breath and retraced her steps to the main staircase, ignoring the Guards. To the right she could hear voices from the city and highland offices, but she had no intention of going there. She could hardly ask the Guards. So she passed them as though she knew where she was going and took the stairs up to the Sejm chamber. That seemed a fruitless venture, but she knew Venezelos and Bronson would criticize her if she didn't check. The Guards did nothing but sweat as she walked up the stairs.

The Sejm chamber was even hotter than the lower floors. It was one large room with three huge flags hung on the wall across from the entrance. In the middle was a simple flag with two horizontal stripes, red on the bottom and white on top. The one to the right had three stripes, yellow, green, and red from top to bottom; and the one on the left had two deep red stripes top and bottom, with a thin white one in the middle. Saoirse supposed they meant something. She hadn't seen flags anywhere else on Daleko Bałtyckie. The rest of the chamber was simple: a podium in front of the flags with a lectern on it facing semicircular rows of chairs, with four rows of dusty benches near the back wall.

As she examined the empty room, a rivulet of sweat rolled down her face. This place needed air-conditioning. Or ventilation. Or a fan. This had been a wild-goose chase. Nothing more than an excuse for that asshole Bronson to adjust the fit on her disguise. She turned and walked out of the Sejm chamber, passed the silent Guards, and took the stairs down to the street and outside.

The wasted trip had not improved her temper. She would drive back to the base, tell Bronson he was hearing voices and needed meds, and then she would forget the whole business.

Then she felt eyes on her. She'd spent enough time on the streets to know when she was being watched. She pretended to reach into her bag while she scanned the block. There it was—a woman staring at her from across the street, standing in the doorway of a brick row house under a sign that said MARIA'S BREAD AND COFFEEHOUSE. The woman was perhaps twice Saoirse's age and dressed far more practically than she was, with a red shirt over pants that looked like denim. She held a half-smoked cigarette near her mouth. When she saw Saoirse look at her, the hand with the cigarette made a small *come here* gesture.

THIRTY-ONE

Saoirse returned the woman's stare. *What the fuck?* she thought. Then she shrugged and crossed the street.

The woman stepped into the doorway to give Saoirse room to enter the vestibule. Up close, her face was that of a woman at least in her forties with the marks of many years in the sun, and there were streaks of gray in her hair. The cigarette was extinguished. Hard brown eyes flicked up and down, examining Saoirse. The woman said something in a language Saoirse did not recognize. When Saoirse made no response, she switched to accented English.

"You are from the peacers." It was a statement, not a question.

Saoirse nodded.

"You might as well have worn your uniform. You look ridiculous dressed like a city girl. Those Guards will have watched you from the moment you approached the Sejm building. No city girl would be going in there today. A swamper girl would wear pants and boots. Because we work. And she still wouldn't have gone in there."

Saoirse hoped the flush in her cheeks wasn't visible in the dimness of the vestibule, with the glare of the sun behind her. Bronson was a fuckup who needed his ass kicked. She halted that train of thought. Now was not the time to get angry.

"I'm sorry if this wasn't what you expected," Saoirse said. "I just followed my instructions. Who are you?"

The woman shrugged. "Alicja Symanski." She eyed her cigarette and relit it. "Fool or not, we need to talk. Come in and sit down."

Hey, I wasn't the fool, Saoirse wanted to say, but Symanski had already turned to walk inside. Saoirse followed her.

Between dim lighting and small windows that needed cleaning, the interior of Maria's Bread and Coffeehouse was in shadow. A dense haze of cigarette smoke did not help. A coffee bar tended by an obese man in a stained white smock occupied the wall to the left of the entrance, and shelves displaying racks of bread and pastry lined the back wall. The floor was uneven brick haphazardly covered with wire mesh mats that scraped against the brick as she crossed them. Symanski led the way to the right, where Saoirse could see a large seating area to the rear. Most of the small tables there were occupied by people smoking, intent on their own conversations. Symanski walked over to a tiny round metal table occupied by a man with a thick beard. Half a loaf of dark bread sat on a cutting board, knife and crumbs indicating that it had recently been a whole loaf.

"This is Piotr Kaminski," Symanski said as the man stood up. She indicated an empty chair, and the three of them sat down. "We are delegates from Boruta and Rokita, on the south coast."

"Saoirse Kenneally," said Saoirse, "and, yes, I'm from the peacers. What did you need to talk to us about, and why are we in a coffeehouse that looks ready to fall down? I understood I was to meet you at the Sejm."

"If that came from the person who told you how to dress, his best service in the future may be as food for the pigs," Kaminski said. "We do not use the offices or rooms in the Sejm building, because it is too likely the prezydent has them bugged. On the other hand, if the man wishes to bug every noisy coffee shop along Pilsudski Road, let him. He will never hear anything he can make sense of. Would you like something to drink?"

"Coffee only," Saoirse said. She thought the look on Alicja's face meant approval. Score one point. "I'll take a cig with that." Bronson was such an idiot, she thought. Why send her to bug offices they don't use, because they're sure they're bugged? She imagined him as pig's food, and smiled.

Symanski pulled a cigarette from a pocket and handed it to Saoirse, then lit it for her. Saoirse let the smoke quiet her jangling nerves while the coffee was brought. She took a swallow and forced a look of satisfaction. At least, the Daleko Bałtyckie coffee was loaded with caffeine.

"Okay," Saoirse said, hoping her nerves were under control, "what is the issue, and why not come to the base? Why the mystery?"

Symanski leaned back and blew smoke at the ceiling. "It is about the upcoming session of the Sejm. The attempt to have a session of the Sejm. About what may happen and about what the peacers can do, which is why we do not wish to be so obvious in our request. The Sejm is like a parliament for our planet," she explained. "The first task of a session is to choose a Marshal of the Sejm. That individual then acts as the executive—carries out the decrees of the Sejm, if you will."

"And the word is that Daleko Bałtyckie will ask the legate to certify it as an independent world and be admitted to the Assembly," Saoirse said. "I assume the Marshal is the one who makes the application. None of this is exactly secret."

"True, and Prezydent Strazdins of Sobieski wishes to be Marshal," Symanski said. "That is also no secret. But we believe that Strazdins has a plan to change the way the Sejm works. Now the Marshal has his office only for the session of the Sejm. When the session ends, so does his term. The next session picks a new one. Strazdins would change this so that the Marshal remains in power until another session of the Sejm picks a different one. Also, he's planning to have it so he can rule without the Sejm being in session."

"I thought the majority of the population on Daleko Bałtyckie is in the coastal and lowland villages," Saoirse said. "You should have the votes in the Sejm to block it. If you don't, I'm not sure what you expect the peacers to do."

"That's not how the Sejm works," Symanski said.

"Or doesn't work, which would be more accurate," Kaminski added.

Saoirse looked from one to the other and blew out another cloud of smoke to join the general haze. "You'd better explain," she said.

Symanski sucked her cigarette down to her fingers and crushed it out. "It is our history," she said at last. "When we settled on Daleko Bałtyckie, we were all dirt-poor refugees. Whether we went to the swamp or the highlands, we had nothing. We were also deeply suspicious about governments—how they acted, what they would do. So we took a page from our history. We said we were all equal, every village or town as good as any other, and decided that no majority would ever be able to tyrannize a minority. We built the Sejm to require consensus. The Marshal is to carry out the consensus decisions of the Sejm, and there is no ruler beyond that."

"Wait a minute," Saoirse said. "Consensus? You mean you all have to agree?"

"Yes." Symanski grimaced. "It worked for a time and then, of course, it didn't."

"*Everything* has to be unanimous?" Saoirse stared at her, the cigarette forgotten until it burned her fingers. "No wonder nothing gets done."

"It's worse than that," Symanski said. "We took the idea from ancient Poland, six hundred years ago. The way it works is any delegate at any time can stand up, be recognized and say *Nie pozwalam*, which means, 'I do not allow,' in English. That ends it. Not only whatever is under discussion, it also ends the Sejm session, dissolves the Sejm, and overturns anything that the Sejm has already done in the session. It was called *liberum veto* in old Poland, and was the ruination of the kingdom. But we ignored the lessons of our own history and talked ourselves into believing we could make it work by virtue of our equality. It is equality gone berserk."

"What it is," said Kaminski, "is a nuclear weapon of parliamentary procedure."

"Give a man a weapon, and you can be sure he will use it," Symanski said.

"Women are just as bad," retorted Kaminski.

"I'm sorry," Saoirse interrupted. "This is insane."

Symanski's smile was wan. "From today's vantage point, I'm sure it is; and I'm sure they said the same thing when the Kingdom of Poland fell apart. Early on here, it worked, though. When the money was raised to build the nuclear plant, we all agreed to restrictions on solar panels and wind so that outsiders would put up the money and build the plant."

"Yes," Kaminski said, "but that is also why, decades since, we cannot remove the restrictions on importing solar or wind. The truth is that it has been nearly ten years since there has even been a full Sejm session. Nowadays, the session starts, someone stands up and says, 'I do not allow,' and it's over. Everyone goes home."

Saoirse could hardly believe what she was hearing. Was their version of the history from Earth correct? She didn't know. Did it even matter? "I can see why Strazdins wants to change the system. You don't have any government at all."

"We would not argue that the system needs to change. We can all see that," Symanski said. "But Strazdins would make himself a dictator. We know where that would lead, and we cannot have that."

"Well, I don't see you have much to worry about on that front," Saoirse said. "All you have to do is have somebody stand up and do your 'I do not allow' thing, and that's the end."

"It's not that simple. If it were, we wouldn't need to talk," Kaminski said. "What has changed is the City Guards and the prezydent. We think they will pack the Sejm chamber with Guards. If you stand up," he pointed his hand at Saoirse like a make-believe pistol and pulled the trigger, "bang. Dead delegates cannot object and they cannot vote. If that fails, he may stage a coup and bet that the legate will certify anyway."

Saoirse looked from one to the other. "I thought that was why you were building up your militia. To prevent anything like that. Bring in your militia."

"And have a battle in the Sejm chamber?" asked Kaminski. "Absurd."

Symanski was shaking her head. "The militia is useless," she said. "I know you have seen them. Children and doddering old men. They cannot stand up to the prezydent's Guards. And that man, Szczechowicz, who commands them? I would not trust him with my life. Or my daughter's."

Saoirse gave Symanski a sharp look. No softness in that face. Saoirse would have trouble arguing that the militia was a battle-ready force, but that comment about Tommie? She might not be feeling too kindly to Tommie at the moment, but it made no sense. "I thought you all agreed on him to command the militia," she said. "Why do that if you don't trust him?"

"There was no other choice," Symanski said, bitterness obvious in her voice. "Anyway, the militia is useless, so what did it really matter? We needed to preserve unanimity among our villages."

"But why? Why don't you trust him?"

Symanski looked at Kaminski, who shook his head. "That is not for discussion," she said. "Not with outsiders. I will say only that men do not change; they do not improve with time."

Tommie had said the argument was personal and over matters that went back to when he had grown up on Daleko Bałtyckie. Saoirse decided there was no point in asking further. "What is it that you want from the peacers?" she asked.

"Disarm the Guards," Symanski said. "While it is still possible. If you will not do that, have your troops occupy the Sejm building and key points in Sobieski and the station at the nuke when they call for the Sejm session. That is how to stop this coup and avoid bloodshed. Tell that to your lieutenant colonel, and tell him the reasons why."

With that, both Symanski and Kaminski stood up. The discussion was obviously over. Saoirse got up as well. She thanked them for the coffee and the cigarette and felt them watch her as she walked to the door.

After the dim light of Maria's Bread and Coffeehouse, the glare of Daleko Bałtyckie's afternoon was blinding. Saoirse stopped at the doorway, squinting, and waited for her eyes to adjust. Her nerves were throbbing from her fingertips to her head, where a squeezing sensation around her temples was building. She wanted another cigarette, but even if she had one, smoking it outdoors would draw immediate unwanted attention. As she stood there, she noticed two burly and bearded men in front of the Sejm building. They wore typical clothes for men in Sobieski: dark pants over imitation leather shoes and lightweight pullover shirts. Those weren't workmen's clothes, and those men weren't going about any business. Or rather, their business was watching for Saoirse. She was sure of it. Her pulse pounded more loudly in her head.

She turned and walked up the street to where she had left the car. Though from the motor pool, it was a plain old car, indistinguishable from half the cars in Sobieski. Bronson had assured her that no one would notice it—the same way he had assured her that her clothes would let her blend in. *Stop that*, she commanded herself. She wanted to run, but she was afraid she would trip over the damned skirt. She settled for a fast walk. The men were walking, too, angling toward her car.

The men reached the car before she could pull the door open. They positioned themselves on either side of her, one blocking the door. She didn't see any weapons. What would happen if she tried to draw her pistol? She decided not to. Not yet.

"One of the delegates from Sobieski would like to speak with you," said the man to her left, in English.

"Care to tell me why I would want to do that?"

The other man said, "That's for him to say. Nothing to be afraid of, little girl." He took her upper arm in his hand.

"Fuck you!" Saoirse kicked him in the shin with the edge of her right shoe. Then she scraped the shoe hard down the length of his shin, its path ending with an audible crack as it drove into the top of his arch. As he let out a howl, she popped her arm out of his grasp and slammed her open palm into his jaw. Lower teeth smashed into upper teeth. She grabbed a fistful of beard and twisted her entire body around to drive his face into her car window, cracking it. The man dropped to the ground, leaving a smear of blood next to the crack in the window.

Saoirse had her hand in her pocket, on the grip of her pistol. She faced the other man.

"*Jezus Chrystus*," the man said. He hadn't moved. As big as he was, she saw no resolve in his face. His weight shifted back and forth; his stance was uncertain. He was afraid of her.

Her head was pounding. "I can just as easily make it two bodies in the street and drive over both of you on my way out. What is going on here?"

"I told you. The senior delegate from Sobieski would like a few words with you. That's all. You didn't have to hurt Jonas."

"Where I come from, two men go up to a woman and one of them grabs the woman, what's coming next isn't a few words."

The man shook his head. "Will you come and talk? It's important."

Saoirse did not want to go. It would be stupid. Right now, she had a gun and the upper hand. She could just get in the car and leave. If she went with him, she could think of all sorts of ways it could end badly. Sure, she had Cyber's little transmitters, but, for the moment, they could only let the base hear how badly it ended. Then again, if she left, Bronson might send Cyber back to the Sejm building to do whatever was involved. Cyber, who was in the Reach because that was the way for her to take care of her family. Saoirse liked Cyber, and anyway, who would care if something happened to Saoirse?

She gestured for the man to go ahead, then followed him back to the Sejm building one step behind. Every nerve quivered, and her eyes darted from one side to the other, looking for attackers to emerge from hiding places that did not exist. At the entrance to the Sejm building, the man stopped for a moment and spoke to one of the Guards. Saoirse tensed, unable to understand them, but the Guard barely glanced at her. Instead, he ran to where she had left the man on the ground.

The other man led her into the brick oven of the Sejm building. The additional time in the afternoon heat had done nothing to improve its climate. Saoirse felt sweat bead on her forehead from the moment she started up the main staircase.

On the second floor they turned left, to the opposite hallway from the one she'd tried earlier. As before, the Guards paid no attention. The hallway ended in a door that looked identical to the other one except its sign read CITY AND HIGHLANDS. Like the other door, it had no faceplate or thumb pad, only a knob. The man leading her turned the knob and, after a click, pushed the door open. Cold air hit her as she stepped inside. These offices had air-conditioning! Whatever happened, at least she would be comfortable. The man led her to the office at the corner of the building where a sign by its door read, CITY OF SOBIESKI, SENIOR DELEGATE. He knocked on the door and, at a voice from inside, opened it and ushered her in.

It was a spacious office with an ornate metal desk in front of corner windows. Two chairs stood in front of the desk, and between those and the door was a low coffee table and two cushioned armchairs. A man stood up from one of the armchairs. He was tall, with a short brown beard and curly brown hair over a long face. The fabric of his clothes was tightly woven. His shoes could have been polished that morning. *Wealthy man*, Saoirse thought.

"You are correct," said the man who had come with her. "She is a peacer. Jonas will need a doctor."

"Always violence where there are peacers," said the man by the armchair. "Rather ironic, given what you are called," he said to Saoirse. "My name is Henriks Ligas. Please have a seat." He indicated the vacant armchair. "Can I get you something?"

"Coffee and a cigarette," Saoirse said. She doubted the caffeine and the nicotine were going to do her nerves and her headache any good, but she needed to occupy her herself with something. She told herself she would be damned and in hell before she'd have her leg bouncing up and down in this office.

"Nojus, if you would," Ligas said to the other man. "Then you may leave us. I will be quite safe."

Saoirse lit the cigarette when it was brought, then took a drink from her cup. She had almost become accustomed to the bitterness of what people on Daleko Bałtyckie called coffee.

"You drink our coffee?" Ligas asked. His eyebrows went up.

"I like it."

"Amazing. Although I must tell you that you look ridiculous in that outfit. Any self-respecting city woman—and those clothes would be worn in a respectable household—would have them fitted better. It's obvious you are not one of us."

Saoirse sucked smoke into her lungs and fought to control herself. "You did not ask me to come up here so that you could comment on my outfit and tell me that I don't fit in. Want to tell me what this is really about?"

"You were meeting with some of the swamper delegates." It was a statement, not a question.

Saoirse blew smoke and waited.

"I do not need you to agree," Ligas said. "You were seen going into Maria's with Alicja Symanski, and in any case, there is no other reason you would be here dressed like . . . that." He waved one hand at her. "That is why I had Jonas and Nojus invite you up here. I will not ask what the swampers said. You will not tell me the truth, and anything they told you will be a lie anyway. What I am going to tell you is what they really intend. They are going to disrupt the Sejm, end the session before it can even begin. I can tell you how they can do that."

"You don't need to," Saoirse said. "I know how the Sejm works. Or doesn't work."

"Then you must understand," Ligas said, his voice urgent, "we must have a successful Sejm. We must get things done."

"As I understand it," Saoirse said, "what you want is to make Strazdins Marshal of the Sejm and change the law so he can rule without the Sejm."

"We want Strazdins to be Marshal, yes," Ligas said. "And why is that wrong? He is prezydent of the only city on the planet, with the largest administrative responsibility on the planet. We must have a functioning government to gain admission to the Assembly as an independent world, with all the benefits that will bring. Why is this a bad thing?"

When she didn't respond, he added, "The rest, though, that is someone's confabulation." He paused. "What they did not tell you, I am sure, is that we want laws that will put a stop to the zombipterisin trade, stop it now and forever. That trade comes out of the swamps, out of their territory, and they do not stop it; they encourage it. We need authority from the Sejm to place units of the City Guard in key locations to stop this trade. They do not want that discussion. But they do not dare oppose such laws openly. Instead, they will stop the session before it starts. One of them will be up before everyone is even seated. *Nie pozwalam*, and it is over."

Zombipterisin. The word rang in Saoirse's mind. Would Strazdins stop it? It had not come up in her conversation with Alicja and Piotr. Who was telling the truth? Was anyone telling the truth?

"And what do the peacers have to do with your local legislative process?" Saoirse asked. "We are not going to run your government for you."

"We would not think of asking you that," Ligas said. "What we need from the peacers is simple. Disarm that militia the swampers have been building up. Without that armed force, they will understand that they need to work with us politically, not try to threaten us with force. We can reach consensus in the Sejm if you will disarm that militia."

The cigarette had burned down to Saoirse's fingers. Hastily, she stubbed it out, blew on her fingers, then licked them. As she did, an idea popped into her head. One that might answer her questions. She tucked her fingers into the waistband of her skirt as if to ease the burn, felt for the thin pocket that held Cyber's little transmitter strips, and pulled one out. She was able to strip the adhesive backing with the fingers of one hand without looking down. While she leaned forward to take another cigarette from the pack on the table with the opposite hand, she stuck the tape on the underside of Ligas' coffee table. There would be a bug in the Sejm offices, just not where Bronson thought it would be. She lit her new cigarette, leaned back in the armchair, and blew smoke at the ceiling.

"Why don't you tell me a little more about how this will work if we do, in fact, disarm this militia," Saoirse said. "I want to understand exactly what I should be saying to Lieutenant Colonel Venezelos."

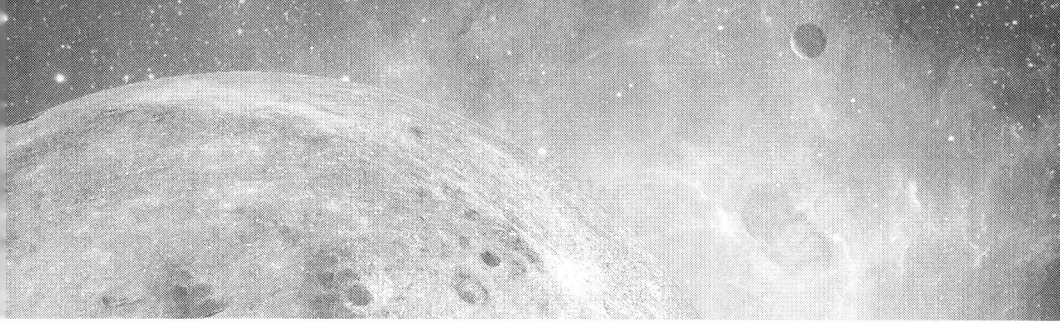

THIRTY-TWO

"Kenneally, the lieutenant colonel wants to see you. Again." Captain Gelashvilli's harsh accent cut through the fog in Saoirse's brain as she stared at her computer screen. What did Venezelos want this time? She seemed to be in his office every day, briefing him on one thing or another. No clue from Gelashvilli.

She stood, saluted, said, "Yes, sir," and left the office.

She was becoming sensitive to the idea that the peacers were perceiving her as Venezelos' pet, or maybe his spy. On Titan Station, she hadn't cared if people thought of her as Mom's pet. The status and the perks had been worth it. But here . . . She was the only female officer, one of the few women in the entire battalion. Her imagination supplied a lot of meaning for some of the looks she was attracting.

No help for it, though. If Venezelos wanted to see her, she would go. She was *not* going to have a conversation with herself about the thoughts that played through her mind. In any case, whatever it was would be better than sitting at that damn computer, trying to decipher why the number of hundred-round magazines for the MK32s that had been off-loaded at the port did not match the number they had requisitioned, and why the supply sergeant had responded to this discrepancy by complaining to her about the number of rounds expended in target practice, and why any of it should matter for a battalion that never left the base except for leave in Sobieski.

Her mind was still on the matter of the magazines when she reached the door to Venezelos' office. She was in the office and had saluted before she realized that Venezelos was not alone. Another man, this one wearing the dark gray of the Guards, had been sitting in a chair by Venezelos' desk. He stood when she walked in. She glanced at him and did a double take. He was gorgeous: tall and slim, with dark-brown hair with a slight wave to it, eyes to match, and both a contrast to the smooth, pale complexion of his clean-shaven face. She could have sworn that his eyes twinkled when he looked at her. Why didn't any of the peacers look like that?

"Kenneally, this is Captain Lukas Petrauskas of the Guards. Captain, this is Lieutenant Kenneally." Having finished his introductions, Venezelos leaned back in his chair and steepled his fingers.

"Hello, Captain," Saoirse managed to say. She didn't know if she was supposed to salute him and she didn't think her arm would move anyway. Petrauskas smiled in return.

"That's plenty of introduction," Venezelos said. "Kenneally, the Guards have heard about you from a few of their sources. They are aware that you are our observer at the militia training site. They would like to have you observe theirs and, I assume, report to me how fabulous they are in comparison." Petrauskas smiled at her again. "As it happens," Venezelos continued, "I would find the comparison useful. The captain will drive you out there, which will make the motor pool happy after what happened to the last two cars you took."

When she didn't respond immediately, he added, "So, how would you like to spend the rest of the day with Captain Petrauskas?"

The question was, obviously, rhetorical, but it wouldn't have mattered if it were real.

"Yes, sir!"

* * *

Petrauskas reclaimed his uniform jacket from the rack outside Venezelos' office and then walked her to a small electric car for the drive out to the Guards' training facility. This proved to be an hour north of Sobieski, in the highlands, on the eastern bank of the Nowy Vistula. Petrauskas had to drive the car, of course, so he had to keep his eyes on the road. That allowed Saoirse to keep her eyes on him. She enjoyed the view. Tommie intruded into her musing from time to time, but it was not as though she were *doing* anything. A girl could *look*, after all.

Petrauskas kept up a running commentary on their surroundings: which branch road led to which town, and how the roads in the highlands had been improved by the city government since Strazdins took office two years ago, which was a miracle for the villages since the Sejm hadn't done anything in more years than people could remember. He stuck in the chatter, on a couple of occasions, how glad he was that of all the peacer officers, Lieutenant Colonel Venezelos had agreed to have her accompany him. He smiled when he said that. She was sure of it.

The City Guard training facility was large. Concrete buildings were arranged around a parade ground, with an obstacle course beyond that. Gunshots echoed from what she assumed was a firing range even farther out. As Petrauskas pulled into a parking area, a platoon-sized unit marched past.

"Come on," he said. "We'll show you some things."

The show started with two platoons running the obstacle course while she watched. Every man was timed, and then the three fastest from each platoon ran it again, with the fastest two being presented to her. A company executed close order drill on the parade ground under her eyes. Then Petrauskas walked her out past the obstacle course to some rough terrain speckled with concrete wall fragments. One platoon took up defensive positions while another one demonstrated how to advance under fire.

"No live ammunition here, of course." Petrauskas laughed.

She laughed along with him and thought back to when she had watched Tommie trying to teach this to the militia. That had looked a bit sad at the time; now the contrast between the ragged militia and the well-organized Guards made it look even worse. The thought made her look away from the demonstration, and she saw a group of half a dozen black-clad men who seemed to be timing, supervising, and directing the activities.

"Those are our contractors," Petrauskas said when she asked. "They're from Romanov. It's a Russian world. They had a conflict, a rather nasty one, when the Chinese tried to put a colony there as well. Then they had a fight with the peacers. Forced them to leave too. They've got the kind of experience we need to train our men, and as you can see, we're having them do it."

Saoirse wondered for an instant if he was trying to impress her. No, of course not, she realized. He was trying to impress Venezelos and was expecting her to repeat all of this at the peacer base.

She was indeed impressed by the time the black-clad men gave the Guards an afternoon break. Every drill, every exercise she saw, had been conducted crisply and well. The contrast to Tommie's scruffy crew of boys and old men could not have been greater. Further, the Guards were careful in the way they behaved toward her. She was saluted, called Lieutenant Kenneally, or *ma'am*, which might be a contravention of peacer standards but was courteous nonetheless. No one called her Irish, and there was none of the adolescent showboating that she had put up with at the militia and that had led to Tommie chewing *her* out. On top of that, she had the feeling that Petrauskas *liked* talking with her. He had stuck close to her side since their arrival, despite several opportunities to go elsewhere.

One question was on her mind, though, as they picked up food from the cooks and took their seats on a concrete bench by one of several metal tables that were roofed over. The cluster of men in black who took a table for themselves reinforced it.

"This all looks great, Captain Petrauskas," she said, "really sharp, really professional. But it looks like you're building an army out here."

"Well, that's because we are," Petrauskas said.

That was not the answer she'd expected. "Why?" she asked. "There are what, less than two hundred thousand people on this whole world, and you have towns on only a small part of this continent. What good is an army?"

"Because of the damned *ruchawka*!" Petrauskas leaned across the table, intensity in his voice and eyes.

"*Ruchawka?*"

"Sorry. That's what we call the damned swamper militia. It sort of means 'rabble.' But that's the problem. Daleko Bałtyckie can qualify for membership in the Assembly of Worlds. Our economy is big enough. The Sobieski Point plant produces enough power to maintain a technology civilization near Earth standard. But we need a planetary government. A real one. That's the third requirement, and the swamper towns are resisting. They're increasing the *ruchawka*; if we are not careful, they will have it as big as our Guards. They block everything we try to do in the Sejm. All it takes is one of them to shut down a session and nullify what's been done, and they do it every time. Prezydent Strazdins should be Marshal of the Sejm, but we can't even get the office filled. Well, we've had enough of it. We're not going to let them keep the planet paralyzed. We're not going to let them cost us a seat in the Assembly as an independent world. Even if we have to fight. And if we have to fight, we're going to win."

That was not the way Saoirse had heard the story from Tommie or old man Nowak, but she could not see contradicting Petrauskas. Instead she asked, "Why would they do this? The, ah, swampers, I mean."

"You have to understand," Petrauskas said, "how things have changed here. The original settlement, the people came from Poland, Lithuania, and Latvia on Earth. Most of them were Polish, frankly. It's obvious, isn't it? Daleko Bałtyckie, that's Polish. Sobieski was the great Polish king. But in the city and the highlands, we kept the Latvian and Lithuanian influence. The swampers are almost all Poles. It's like, living just by themselves, they're losing civilization. And it's the zombipterisin. The swampers harvest it, smuggle it. They fight to keep us out of the areas where they're doing it. When we try to do anything in the Sejm, they dissolve it. If Strazdins can be Marshal, we'll put an end to that. We'll control the spaceport, too, so the smuggling will have to stop. They're going to fight us on that. We know it and we're going to be ready."

Tommie was fighting for zombie smugglers? That didn't seem right. But she couldn't say that to Petrauskas. Not here, maybe not anywhere. "What about the peacers? What about us?" That she could say. "We have a battalion here. We can stop any fighting."

Petrauskas smiled at her. "Maybe," he said. "Nothing against you or your lieutenant colonel, but who knows what orders your battalion will have. There is a saying I heard from one of the Romanovs: 'A man who bets his life on what the peacers will do doesn't live long.'"

Saoirse flushed. "I'm sure we're not here to fight you." She wanted him to believe her. "And for sure, we're not going to side with zombie smugglers."

"I'm sure not." Petrauskas smiled again. She wanted to melt.

Their conversation was interrupted by another Guards captain. Word had reached the Guards about Lieutenant Kenneally's marksmanship. Would she agree to a contest with three of their best shots? Since the Guards used the same MK32 rifle and ammunition as the peacers, she would be familiar with the weapon. Saoirse smiled and accepted the challenge.

Saoirse won that contest. She was certain she saw Petrauskas smile at her as she walked over to him afterward. Equally clear was the frown on the face of one of the Romanovs as he looked at her final score.

. . .

Saoirse recounted the visit to the Guards training camp for Tommie when she saw him two days later, although she left out any mention of Petrauskas. At least she was pretty sure she'd left him out of the story. In any significant way.

"*Ruchawka*," Tommie said, his voice bitter. "It's a Polish word. Look it up; it means 'riot.'" He laughed, but without humor. "It was used to describe the Polish militia of the time back during the Napoleonic Wars on Earth. I suppose we are no better disciplined than they were, although we are not the thieves they were. As for the rest, I hope you do not believe any of the bullshit he was handing you. As if I would be working to protect zombie smugglers."

"I don't believe any of it," Saoirse said quickly.

She thought Tommie was distant that afternoon, or maybe he was only distracted. The afternoon did not turn into an evening, because a message on his comm signaled business he needed to attend to. After they had parted and Saoirse was driving back to the base, she wondered if he could have heard about Lukas Petrauskas. Had she said anything wrong? Looked too happy on those few occasions when she had no choice but to mention Lukas, as she was starting to call him in her mind? Even if Tommie had a spy in the Guards' camp, what could he have heard? She hadn't done anything! Except look. And think . . . a bit.

Her comm buzzed as she passed through the main gate of the peacer base. According to the message, Captain Lukas Petrauskas of the Guards had asked to show her some of the highland farms and villages tomorrow. Venezelos had approved and forwarded it to her.

THIRTY-THREE

Petrauskas picked her up at the base the next morning. At first they drove north of Sobieski, then instead of continuing up the Nowy Vistula to the training base, he turned east, away from the river. Large stands of trees, fifty feet high and shaped like cones, alternated with fields of flexi-ferns that stood three times the height of the car and leaned over the roadway, creating tunnels of leaves for them to pass through. Tinkerbells flitted through the ferns, wings iridescent in the sunlight. Occasionally, one splattered against the windshield. Twice they came into the open to see meadows of the little chartreuse fern-clovers that shone in the sun.

"I know this is not as exciting as the training camp," Petrauskas said, "but we thought it would be a good idea for you to get an idea of the culture we have here. What is at stake. What we will fight to keep." He paused. "Also, it seemed like a really good excuse to spend most of the day with you. And you can call me Lukas, if you like, rather than Captain Petrauskas." He looked over at her with a smile and a laugh, his white teeth flashing.

Saoirse laughed as well. She would like that very much.

They passed through two villages, both little more than several gaily painted concrete buildings along the road with one or two cross streets, each ensconced in a wide belt of open land.

"Firebreaks," Lukas said. "We respect nature's power on Daleko Bał-tyckie, especially fire. Our villages put in the effort to keep a safe open zone. If fires threaten to overrun the farm firebreaks, our people can shelter in the villages. You won't see this kind of careful management in the lowlands. There, the swampers are at the mercy of the planet."

They stopped in the second village to buy a pastry and a mug of Daleko Bałtyckie coffee. Lukas professed to be astonished that she drank the coffee with a smile, and the shopkeeper pressed a second pastry on her as an expression of his own amazement.

After leaving the shop, Lukas turned the car onto one of the cross streets. That rapidly turned into a narrow country road. The trees and ferns were replaced by farmland, with fields filled with Earth crops or open pasture.

"Families up here manage large farms," Lukas said. "We grow everything we need, but we take care not to let Earth plants get into the wild and we use mini-bots for the necessary pollination. We also raise animals on most of these farms. Pigs and goats do very well. They eat anything, Earth or native. We have also started to have success with cows, although that is only in the last few years. We have cow's milk now and, occasionally, steak, although we need to be careful there. The cows are too precious to use many for meat, so that is only on special occasions.

"The one animal I'm afraid does not do well here is horses. They're finicky about what they eat, and we can't get them to thrive. They die as colts. Well, donkeys don't manage here either. We tried hard early in the colony because it would have helped with transportation." He laughed. "And I've seen pictures of cavalry. Don't you think it would look grand if the two of us were riding down this road on horseback, side by side?"

She could picture it. "It might look grand, but I'll bet it's not all that comfortable."

That brought more laughter from Lukas, and Saoirse flushed with pleasure. She had never been on a horse herself, but was willing to bet on the lack of comfort. If it made Lukas laugh, that was a bonus. Anyway, there was no risk of having to get up on a horse here.

"I'll take you to one of the farms near here. You won't see anything this prosperous in the lowlands or on the coast. The swampers don't know how to manage their land properly."

Saoirse ranked inspecting a farm as just above contracting dysentery on her interest scale, but she was not about to disappoint Lukas. "I can't wait," she told him.

They turned off the road onto an even narrower lane that led through a firebreak to a flat-roofed farmhouse painted bright red. Fields of what was probably wheat stretched out behind it as far as Saoirse could see. To the right of the house, a large structure, also concrete painted red, had a wide, open sliding door. That must be the barn. The sound of pigs came from behind it.

Lukas parked the car and walked up to the front door, Saoirse a step behind. The door opened as they reached it. On the other side stood a stout woman wearing an apron, her short brown hair streaked with gray. She and Lukas exchanged greetings in a language that was not English. Saoirse hastily stuck in an earbud and set her comm to Translate.

Agnieszka was the name of the lady of the house, and she had just finished putting a pie in the oven for later. Indeed, she had a little time to chat and would be happy to show them around. They started in the kitchen, already redolent with the smells of baking. Agnieszka showed off her electric stove and oven, her refrigerator and her freezer. To Saoirse's eye, the appliances would have been equally at home in a Chicago dwelling. The interior of the home was small but tidy. A little floor bot scooted from room to room with them, picking up any stray particles that landed on the floor. Outside, Agnieszka showed off the pigpen and the chicken coops.

"We are fond of bacon," she said to Saoirse through the comm's translator, and then made it clear that Saoirse should eat more heartily.

That was when a loud, "Moo!" from behind Saoirse made her jump and spin around. While she had been watching the pigs and considering the possibilities of real eggs with real bacon, a large brown cow had ambled up behind her. It dipped its head to crop some of the fern-clover, then looked up at her again with its large eyes. She reached a tentative hand toward its head.

"Cows don't bite," Agnieszka said. "They give milk."

Lukas and Agnieszka laughed, and Saoirse turned red. She reached out farther with her hand and scratched the cow behind one ear. It seemed happy enough and made her giggle.

※ ※ ※

"Except for no flowers in front, that place could have been in the Midwest of the US back on Earth," Saoirse said when they were back in the car.

"And that's the point," Lukas replied. "Now, what you said about flowers—and I know them from pictures—Daleko Bałtyckie hasn't evolved flowering plants, and since they aren't necessary—I mean, yes, they're pretty but we don't need them for food—we aren't going to introduce them. We're good stewards here. But for the rest, you are right. Our standard of living here is on a par with Earth. We've worked hard, very hard, to get to this point. You won't find anything like this with the swampers. They keep falling farther and farther behind; they're barely civilized anymore. It would be sad, if they weren't so threatening."

Saoirse was quiet. She didn't know what to say. Agnieszka seemed nice; her farm was beautiful.

"Look," Lukas said into the lengthening silence. "I didn't mean to sound so glum. My comrades and I, we'll do what needs to be done, and that will be it. Please don't worry about it, and you can tell your Lieutenant Colonel Venezelos that he shouldn't worry about it either." He turned the car back onto the road. "I have a thought. Can I ask you to come to dinner with me tomorrow night? I know a good restaurant by City Center Plaza, and I understand, you know, no alcohol. I won't have any either. We'll just have dinner and talk, and maybe there could be some ways you could help us. Would that be okay?"

Saoirse's yes came almost before Lukas had finished his question. "I'd like that very much," she added.

She reflected on the drive back to the base that she wasn't cheating on Tommie. This was dinner. And gathering intel. For now.

THIRTY-FOUR

Saoirse was tugging at her uniform jacket while trying to get a wide-enough view in the tiny mirror on the wall of her room. She had found a man in A Company who was apprenticed to a tailor on some planet in the Reach before becoming a peacer, and he had volunteered to modify a male dress uniform to fit her. This was the first time she had tried it on. She needed to see that the jacket fit properly across her chest, but no matter how she turned, she couldn't see it well enough. That was when her comm buzzed.

LIEUTENANT, the message read, NEED TO SEE YOU ASAP. URGENT MATTER. It was from Juliana Hopkinson.

Saoirse looked from the comm to the mirror. What was urgent was the fit of her jacket. NOT NOW, she sent back.

The response was immediate. SIR, I NEED TO SEE YOU.

Saoirse sighed and gave up. She knew Hopkinson well enough by this point to realize that continued refusal would only lead to the woman doing something insubordinate. Saoirse did not want to deal with that. OKAY, she sent. IN MY QUARTERS.

Her door opened almost immediately, a clear sign that Hopkinson had been sending from the hallway right outside.

"What is the crisis, Corporal?" Saoirse asked. "Have aliens invaded?"

"It's about the dinner you're going to," Hopkinson said. "Or, more precisely, about Captain Pretty Boy you're having dinner with."

Saoirse stared. "How do you know about that? Him? Both?"

"Well, sir," said Hopkinson, "I could say that it's obvious because, until today, you haven't done anything with your hair since the day you arrived." She flicked her own elaborately braided and longer-than-regulation ponytail over her left shoulder for emphasis. "However, the fact is that the first day Captain Pretty Boy was here, Venezelos had him hang his uniform jacket outside his office before he came in. That gave Cyber a chance to slip a micro-thread receiver net into the fabric while Venezelos kept him talking. I must say, there's a lot of stuff we don't have, like armor, artillery, and planes, but Cyber's got some nifty tech. Turned the man into a goddamn microwave transmitter."

"Oh God," Saoirse said weakly. "You bugged Lukas." Her back against the wall, she slid down to sit on the floor.

"There's something you should hear, sir. From about lunchtime today. Cyber ran it through the translator, but you can hear the actual voices. You'll recognize his." Hopkinson held out an earbud and a control wand.

Saoirse did not want to listen. She did not want to hear whatever had been recorded. All she could think of was a similar stunt she had pulled in high school. She had bugged a specific bathroom in the boys' dorm with a net of directional microphones that fed directly to her comm. She had heard rumors that they did drugs in that bathroom after dinner and had set it up for her comm to broadcast the feed to the girls on her floor. However, what came through that evening had been a loud discussion about one particular girl—Saoirse Kenneally.

The boys had commented in detail on each part of her body. They had talked about her tits (too small), her ass (too flat), whether she could kiss properly (probably not), and whether she did other . . . things. The girls on her floor had laughed themselves hysterical. They had demanded that Saoirse take off her clothes so they could compare her body to what the boys were saying and guess if the boys had really seen it. They demanded to know what she had done and with which boy. Saoirse had wanted to scream, but she wasn't able to get any sound past a throat struggling to draw breath. She had wanted to kill someone—preferably herself. She had settled for drinking until she passed out, but unlike other times, when she woke the next day, she remembered every detail.

"You really need to hear this now, sir. It's only a short clip. Cyber just took what you need to hear, she didn't edit anything. Please."

It was the *please* more than anything else that got Saoirse to take the earbud and put it in her ear. Then she hit the On button on the control wand.

"So, how's Operation Peacer Girl going?" said a voice Saoirse did not recognize.

Clinking noises and conversations in the background made her think this was taking place in a dining hall.

"Really well." That was Lukas' voice. Saoirse wanted to hit the Off control, but she did not. "Our Romanovs really know what they're doing. They said, based on her profile, she would be attracted to me, and she is. She's like a little schoolgirl with a crush. We'll have dinner tonight, and we'll start finding ways for her to help. She'll do it. She's just the tool we want."

"Typical woman," said a third voice. "No emotional self-control. I can't believe she's an officer."

"Neither can I," said Lukas. "And my God, you should have seen her at the farm. The Romanovs said she would like farm animals, and she was so gooey over that cow. I thought she wanted to get down and milk it."

"I didn't want to go to the farm," Saoirse whispered. "I only went because you wanted me to go and I wanted to do what you wanted."

The first man laughed. "More to the point, Lukas, did you get to milk her udders?"

"Not yet, Matis, not yet." Lukas laughed as well.

"It hardly seems fair," said the third man. "You get selected for this special project, and you'll get to fuck her as part of doing it."

"I would say it hardly seems worth it," said the man called Matis. "A real man needs strong drink, not weak beer."

That brought another laugh from Lukas. "Even weak beer is worth chugging."

The clip ended. Saoirse thumbed the control wand to Off and took out the earbud. Her mind was whirling. It had all been a setup. The Guards, or the Romanovs, had picked Lukas to get her based on her profile. Her profile! Of course. That was how Lukas had known about alcohol when he asked her to dinner. He had slipped, and she hadn't paid attention. And the whole damn thing was in a digital file.

"Who else has heard this?" She asked in a dull voice.

"Cyber, of course. She gets all the transmissions. And when she heard it, she had me come and listen to it. That's it. Bronson hasn't heard it; Venezelos hasn't heard it."

Yet was the word Saoirse's mind said should have been at the end of Hopkinson's last sentence. "What do you want me to do?" Saoirse asked.

Hopkinson shrugged. "Whatever you want."

You are teetering on the edge of disaster. Just as usual. It's always the same with you. A bad decision, followed by a worse decision, and then a truly horrible one after that. Just like that time you ended up in jail— Shut up, Saoirse, this is not the time.

Saoirse looked up at Hopkinson from the floor. "Let me be really blunt," she said. "What do I need to do, for you or anybody else, to keep this little clip from going viral?"

She steeled herself for all manner of possible answers and demands, but having Hopkinson burst out laughing was not one of them. "You're a strange one, Lieutenant," she said when she could talk. "I mean, we've all figured there's something odd about how you got here, but let that be. No one cares now. So listen to me, sir. Since you got here and started working with Sarge, this platoon's in better shape than any time since I got here—better than any of us remember. You pay attention to what we need. And, shit—for me, that day you got up with Mwesigye to demo hand-to-hand . . ." She shook her head. "You kept getting up. I couldn't believe it. So you do what you want to do and don't worry about me or Cyber. Not Bronson, either. He'll never hear it. Trust Cyber on that."

"Thank you." Saoirse extended her hand. Hopkinson grasped it and helped her back up to her feet.

Saoirse checked herself in the mirror and tugged the uniform jacket as straight as it would go. Then she opened her closet and pulled out a wide belt with a holster attached to it. She buckled that on, then reached up to the top shelf and came down with a pistol. She checked that it had a full clip and then slipped it into the holster.

"Are you planning to shoot him, sir?" Hopkinson asked. "If I may say so, that would be only a moment's pleasure and it will cause talk."

"I don't know what I'm planning to do, Corporal," Saoirse said. "I think I'm going to make it up as I go along. But thank you for your assistance with this, ah, delicate matter. And thank Cyber for me as well."

. . .

Half an hour later, Saoirse parked a Gemav she had taken from the motor pool in the plaza by the statue of Jan Sobieski. The restaurant Lukas had messaged her about was right on the square. It was the one she had walked past that first night she went into town to meet Tommie. The outdoor tables, with their little signs that said smoking was allowed only indoors, were all filled. The front door with its NO SWAMPERS HERE sign in the lower left corner was the same, but it meant more than the last time she had seen it. She pushed the door open and went in.

Lukas was seated at a table for two in the middle of the room. He favored her with a broad smile and a wave when he saw her enter. *Smile while you can*, Saoirse thought.

She pulled out the vacant chair and joined him at the table. The tablecloth, she noticed, was a heavy white fabric, smooth to the touch. It would not have been out of place in a high-end Chicago restaurant. She glanced at the menu and the prices. No young captain in the Guards would be taking a date to a restaurant like this. Had anyone thought that she might notice? Or would they never expect a woman to figure it out? Especially not a silly schoolgirl with a crush. She wondered who had given him the money for the dinner. Fuck the Romanovs and their profiles. She didn't care about any of it.

"I was worried," Lukas said. "I was afraid something had happened at the base."

"Sorry I'm late. In a sense, something did come up," Saoirse said. "But I figured it would be okay because I understand that you're perfectly fine chugging weak beer."

At first, Lukas looked puzzled; then his eyes narrowed. "Do you want to tell me what the hell you mean by that?" His voice was no longer so nice.

"Certainly. But first, I want to give you some important information."

"What?"

She smiled at him. "My hand is on the grip of a Glock-Winchester 7.5-millimeter automatic pistol. It has a full fifty-round magazine and will fire at the rate of sixteen hundred rounds per minute. Each bullet will leave the muzzle at the velocity of thirteen hundred feet per second. All of which is a long-winded way of letting you know that you could be a bloody corpse in the time it takes my face to change to bitch look. Be very careful about making any movements or noises. Got it?"

He blanched. Saoirse could read fury in his face, but she could also see fear. "Yes."

"Please tell whatever puppeteer is pulling your strings that you failed miserably. Tell them that the silly woman officer isn't going to be your tool. Not now, not ever. And you don't get to fuck her."

"You are making a big mistake." His lips pressed together so tightly they turned white.

She smiled. "I don't think so. I've made enough mistakes to know the difference. Now, why don't you enjoy your dinner. Somebody put up a lot of money for it." She stood up and her hand was on the pistol grip, finger next to the trigger. "One last thing," she said. "If I ever see you again, I will kill you."

THIRTY-FIVE

Saoirse had barely gotten dressed the next morning before her comm buzzed.

"My office. Now." It was from Venezelos.

She cursed under her breath. It wasn't as though she had actually shot Lukas; she had only threatened to kill him. Wasn't that good self-control? Of course, she had done it in public. In a restaurant in the center of Sobieski. She left her quarters and hurried over to the battalion HQ.

Venezelos had another man in his office with him when Saoirse arrived. Tommie.

Awkward. She almost forgot to salute.

"Colonel Szczechowicz says that there is something we need to see regarding the zombie trade," Venezelos said. "It's out in a coastal village called Wałęsa. I don't trust vid; I want actual eyes on it. You're the liaison with the militia, so I want your eyes. Based on the distance, you should be back by evening. Report to me in person when you return. Don't worry about the time."

Back by evening. The whole day in a car with Tommie. On this day, of all days. Could life get more awkward? She had decided that she was over being angry at Tommie for his being angry at her, but she didn't know how he felt about her, and she didn't like the uncertainty. Why did everything have to be so complicated?

They walked to the car in silence, and the silence continued as they drove out from the base and along the highland road down the slope to the coast. When they reached the intersection with the Coastal Highway, Tommie turned north. To the left of the car, she glimpsed the ocean intermittently and heard its waves breaking noisily on the rocky shore. A solid layer of gray clouds hung over the water, mirroring her mood. Then they came around a curve, and a mile-wide expanse of river lay in front of them. The highway crossed it on a narrow two-lane bridge. Just before the bridge, Tommie pulled over.

"This is the Lower Nowy Vistula," he said. "If you follow this bank of the river northeast into the flexis and the forest," he pointed to a wall of yellow-green in that direction, "you come to the base of Sobieski Falls." He hesitated for a minute. "It's magnificent, a drop of nine hundred forty-three feet from the Point, where the nuclear plant is. I want to take you there. Not today, of course. But sometime. There's actually a trail up the cliff along the side of the falls. It's pretty near vertical itself, lots of switchbacks and scrambles over rock, but it will take you all the way up to the Point."

"Thank you, but not for me. The trail, I mean," Saoirse said. "Over nine hundred feet straight up? I'd be scared shitless."

"How about if I do it with you?" Tommie asked.

Saoirse looked over at him. His eyes were fixed on the road ahead.

"That would be okay," she said slowly.

"Good."

"Have *you* taken that trail?"

"Yes." Tommie paused again. "The boys from the villages up and down the coast have done it since there were boys on this planet. It's—what do you call it in English?—a rite of passage. Of course, it's a bit of an issue today. The mothers worry boys will fall and get killed, and that has happened, but what's a rite of passage without risk? Also, the Guards built a wall across the Point to turn the control station into something of a fortress. That wasn't there when I was climbing age. Now the trail comes up inside the walled-off area. Not a great place to get caught."

"You said the boys climb this trail as a rite of passage. What about the girls, do they do it?"

"No. Not that I've ever heard of."

"So what is the rite of passage for girls?"

Tommie didn't look at her. "Childbirth."

Saoirse bit back the words that wanted to jump immediately out of her mouth and reflected for a minute. Yes, she thought, childbirth would be as scary and painful a transition as climbing up a cliff, particularly in a small village. She would admit that. *More* scary. And a lot more responsibility. A cliff hike lasts however long it lasts, whereas having a child lasts until you die—if you're lucky. Then she hit him anyway, a solid punch on his arm. She couldn't really blame him for the culture on this planet, but he was handy. "Why don't you restart the car and get going, so we can get back before tomorrow?"

⁂

At the other side of the bridge, an ugly concrete blockhouse stood at the center of a cleared and partially paved zone. Behind the blockhouse rose a tall mast of antennae. The gate across the roadway had been raised, and no one came out to challenge them as Tommie drove past.

Past the cleared zone around the blockhouse, the road ran into swampland that stretched out ahead as far as they could see. Glistening pools of standing water were separated by short stretches of muck, but vegetation hid most details of the ground. Low to the ground, flexis with long, waving leaves sprouted from every patch of mud above water. Amid the clumps of flexis, trees with broad lower branches and tiny leaves stood sixty feet tall. Other trees, if that is what they were, stood out of the standing water on twisted, elevated roots that resembled an earthly mangrove, except these trunks and roots were a fuzzy green. Everywhere, tree trunks as straight as a pipe and devoid of branches rose from low bushes of floppy yellow-green leaves. These pole trees were also a fuzzy green all along their height. While some were only a few feet high, others reached fifty, a hundred, even two hundred feet in the air. Those over twenty feet sported a bulbous green crown—the taller the tree, the larger and bushier its crown. On those trees taller than fifty feet, long branches drooped from the crowns, each sporting a myriad of tiny leaves that flashed yellow-green in the sunlight. Fallen trunks of pole trees littered the ground and were partially submerged in pools in all directions. It was a forest painted in chartreuse, but because the leaves were tiny, sunlight reached the ground despite the density of the growth.

The road became a causeway, its paved surface jutting from the water and the soggy mud. Multi-wing fliers, many times larger than the tinkerbells Saoirse was accustomed to at the base or the city, buzzed through the trees and around the car as they drove. A loud belch from a pool to the right of the roadway seemed to come from a log, but then Saoirse saw a mouth open that could have fit her whole leg.

In a stretch of swamp that looked no different from the swamp they had already crossed, Tommie stopped the car. He pulled out his comm, checked the screen, tapped out a message, and checked the screen again, as if willing a message to appear. When none did, he let out a sigh and stared up at the clouds.

A flier landed on the hood of the car. This was a huge specimen. Its spindly legs gripped both sides of the car's hood. Eight gossamer wings on each side stretched well past the sides of the car. When sunlight broke through clouds, the wings shimmered. The flier cocked a flattened crescent of a head, adorned with little spikes, at Saoirse, who stared at it with rapt attention. Then it opened two sets of mandibles, each one a foot wide.

Saoirse gasped. Tommie, his reverie broken, laughed.

"Those fliers eat only leaves and smaller tinkerbells," he said. "Even if he did try to grab you, there's not enough strength in those pincers to mark your skin."

"Easy for you to say."

At her words, the flier leaped into the air, flicks of its wings and wafts of breeze taking it high among the pole trees. Saoirse watched it until it was too high to follow.

With the flier gone, she expected Tommie to start driving again. He didn't, though, and when she looked over, he was again staring at the screen of his comm. Tension showed on his face, at his eyes, in the furrows on his brow. His fingers tapped the steering wheel. With an oath, he shoved the comm into a jacket pocket, and his hand came out with a cigarette. He lit it and smoke bellied against the windscreen. They had to keep the windows closed to keep the flame within the car.

"Tommie, what's wrong?"

"Nothing."

"Bullshit."

"Yeah." He sighed again. "It's about the person we need to speak to, the one who can show us what we need to see—what you need to see."

"Did he ghost us?" Saoirse asked. "Did we come all this way for nothing?"

"No. He'll meet us. A bit later than planned, although maybe that's just as well."

"Then I don't understand," Saoirse said. "We'll still get this done, whatever we came for. Venezelos doesn't care how late we come back."

"That's not the problem." Tommie turned away from her and puffed on his cigarette. He spoke in the direction of the vegetation outside his car door. "The person is my *tata*, Aleksander Szczechowicz. My father."

Saoirse was silent for a minute. She'd been assuming the strain between them involved either the incident at the training camp or her time with Lukas. She had never thought of this.

"You never mentioned your family," she said. "All you told me was that your story started with the peacers. If you don't get along with him, God knows, I understand what that's like."

He didn't look at her. "No, you don't. I haven't seen or spoken to him since the day I ran away. We haven't been in touch at all."

"Since you ran away? Wait." Saoirse paused. "You mean you haven't had any contact in eight years?"

"Correct."

"Tommie." Saoirse stopped, searched for words. She knew all the formulas, but it had always been someone else saying them to her while she pretended to listen. "Tommie," she started again, "maybe it's time. Maybe there are some things you need to say to each other."

"I'm sure there are," he said. "However . . ." He shook his head. "I'm sorry you had to come along. I knew the Guards would feed you their propaganda, their story about zombipterisin, so I reached out to people who would talk to me, asked for a person who could find evidence that would matter. I didn't expect it would be him. Sorry I involved you in this."

"I'm not sorry," she said. "Eight years. You need to talk to him, Tommie."

"I need to talk to him about our business. About the zombie trade. That's important."

"I'll bet some other things are important too."

Before he answered, Tommie started the car. "There's an old saying that goes, 'It's the job you don't start that takes the longest to finish.'"

"So maybe you should start." Saoirse glanced over at him. "I'm here for you, Tommie." She realized that she meant it. For the first time that she could think of, she meant those words.

Tommie reached out and squeezed her hand gently. "Thanks, Irish."

.   .   .

The land sloped upward at a gentle grade, and the swamp dried out. Standing pools of water were replaced by a profusion of man-high flexi-ferns and cone-shaped trees that stood fifteen to twenty feet high. The buzzing of the tinkerbells and the big multi-wing fliers, incessant in the swamp, disappeared completely. The causeway changed back to a paved road. From the left, they could hear the slap of waves against the shore, which told them that they had come back to the coast. Finally, the road ran up a low bluff between banks of flexis, and as they crested it, they saw the village of Wałęsa across cleared ground.

The road led them to an open square that had been the center of the original settlement. A painted sign in Polish and English on a two-story building on the right side of the square identified the offices of the village administration and the mayor. On the side of the square directly ahead of them stood a larger concrete building with a flight of stairs leading to a small porch and double doors. A steeple with a cross identified it as the village church. The left side of the square was occupied by storefronts. All the buildings were painted in a variety of bright colors, similar to the ones in Sobieski. The roofs were dark brown and, from their shape, made from sections of pole tree trunks with the green fuzz shaved off. To the left, the ocean crashed and roared beyond a line of low buildings and rows of solar cells. A few people were going into or coming out of the stores along the square. They paid no attention as Tommie parked in front of the village offices.

"Pretty quiet place," Saoirse said.

"It's midday," Tommie replied. "Most people are having lunch or are at work, and much of the work in a village like this is at sea or on the docks. Sea life is plentiful here; it's the key to our food supply and economy. Native animal life on land doesn't go beyond large amphibians." He looked at his comm. "We still have some time to wait." He looked out through the windshield of the car at nothing in particular. "It looks the same as it did the day I left."

A boom sounded across the town, and Saoirse jumped.

Tommie smiled. "Come with me," he said. "While we have time, there's something I want to show you."

He led her toward the sound of the ocean, past the church, down a street flanked by rows of low concrete houses in bright colors that had weathered over time. The houses ended at a road that ran around the border of the town. Beyond that lay a stretch of bare, rocky land that rose first into a low hillock and then into a pile of jumbled rocks right at the water's edge. A cool breeze blew in off the water. Again, the boom sounded, apparently from the rock pile in front of them.

"Come on!" Tommie sprinted across the flat and began to climb the rocks.

Saoirse followed close behind. The rocks were gray with veins of brown and varied from the size of bricks to curbstones. It was as if a giant had taken a sledgehammer to a staircase built for giants and left the jumble of debris at the shoreline. The boom sounded again as they were halfway to the top.

"What is that?" Saoirse asked.

"A thunder hole!" Tommie shouted over his shoulder. "This is one of the places I used to come to when I was a kid and was supposed to be in school."

Tommie reached the top of the rock pile and picked his way carefully to the edge that faced out over the ocean. He motioned for Saoirse to join him. She did, but more slowly, picking her way over. The rocks were wet with spray, and her boots slipped in places. From the flat land by the village, the rock pile did not look that high, but with each step near the top, the way down looked longer and longer. When she finally reached Tommie, she took a long, slow breath.

He pointed down at a narrow crevasse in the rocks below them. "The waves have created a narrow channel down there. When the wave floods in, the water blocks the outlet and compresses the air behind it. That noise you heard was it booming out the top. The best spot to see it is here." He indicated a spot two feet behind the opening of the crevasse, and Saoirse walked over to it. "Wait just a minute," he said.

The next wave came almost exactly a minute later. The water rushed in and sprayed around the rocks. A boom that would have done justice to a howitzer blasted from the thunder hole, followed by a spout of water into the air. Three seconds later, another spray shot up from cracks in the rocks behind Saoirse and drenched her from the back with cold water.

She shrieked and jumped up. "I am fuckin' soaked!" she shouted, trying to balance on the slippery rock.

Tommie burst out laughing. "You should have seen your face!"

She glared at him. "My face? You fucking bastard, you knew that would happen! Would it have been even funnier if I had fallen into the ocean?"

"No, no one falls." He put his hands up. "I'm sorry. We used to play that trick when we were children. Only works once on a person, of course."

"Well, I'm not one of your fucking village idiot kids. Shit, I'm wet all down my back. Better keep your hands up. I may rearrange your face. I suppose this is my payback for going around with that stupid Guards captain, which I'm sure you heard about." *And if you hadn't,* she thought, *I just told you.*

He looked startled. "What? No, no. I mean, yes, I heard all about Captain Petrauskas. I wish I could have seen his face when you had your hand on the pistol. But, no, this isn't about you or what you did; this is about me and what I did. What I need to tell you." Suddenly, his face fell. "I told you I'm not good at this stuff, but that's just a handy excuse. The truth is . . . I don't deserve you. Or anyone else, for that matter." He stopped to catch a breath. "I want to tell you why. No, I need to tell you why. When I heard the boom, I knew this was the place. I only used the old trick as a way to get up my nerve."

"What?" Saoirse's anger was replaced by confusion. Tommie, the combat peacer who wore red and gold, needed to get up his nerve?

"Marta punched me when I pulled that trick," he said abruptly. He turned around to look at the water. "She split my lip, bloodied my mouth real good."

The abrupt shift in the conversation took Saoirse by surprise. For a moment, she stared at his back, not knowing what to say. When the silence continued, she said, "Marta?"

"That was her name." Tommie looked out over the water. "When I was fifteen, I had a girlfriend here. She was from the next village up the road."

"And?" Saoirse asked. "Most fifteen-year-old boys have girlfriends, if they are hetero. So she punched you in the mouth when you did this. I like her already, even if she was your girlfriend. Was she pretty?"

"I thought so. She was a little wild, a little crazy; I thought she was special. Her family hated that she liked me." His voice sounded strange.

"Something happened," she said. "Tell me."

"Yeah." Tommie glanced at her. "That's what I'm trying to do. It's just harder than I thought. Okay. So, what happened is . . . we have a boat race here every year, out of the harbor. The course goes out through the rocks you can see sticking up beyond this point." He pointed far out, to where the water foamed and surged around clusters of rocks and tiny islands that stuck up out of the waves. "The finish is on the beach far down to the right. We race in two-person sailboats. When you reach fifteen, you can compete."

At her look of surprise, he explained, "Well, this is a fishing village. Boys and girls grow up in boats; it's a big thing. Anyway, Marta was going to race with me in my boat, the first race for both of us. Except I got really drunk the night before. Couldn't wake up to make it to the harbor on time. She wasn't going to miss it, so she went with another guy—not that good a sailor, not that good a boat. He wasn't even going to race, but when she asked him to take her on, he said okay. Not a bad guy, but not a good sailor. Currents and winds are tricky here, can be dangerous going through those rocks. That's part of why it's a big competition."

He turned back to the ocean and pointed out to the waves and distant rocks. "They capsized out there. Drowned. Nobody realized quite where they were; they were so far behind and off course. Everybody was focused on the boats finishing. By the time an alarm sounded, it was too late. I didn't even know what happened, not at first. When I got up and realized she'd gone with someone else, I stole some liquor and went into the swamp to sulk. I wasn't even here when they got in trouble; I was getting drunk. If I had been here, I would have had my eyes on that boat. I was the best goddamn sailor in any of these villages, and I wasn't even here to go out for them. If I wasn't such a drunken ass, she would be alive." His voice broke and he stopped.

Saoirse looked at him, still facing away from her and intent on the water, fists clenched at his sides. "Tommie," she said, "you can't do this. You didn't make her get in that boat with the other boy. You didn't make the boat sink. Everybody else who was here had a responsibility too. It can't be all on you and they can't put it all on you. Even if you had been in the harbor, how could you have gotten out that far fast enough to save them? It's horrible that it happened, but you didn't cause it."

"No," Tommie said. "If I had been here, I would have seen them in trouble. I *would* have gotten to them in time. She should have been with me in the first place. It happened the way it did because I'm a drunk. I can't change that, just like I can't change what happened. I own it. Everyone in the villages up and down the coast knew about it. They still do. That's why there was all the argument about the command of the militia. They don't trust me. And why should they? Marta did." He took a long, shuddering breath. "Hardly a day goes by I don't think of what she must have been thinking when she was in the water, praying Tommie would come for her. And I didn't come. I can't change what I was and what I failed to do. All I can do is do better now. So, there's the truth, and that's why I can't be involved with anyone, don't deserve to be."

Tommie's eyes were still on the ocean, focused on those distant rocks. Saoirse thought of the Valor Star he wouldn't discuss, the star that had been given for a near-suicidal rescue of kids held hostage and threatened with death. *When have you atoned, if an implacable judge sits in your own mind?*

She clambered over the rocks to him and put her hands on his shoulders. His muscles tensed, and she pressed him to turn around. When he did, she closed the remaining distance and kissed him. He returned the kiss with even greater intensity and a promise of so much more. It was as though the last wall of reserve had come down. She wanted it to never end.

When their lips at last broke apart, Tommie looked into her eyes, his hands on her hips. "You are special," he said. "You're the only one I can tell this to. You're the only one I can laugh with. And you're the only one, now, I could play that trick on." He smiled. "Maybe . . ."

Saoirse was sure she knew what he was going to say next. She wanted him to say those few more words. When he was silent, she thought maybe she should say them for him. She didn't, though. She should let him get there himself.

"I said I was here for you, and I meant it," she said. "Now, we better get back down there before you have even more trouble with your father."

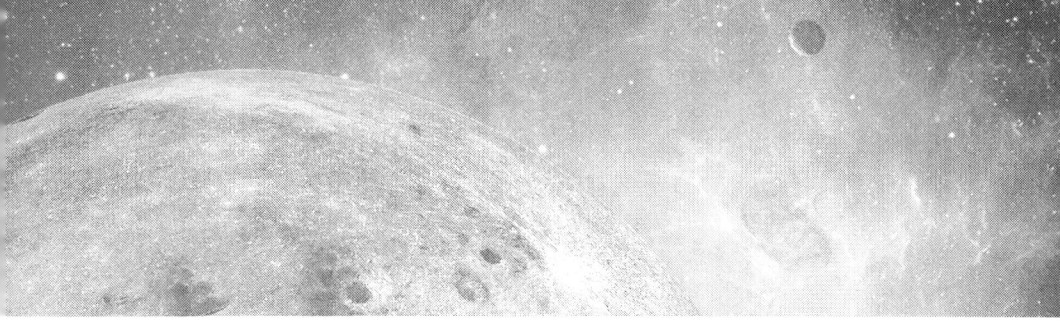

THIRTY-SIX

By the time they returned to the square, a man was standing in front of the village offices, his arms folded across his chest. This could be no one other than Aleksander Szczechowicz, Tommie's father. In appearance, he was an older version of Tommie: the same height, the same broad shoulders straining the seams of his shirt, and only a bit thicker in the midsection. He wore a battered broad-brimmed hat that shadowed a face that was a copy of Tommie's, different only in scattered irregular dark patches and deep lines from a life in the sun. His pale blue eyes, however, gave no hint that they ever twinkled.

"Late," said Aleksander. "Typical."

"Now, Tata," Tommie said, "you are the one who messaged you would be late. Why did the villagers have you handle this, anyway?"

Aleksander shrugged. "What you need to see is outside Wałęsa, and I may have been selected as punishment—although for which one of us, I cannot tell. More likely, since my father saw to my education, a task in which I so obviously failed with you, and I am the swampland expert here, I am the logical one to do it." He paused. "You were to meet me here when I arrived. What happened?"

"I only . . . we . . . took a walk in the meantime."

"Still drinking?"

Tommie flushed across his entire face. "I haven't had a drink in seven years."

Aleksander grunted. "Well, that is some good news." He paused, stared at his son. "Your *matka* died three years ago, Tomasz. You should have been here."

"I know. I'm sorry, Tata. I was in the hospital. I didn't find out until much too late."

"It was not the first time you were not where you should have been, as several villages reminded me. Still, you could have come when you learned."

"I'm sorry. It wasn't possible."

Aleksander let out a long breath and then shrugged. "I know the answer. You went where your peacers went. Bringing much peace to the Reach, are you?"

Tommie stiffened, the hardness in his father's eyes reflected in his. "We try, Father."

"Maybe you need to try harder." Aleksander looked past Tommie at Saoirse, as if noticing for the first time that his son was not alone. "This is the peacer lieutenant I was notified about?"

"Yes," Tommie said. "Lieutenant Saoirse Kenneally." He turned back to Saoirse and indicated Aleksander with his right hand. "My father, Aleksander Szczechowicz."

Saoirse put out her hand. "Pleased to meet you," she said.

"That remains to be seen," Aleksander said. At least he shook her hand, his palm rough and calloused. "I won't give you the line about how my son was really always a good boy, because he wasn't. Rarely, if ever, would be more accurate. Five daughters and one son, and he was the son." He turned back to appraise Tommie with a critical eye. "It does seem, though, that he has done something with his life, which is more than any of us would have thought."

Tommie flushed again, but Aleksander seemed oblivious to the effect of his words. "Come with me, please." He gestured toward the road out of the village. "We must talk privately, and I need to show you something in the swamp forest. You are free to record vid, and you probably should. I will trust you not to record my voice, although it is a valid question how much I should value my life at this stage of things."

With that, he turned and led them on foot through the streets behind the village offices and into the open land beyond. The sound of surf on an unseen beach came from below bluffs to their left. Rows of solar panels stood on the bare land between them and the ocean. Farther off, Saoirse saw fences. The bleating of goats came from that direction to mix with the sound of the waves.

"We maintain a firebreak around the village, Lieutenant," Aleksander said, "no different from the damned highlanders. Have to. No matter how careful we are, lightning strikes start fires. With Daleko Bałtyckie's atmosphere, stopping them is chancy. Our goats and pigs help keep the land clear, just as they do on the highlands. I grant that cows do not like the lowlands, so we drink goat milk not cow milk down here, but that may be the one difference. That, and the fact that women work the same as the men here, although the highlanders will tell you that is a mark of our degeneration."

"There are no women in the militia," Saoirse said.

"Probably a mark of superior intelligence," Aleksander replied. The wind changed, and the sound of pigs and goats intensified. He glanced at the distant fences and said, "We set the children to watch the animals as a chore, and scare them into paying attention by warning them that if the goats escape, with the high oxy here and the way everything grows, the kids will come back eight feet tall with horns like lances, and go hunting the children who didn't watch."

Tommie laughed. "They told us that when I was a child," he said. "I never believed any of it."

"You never listened to anything else, either." Aleksander turned away from Tommie and pointed at the solar panels. "Those panels are all that stand between us and complete dependence on Sobieski Point for electricity. They do not supply enough to make us *independent*," he added, "although we can at least afford what they charge us for the extra power we need. We cannot grow beyond where we are, though, not without going broke. And many villages do not have even this much. Almost all of this was bought illegally, at least according to the old law of the Sejm. That law was the price we paid to have the plant built in the first place. A myopic decision if there ever was one."

"When you say you bought the panels illegally, you mean you had them smuggled in," Saoirse said.

"Yes. We paid a high price to certain ships, paid even more to certain inspectors and people who worked at the port and in the city government."

He stopped there and looked directly at Saoirse, as if waiting for her to speak.

With that, something clicked in her head. "You had to pay a high price. And you paid that price by selling zombipterisin."

"There are no saints anywhere on Daleko Bałtyckie," said Aleksander. "At first, nearly a decade ago, we sold it when Earth found its value in treating schizophrenia. But, yes, we sold more when its other properties became apparent. We felt we had no choice then. Without these panels, we were at the mercy of the prezydent of Sobieski. He could cut off the power as he pleased; that did not require a decision of the Sejm."

"And you hid what you were doing," Saoirse said. "Because you knew it was wrong."

"Everyone has something to hide, Lieutenant, and most of what is hidden is wrong," Aleksander said. "Even you, I imagine. What dark secret are you hiding?"

Startled, Saoirse wondered if those hard blue eyes had somehow looked into her soul and divined the truth. She was hiding plenty. She fought to stop inner Saoirse from reciting every last piece of it. She had no time to listen to it. At least none of her past had killed little Caitlyn.

They exchanged hard stares.

"Why can't you make the solar cells here?" she demanded. "It's not as though it's a mystery how to do it."

"It is not a mystery," Aleksander agreed. He turned back to look at the panels that stood against the sky. "Not a mystery, but it requires a manufacturing plant with clean rooms—not easy to build in fishing villages and swamps on a frontier planet. But even if we could do it, we couldn't do it. Modern, cheap solar cells are made of organic polymers. Even the oldest silicon cells are encapsulated in plastic. And where do the organic polymers and the plastic come from? The starting molecule is ethylene, and that comes from petroleum and natural gas.

"And in case you were unaware, there is no petroleum or natural gas on Daleko Bałtyckie! That's why almost all plastic that you see here comes here on an interstellar. That's why Daleko Bałtyckie is a Class Two world, left available for economic refugees from Eastern Europe, and not a Class One world that the Americans, and Russians, and Chinese, and others fight over. None of this excuses what we did, I realize, but that is why there was no choice."

Tommie spoke up then, his voice soft. "There is always a choice, Tata," he said. "You can fight. *We* can fight. I said that even when I was a boy, when this started nine years ago and everyone moaned about the useless Sejm. I say it again now."

"Ah yes—my son, who at sixteen knew everything there was to know before you ran from here for reasons we do not need to discuss. You would fight. Just like you fought with every boy and half the young men in the village. And what would we have fought with back then? And how would we have paid for our weapons then? You know how. And I'll tell you what fighting gets you in the end. You get dead men, raped women, and burnt-out homes. Tell me you have not seen that across the Reach! That's why our grandparents and great-grandparents came here. To get away from that."

"But it has come with us," Tommie said quietly. "Sometimes you have to fight, Tata. That is why we must have a militia, a real force. Why I am back here. Despite everything."

At that, Aleksander's shoulders slumped, his whole posture a balloon that had lost its air. "Yes, and again, there is no choice about it. And so, maybe, there was no choice before. This prezydent of Sobieski, Prezydent Strazdins, has set his sights on being dictator of Daleko Bałtyckie, with or without the title of Marshal of the Sejm. We know this because he has decided to build an army. Call them City Guards, it is an army—and there is only one purpose for an army. We have enough solar panels. They cannot compel obedience by switching off the power, so they will do it the old-fashioned way. By force.

"They will do it. And they will use that army to take over the zombipterisin trade. They are doing it now. We stopped the trade five years ago when word got back here of what it was doing. The Guards have been the ones expanding it for the past three years, no matter what they say. They do not care, as long as money flows to the prezydent and to his army. And so now we will fight. Maybe our chances would have been better before, but we can't go back in time."

He turned his eyes on Saoirse. "Are you sufficiently depressed, Lieutenant? Are you sufficiently sick of all of us?"

"Wait." Tommie stepped between Saoirse and his father. "The coastal and lowland villages did stop the trade five years ago, and they have agreed to keep it stopped. We cannot change what we did in the past, but now we are doing what is right."

"And that is true," said Aleksander. "As my somehow virtuous son points out, we stopped it. Enough of us, myself included, had long been uneasy about it, and although it takes time for news to come from Earth, it does come. We will not purchase our own freedom with a drug that enslaves others. My son and I see eye to eye, for once. The problem now is Strazdins and those who flock to him. Come with me and see what you must see."

From that point, they walked in silence. Aleksander angled the path away from the coast and led them down a slope. The land became boggy, and they entered the swamp forest on foot. The ground sucked at their boots. The air was close and damp. They were in among the pole trees; all around them were giants reaching for the sky or dead logs on the ground. Other plants grew thickly, either from the mud or from the standing water, more varieties than Saoirse could guess at. Fliers on wings wider than a man's arm span glided past, and tinkerbells circled their heads. A splash sounded from a pool to their right and a fin slid across the surface of a pond. The rest of the animal was hidden beneath the surface.

"What do you see there? At the top?" Aleksander pointed to the top of one of the pole trees.

"It looks like a green ball balanced on top of a green pole," Saoirse said. "What am I supposed to see?"

"Just that. What you see is the crown of the pole tree. When the tree matures, it forms that crown on the top. It has to be about seventy feet high before it's mature, although you see the ball earlier. When the crown is mature, the tree makes hundreds of thousands of spores under the branches that come out from the crown. They're spread by the wind, and we get more pole trees. That crown is the answer."

"I don't understand," Saoirse said.

"We don't know what the trigger is to make the pole tree grow its crown and make spores, but we do know the chemical that fuels that change and growth: zombipterisin. Something triggers the pole tree to make zombipterisin, and that makes the crown grow so the pole tree can reproduce. In other words, the crowns are loaded with zombipterisin, and that's the only place you can find it. Scientists say a chemical so complex should not occur here, but it does. It is so complex that it is cheaper to ship it between stars than make it in a lab. And you can see why you cannot grow these elsewhere. This is why the trade started, first as a lucrative drug for schizophrenia, then as a more lucrative drug of addiction."

"Thank you for the lecture on pole trees and where zombipterisin comes from," Saoirse said, "and I certainly understand that people aren't going to grow these in their backyards on Earth, but why did we need to come out here for this talk? Is that all you wanted to show us? We're standing in a swamp, my boots are sinking into the mud, and my feet are wet. What's the point?"

Tommie winced at her tone.

"You are impatient," said Aleksander.

No shit. You've been impatient for every one of your twenty years, which is half the reason you're always in trouble and drove your family crazy to the point that . . . Saoirse, will you shut up?

"Sorry I seem impatient," Saoirse said. "But I understood that you had something you had to show us, something I needed to see and report back on, and I'd like to see it before I sink up to my knees."

"You needed to understand the pole tree first," Aleksander said. "Now, the bark of this tree is very tough. It must be, to support the weight of the tree, because these trees do not make wood. Only pulp inside. It will also resist fire to some extent, enough that we use it for roofing on concrete buildings. Now, I told you, zombipterisin is produced in the crown. By the time the pole tree dies and falls down, the zombipterisin concentration in the crown is very low, almost gone. If you want to harvest zombipterisin, you need young crowns. That means you need to cut the pole trees down, and that's like chopping through steel. Look at the bases of the pole trees over there. See how they are cut?"

He led them over for a closer look. The bases of the pole trees had been smoothly cut, not snapped or broken. The stumps were hollow; whatever pulp had been inside was gone. The cut surface might have been polished, the way the sunlight glinted off it.

"These were cut down with a laser saw," Aleksander said. "We don't have tools like that. The Guards do."

Saoirse stared at the cut stumps and recorded them on vid. "The pole trees were cut down with laser saws. I'll buy that. And I'll accept that the Guards have laser saws. That's not exactly a new invention. But you can't tell me that it means the Guards cut them down. That's a false syllogism.

You could have gotten laser saws, just like you got the solar panels you're not supposed to have."

To her surprise, Aleksander grinned. She'd figured he didn't know how to smile. "True. Now you need to get your feet wetter."

He slogged farther into the mire and standing water and pushed through a bank of head-high flexi-ferns. Saoirse cursed under her breath, pulled her boots out of the sucking mud, and followed him. Tommie brought up the rear. She felt water come over the top of her boots and fill them. The smell of rotting vegetation filled her nostrils and stuffed her sinuses.

On the other side of the flexi-ferns, a truck lay half sunk in the bog. A pole tree had fallen across the cab and smashed the windshield. The upper part of the logo of the City Guards could still be seen on the driver's door.

"The idiots they sent thought they could drive a ground effect truck into here to load pole tree crowns," Aleksander said. "They tried to pull it out, and only made it worse. A pole tree happened to fall on it." He laughed without any mirth in it. "I doubt anything is going to move it now."

"Someone could still say that you planted it here," Saoirse said. "I've heard the Guards talk about how the zombie trade is all due to your villages, and how they're the ones who will stop it. I know you say otherwise, but they'll claim you stole this truck or got some other truck and painted it to look like a Guard truck."

"Your lieutenant is a good devil's advocate," Aleksander said. "Or maybe only suspicious of us, after all I have said. However, ground effect trucks are closely tracked here. They are imported, expensive, and hard to replace. So this vehicle has a registration code, and there will be a Guard truck with the same registration code. There will be a face and thumb that unlock the vehicle for driving, and you can find who that was. Even without a satellite system, the vehicle will track where it went and how it got here."

Saoirse splashed around the truck, wet to her knees, recording the entire scene and, in particular, the registration code the truck bore. The cargo area was empty, but scattered across its decking were leaves that matched the ones on the branches that drooped from the pole tree crowns. There had been crowns in the cargo bay of the truck.

"I'll show all of this to the lieutenant colonel," she said as she was recording. "I will bet, though, that he will need independent confirmation of all the things you just told me."

"We have connections in the Sobieski offices," Tommie said. "We'll find out where they keep the vehicle information and let Venezelos know. That way the peacers can get it and no one can claim we faked it."

Saoirse felt herself relax a little. "Good," she said. "That should do it. Now, can we get out of this swamp before I sink to my hips?"

"Of course," said Aleksander. "We'll go back to the village, and we can have a little refreshment before you leave."

As they pulled themselves to drier ground, Aleksander grabbed one of the trunks of a leafy bush that reached past his head. The trunk looked the same as that of the pole tree, but the circumference was much smaller. He scratched a cushion of tiny green leaves off the trunk to reveal the dark bark below. "This is our coffee bush," he said. "What we call coffee comes from brewing this bark."

Saoirse nodded. "Tommie told me about that. It's not that bad. I drink it."

"You have a taste for it?" Aleksander's eyebrows went up. "I must tell you I find that almost as surprising as what they're saying in the militia: that you have a taste for him. It is a strange universe."

Saoirse felt heat rise in her face. She looked over at Tommie and was gratified to see color in his cheeks as well.

"What about that plant over there?" she said to change the topic, pointing at a brownish ball that stuck out of the mud. She hoped she sounded nonchalant, as though Aleksander had not said anything about her and Tommie. The ball gave rise to a shock of long drooping leaves and a number of gray stalks that ended in a slightly concave paddle.

"We call it a wivesplant," Aleksander said. "It is interesting only in that those gray clubs are actually wood—a bit like ash from Earth, according to the references. The source of the name should be obvious: the wife can use them on the husband. No other particular interest. Why did you ask?"

"Because it looks like a bunch of hurleys growing out of a plant."

"Hurley? What's a hurley?"

Saoirse smiled. The tension among them had relaxed, at least a bit. "A hurley is like a club. It's used to hit a *sliótar*, that's like a ball, in hurling and camogie. Those are Irish sports. You hit the sliótar between the goalposts and over the crossbar to score a point, or through the posts and under the bar for a goal and three points."

"She's Irish, Tata," Tommie said. "That's why we call her Irish."

"No, it's you who calls me Irish," Saoirse retorted.

"Everyone does now," Tommie said.

"Well, you started it. It's your fault."

Aleksander laughed. "If this is the one with a taste for you, Tomasz, then I would say you deserve it. Should we go back for coffee and cakes, or will I get to watch how she uses what she calls a hurley?"

• • •

In the end, they had little coffee, less cake, and fewer words. Tommie did not want to go to his father's house, and Aleksander looked uncomfortable even as he made the offer, so the three of them sat in a little bakery across the square from the village offices. While the coffee cooled in their cups, Aleksander stared across the table at his son. Tommie stared down at his coffee cup, and although he picked it up twice, it never reached his lips. Saoirse knew that Tommie and Aleksander needed to talk to each other, but it wasn't happening, and she couldn't figure out how to get that conversation started. The brief window of relaxation she had manufactured with the talk of the wivesplant and Irish sports had closed.

The thought crossed her mind that she should get up and leave the two of them alone. But no sooner had she thought it than she decided it would be a very bad move. What would they do without her there to keep things civil?

Finally, Tommie mumbled a few words about it being a long drive. They each had reports to make, he added.

The parting was awkward and mostly silent. Saoirse felt an almost palpable relief from both Tommie and Aleksander as they said goodbye.

The little car went down the bluff outside the village, and soon the houses were hidden from view. Tommie seemed to have retreated back behind a wall, the one he held against the world for so many years, the one she thought she had broken through only a little while ago.

Say something, she told herself; *break it again*. "I'm glad you wanted to fight, Tommie," she said. "I'm glad you were ready to fight the prezydent and the city even all those years ago."

"Do you think I ran away because of that argument over fighting?" Tommie asked sharply. "Don't. I ran away because I was a rebellious, drunken little shit. I ran away from what happened to Marta. Don't make me out to be a hero over this. I'm not. Most of what my father said about me is true. Maybe all of it is."

Saoirse looked for a fingernail to bite, mostly to give herself a moment to think. She had made it worse, not better. "You need to talk with your father about all of this," she said, trying to sound emphatic. "The two of you need to talk. It's eating up both of you."

"I know that, Irish," Tommie said. "Today would have been a bad day for it, that's all. I'll be back here soon, and I'll do it. I promise."

"I told you I'll be here if you need me, and I will," she said. "Just let me know."

They made a little idle chitchat after that, but Tommie seemed to retreat into his own thoughts while he drove the vehicle as fast as the road would permit. That left Saoirse to deal with the flood that swirled through her mind. It contained much more than thoughts of Tommie and Aleksander. Everywhere she turned, it seemed, someone was dealing zombipterisin. She had been ready to kill Moore and Mouse back on Titan, no matter their protestations of how "necessary" it was. And was it any different here, where it had been "necessary" to allow the villages to stand up to the prezydent? And was that any different from the plausible explanations—or at least, ones that might sound plausible—she had come up with for all the awful things she had done?

She stared out the window as the land sped past. She had to own what she had done, but at least none of it had wrought the horror that zombie did. She couldn't help but see Caitlyn, and tried to push the image out of her mind. She didn't want to think about zombie anymore. Not right then.

She wanted to think about Tommie and not about his relationship with Aleksander. She wanted that feeling back, the one she had had when they kissed by the thunder hole. She wanted to tell Tommie that she loved him. She did, she was sure of it. But one look at his face told her she should wait for a better time. She wanted to hug him and tell him that what had happened to Marta was a tragedy, that he needed to forgive himself, and that he could love somebody now. He could love *her*.

But she couldn't hug him while he was driving, his hands clenched on the wheel, clearly brooding about his father and his past.

He'd said she was special. He had said that and she had heard it. She turned the word over in her mind, each syllable, and remembered the way he'd said it. There would be plenty of time for him to say more. She had only to wait for the right time. Those thoughts were enough to set up a roseate glow in her mind for the rest of the ride back.

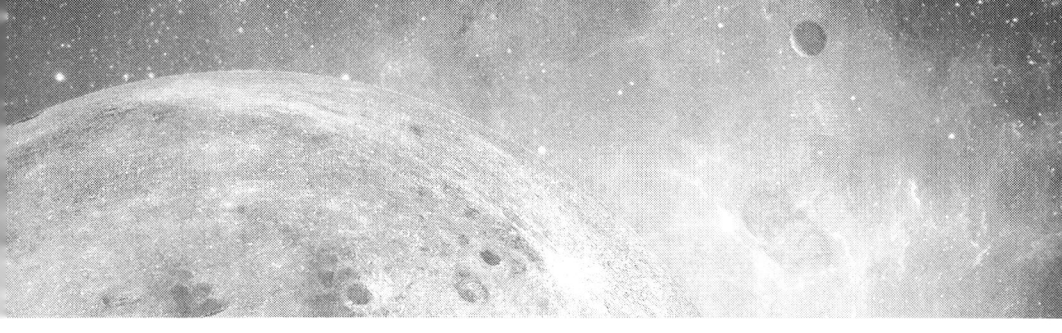

THIRTY-SEVEN

Third Platoon, Company C of the Thirty-second Battalion of Peacemakers rolled into City Center Plaza shortly after dawn, two days after Saoirse returned from Wałęsa. Aside from two of the Guards, visible by the front door of the office building that housed the prezydent's offices, the plaza was quiet and deserted. Even the buzzing tinkerbells had gone home for the night.

Saoirse sat in the front seat of the lead vehicle with a hand clamped on top of her right leg to keep her knee from bobbing up and down. She had decided she would be damned and in hell before she would let any of the peacers see how nervous she was. Nervous? Excited too. Even a bit giddy. This was the first time she had worn the body armor and helmet over her camo. It was her first operation as a peacer, the first time she had led people on a mission. True, all they were doing was searching the prezydent's offices and taking any computer equipment they found there, but the office did have Guards. Also true, before they left the base, Mwesigye had given precise instructions to each of the squads. But still . . . those Guards were armed. Would they shoot at the peacers? Saoirse had been in plenty of fights, had been beaten up more times than she remembered or wanted to count, but no one had ever deliberately tried to shoot her dead.

Well, there was that guy in a bar you've forgotten the name of in some town you can't remember either, but he didn't start out intending to kill you. It was only after . . . Goddamn it, Saoirse, why are you dredging that up now?

They pulled up in front of the office building, the statue of Jan Sobieski behind them. The other vehicles drove to their planned positions and stopped as well, with only a few squeaks from the brakes to disturb the silence. Peacers jumped out of their vehicles and ran to the positions that had been planned for them, blocking the other streets leading into the plaza. Saoirse got out as well, Mwesigye and Cyber Alves next to her, and Hopkinson with her squad behind. The two Guards watched them, but neither moved. She wondered what they were thinking. She wondered if either of them would recognize her from her visit to their training facility. Didn't matter. It was showtime.

Saoirse took a breath and strode toward the pair at the doors.

Both Guards shifted nervously as she and the other peacers approached, but they kept their positions. They wore the City Guards uniform: light-gray berets, dark-gray pants and jacket, with a red collar tab showing a plumed helmet stitched in gold. Their black boots came to mid-calf and looked like real Earth leather, even though they probably weren't. She thought it was odd that she noticed those details as she walked up to them. Both of them held rifles, but they did not point them in the direction of the peacers. My God, she thought as the growing light showed their faces, they were really young. Younger than she was. Mid-teens, at most. She walked right up to them and stopped. One of the boys licked his lips.

"We have been informed," she said in a voice she willed not to waver, "that this office contains evidence of illegal trade in zombipterisin. We are going to conduct a search and will remove computers, memory, and any other material we think could be evidence. A copy of this order is being sent now."

At her words, Cyber pressed Send on her comm.

"We cannot allow anyone in this building without proper ID or a pass," said the boy who had licked his lips. His voice shook. "You can't come in. You just can't."

Saoirse stepped close to him, practically nose to nose. "Listen to me, fucktard." She knew how a command voice sounded. She adopted it. "You two can put your play rifles down and go home, or I am going to jam the barrel of my fucking rifle up your right nostril and pull the fucking trigger."

She brought the rifle up so the end of the barrel made contact with the Guard's nose. He pulled his head back, eyes as wide as they could go. The other Guard stared, transfixed.

"Move! Now!" Saoirse shouted.

As one, both Guards dropped their rifles and bolted for the street. Saoirse glimpsed a hint of a smile on Mwesigye's face as she turned around to look at Hopkinson and her squad.

"Okay," she said, "let's do our job."

* * *

Later that afternoon, Saoirse received a summons to Venezelos' office. She found the lieutenant colonel seated behind his desk, apparently contemplating the ceiling.

"I have an interesting situation," he said after her salute. "I've been reviewing your records. Again."

He paused while her heart sank. *Not now*, she thought. *Not after all this.*

"According to these records," he went on, still gazing upward, "you're very good with computers. No education past high school, but they had you in an acting sysadmin role on Titan Station. That would make you some real self-taught hacker. Is that correct?"

"Yes, sir. Self-taught and parent-taught." Mentally, she exhaled. He was questioning a part of her record that was actually true.

"Whatever," Venezelos grunted. He leaned forward and looked straight at her. "For all I care, you took some hallucinogen, and when you woke up, you were a computer genius. I don't care. What I do care about is that of all the shit your troops hauled out of the prezydent's offices, there is one drive with nothing on it. Nothing. Everything else has the usual junk you might see in a government office—not that we've read everything they wrote—but nothing turns up on searches that could be zombie related. More specifically, there is nothing about their vehicles: no registration numbers, no driver records, no trip records. Now, those records were supposed to be there. They aren't. And there's nothing that looks like a code for that information. Except there is this one drive that is as empty as the space between the stars."

He tapped his desk. "Remember, this is Daleko Bałtyckie. There's no distributed network here. No cloud. Anything and everything to do with computers is on local storage, and this drive is empty. IT in the legate's office thinks it's a new drive. *I* think the legate's IT is incompetent. I want you to have a look at it. Tell me what was on it—if there ever was anything on it."

"I hack, sir," Saoirse said. "I'm good at that. And I did do the sysadmin job. What you're asking, though, that's forensics. I've never done that, sir."

"Neither has anyone else within God knows how many light-years." Venezelos looked tired. "Kenneally, Prezydent Strazdins and the Guards say they are stamping out the zombipterisin smuggling. That's part of their reason for building up the Guards. They're the good guys. The legate agrees. Your Colonel Szczechowicz says the opposite, and what you brought back from Wałęsa would back him up if that truck truly came from the Sobieski City Guards. The tip that came in through Bronson's sources was pretty specific about where to look and what to take. But so far, we've got nothing except this empty drive, and this raid we just conducted is going to stir a hornet's nest." He sighed. "Cyber is pretty good with the tech too. Look at it with her. Do the best you can."

. . .

Cyber looked morosely at Saoirse. "I'm glad the lieutenant colonel thinks I'm good. I only wish I were that good. I've got some tools, yes, but I've never done this."

Saoirse shrugged. "Same is true for me. Why don't we try together?"

Two hours later, Alves closed the last window on her screen and pushed her chair away from the desk, eliciting a screech from the concrete floor. "This drive has been wiped," she said. "Wiped really, really thoroughly. I don't think you could wipe it any more, unless you just ground the drive to dust. I mean, I'm pretty sure there was data on it, but I can't pull anything back. I'm sorry."

"Don't be sorry," Saoirse said. "You knew a lot more tricks than I did. Someone made sure it was clean, even if you can tell it's not new. Who would have software that good? I can't believe a city mayor on a Class Two world has access to stuff like that."

Alves nodded. "No way. We're talking military grade, peacer command maybe—I'm not even sure. The big national armies: US, Russia,

China, maybe some others. And they don't leave that kind of software lying around."

"If we sent it back to Earth, do you think they could read it?"

Alves shrugged. "I can't be sure. I doubt it, though. Whatever was there is gone for good."

"Unless the prezydent has a copy on a memory stick stuffed in a sock at the bottom of a drawer." Saoirse sighed. "I don't think we're going to be able to look through his dresser, though. I'll go give the lieutenant colonel the bad news. Thanks for trying, Cyber."

· · ·

At midnight that night, a truck stopped in front of the main entrance to the peacer base. Two men hauled a large bag from the cargo bed and dumped it on the ground. Then they drove off. When the base guards opened up the bag, they found a young man, bound hand and foot and shot between the eyes.

· · ·

The next afternoon, Saoirse's comm displayed a message ordering her to the conference room in the headquarters building. When she entered, she saw all the peacer officers except Captain Janssens of Company A, who was in the base hospital with nail-joint syndrome. To her surprise, Tommie was there as well, in the dark-blue uniform of the militia; the only one there wearing red and gold. The only person not in a uniform was Liu Honghui, the Solar Council's legate on Daleko Bałtyckie. He was also the only one standing. His posture was as tense as his face as he braced his hands on the table to lean forward and glower at Venezelos. Saoirse was glad all eyes were on the legate, allowing her to slide into a vacant chair without attracting any notice.

"Dimitris," Liu said to Venezelos as though no one else were present, "your peacers have made a complete mess. This was a tenuously balanced situation here. I need to point out that I had Prezydent Strazdins storm into my office this morning to personally file a complaint. It starts from your lieutenant threatening the life of the uniformed Guards who were carrying out their duties at his office!" At that, he scanned around the table, spotted Saoirse, who was the only woman in the room, and pointed at her. "I expect some action to be taken about her behavior."

Before Venezelos could respond, Tommie broke in. "I would expect some action," he said, "about the man who is actually dead rather than the one who ran away from his post when he was threatened. I'm sure that if Lieutenant Kenneally had actually intended to kill the Guards, they would be dead. Let's talk about the one who is dead."

Saoirse wasn't sure she could ever be as cold-blooded as Tommie was suggesting, but she was grateful for his intercession anyway. It did divert Liu from her.

"Yes, the dead man," Liu said, now focused on Tommie. "A swamper clerk in the prezydent's office. The prezydent has told me that the Guards suspect other workers blamed him for your peacers' raid. He assured me they will get to the bottom of it soon, although he did say that he considers this a part of an open rebellion—those were his words—now taking place in coastal and lowland villages. He blames this state of affairs on *your* militia, Colonel."

"Attempts at armed oppression often beget armed resistance," Tommie said. "The City Guards are not welcome in the coastal and lowland villages."

"The City Guards are the armed forces of the legitimate government of Daleko Bałtyckie!" the legate replied.

"No," said Tommie. "The government of Daleko Bałtyckie is the planetary Sejm and its elected Marshal. The facts that the Sejm has not functioned for years and the Marshal position is vacant do not change what the legitimate government is. Boris Strazdins is Prezydent of Sobieski, and the City Guards report to him in that capacity. The Guards are not the armed force of the planetary government."

"I do not need a lesson in local politics," Liu snapped. "This prezydent and his Guards represent the best chance, maybe our only chance, to bring the zombipterisin smuggling under control, a drug that comes out of *your* coastal villages and towns. If we find, as I am suspecting, that your militia is protecting the smuggling operation, I can assure you there will be very significant consequences. I have had you called here today to make sure you understand this."

Venezelos rose to his feet. "I think this meeting has deviated from its stated purpose, Legate. While I respect your concern about the prezydent's complaint, I must note, as I did when you called, that we received a very credible tip that the prezydent's offices contained information relevant to the smuggling operation and, in particular, about a ground effect truck found in a swamp that appears connected to that operation. Captain Bronson?"

Bronson appeared unruffled by the attention that focused on him. "That is correct, Lieutenant Colonel. The information came from a man working in the prezydent's offices. His position would have involved work with their vehicles. We verified his position. He has not been trading information for money in the past. He gave enough details that we could check, or knew of, that the information seemed credible."

"Thank you," Venezelos said. "Curiously, there is no information anywhere in those offices about motor vehicles, wheeled or ground effect, and no information on the people who have access to them. There is, shall we say, an unexplained blank computer drive from that office."

"For all I know, Dimitris, that drive contained a list of the prezydent's mistresses," Liu said. "This culture is straitlaced and prudish. Enough so that maybe somebody would wipe it, if that is what was actually done."

"And the killing?"

"He was our source," Bronson said. "However, I cannot say much more than that, because, ah, people are not talking to us right now."

"What we know about the situation is as Bronson and I said before," Liu said. "And you are right, Dimitris, we have strayed from our purpose. Our need is to bring the zombie situation under control. Which your militia," he again turned to Tommie, "was supposed to assist with, instead of organizing to fight the City Guards and protect the smugglers. I am telling you, I want and expect the cooperation I was promised."

Before Tommie could respond, Venezelos put his hand up. "For a Class Two world with limited settlement, the complexity of affairs is starting to resemble a Gordian knot."

"The solution to that was a sword," Saoirse said into the brief silence that followed Venezelos' statement. The comment earned her a glare from Liu, but the tiny smile on Venezelos' face was more important. Slogging through the books on Greek history and culture had been worth it.

"Well put," Venezelos said. "We are not going to continue this argument about which side is working with the smugglers when we do not have any further information. I believe it is time to use Lieutenant Kenneally's approach. We have a peacer battalion here and we need to deploy it. All Daleko Bałtyckie units need to disarm." He looked between Tommie and Liu. "All of them. While the battalion cannot cover all the coast and lowlands, we can identify hot spots, bring them under control, and seal the port. Let us put an end to it."

"Typical peacer," Liu sneered. "Dimitris, I thought better of you, but your only solution is to send the peacers into battle against everyone. You don't have the resources, and HQ on Earth is not going to give you the resources. What is more, Daleko Bałtyckie stands on the verge of admission to the Assembly of Worlds. All that is missing is for the planetary government to elect its Marshal and submit the application. Then it is for me to certify it. You would set this back years by the action you propose, and we would need to keep the peacers here for all those years too. Need I remind you of the expense involved and the need for troops elsewhere in the Reach?"

Venezelos frowned. "I am well aware of what it takes to maintain the battalion here. I am also aware that a setback to Daleko Bałtyckie's progress would deprive you of the status that comes from promoting a world to independent rank. Let us be transparent about all our interests."

Liu stiffened. "Lieutenant Colonel Venezelos, I am the legate of the Solar Council in this system, and I am exercising my authority now. You will not order this battalion or any elements of this battalion to undertake any mission outside this base without my prior agreement. Is that clear?"

Venezelos was quiet for a minute. Then he said, "I acknowledge your authority as legate. I will not order any elements of the Thirty-second Peacemaker Battalion on any mission outside of the base without obtaining your agreement. Is that satisfactory?"

"Perfectly."

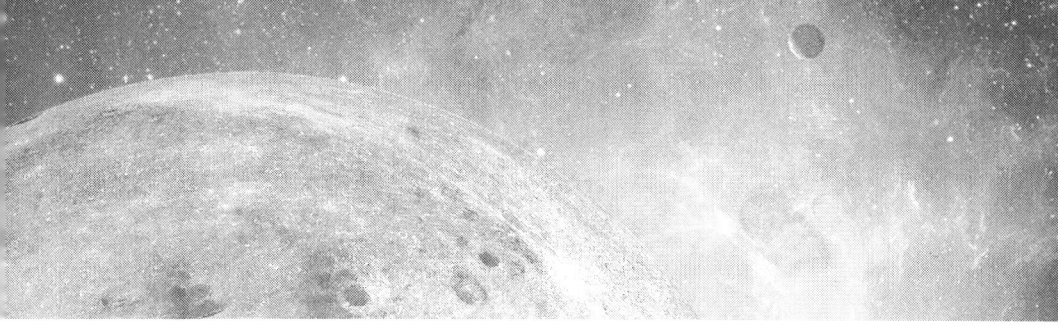

THIRTY-EIGHT

The next two days were quiet. Electric-powered drones that the battalion sent over the Sobieski area showed more Guards than usual at their training camp, but nothing to suggest they were doing anything other than training. The quiet ended early in the morning of the third day with Alves bursting into Venezelos' office in a near panic, huffing and puffing as though she had run two miles to deliver her report rather than down the corridor from the headquarters company office. Venezelos showed no emotion; his face gave no signs. With a few terse words, he ordered the long-range drone into the air. Then he watched the drone's data feed. When it stopped, he stared at the screen that showed the track of the drone. He did not like where his thoughts led. The meaning of what he had heard and seen was clear. Equally clear was what he needed to do.

The more vexing question: What was he going to use to do what he needed to do? Captain Janssens of Company A was still in the base hospital with that damned nail-joint syndrome. The docs said he would recover fully, but he would not be leading troops anytime soon. Three percent of humans who came to Daleko Bałtyckie developed nail-joint; why did Janssens have to be one of them? It was more than inconvenient. As well, Company B still did not *have* a captain, and those platoons were understrength, raided for troops to fill the holes in Companies A and C when requested replacements never arrived.

That left Company C under Gelashvilli. The company was close to full strength, and Lieutenant Mohammed in First Platoon was solid. Unfortunately, Second Platoon had lost its lieutenant to a transfer with the last ship in port, and it was also missing a squad leader. Then there was Third Platoon under Kenneally. Why couldn't she be the one in the hospital with nail-joint? True, she hadn't fucked it up, at least not yet, and the training scores for the platoon had actually improved. She had made herself useful as liaison with the militia and with the Guards. Put her in the field, though? With what was in her record? Briefly, he thought about moving Gelashvilli to Company A, then discarded the idea. Why Gelashvilli hadn't gone to a Russian-speaking unit was a mystery, but at least Company C was used to him.

Venezelos' image in the screen stared back at him with unblinking eyes. A man used the tools he was given. And made it sound like the best approach anyone could think of. And did not complain.

He reached for his comm and tapped in a message to Colonel Szczechowicz.

· · ·

The order to assemble for a briefing and orders in the HQ conference room hit Saoirse's comm when she was in the motor pool. No explanation came with it, but the word *immediately* was underlined. Mwesigye was standing next to her at the time, as they had been arguing with the sergeant in the motor pool that their Gemav engine needed an overhaul. She showed the order to him.

"I'll have the platoon ready to move out, sir," Mwesigye said, and then he left to do that.

Saoirse had lost track of the number of times she had given thanks for the existence of First Sergeant Mwesigye. She had no idea how to get the platoon ready to move out, had not gleaned the need from the terse order, and doubted she would have had the time to do it even if she had known.

When she arrived at the conference room, the occupants were Venezelos, Cyber Alves, Captains Gelashvilli and Bronson, and Tommie. Right behind her through the door was Lieutenant Mohammed, who led First Platoon.

"Close the door, Lieutenant," Venezelos said with a gesture to Mohammed. "No one else is coming."

When the door had shut and the security privacy light on the table was illuminated, he continued. "Cyber, please brief this group on what you told me."

Alves looked as though she wanted to be somewhere else, anywhere else. "We have been having difficulty maintaining electronic surveillance at the prezydent's offices, thanks to their Romanov contractors. They sweep their building and the ones the Guards use regularly, and they are pretty thorough. However," she looked at Saoirse in a way that made everyone else look there as well, "we have been able to bug the offices of the Sobieski delegates in the Sejm building, and those bugs have stayed in place.

"One is in the office of the senior delegate from Sobieski. A number of delegates from the city and highland villages have sons in the Guards. Ligas, the senior delegate from Sobieski, is one. I picked up conversation about the upcoming Sejm session. The Guards started to mobilize all their men two days ago. That's the activity we're seeing at their base. They're planning to take hostages from the coastal and lowlands villages. Then they'll call for the Sejm session. That's how they're going to make it work. They're going to take children from the villages to do it." Alves looked ready to cry.

Venezelos signaled her to stop and took over speaking. "Early this morning, our surveillance drones showed a significant troop movement by the City Guards. Six trucks and a Gemav left their highland training camp, passed through Sobieski, and took the road down to the coast. Obviously, we cannot see into the trucks, but we need to assume they are moving between one hundred fifty and two hundred soldiers."

Saoirse stiffened. She had never heard Venezelos refer to the City Guards as soldiers before. She doubted it was accidental.

"I ordered our long-range drone up to track the convoy. We followed them to the bridge over the Lower Nowy Vistula, where the Guards have that blockhouse on the road. We believe that they are traveling to Wałęsa and then to the villages farther up the coast, but at that point we lost contact with the drone."

"Communications failure, or mechanical?" asked Gelashvilli.

"Either is possible," said Venezelos in a tone that said he did not believe either. "We need to consider the possibility that it was shot down."

The room was completely quiet for a minute.

"That drone has attack and defense capabilities. Are the Guards capable of taking it down?" Gelashvilli asked.

Venezelos turned to Alves. "Cyber?"

"Romanov, where the prezydent's contractors come from, gave a peacer unit a hard fight four or five standard years ago. Based on our records, yes, they would have the tech and the know-how to do it."

Venezelos nodded. "So, the Guards have mobilized, they are moving troops in numbers they have never done before, and we have reason to believe that their solution to the impasse at the Sejm is hostages. And our long-range surveillance drone is suddenly off the air. Our only other long-range drone is in for repair, and as you know, our request for additional such drones and fuel was not filled with the last supply ship. Additional drones are not considered necessary for our mission here, especially given the difficulties with fuel for the long-range ones."

"Bronson, how is it possible we are sitting here with this information only this morning?" Tommie broke in on the tail of Venezelos' words. "You have information that they were mobilizing their men two days ago."

"It is hardly as clear as Specialist Alves has made it sound." Bronson fixed Alves with a glare, and it looked as though she wanted to shrink under the table. "Information from our devices at the Sejm building has been of very low quality. Actually, I was not aware one was located in the office of the senior delegate from Sobieski, which is a topic of another conversation, but the point is, what we have had from that location has been low quality and was not consistent with the information I have received from other sources. It is unfortunate that on this one occasion, it has yielded accurate information."

"Unfortunate." Tommie delivered the word like a sledgehammer. "That is an interesting characterization of the situation we have as a result. I brought Stanislaw's north coast company in for training because the situation was quiet, nothing was happening. The southern coast villages have their companies in place, but there is only one company for the northern coast, and those villages are open to attack now. And that is where this column appears headed. I would say that this is more than 'unfortunate.'"

"I must point out," Bronson said, "that it is clear whose fault it is for our lack of good current intelligence." He pointed at Saoirse. "We had a golden opportunity to establish an information channel by taking advantage of a relationship with one of the rising officers in the Guards. That would have certainly helped in this situation, but we lost it because this lieutenant got upset and threatened to shoot the officer in the middle of a Sobieski restaurant. I mean, there are times a woman needs to do the things a woman can do, and somehow, the idea that she was guarding her virtue and virginity is ridiculous."

Saoirse tried to clamp a mask over her features to hide the emotion that boiled up. She wanted to leap across the table. She wanted to draw a weapon and use it. It was fortunate that she had not brought a weapon into the conference room.

"That will do, Captain Bronson," said Venezelos with a tone of finality. "I am aware of the legate's confidence in your ability and his belief that you should be given great latitude; however, you are an officer in my battalion. If Lieutenant Kenneally kills you in my conference room, I might be forced to take official notice of it. Sparse as it is, the intelligence we have is what we have to work with."

"Yes, sir. But, Lieutenant Colonel, why is this man here?" Bronson pointed at Tommie. "He does not belong here and should not be privy to our intelligence or its limitations."

"He is here because I messaged him and told him to be here," Venezelos snapped. "If you need further justification for my action, *Captain* Bronson, recall that we have been clear to both the prezydent and commanders of the Guards and to Colonel Szczechowicz that if we detected aggressive action by either side, we would share that information with the other. That seemed a useful deterrent. Now it seems there is a clear risk that the peace, such as it is, will be breached. You do agree, do you not, Captain, that we are here to maintain the peace?"

"Of course, sir."

Venezelos stopped and fixed each of the others in turn with an unblinking stare from his close-set eyes. "I am glad this is all clarified so that you will understand the step we are going to take. Captain Gelashvilli, I am detaching you and the First and Third Platoons of Company C from the battalion and assigning you to Colonel Szczechowicz of the militia. He will order your movements and actions. Colonel?"

"Thank you, Lieutenant Colonel Venezelos," Tommie said. "I will take the northern coast company of the militia under my direct command, along with your platoons, to Wałęsa. Our objective is to determine what the Guards are doing and to prevent any punitive actions against the villagers. With your platoons, we will have approximately one hundred sixty effectives, and that should be adequate to deter the Guards. I was able to send a message to Wałęsa immediately after I received yours. They will have taken the children, and I hope themselves, into the swamp. That should do for the immediate term. When we arrive there, the rules of engagement will be straightforward. We will not initiate hostilities, but we will not permit hostages to be taken. If we are fired upon, we will return fire and take such action as is appropriate. Captain Gelashvilli, these rules will apply to your forces as well."

"And the legate, sir?" Gelashvilli said to Venezelos. "What about the orders he gave when he was here a few days ago?"

"Thank you for raising that point," Venezelos said. "The orders I received are not to order any unit of this battalion on a mission outside the base. I am obeying those orders. What I have done is to detach your company from the battalion, and I have put you under the command of Colonel Szczechowicz. You will, of course, obey the orders he gives you. This may be a fine point, but I think the distinction is clear."

"It is very clear, sir," said Gelashvilli.

"Alves," Bronson said, "you go with Gelashvilli. They will probably need your skill set, and I do not need you here. I'll handle intelligence and coordinate with the legate's office."

Alves looked as if she hoped Venezelos would object, but he did not. Venezelos only glanced around the room to see if there were any other questions. None were proffered.

"Thank you for the loan of your troops, Lieutenant Colonel Venezelos," Tommie said. "This is the right decision, and not one the Guards and their Romanov friends will have anticipated."

"I hope so," Venezelos replied. "Do what you need to do."

Tommie nodded. "Captain Gelashvilli, be on the road in thirty minutes. My militia unit will join you on the road down to the coast."

Saoirse felt a lump in her throat that would not go away, even with a hard swallow. This was not supervising a raid on an office when there was no force that could truly oppose the peacers. This time, they might be riding into a real fight. How was she going to know what to do? Would she be able to figure it out? She desperately wanted to talk to Tommie. When she looked for him, however, he was already gone. The only thing for her to do was to find Mwesigye and her platoon and pray that she looked like a tough and ready peacer, regardless of how she felt on the inside.

. . .

Saoirse rode in the front seat of the first wheeled peacer truck, right behind the Gemav that carried Captain Gelashvilli and Tommie. By the time they reached the junction of Highway 1 from Sobieski with the Coastal Highway, the third cigarette from the pack she had bought from one of the militia had burned down almost to her fingertips. Her mind was focused on minimizing the up-and-down bounce of her leg so that Mwesigye, who was driving, wouldn't notice it. Her free hand checked again for her little leather journal; she had stuffed it into the left breast pocket of her camo, now under the body armor. She'd been sure she would have feelings or make mistakes that she should note, but now it seemed silly to have brought it. When was she going to have time to make notes? Then the ash did reach her fingers and she gasped and crushed the butt out on the dash. Even with the retardant, cigarettes burned fast on Daleko Bałtyckie.

She swore—under her breath, she hoped—and pulled out another one. It was plump and irregular, hand-rolled Earth tobacco grown on Daleko Bałtyckie, strong and harsh on the throat. She fumbled with the hot-stick lighter she had also bought, still not accustomed to cigarettes that had to be lit and not merely inhaled.

Mwesigye chuckled. "May want to watch those, Lieutenant, in case you need your wind. Looks like you're going to make your stars soon enough."

"My wind will be fine," Saoirse said. "If nothing else, the oxy here will cover me."

She leaned out the window to look at the three trucks with the platoon and Tommie's militia company and a Gemav behind them. Bringing up the rear was the comm car, a wheeled vehicle bristling with antennae, a signal booster, and a converter to guarantee their communications with the base. One hundred sixty peacers and militia to do . . . what? Impress the Guards? Overawe the Guards? Fight the Guards? The loaded weapons and body armor she and the peacers wore said they were ready to fight. The militia were not wearing body armor, but that was because they didn't have it. Their weapons were loaded as well. She pulled her head back in. Most of the panels on the dash of the truck were dark, but that was not because a fight wasn't imminent. Mwesigye had shut off the panels and screens because there was no satellite overhead to transmit GPS or enemy positions, and no drone in the air ahead to send vid of what was in front of them.

Mwesigye, his face relaxed, looked as if he were out for a drive in the country—until she glanced at the armor, grenades, and weapons that adorned his frame. Was she going to make her stars? Jesus Christ on a stick! That wasn't why she had come to Daleko Bałtyckie. The fourth cigarette was almost finished.

The convoy swung onto the Coastal Highway and came to the Nowy Vistula, across the bridge from the blockhouse and its comm antennae. Unlike her drive of a few days ago with Tommie, they found the gate down, barring the road to traffic. Two armed Guards stood by the gate, one with his hand up in the universal *stop* signal. Two more Guards came out of the blockhouse behind them. Their rifles were at the ready. The Gemav in front of Saoirse's truck crossed the bridge, then slowed to a stop, its nose almost touching the gate.

"By order of the prezydent of Sobieski, this road is closed to traffic beyond this point!" shouted the Guard with his hand up.

"I do not think that is correct," said Captain Gelashvilli in his heavily accented English.

He raised a hand, and the roof over the rear of the Gemav retracted. A recoilless rocket launcher rose into firing position, manned by a peacer behind a shield. The rocket tube aimed at the blockhouse. Mwesigye loosened a pistol in its holster on his belt.

"My friend, are you planning on dying today?" Gelashvilli asked.

The Guard who had his hand raised looked at his mate, who tapped his comm and then pressed on his earpiece. He looked back at the first Guard and shook his head. At that, the first Guard's stop signal changed to a *go-ahead* wave. All four Guards walked back to the blockhouse as the barrier swung up and out of the way to leave the road open.

Mwesigye grinned. "Sensible man. They want to live to go home for dinner. Word's gone on ahead, though, Lieutenant. Count on it. You're making your stars this trip for sure now."

THIRTY-NINE

Something was wrong in the village of Wałęsa. Saoirse sensed it as soon as the truck topped the low rise in the road up from the swampland and crossed the village's firebreak. She couldn't tell what had set off her internal alarm, not at first. It was a feeling of wrongness, and she'd had it before in other places and times. She remembered vividly the time it had warned her not to go into that alley with the guy who was urging her on. It had probably saved her life more than once.

Of course, people might have differing opinions on whether your life is worth saving, and your parents might well be among them— Goddamn it, Saoirse, now is not the time. Shut up!

She took a furtive look over at Mwesigye. He seemed to have the same feeling. The relaxed posture from earlier was gone; he was alert behind the wheel, his eyes sweeping the road and surroundings.

Saoirse studied the outlying parts of the village as they drove in, trying to get to the root of her unease. No one was out, working or otherwise. No kids were playing tag around the solar panels. Tommie had said that he messaged the village to take their children and go into the swamp. Maybe that was all it was.

"I'd have your rifle ready, Lieutenant," Mwesigye said.

Saoirse checked it, her mouth suddenly gone dry. The little convoy turned onto the street that led to the village square and came to a sudden halt. She could see bodies on the ground in the square—counted eight of them, two in militia uniforms and six in the uniform of the Guards.

Tommie spoke into his microphone, ordering his northern coast company to spread out and watch the flanks.

"First Platoon," Gelashvilli's voice sounded in her earbuds, "stay with the vehicles. Third Platoon with me. Let's see what happened here."

Tommie left his vehicle and walked over to the bodies. "Something is wrong," he said. He bent over the two bodies in militia uniforms and studied their faces. "I do not recognize either one. I know my men. Makes me wonder if the ones in Guards uniforms are really Guards."

Gelashvilli gestured for some of the peacers to check the stores across from the village offices. He turned toward those offices with his sergeant major. Saoirse and Tommie were alongside him.

Before they could reach the building, the front doors opened and two men walked out, one an officer in the Guards with major's tabs on his collar and a pistol in his hand. The other wore a black uniform, like the Romanovs Saoirse had seen at the training camp. He had no sign of rank, held a rifle in his hands, and wore a helmet with a dark combat visor that covered most of his face.

"Ivars!" Tommie shouted. Saoirse recognized the name as that of the man who had not shown up the evening she interrupted Tommie's meeting at Nowy Zoni. "Now we see your true colors. What has happened here?"

"I should think it is fairly obvious," Ivars said. "Your militia launched an unprovoked attack on the City Guards. The peacers joined you in the attack. The casualties," he swept the pistol around the square, "speak for themselves."

That drew a harsh laugh from Gelashvilli. "Pure bullshit," he said.

"I don't think so," Ivars responded. "We have vid. It may not be terrific quality, but we will note that the people who took it were being shot at."

"You say you have vid," Gelashvilli growled. "What do you think we have?"

"Not much," Ivars answered. "Considering you are surrounded."

The man in the black uniform spoke into a microphone by his mouth. His voice was too soft for Saoirse to hear, but immediately afterward, the church doors opened and three more men in black came out onto the top step, leveled rifles in their hands. More rifles appeared at the windows fronting the square, and more men appeared from behind buildings at the entrance to the square, trapping the arrivals.

"Peacers and militia!" Ivars' voice rang out, amplified by a small microphone at his jaw. "Drop your weapons immediately! You are surrounded. Anyone raising or continuing to hold a weapon will be shot." Across the square, rifles tumbled to the ground, Saoirse's among them. "The coastal and lowland villages will provide their children as hostages for the good behavior of their delegates," Ivars said. "Once this is done, the Sejm will be called into session. Boris Strazdins will be elected Marshal, and the Sejm will grant him full power of government. In view of the massacre here of our Guards, I expect the Marshal will dissolve the militia and demand that the legate order the peacers off the planet. We will have peace and order then."

"So this is your grand plan," Tommie said. "You are going to make war on children."

"Hardly," Ivars replied. "They will be a pledge of good behavior. Nothing more than that. We know they have been taken into the swamp. They cannot stay there very long." He paused. "When it comes to putting children in harm's way and leaving them to die, you would be the expert. Do you plan to do that again?"

Tommie stepped closer to Ivars. "As a man," he said, "you look like an abortion."

Ivars smiled, then shot Tommie twice in the stomach.

Saoirse screamed, dashed forward, and threw herself down at Tommie's side. She pressed her hands over the wounds to try to stop the bleeding. It was futile.

From above her, she heard Ivars say, "Go to your lover, you stupid little girl. That's all you are and all you're good for."

Saoirse looked down, saw Tommie's blue eyes looking up at her. "It doesn't hurt so much," he said.

The man in black spoke into his microphone again, and the men at the church fired a series of shots at the peacers and militia. Gelashvilli and the sergeant major fell. So did the other officers, peacers and militia.

"We know who your officers are," Ivars said, his voice amplified, "and they are dead now, all of them. If you surrender and follow all instructions, you will be treated well. Peacers will be released unharmed for transport off-planet. Hands on your heads and surrender! Or you can all die now!"

Saoirse heard the words as if from a great distance. Time seemed to have stopped. All the officers were dead? What about her? Of course, they thought she was only a stupid little girl who didn't count. She looked back down at Tommie. His breathing labored. One of his hands tugged weakly at her arm.

"Irish," he whispered, "save my world, Irish. Please save my world."

Saoirse blinked, tried to focus. Tommie's blood was on her hands, on her camo. She looked at the blood. In that instant, a white-hot rage exploded inside her. It was different from her usual inchoate anger, different from any burst of anger she had ever had. It was focused. She wanted to kill.

She looked around. Guards were coming into the square to round up the disarmed militia and peacers. No one paid attention to her; no one was even looking at her. Her rifle was where she had dropped it, not too far away. She got her legs under her and, with a scream, launched herself into a dive for the rifle. She grabbed it, rolled, and came to a stop on her knees with the rifle in her hands. Bullets sprayed the ground ahead of her, where her roll would have taken her had she continued it. She brought the rifle up, sighted, and fired three quick shots. Bloody red comets burst from the heads of each of the riflemen in black in front of the church and splattered across the church doors.

Pandemonium erupted in the village square. City Guards fired wildly, hitting peacers, militia, and other Guards who had gone into the square to get their prisoners. Peacers and militia scrambled after the weapons they had dropped and returned fire just as wildly. Men screamed and fell and screamed some more.

"You should have killed the stupid little girl!" Saoirse yelled. She looked for Ivars to kill him and for the man in black who had stood with him. She did not see either one.

Bullets whistled around her. One struck a glancing blow at her chest, across the body armor. It spun her to the side and staggered her, but she stayed upright. Only a groove in the body armor, and no blood showed. She saw a head at a window across the street and shot it. Bullets flew all around. She should get down, take cover, do something. What?

Voices yelled, "Lieutenant!"

"Lieutenant, get out of there!" That bellow was from Mwesigye. "You have to leave them."

That penetrated. She focused again. Saw bodies on the ground, one across a windowsill. She found her voice.

"Peacers! Militia! To me! Retreat!"

A rocket streak flashed from a window, hit the comm car, and detonated. The car was blasted into the air, landing in ruin. Bullets riddled the tires of all their wheeled trucks.

"Retreat with me!" she shouted as she backed down the road, firing whenever she saw movement. She wanted to kill Guards, and she didn't care about their bullets.

. . .

That retreat was more like a helter-skelter dash out of Wałęsa that ended with the peacers and militia crouched in the shelter of the low rise where the road came up from the swamps. Some of the troopers looked as if they were trying to dig themselves into the dirt. Others held their rifles above the bluff with their heads down and fired blindly in the direction of the village. Saoirse remembered Adelayo scornfully calling that type of shooting "spray and pray."

"Stop it!" she shouted. "Stop it! It's a waste of ammunition." She was joined by Mwesigye, and she had to admit, his roar was far more effective.

Once the spraying and praying had ended, quiet fell. No shots reached out for them. A cautious peek over the top of the bluff revealed no enemies. The Guards were still back in the village.

Saoirse took the time for another glance at where the bullet had struck her body armor and poked at it with a finger. There was a hole in the armor; the bullet had penetrated. Right below was her leather journal. The bullet had struck the spine of the journal and deflected. Instead of ending up in her lung, it had made an exit hole in her camo over her abdomen. She shook her head with a sense of wonder, as though this had happened to someone else and she was looking at them. Apparently, God did not want her to die. Yet.

"The Guards had four Romanov contractors with them," Mwesigye said. "You killed three of them back in the square. They may be pretty confused and scrambled right now, but they will come after us. It will only take them a bit to get reorganized. Our vehicles are blown, even if we could get to them, and I do not think we can. This slope gives us a little protection, but the flanks are open; it will be easy to get around us when they think of it. What are your orders, Lieutenant?"

"What?" Saoirse's head snapped around and away from the hole in her armor. She stared at Mwesigye.

"You're the only officer left," he said in a quiet voice. "The others are dead, peacer and militia. You are in command."

The words sank like a stone in Saoirse's stomach. She was in command? The first thought through her mind was that this was a very, very bad joke. But it was no joke. Mwesigye's face was serious. What the fuck was she supposed to do?

"Cyber!"

"Yes, sir."

Somehow, Alves was at her elbow, face pale, eyes wide, pupils the size of black coins. Alves hadn't made her stars yet. She would today, if she lived through it. *Well, that makes two of us*, Saoirse thought.

"Are you in contact with the base?" Saoirse asked.

"No," Alves answered. "The comm car . . . My God, if I hadn't gotten out before—" She caught herself and stopped. When she started to speak again, for all the strain on her face, her voice was steady. "Without the comm car, we need the tower at the blockhouse on the Nowy Vistula for relay, and they're blocking us. I can't reach anyone." She bit down hard on her lip.

Saoirse was spared from coming up with an immediate response by a scream from behind her. One of the teenage militiamen had been shot in the arm, and the peacer medic was bandaging it.

"Put a man face on, boy," growled one of the older militiamen. "You have to deal with it, so no point crying."

"We'll get home," said another boy standing next to him. Saoirse recognized Andrzej from the training ground. "Irish will get us out of this. Be sure of it."

Fuck. That was the only word Saoirse could think of. Fuck, fuck, fuck. *She* was going to get them out of this mess? How? She hefted the comm in her hand. Before she had lost her comm on Earth, she was accustomed to finding five, ten, or even more how-to vids on anything she wanted to do. Even if the Guards were not blocking their connections, she doubted she would find a vid on how to extricate a surrounded company from disaster. She stared at the comm. And it struck her.

"Cyber!" she yelled. "Shut down the electronics. All of it! Everyone, comms off! We may not be able to connect, but they can track us by the electronics."

Mwesigye repeated the order, and she saw troopers hurry to comply. One peacer grumbled, "Was that something they taught in the Officers' School you supposedly went to?"

He was immediately challenged by Andrzej. "You listen to Lieutenant Irish! Our colonel respected her. You need to do the same."

For a moment, it looked as though a fight would break out, but then the peacer only shook his head and turned away. He did shut down his comm.

What, Saoirse wondered, had Tommie told his militia about her? That thought brought up other thoughts of Tommie, and she tried to block them behind a wall. She had no time for feelings. Even if she could see his blue eyes looking up at her, even if she could hear his last words to her, she could not afford to feel anything. She needed to do something. Anything was better than nothing.

"Sergeant," she said to Mwesigye, "we're going to retreat back into the swamp, back down the road."

"Yes, sir."

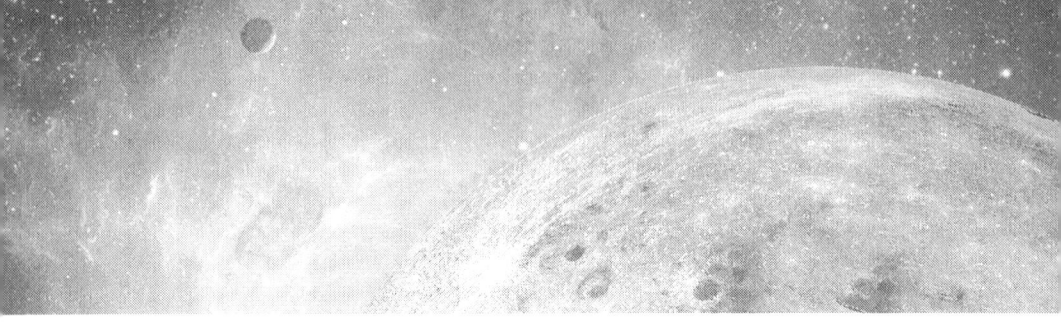

FORTY

The troops strung out along the road in a ragged column. Saoirse walked point with Mwesigye because that was where she thought she should be as the *de facto* company commander. Her platoon followed, with the remnants of First Platoon, now under Sergeant Stephenson, behind them. The peacers had lost thirteen, in addition to their other officers, in the fight at Wałęsa, but enough sergeants and corporals remained that the organization of Company C was unchanged. The militia walked behind the peacers, in no particular order. Without any body armor, they had lost more heavily; only forty-eight remained. As with the peacers, the officers had been targeted and gunned down at the beginning. Only one sergeant had survived the bloody firefight. Saoirse was sure that they needed to be reorganized in some fashion, but she didn't know how to do it and was afraid to ask. Since the militia came along of their own accord and without questions, she pushed that issue to the back of her mind with a promise to worry about it later.

Soon they were back in the swamplands. One person in each peacer section carried a laser saw, so they felled pole trees here and there and dropped them across the road to slow down any pursuit. The pole trees grew thickly all around the road, but their tiny leaves at the crowns and tops let plenty of light down to the swamp below, where shorter trees and other vegetation grew profusely. Despite the light, the day darkened rapidly as the sky above became a sold mass of thick gray clouds that promised rain. *Just what we need,* Saoirse thought sourly, *a drenching rain with no vehicles, no shelter, and swamp on both sides.*

Just as concerning was the matter of food. If they maintained their pace, they would cover the distance to the blockhouse on the Nowy Vistula in two days, three at the most. They had enough rations in their packs for that, but there would be no help from the Guards there. Was there a way to sneak around the blockhouse, or would they have to fight their way across the bridge? She didn't know, but either way, they would have a full day's march on empty stomachs from the Nowy Vistula to the base outside Sobieski. That assumed that the distance and their rate of march were what she thought. She was not going to have Cyber turn on any of the electronics, and she was equally unwilling to check any of her assumptions with Mwesigye. It was bad enough that the peacers probably thought she didn't know what she was doing. She didn't want to make them certain of it. All that calculation assumed that the Guards back in Wałęsa allowed them to stroll away down the road. Her thoughts kept circling back to that question until her concern about it exceeded her fear of looking ignorant.

"Do you think they will let us get away without a fight?" she asked Mwesigye.

"No, sir." He paused long enough for three long strides. "I don't think we hurt them bad enough to keep them from coming after us once they get organized and get their vehicles around where ours were shot up. Once they do that, they'll come fast. I don't think they have a choice."

"They don't have a choice?" Saoirse asked. "Why?"

"They shot up a peacer company," Mwesigye said. "Killed our officers in cold blood. If it were just militia, and maybe that's all they thought was coming, maybe that wouldn't be such a big deal. We all heard what they said in the square about having vid of militia killing their Guards, never mind that it's fake. They stage their election, tell their story, bribe some people, stall until they apply to be an independent world, maybe they get away with it. But they attacked peacers. They can only make that story work if we're prisoners with no officers, or better yet, if we're dead. So they have to come after us. How does that sound, Lieutenant?"

"Bad," she said, "as in bad news." Had he emphasized the word *lieutenant*?

"What are you thinking, sir?"

Her thoughts went back to the streets and shelters where she had lived for a while. What would happen without any police on the street or any authority in the shelters? She knew the answer. Maybe there were many things she didn't know how to do, but she wasn't squeamish about what she knew she had to do.

"When they come, we kill them first." She didn't look at Mwesigye. Was he surprised? It was a grand statement, but she couldn't simply tell Mwesigye to make it happen. Or, maybe she could. Or should.

If you weren't such a miserable liar and a fake and had ever paid attention and learned anything, you would be okay asking for help, but you can't, because then everyone will know you don't know shit and— Shut up, Saoirse!

She shut down the inner recriminations and told herself to think about what they should do. The road was more of a causeway now, with standing water on both sides. Flexi-ferns, low trees, coffee trees, and wivesplants grew thickly among the pole trees on both sides of the road. The air felt as thick as the foliage, like a veil of mist that merged with the pools and puddles on the ground. Tinkerbells and bigger fliers clouded the air around them. Up ahead, the road curved right to go around a thick stand of pole trees. The Guards would be coming in trucks and cars.

"Let's do it here," Saoirse said. She stopped and turned around. The column bunched up behind her.

"Hopkinson," she pointed at the corporal, "take your squad and chop down a bunch of the pole trees just past the curve so the road is blocked, and blocked good. Chop 'em so it's not obvious from here. Then get your squad behind the barricade and cover the road. Everybody else," she raised her voice, "off the road on the left side, all along the road up to the blockade. Make sure you can see the road. I fire the first shot; nobody shoots until I do. Then kill them all. Militia, do you understand me?"

She heard scattered shouts of "Yes, Irish!" from the back of the column, and the militia moved off the road. Among the peacers not in her platoon, she heard one grumble, "They'll just run off to the other side and shoot us when we go after them. We should get them from both sides."

"Idiot," she heard another say in response, "then we'd wind up shooting into our own. Do what you're told."

Was she right? Saoirse wondered. Or did the idiot have it right? Too late to change her mind. She looked for Mwesigye to see if she could read approval in his face, but he was already moving down the line, making sure the peacers and militia were off the road in good positions. She took that as approval. He wouldn't do that if he disagreed. Or would he?

She shook herself and moved to a position by the curve in the road. From there, she could see down the road they'd come from to her right, and she also had a good view of the growing blockade of pole trees to her left, where Hopkinson's squad would be hidden. All she had to do was pick the right moment to fire the shot that would trigger the ambush. Ironic, she thought, that she had chosen for that task the peacer who was least likely to know when to fire. She could hardly ask Mwesigye when to shoot. Another bad choice. No, it was worse. It was unclear. She didn't know if it was a bad choice.

It was hot and sticky where she crouched among the plants. Moisture from the air condensed on her armor and helmet and soaked into her camo. The wait felt interminable. She rolled up the sleeves of her camo in a futile attempt to get comfortable. Maybe they should have kept going. Maybe the Guards were stuck behind the pole trees they had cut down before. Maybe they weren't coming after all. How long would her troops be standing wet and miserable in water and muck because of a choice she had made? How long would they wait? And what would they do if they got back on the road and *that* was when the pursuing Guards arrived? However it went wrong, it would be her fault. Again, she ordered herself to stop dwelling on her inadequacies.

She felt herself shaking. She wanted to go somewhere else so no one would see her shake, even though the screen of plants was so thick that she could not see anyone on either side.

No. She knew what she had to do. For once, she would have to shut off her fears and her stupid emotions, and she would have to do it without alcohol or drugs. She told herself that for the first time in the entirety of her useless and miserable existence, she would have to be worthy. Worthy of what? Of the men and women who might die in this swamp because *she* had decided they would fight in this place, and in this way. She could hear herself saying she couldn't do that. She heard her inner voice again, the one that told her she was weak, different, an outsider, a failure; the one she always listened to.

"Shut up, Saoirse." Shocked, she realized she had said it out loud.

"Lieutenant?" That was Mwesigye, a little to her right, completely hidden. "I couldn't hear what you said."

"Nothing, Sergeant. I was only thinking out loud."

And then something clicked in her mind. *This is not all about you*, she told herself. *It's not all about Saoirse Kenneally.* It was about Caitlyn, a little girl she never knew. It was about Tommie. She saw them both in her mind's eye. It was about the men and women who lived on Daleko Bałtyckie and those in the peacers and militia who followed her. She would give it her best effort, and that would be what she could give them. Because it was about them, and not about Saoirse Kenneally. She patted the snake on her arm. It was going to be okay. She should think of a name for the snake while she waited, but then she saw the cab of a truck appear on the road that led back to the village. It was almost time.

Wait for it, she thought. *Wait for it. Wait for it.* The truck seemed to inch forward at a crawl. From her position at the curve, she could see a line of vehicles behind the truck: four more trucks and two cars. She could see the Romanov, the man who wore black, in the car immediately behind the lead truck. She thought Ivars was seated next to him but could not be certain. She worried that one of the militia boys would open fire before the line of vehicles was completely in the trap, but that did not happen. Those boys obeyed the woman they called Irish even as she had trouble believing that woman was her. *Wait.*

The lead truck rolled into the curve and came to a stop as the driver saw the barricade of felled pole trees across the road.

"Wozinski, take your men and clear those damned trees." The words, in a harsh accent, came from the Romanov.

Half a dozen men jumped out from the back of the lead truck. Saoirse wanted to shoot the man in black. Instead, she shot the driver of the lead truck through the windshield.

Hellfire erupted from the barricade and the side of the road where her troopers were concealed. The men who had gotten out of the truck fell immediately. Gunfire shot back from the vehicles. Screams and groans filled the air. The road was a scene of chaos.

The Romanov, his voice amplified, screamed for the Guards to charge into the vegetation where the attack came from. He had an automatic rifle in his hands and sprayed bullets into the cover at the curve of the road where Saoirse and others were hidden. Bullets ripped through the leaves around her. She dropped into the muck, heard screams nearby. She popped back up, unscathed, felt tingly, felt *alive* on top of the fear. She saw the man in black firing into the bushes to her right. She shot him then.

Saoirse spotted Ivars as he jumped off the edge of the road into the water and charged into the bushes with other Guards, trying to get at their unseen assailants. She moved at an angle to cut off the path she thought he was taking.

Rifle at the ready, Ivars burst through a screen of flexis almost directly in front of her. Before he could bring his rifle around to shoot her, she swung hers like a club and caught him across his chin. He dropped his weapon and fell on his back in the mud. Saoirse stepped over him and slammed the butt of her rifle down on his head. She brought it straight up and slammed it down again.

And again.

And again.

Bloody droplets spattered across her camo, her body armor, her face. She drove the butt of her rifle back down into his head again.

And again.

And again.

"He's done, Lieutenant." Mwesigye's voice.

Saoirse stopped, straightened up, and looked down at the bloody pulp that had been Ivars' head. She thought she was supposed to feel revulsion or nausea, but she felt nothing. She was sure she should not have felt that tingly, excited sensation she had when bullets were flying, people were shooting at her, and she was shooting them. One more thing wrong with her. But she had no time to worry about it. She grabbed a bunch of leaves and wiped as much blood as she could from the stock of her rifle and her hands. Plenty of blood remained. She turned around to look at Mwesigye.

"It's over," he said. "A few of them got away into the swamp. Not many. I wouldn't bother trying to chase them."

Saoirse nodded without saying anything and moved for the road. It was an effort to pull her boots out of the sucking mud to take a step. Where had her energy gone?

The roadway was littered with the bodies of dead Guards. They were strewn on the road, hung over the windows and doors of vehicles, and lying dead inside those vehicles. All the bodies she saw were Guards. The dead peacers and militia were still hidden in the swamp. The Romanov in the black uniform lay sprawled where Saoirse had shot him. Mwesigye walked over to the corpse and prodded it with his foot.

"Not worth your contract, were you?" he asked rhetorically. "You came on fast to be sure we didn't get away, so you didn't have flankers out who could have found what we were doing. Too damn sure of yourself."

Beyond Mwesigye, other peacers and militia were emerging onto the road, checking bodies to make sure they were dead, and looking into the bullet-riddled cars and trucks.

"Plenty of food here!" a peacer from the First Platoon shouted from one of the trucks. "I won't say it's good, but it's enough to get us home."

"Not just food," another voice replied. "There are comms here. Bastards won't be blocking their own comms. We hack them, and we can contact the base."

At the word *comms*, a chill went down Saoirse's spine. "Nobody touches any of the comms!" she shouted. "Cyber, where are you?"

"Here, sir." Alves clambered up onto the roadway and ran to where Saoirse stood. "I heard. I can hack them; I'm sure."

"Wait. Our electronics have been off," Saoirse said, "so the Guards couldn't track us. But back in Sobieski, they're going to know where this unit was, where the vehicles *are*. Even if these Guards had no chance to tell their bosses what was happening when we opened fire, the ones in Sobieski are going to figure it out pretty quick when nobody answers a message and the position of the vehicles doesn't change relative to the tower at the crossing. Right?"

"Yes," Alves said.

Saoirse turned back to Mwesigye. "Do the Guards have any aircraft?"

"No warplanes, no," he said. "They can't make them here, and they can't ship them here—not just for the space they would take up on an interstellar but because of the fuel and the maintenance facilities they need. But they do have a few light planes and helicopters. Nothing big, due to the fuel situation, but they would be able to fly over. You could put a machine gun in something like that, like they did in the First World War on Earth. And anybody can make a Molotov cocktail and toss it. You don't need gasoline."

"*Meu Deus!* My God!" Alves screamed. "Fire! With the percent oxy in the atmosphere, even wet plants can burn!"

"Everybody away from the road!" Saoirse shouted. "Out into the swamp, into water. Now! Move! Move!"

Saoirse saw confusion and doubt on the faces of the peacers near her. Would they obey her and follow her? The militia showed no hesitation. Those who were on the road jumped off immediately. That was enough to sway the peacers. First singly, then in groups, they left the road carrying any wounded they had just brought out of the swamp. Any hesitation ended when a buzzing sound came from above. They watched from the swamp as a small plane, flying not much higher than the top of the pole trees, came into view. The side doors of the plane were open. The same tiny leaves on the pole trees that allowed sunlight to the floor of the swamp forest opened the road to the occupants of the plane. The rat-a-tat-tat of a machine gun hosing the road and the surrounding swamp with bullets came soon after. Peacers and militia on the ground fired upward, but only forced the plane higher. It circled around, and two small objects trailing fire tumbled out. Where they hit, fire caught among the greenery. The peacers and militia were already on the move, but the fire grew fast.

Quickly, the flames leaped high and jumped from plant to plant. The entire stretch of road where the ambushed vehicles stood was engulfed in fire, and it kept spreading. Pole trees caught despite their resistant bark and turned into columns of fire, flames and smoke a hundred feet and more in the sky. As the crowns and fronds of the pole trees caught fire, burning leaves and branches fell into the swamp. Flaming pole trees fell, and the fire spread even faster.

Saoirse ran from the inferno as fast as the gooey muck would let her go. The heat on her back built up and spurred her to greater effort to put distance between her and the flames. Alves and Mwesigye were with her, but she could see no sign of anyone else. She could only hope they were staying ahead of the flames as she was, but how long she could do so was unclear. Sooner or later, the fire would leap ahead of them or their strength would fail.

Salvation came from the skies. Thunder boomed. The heavy gray clouds released their first fat drops of rain. The intensity of the rain built swiftly, until they were surrounded by sheets of falling water that hid all the forest more than a few feet away behind a curtain. Where they had dreaded the thought of being drenched on the road and having to march soaked to the skin, now they welcomed the rain as a savior. Saoirse dropped to her knees in a puddle of water and raised her arms to the sky. The rain spattered off her armor, ran down her back, and soaked all of her as thoroughly as the bog did her legs, but the fire no longer chased her.

The downpour continued for nearly two hours and smothered the flames.

PART IV
THE POINT

Attack where he is not prepared; go by way of places
where it would never occur to him you would go.

SUN TZU
The Art of Warfare

Why is it that in battle, within sight of thousands of horrible deaths
nearby, there was no trace of fear in my soul? What does it mean?

NADEZHDA DUROVA
*The Cavalry Maiden: Journals of a Russian Officer
in the Napoleonic Wars*

FORTY-ONE

After the rain stopped, the clouds moved off, leaving a bright, blue late-afternoon sky. The smoke had been washed out of the sky, although its smell remained at the floor of the forest. Saoirse staggered over to a charred pole tree and leaned against it. Mwesigye and Alves were still with her, but no one else.

"How can we reassemble?" Saoirse asked.

"I can turn on the electronics and all the comms by remote," Alves said. "Do you want me to do that?"

"No," Saoirse said. "They'll ping the tower at the Nowy Vistula. That's only giving them another chance to kill us."

Mwesigye nodded. "The troops will all head back to the ambush site," he said. "That's the only move that makes sense."

The swampland they crossed on the way back to the road was an open-air charnel house. All that had been bright and yellow-green was black. Ash floated on the standing water and coated the ground. The remains of pole trees stuck up into the air and reminded Saoirse of the charcoal sticks she had drawn with in elementary school. The occasional charred body of an amphibian floated in a pond here and there.

The roadway, when they reached it, was no better. The concrete surface had been blackened and cracked from the extreme heat. One section had fallen into the swamp below the causeway. The vehicles they had ambushed were little more than blackened metal skeletons, and the bodies of the men who died there had been reduced to shapeless lumps.

"Jesus," Saoirse said softly as she turned around. The view was the same in all directions. "I understand why they're so paranoid about fire here."

Slowly, singly, in pairs and small groups, others made their way to the road through the wasteland of burnt swamp forest. After about two hours, forty-one peacers and thirty-six militia had mustered on the road, not quite half the troops that had ridden to Wałęsa what felt like an eon ago. The peacers stood grouped by their squads and sections, whatever was left of them. The militia showed no order, an amorphous group of boys and old men.

All of them were looking at Saoirse. No, they were looking *to* her and waiting *for* her. It took her a moment to realize why. She was the *officer*; she was *in command*. That mattered to the battered fragment of the troops on the road. She thought about that and decided that this wouldn't be the first time she had made up everything as she went along. She had promised to do her best, and she had to do it.

"Sergeant Mwesigye," she said, "match up the militia with our units. We're not much more than two platoons altogether. It will go better if they have some organization."

Then she held her breath. Should she have told Mwesigye how to divide up the militia? However, he said only, "Yes, sir," and walked down the road to carry out her order. She looked at the troops—*her* troops, she reminded herself—while Mwesigye was doing the organizing. At first they looked dazed by the destruction around them, but that wore off quickly. They looked, in fact, ready to fight, even if they had nothing to fight with except what they carried. They were uniformly filthy, covered in mud and ash, although the mud was drying in the sun. Saoirse was as dirty as they were. She looked at one of her hands and saw dirt in every pore. Each fingernail was outlined in black. The sight brought a grin to her face. At least the nails had never turned black.

"What do we do now, Irish?"

The question came from Andrzej. Saoirse found a second to be glad he was alive. The question demanded an answer, though, and a quick one. Another one of the militiamen took it up and suggested a return to Wałęsa.

"Our homes, our families are there and in the villages farther north on the road. We need to be there to protect them, for when they send more bastards to do the job this lot started."

"No," Saoirse said. "That's not the way to protect your families. There are not enough of you to defend Wałęsa, even if the peacers stay. And we can't. You have no real defenses there. It would only turn your homes into a battlefield. That's a battle you can't win."

"Then what are you saying we should do, Lieutenant Irish?"

"We need to move up the road to the bridge on the Nowy Vistula," Saoirse said. "Strazdins can't send the Guards up the road north if we're there, and at the same time, we have options. The road to the peacer base and to the southern coast will be open. For all our losses, the Guards lost a lot of men too. Strazdins doesn't have enough men to cover everything. Let him worry, for a change. We're not going to let him get away with murder." That last sentence in particular found general agreement. She heard, "Yes, sir," from the peacers and from the militia. That consensus lasted until some of them shouldered their packs and looked at the blackened surface of the road in front of them.

"Use the road, Lieutenant?" asked Corporal Rege from the First Platoon. He looked down at his feet, then back at her. "I mean, you were right about the electronics so they couldn't pick us up. My God, look at this." He swept his hand across the road. "But if we use the road and they send another plane, what's to stop them from firebombing us again?"

"That's a risk," Saoirse said. "No argument on that. But if we use the road, we can be at the crossing in two days. If we try to trek through this swamp, God knows how long it will take, and we don't have enough food."

"My electronics package has Big Ears," Alves said. "It's passive, so no ping or signal they can pick up, but we'll know about one of those planes before they can see us. I can rig it so nothing else turns on."

"Do it, Cyber," Saoirse said. "Andrzej. Take two of the boys and run up ahead of us. If they send more Guards down the road, give us three warning shots so we can be ready for them."

"We'll do it," Andrzej said, "but it won't be three *warning* shots. It'll be three dead Guards."

He snapped his fingers at two boys, and they slung their rifles and followed him down the road at a jog. Saoirse watched them go with a sense of amazement. It wasn't only the boys. She said, and they did. What had happened here?

Alves' Big Ears proved their worth on the march to the river. They gave an alert the next morning, and the company scrambled off the road into the surrounding foliage. Several minutes later, human ears picked up the buzzing of a light plane. Saoirse maneuvered herself so she could look skyward without, she hoped, revealing herself. It meant lying on her back in muddy water, but it was worth it. The little plane buzzed overhead, following the road north. Guards crouched at open doors on each side, with machine gun muzzles poking out into the air. A little while later, the plane came back headed south along the road. No shots were fired; no Molotov cocktails were thrown. Ten minutes after Saoirse could no longer hear the sound of the plane with her own ears, Alves gave the all clear, and it was passed, person-to-person, through the whole company. The troopers reassembled in the road, again wet and wearing fresh mud, and continued their trek south.

With the star at the horizon and twilight soon to come, they rounded a bend and found Andrzej in the middle of the road, waving for them to stop.

"The clearing for the blockhouse firebreak starts after the next curve," he said. "We can't go any farther without being seen."

"Okay." Saoirse held up her hand and stopped. The others came up and clustered around her. She had a quick internal debate. Would asking a question of them look weak? No, she decided, they would not expect her to know all the answers all the time. "So, how do we do this?"

"We can't go around it." That was Nowak. "There's no ford on the Lower Nowy Vistula below the falls. If we're crossing, and we have to cross if we're headed for either the peacer base or the southern coast, we're either building boats or using the bridge. No way we can build boats."

"That's why the blockhouse is there," said one of the other older militiamen. "It controls the road to the villages on the northern coast. It also splits them off from the ones on the southern coast."

"So, we have to take it out," Saoirse said.

"I've been inside it," Mwesigye said. "They invited the lieutenant colonel there four months ago, and I doubt it's changed. Usually has eight Guards posted there, but it can hold ten, so assume ten. One room in back, that's sleeping quarters. Front half has three rooms: an eating area, an office with their computers and comm gear, and a guard station for whoever is on duty. The windows are barred and screened, so we can't climb through but they can shoot out. It's not like firing slots, though; we can still shoot in pretty effectively. Not sure how easy it would be to put a grenade through. The door is a door, reinforced maybe, but it has a mechanical lock same as all the buildings here. This is a concrete house, not a fortress."

"The problem is the comm tower," Alves protested. "No matter what we do, the moment we attack, all they have to do is call for help. That plane, or more than one, comes and we're dead."

"They won't risk firebombing this area," Nowak said. "Too likely to destroy the bridge, maybe even the blockhouse and tower, even with the firebreak."

"It doesn't matter," Juliana Hopkinson said. "They have machine guns in those planes. Primitive, but I've been attacked from the air. You haven't. Cyber is right. Once they call in the air support, we're screwed."

"Then we have to get inside before the planes get here," Nowak said.

"That's crazy." That was Stephenson from First Platoon. "To do it that fast, we have to make a dash across the firebreak. Even with covering fire, we have to go for the door, and I bet half of us are gunned down on the way."

"Wait," Saoirse said. "If we knock out the comm tower first, then they can't call for help. Correct?"

Alves nodded. "Their comms won't connect to Sobieski without it, same as ours."

"But how are we going to do that, Lieutenant?" Hopkinson detached a grenade from her body armor and hefted it in one hand like a ball. "It's got to be two hundred feet, more even, from cover to the blockhouse, and the damn tower is built off the back part of the roof. Maybe if I stood in front of the door, I could throw a grenade up there, but not from across the firebreak."

An image popped into Saoirse's mind. She wished it hadn't because it was crazy—suicidal, even. But she had made promises. "How much does that weigh?" she asked.

"Hundred grams."

"And detonation?"

Hopkinson shrugged. "I can arm it," she pointed at a depressed button on the grenade, "and it blows in five seconds. Or we can detonate remotely. Cyber can do it."

"I can do that," Alves said. "If it's set for remote activation, you can pound it with a hammer, and nothing will happen until I send the signal. Then, *boom*."

Saoirse took a deep breath and let it out. She looked around for a wivesplant and spotted one growing near the side of the road. "Okay," she said, "somebody cut me one of those," she pointed at the clubs growing out of the wivesplant, "so it goes from the ground to my waist when I'm standing with my hand at my side. And give me some tape."

Puzzled looks followed her words. Saoirse stood at the center of a circle of quizzical faces.

"What do you have in mind, Lieutenant?" Mwesigye asked.

She grinned. "I'm going to play camogie."

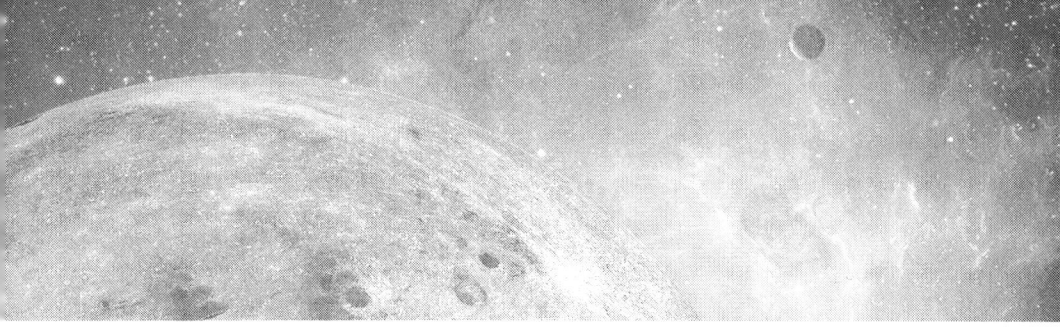

FORTY-TWO

Twenty minutes later, Saoirse stood behind the last screen of greenery before the open ground of the firebreak. Her right hand gripped her improvised hurley, and her left held her high-explosive sliótar. She studied the ground ahead of her as she reviewed in her mind what she would need to do.

Behind her, the road came out of the swamp at a gentle slope. The ground alongside the road as it entered the firebreak was solid. She would be able to run across it for her strike rather than have to splash through mud and water, which would have made an already difficult task an impossible one. It was going to be a long shot, maybe at the limit of what she could have done in school, but she was much stronger now. The problem was that while she would have a good surface to run on, she would be out in the open with no cover while she made her strike. The trees and flexi-ferns across the arc of the firebreak from her were maybe forty yards away. It looked like forty miles.

I am going to get my ass shot off, she thought. *I am going to die. Which might be a great relief to a number of people.* Her mind wanted to catalog all the individuals, but she cut off the thought. She decided she wasn't going to die today. Fuck all of them. She had promises to keep. She was going to do her best.

She waited while Mwesigye and four others worked their way through the swamp around the perimeter of the firebreak to the trees where Saoirse's run would take her, assuming she wasn't shot down first.

Her breaths came faster. She saw the signal, nodded, if only to herself, and reminded herself not to toss the sliótar at the fourth step the way the camogie rules required.

Saoirse burst from concealment in a desperate sprint, legs and arms pumping for all they were worth. Nothing happened at first. Maybe no one was looking. That lasted almost to the patch of ground she had decided was where she would strike. Then gunfire burst from the blockhouse. It kicked up dirt behind her. Her company opened up from behind her on the left, and bullets peppered the front of the blockhouse. She tried to ignore the shooting.

She needed two more steps. Toss the grenade just in front of her.

More shots flew. Grip, swing, and strike with the hurley.

She heard a sharp crack as the blade of her hurley hit the sliótar grenade. She launched the grenade high, as if for a point, and it felt good as she struck it. More shots.

She dived headfirst for the line of green just past the firebreak. She slid across rough ground into the trees, bullets hitting the leaves above her. The ground dropped out from under her, and her slide ended in a fall face-first into mud and water.

Cyber? she wondered, and in that instant an explosion echoed across the area. Saoirse struggled to her feet and pushed past leaves to see what was happening. A cloud of smoke billowed around the comm tower. While she watched, pieces of tower and antennae rained down on the roof of the blockhouse.

"Yes!" Saoirse screamed and pumped her fists. The comm tower was down, and somehow, she was alive and intact.

"Nice shot, Lieutenant." Mwesigye was at her shoulder. He handed Saoirse her rifle. She had forgotten all about it.

"Any chance they got a message out?" she asked.

"Doubt it," Mwesigye said. "They had maybe three seconds, less if you figure they didn't know what was happening at first."

"Good. But we still have to get them out of there. How do we do this?"

Mwesigye grinned. "It's a lot like Stephenson said before. The company back there will fire at the windows, make them keep their heads down. Namelok and Hendler, who came around with me, will do the same for the windows on this side. While they're doing that, I'm taking Kimayo and Heikkinen and rushing the door."

"I'm going with you."

She hadn't planned to say that. The words simply popped out of her mouth.

Mwesigye gave her a hard look, then shrugged. "Come with me."

He led her to a short rise past the drop-off she had fallen over when she landed in the mud. Up that slope, the other peacers crouched amid flexi leaves. Mwesigye looked at a countdown running on his wristband. When the numbers reached zero, a storm of fire directed at the blockhouse erupted from across the firebreak. At the same time, to their right, gunfire targeted the windows on that side of the blockhouse.

Mwesigye and the other two jumped up and ran across the open ground to the door. Not so prepared for the jump-off, Saoirse was a step behind at the start. She was a faster runner, though, and pulled ahead of the others, rifle in one hand, head down, and a hand on her helmet as though she needed to hold it in place. A bullet took down Kimayo. He flopped and rolled on the ground and screamed for help until another bullet silenced him.

Saoirse, Mwesigye, and the peacer named Heikkinen gained the precarious safety of the blockhouse wall next to the door. They were all breathing in deep, heaving gasps, whether from the dash or the air full of bullets was not clear. Mwesigye gestured Heikkinen and Saoirse to stay clear of the door. Then he took a step back, trained his rifle on the lock, and blasted it. Immediately, he flattened himself against the concrete wall as a cluster of bullets ripped through the door from the other side. He swung back in front of the door, lifted his boot up to chest level, and crashed it into the door with all his weight behind it.

The door flew open. Mwesigye again swung away, flat against the wall. Firing came from the inside. Heikkinen tossed a grenade. The explosion blew smoke and debris out the door. Right after the explosion, Saoirse charged through the doorway, rifle blasting on full automatic. She was the first one through. A thick haze clouded the room inside; the lights were out. Where she perceived movement, she fired. Muzzle flashes, seen even with the flame caps, lit the haze from the back. Mwesigye and Heikkinen were in the front room as well, and shooting. Saoirse rushed to the back, found a door in front of her, kicked it open, and fired into the room beyond. A scream echoed. In scant seconds, the only shooting was theirs.

"Cease fire," Mwesigye said.

Heikkinen stopped immediately. Saoirse did as well because her magazine was empty. Silence descended on the blockhouse.

As the smoke cleared, they found the bodies of ten Guards. Whatever equipment had been in the blockhouse was wrecked. They spent no time checking any of it. What was more important was spare ammunition and food.

"Can never have enough ammunition," Mwesigye said. "The food is good too."

The company packed everything they could carry as fast as they could and were back under the cover of the vegetation in only a few minutes.

"We need to be away from here," Saoirse said. "Sobieski knows the tower went down because they'll have lost its signal. Assume they send a plane to look. We want to be gone."

"It will be dark soon," Stephenson said. "Once we get across the bridge, we can get off the road and into the flexis. They're tall enough to hide us, and no way will they firebomb that side of the river. A firestorm could run all the way to the city. We can reach the base."

"We're not going to the base," said one of the older militia. "If we hold this crossing against the Guards, we can defend the road north and threaten them to the south."

"We're not going to the base or staying here," Saoirse said. Dead silence reigned. All of them stared at her. "I said, we're not doing either."

She knew the move they had to make. All the books Tommie had given her, the ones she read *because* he had given them to her, screamed out the answer in her mind. The idea had been taking shape ever since the ambush. It was right. The time for decision was now. She was not going to let Strazdins get away with murder.

"Listen to me," she said. "If we go back to the base, all we do is put all of us together in one bottle where the prezydent and his Guards can watch us. Same reason we can't stay here guarding a crossing that, maybe, they don't try to use. We won't be able to stop what's happening."

"Sure we can, Lieutenant," Stephenson said. "We tell our story. The lieutenant colonel will listen to us."

"That won't change anything," Saoirse said. "Listen to me. They'll spin a story. The Guards are out to stop the zombie trade; the militia fought them; the peacers got in the middle. It'll be enough to stall for time. They have enough troops to beat us, one piece at a time, if they move as a unit and we're splintered into multiple places. They'll still take their hostages, and Strazdins will force the Sejm into session and make them hold this election. The Sejm will have no choice; they're not going to sacrifice their children.

"Strazdins will be Marshal and he'll get the powers. Or maybe, they simply declare Strazdins Marshal and dare us to do something about it. Daleko Bałtyckie will apply for membership in the Assembly as an independent world and demand the peacers leave. Strazdins gets to be tyrant and they'll keep shipping zombie and they get away with murder. Do you really think the legate is going to declare war on the planetary government of Daleko Bałtyckie? Even if they deserve it?"

"That'll be the day after there's peace in the Reach," Mwesigye said. "This is the Reach. The bad guys often win."

Nowak spoke up for the militia. "What you say makes a sad kind of sense, Lieutenant Irish. But I don't see what we can do. Go back to the peacer base, stay here, or go to the southern coast, it sounds like Strazdins wins."

"Not this time," Saoirse said. "The way to stop Strazdins is by making a move the Guards must respond to, to give them no choice but to come at us with all their force so they have nothing left for anywhere else. We have to bring it all down on us. We have to do it right now. Going back to the peacer base, staying here, doing anything else—all we might do is save our own asses and give this world to a murderer. That would be the price of our safety."

She hadn't said they would be cowards if they took any choice but hers. Not quite. But she could see from their faces that they understood her meaning. She waited for a response.

Cowardice is something you know all about, isn't it? Feel awkward? Get drunk. Got a problem? Get high. Life's tough? Do both. Not solved? Repeat, until getting drunk or high is all that matters. Go too far, end up in trouble, get rescued, go to rehab.

Her inner Saoirse spoke the truth; she could not argue with herself. But it was as Tommie had said, what seemed so long ago. She could not change what she had done in the past, but she could do better now.

The silence lasted for minutes that felt like hours. She wanted to have a cigarette, even to hold an unlit one. After that fire, she didn't think she'd ever smoke again, but she wanted to have one and didn't. She ignored the urge. Time passed. She studied their faces. No one was laughing at her. No one was sneering. No one did anything. They were thinking about what she'd said.

"We're with you, Irish!" Andrzej burst out at last.

"Of course we are with you," Nowak said.

Saoirse smiled.

Mwesigye spoke. "What would you have us do, Lieutenant? We will follow your orders."

For an instant, Saoirse wished he'd turned his back and walked away, taking the rest of the peacers with him. It would have been easier. Now she had to make her crazy idea work.

"I heard a story that there's a trail from here along the Nowy Vistula, which leads to the base of the falls. And from that spot, there's a path up the cliffs right next to the falls. I heard swamper boys know it and climb it."

"It's true," Andrzej said. "I've done it!"

"I as well!" The shouts came from all the boys.

"I've done it three times," Andrzej said, "and once in the dark."

That brought a chuckle from Nowak. "I think almost all the militia can say that they have done it, and I do not think we need to ask each of us how many times. I will be honest, however, and say that years ago it was not nearly so well marked as it is today."

That brought laughter from the older militia and a glare from Andrzej. Even many of the peacers were grinning.

"There's the answer, Sergeant Mwesigye, Mx. Nowak." Saoirse put her hands together and stood in front of all of them. "That path leads to the plant at the Point, and without that plant, Strazdins has nothing. We're going to climb the path next to the waterfall, then we're going to storm that nuclear plant from the rear and take it."

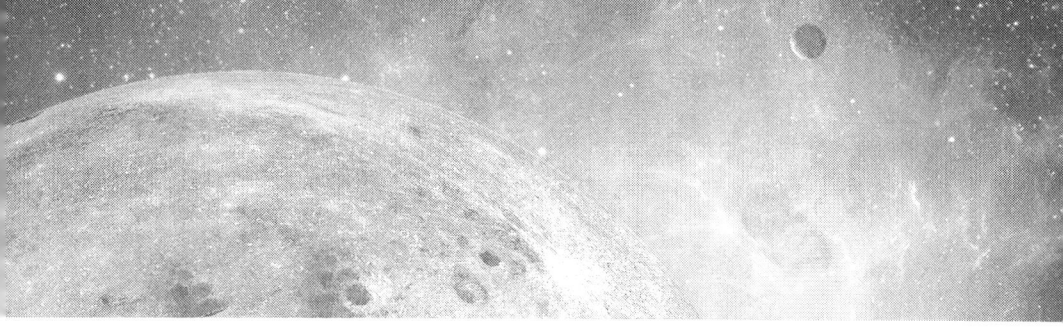

FORTY-THREE

The combined company of peacers and militia left the road immediately after they crossed the bridge. From there, they headed inland along the southern bank of the Nowy Vistula. Andrzej and three of his friends led the way, claiming to be the most familiar with the trail. Saoirse couldn't see any trail in the failing light, but she wasn't certain they needed pathfinders at this point—they kept close to the river on their left, and even in the dark they could hear it. Still, it was obvious Andrzej wanted to lead. If she let him do it now, he wouldn't be sulking when they needed him to guide them up the cliff.

Pole trees grew along the southern side of the river, most thickly in the mud by the riverbanks. The trees thinned out as the ground became higher and drier farther to the south. Replacing them as the dominant tree were forty-to-fifty-foot-high trees with widespread lower branches tapering to a narrow top, giving the impression of a cone. Their trunks contained true wood and their bark looked more like that of an Earth tree. More important to the peacers, their branches had numerous leaves that were bigger and provided more cover from spies in the air than the pole trees did. Once the column was under those trees, the sky was shut away.

"Just as well," Juliana Hopkinson said as she looked up at the roof of leaves. "It's like a sauna under here, but nobody is going to spot us from one of those planes."

Saoirse grinned at that. She felt as wet from sweat as she had from her falls into the swamp, but it was worth it to be screened from the air.

They made camp that night under the trees and chewed their way through uncooked ration sticks. No one complained, however. No one was eager to turn on a heating element to cook, even if it wasn't an open flame. Fortunately, the temperature in the woods meant that no heat was needed at night.

The increasing roar of the waterfall dominated everything from the moment they set out the following morning, becoming louder, it seemed, with every step forward. The trail angled to the left, toward the roar, while the ground became rocky for the first time since they had left Wałęsa. Then, with the abruptness of a curtain being pulled back, the screen of trees and drooping leaves parted. A few feet of jumbled rocks packed into dirt separated them from a flood of rushing water. The Nowy Vistula boiled past, white foam bubbling where it dashed over rocks, a torrent on its way to the distant shore.

Saoirse stepped out to the edge of the water. To the right was the base of the falls. A wall of falling water slammed into a pool, the impact sending spray and mist fifty feet into the air and coating everything with fine droplets. Saoirse wiped her face and looked up. And up. Nine hundred and forty-three feet above them, the Nowy Vistula poured over the edge of the cliffs, an entire broad river tumbling down through the air. A pebble skittered across the rock next to her, and she turned to see that Mwesigye had joined her. His face turned upward as well.

"You know, Lieutenant," he said, "that first day I met you, the thought crossed my mind that you might be crazy. When you went charging into that blockhouse back at the crossing, I was pretty sure of it. But this . . . this removes all doubt."

"Thanks," she said. "You're not the first to say that, by the way, but the way you put it is the first time it sounds like a compliment."

Mwesigye laughed softly. "Well, before we can get crazy, we're going to have to cross that."

Directly in front of them, the river had cut a side channel out of the pool at the base of the falls. That channel, a small river in its own right, ran off to the right, hugging the base of the cliffs in front of them. The only solid footing on the other side was a small patch of rocky beach between the pool and the cliffs. That beach looked as if it ran behind the falls as well, but the water and spray blocked the view.

"That's where we go!" Andrzej shouted above the roar as he came over to the two of them. "I'll show you how we do it. You don't want to try wading across. See the yellow on the rocks under the water?" They looked where he pointed and saw stringy tendrils clinging to stones and waving in the strong current. "It's a moss," he said. "You can actually dig it out and eat it, but the problem is that it's slippery. The current swirls, coming out here. It makes whirlpools and sinkholes that shift over time. Slip on moss, go down, hit your head—bad. Watch what we do."

Andrzej shouted for two friends to join him. They picked up large rocks from the shore and heaved them to shallow spots in the little river. One vanished from sight after it broke the surface, proof of a sinkhole at that spot, but the others came to rest on rock only a little below the water and stuck up into the air.

"Stepping-stones," said Mwesigye.

"*Tak*," said Andrzej. "Go from one to another. Stay dry. No risk of a bad slip on the moss. The river will wash them away soon, so unless you come right after someone else, you have to do it again. But there are always more rocks coming down."

With that, he sprang for the first of the rocks and then jumped from that to the next, and again until his last jump took him to the ground at the base of the cliff. His two friends followed him just as easily. Nowak stepped to the water's edge and crossed as well, perhaps not so fast, but as sure of his feet.

"Fuck this shit," said Juliana Hopkinson. She had brought her squad up to the river's edge while Nowak crossed. She unslung her rifle and heaved it across to Andrzej, who caught it. Her two bandoliers, with their magazines and hand grenades, followed. Then she went for the stepping-stones. She teetered a bit on one in the middle, but finished with a jump to the other side and raised her arms like a gymnast at the end of a routine. Then she turned back to face her squad.

"Let's go, peacers," she said. "If you can't do this, you deserve to grow moss."

After Hopkinson's squad had crossed, Saoirse decided to take her turn. It wasn't so easy as the others had made it appear. Her boots seemed too big to fit on the stones, although they were no larger than the others, and instead of giving her a flat base, it felt as if each boot provided only a narrow ridge of support for her body. The result was that each boot wobbled on a stone that also wobbled beneath it. She knew she was going to fall. A large rock sat near her, maybe half an inch below the waterline. It looked flat. She stepped on that one. She slipped on the moss. Reached with her foot and found nothing. She went down, and cold water closed over her head. Boots, camo, and body armor all weighed her down. She kicked hard, frantically, and thrust her arms up into the air.

A hand clamped on one of her wrists and hauled her upward. Her head broke the surface and she gasped for air. Hopkinson was there, one foot on a stepping-stone, the other calf-deep in water with her boot wedged between two of the moss-covered rocks. She kept her grip on Saoirse's arm while she reached down with her other hand to grab a fistful of Saoirse's camo. She swung Saoirse toward the far bank like a dockworker tossing a sack of grain. The momentum was enough to propel Saoirse into shallow water. She staggered, more than walked, the rest of the way up the bank.

"Thank you!" she yelled out to Hopkinson.

"My pleasure," Hopkinson replied. "It wouldn't do to let our commander drown before the next battle, would it?" Hopkinson looked down, rebalanced her weight on the stepping-stone, and extracted the foot she had wedged below the water. Then she made two jumps back to land.

The stone that Saoirse had fallen from was no longer visible in the river. The crossing paused while Andrzej and a friend scouted out a larger rock that took both of them to heave in. By the time the entire company was across, three more peacers were fished out, but none were any worse than wet.

The pool did prove to have a small dirt beach that ran behind the falls. There, completely hidden by the wall of water between them and the rest of the world, the company organized for the climb up. Large packs had to be left behind, as Andrzej and the other militia warned against extra weight and anything that might unbalance a climber. That led to some grumbling about the amount of food that was being left, but Mwesigye yelled that if they fell off a nine-hundred-foot cliff, they wouldn't have much of an appetite afterward. Priority had to go to weapons and ammunition. As it was, two light mortars and rounds for them that they had found at the blockhouse and carried from there had to stay behind. They had a brief argument over the shoulder-launched rockets.

"I can manage with one," said Hopkinson, "and I'll find another who can. We're going to need these."

The path upward started from a crack in the cliff wall at the base and climbed steeply from the outset. Within twenty feet above them, the trail was no longer distinct from the cliff wall.

"Cyber," Saoirse asked, "what's the risk of being spotted while we do this?"

"Very low, I think." Alves was one of the ones who had fallen in the river, and her teeth chattered as she stood in her wet uniform, examining the cliff face above them. "No surveillance satellites around Daleko Bałtyckie, so no risk of that. There is plant growth coming out of the side of the cliff that looks like it will overhang our route. With good cameras, maybe they could pick us up if they flew a plane in here or, more likely, a drone. But they would have to be looking for us here."

"Which isn't likely," Mwesigye said. "Once they find out what happened at the crossing, which they probably have, the first places they'll look for us will be toward the base or the southern coastal villages. The one advantage of that damned swamp and being on foot is that there's no trail to find until a long way from the crossing."

"If we go up after dark, there's no way they can see us," Andrzej said.

"No," Saoirse said. Maybe Andrzej really had done it at night as he claimed, but she would bet they would lose most of the troopers to falls if they tried. Besides, if the Guards were going to look for them at the falls by plane, they could just as easily use night vision or infrared cameras. Daleko Bałtyckie might be short on military equipment, but good cameras would be around for other reasons. "It's a hard-enough climb as it is. We're doing it in daylight. More important, what's the risk of a guard or a wall being there when we get to the top?"

"*Nie*, no," said Andrzej. "It's just an occasional guy coming up, and since they built the wall across the Point, we take a branching trail near the top that goes past the wall. There won't be anybody at the top of the trail, and nobody will be looking."

Saoirse wished she could be as confident as Andrzej, but it didn't matter. There was no place else for them to go. They had to finish what they had started. No, they had to finish what *she* had started. Just in case there was any question about whose fault this was.

"Andrzej," she said, "you lead us up. I'm going to be right behind you. The rest of you in a single file. Sergeant," she pointed at Mwesigye, "you set the order. Make sure we have good shots at the front."

The line formed rapidly and mostly of its own accord. Meanwhile, Saoirse and Mwesigye huddled with Andrzej and Nowak around a stretch of smooth dirt. There, Andrzej and Nowak used sticks to diagram their target in the dirt. Nowak was the better artist, but Andrzej had the more recent memory. Between the two, with some rubbing out and redrawing, along with a little argument, what emerged was a dirt drawing of the tip of the Point. They studied where the station building stood, where the entrances were, where the trail would come up, and what the distance from the top of the trail to the closest entrance would be. Saoirse and Mwesigye asked some questions and then looked at each other.

"Looks simple enough, sir," said Mwesigye. "Get a dozen of us to the top and rush the back door before they figure it out."

"Yeah, I could do it in my sleep," Saoirse replied.

Mwesigye grinned. They walked back to the line of peacers and militia. "Look at the bright side!" Mwesigye shouted at them. "If you fall off, you don't need to worry about screaming. The falls are so loud no one will hear you."

Quite a few of the peacers and even some of the militia laughed at that. As she claimed the second spot in line behind Andrzej, Saoirse shook her head. Was that peacer humor? Or was that what men did in front of other men to look braver than they felt? *I'm scared shitless*, she said silently to herself, *but it's too late to do anything except climb*. Her mind tried to start its usual trick of listing people who would be happy to hear that she fell, but she stopped it. It was not very useful. Instead, she looked back at the people who made up her little company.

For all the disaster they had faced, they were in good shape physically, but that was due to the fact that those with significant wounds had either not escaped from Wałęsa or had perished in the inferno on the road. The fight at the blockhouse had cost them only two men and given minor wounds to a few others. Probably the worst of the wounded was the boy with the arm wound she had seen being tended to outside the village. He was standing in line but protesting that he could not climb that cliff with only one good arm.

Nowak was next to him. "You just use that arm no matter how much it hurts," Nowak said. "You can brag about it to the girls afterward."

"You can't stay here, you know," said a boy of similar age on the other side of him. We'll rope you in with us and help you across the really tough spots."

Saoirse didn't see if the boy made any reply, because at that point she heard Andrzej say, "Here I go!" With that, he pulled himself up into the crack in the wall that formed the beginning of the path. Saoirse hastened to follow.

At first, they had a real path of dark packed earth to follow, albeit on a steep upward traverse of the cliff wall. It was almost wide enough at the base to put both feet side by side. As they went up, however, that little ledge shrank to the width of a single foot and then narrowed to the point where they flattened against the wall and dug in with fingers and toes for whatever purchase they could get. When it seemed that the ledge would vanish entirely and leave them clinging to the cliff by their fingers, a switchback appeared, leading back toward the falls. The dirt was softer there and had the look of having been widened with tools. The respite was temporary, however. Another switchback appeared, taking them away from the falls again along a thin, stony ledge. Even that tiny ledge ended.

"We go up from here," Andrzej called back to Saoirse.

It was a steep vertical wall they had to climb, gripping protruding rocks or tiny recesses with their hands and feet to gain the necessary leverage to pull themselves up to the next excuse for a ledge that would serve as a switchback.

To Saoirse, the climb went on forever. She was pressed against the cliff, seeing nothing beyond the next fingerhold or toehold. One switchback followed another, distinguished only by how narrow they were and whether anyone had used a tool to improve the purchase. More vertical climbs were interspersed among the switchbacks and differed only in how high they were and how desperate she felt as she fumbled for the next place to put a hand or foot. She didn't think anyone fell during the climb, although she wouldn't have known if someone did. Mwesigye was right about the din of the falling water. No one would have heard a scream.

Every muscle, from the tiny ones at Saoirse's fingertips all the way to the deltoids at her shoulders, seemed locked in cramps by the time she clambered up behind Andrzej onto a broad shelf of packed dirt. The top of the cliff was no more than ten feet above their heads. The way Saoirse felt, it could have been another thousand feet to go. At least she found it gratifying to see Andrzej breathing hard.

"This is where the trail splits," he panted. "The new branch is to the right; it leads past the Point, past where the Guards built the wall out to the edge of the cliff, and comes up in the flexi-ferns along the edge they don't bother to clear. That's how we can climb the cliff without coming up inside the wall and without being seen."

"That does us no good," Saoirse said, "because we need to be inside the wall."

"Right." Andrzej pointed the other way. "That is the old track, going back in the direction of the river. We'll come up behind the building, like I showed you. Nobody has done it this way for a year and a half, since they built the wall, because then you can't get out."

"We're not getting out," Saoirse said. "Now, let's go. There isn't room here for any more of us, and the others are coming up." Indeed, in the time they had talked, three more had reached the shelf, and it was full.

The old track ended, thankfully not in a vertical wall the way Saoirse had imagined it, but as a steep slope of packed dirt and stone. Decades of boys scrambling over the top had eaten into the cliff at that point and eroded it.

"I'm going first," she said, "in case someone up there needs to be shot." Then she squeezed past Andrzej onto the last slope, once again feeling that tingly feeling of excitement mixed with fear.

She crawled up the slope, then halted with her helmet almost even with the lip. The next movement she made upward would expose her to whoever or whatever was at the back of the control station for the nuclear plant. Would it be an empty field, as Andrzej and the other boys were convinced? Or would there be a guard there? Would the guard have a rifle pointed at the precise point where her head came up? A shiver went through her. *I'm scared*, she thought. *I'm really, really scared. But I'm excited too.*

Saoirse pulled her legs up under her, grabbed the dirt at the lip, and jumped over the top. She hit the ground, rolled to the side, and flattened herself against the dirt. Nothing happened. She listened, not daring to lift her head. No shouts. No gunshots.

Finally, she looked up. In front of her was about forty yards of open ground to the back of the control station. It was flat and completely devoid of cover. There was nothing there except the tiny fern-clovers covering the ground. The windows on the first and second floors were blank. She couldn't see any sign of people through them. A single door in the lower story was closed—it was where Andrzej and Nowak had put it in their drawing, so that was a good sign. To her left, she could hear the river as it went over the falls. The cooling towers of the plant loomed over the control station.

Behind her, Andrzej came over the top. She waved him on and then to the side to make room for the next one. Another trooper came up. Then another. Soon, six of them hugged the ground at the cliffside.

She looked back at the control station. Someone was standing at one of the second-floor windows where, a moment before, there had been no one. They were looking at her. They turned, as if speaking to another in the building, then pointed out the window.

There goes the fucking plan! Saoirse knew what would happen next. Whoever had seen them would call to the Guards at the front of the station and along the wall. They would come running around the building and trap Saoirse and the half dozen with her against the edge of the cliff. They didn't have enough troops up; they weren't ready.

Saoirse stopped thinking. She jumped up and fired at the windows. Glass shattered and rained down on the ground. Nobody was going to stick their head out right away. Then she launched herself into a frantic dash for the back door, covering the ground in a handful of seconds. The door was hinged to swing inward. She brought her knee up to her chest, as she'd seen Mwesigye do, and smashed the sole of her boot into the door. The lock broke and the door slammed inward. She landed forward, rifle leveled, and fired through the opening. She heard a scream, ignored it, and charged into the corridor. A body lay unmoving on the floor. She didn't even look to see if the man had been armed.

A door opened farther down the corridor. A man looked out. He had a pistol drawn. His eyes went wide at the sight of her, and his shot went high into the wall behind her. Saoirse shot him down. Then she rushed to the open door and sprayed the area beyond it with gunfire. The door at the end of the next corridor was opening. She ducked into the doorway she had just fired through and shot into the door at the end of the corridor. A thump heralded a body falling to the floor on the other side. Seconds later, gunshots echoed and bullets sprayed across the corridor. Saoirse dropped into a crouch and fired low into that doorway. Another yell followed. She found a second to hope that her troops had rushed to the building behind her.

That was when a fusillade erupted outside. She could hear shots and screams through the walls. Another volley of shots, then silence.

Saoirse risked a peek through her doorway and saw a white towel dangling from a pole thrust through the opening of the door at the end of the corridor.

"Okay!" she shouted. "Slide your weapons through the door on the floor. All of them—pistols, rifles, whatever. Then come through with your hands on your heads."

FORTY-FOUR

Ten minutes after the control station surrendered, Saoirse stood at the receptionist's desk by the front entrance. The victory was as complete as it was total. The peacers and militia had taken no casualties. Thirty-eight employees of the Sobieski Point Nuclear Plant were under guard in the administrative offices upstairs. Two others were dead. Saoirse had killed one when she fired through the window, the other when she burst through the back door. Their bodies had already been dragged out back, and she had no time to think about them anymore. A squad of fifteen Guards were stationed at the plant, but they had clearly not been expecting an attack, and certainly not from attackers scaling the cliffs of Sobieski Falls. Now six of the Guards were dead and the remaining nine sat, hands bound behind them, on the floor of the reception area in front of Saoirse.

"What would you like to do with them, Lieutenant?" asked Mwesigye.

"You should let us go," said one of the captives. He wore the insignia of a captain in the Guards. "Your attack was brave and clever, but it will accomplish nothing for you in the end. The prezydent will send more Guards from the city and the highlands. The ones from the city will be here soon, I should think, and you will not hold this place against them. If you let us go, we can convince them to accept a surrender that will save your lives."

Saoirse had to laugh. "That is off the charts on the bullshit meter. We're not letting you go so you can tell your friends how many of us are here and what we've got."

The captain scowled. "If the Guards don't kill you when they take the station back, they'll kill you afterward."

"And take on the rest of a peacer battalion?" Saoirse shrugged. "If that's what's going to happen, I might as well shoot you now. I'm not known for my self-control."

She was rewarded by a flash of fright on his face and she laughed again. Then she turned to Mwesigye. "There's got to be a storage area in the basement. See if we can lock them up there, safe and out of the way. The employees, too, except for the ones who know how the systems work. We need to talk to them. In the meantime, I'm sure the Guards are on their way."

"I've reinforced Hopkinson's and Nnadi's squads and have them on the walls and covering the gate," Mwesigye said. "That wall," he shook his head, "was designed to keep rioters out, not to stop a determined assault. If they decide to retake this place, and they will, we will need the battalion to get here. And that's the next problem, sir. Nobody can connect to the base on the comms. They're fine in here, but we can't send or receive from the outside."

Saoirse pulled out her own comm, the Peach Mom had given her what seemed like a lifetime ago. It picked up the access point inside the control station, and she could contact the peacers and the militia, but it was as though the world outside the station did not exist.

"Odd." She selected a contact from the list. "Cyber," she said when the comm connected, "I need you in the reception area. Now, please."

In the time it took Alves to hustle to the front of the station, militiamen had cleared the prisoners from the room. Saoirse and Mwesigye were alone when Alves showed up.

"What's with the comms, Cyber?" Saoirse asked. "We should be able to pick up the base from here even if the Guards are denying access to any of the signal towers."

"We're being jammed, Lieutenant," Alves said. "Actively blocked."

"What? How is that possible?"

"I don't know, sir. It's not supposed to be possible. To jam us like this, they'd have to be on our reserved frequency and be able to crack our codes. They shouldn't be able to do it."

"Except they are," Saoirse said. "We can't call for help or transmit what we know." She stared off into space for a moment. She had figured that Strazdins would assault the station with every man he had. But she'd also thought that once they spoke with Venezelos, the legate would have to let the battalion relieve them. Then Strazdins would be caught, the plant out of his control and the rest of the battalion in his rear. Now another plan had gone down the drain. She wanted to knee Prezydent Strazdins in the balls.

That was when she had an idea. "Cyber, have you found the main control room for this place?"

"Yes." Alves nodded. "There are two levels to this building belowground. The control room is on the lower one."

"Good." Saoirse grinned. "Go downstairs and turn off the lights."

"Excuse me, sir?"

"Shut off the power. Cut the transmission from the plant. I'm sure you can persuade one of the employees to help you if you need it. The lowland and coastal villages, most of them, put in solar cells to decrease their dependence on the plant, in case the prezydent did exactly this. The city and the highlands, though, they depend on it. We're going to turn the tables and see how the prezydent likes being in the dark."

That brought out one of Mwesigye's laughs. "I imagine we will have guests at the door even faster."

* * *

The wall that protected the control station of the Sobieski Point Nuclear Plant ran from the river, close to the cooling towers, to the cliffs past the place where the trail came up. It was ten feet high, built of the same structural concrete as almost all buildings on Daleko Bałtyckie. People had decorated it, both inside and out, with murals of farms and villages painted in bright colors. The pastoral look was spoiled only by the coils of razor wire that ran along the top. Near the center point of the wall, as measured from the river to the cliff, was a gate where Pilsudski Road from the city entered the control station yard. Two concrete barriers, three feet high and a truck length apart, formed the primary obstacle to entry. A vehicle needed to stop at the first barrier for an initial check; then that barrier would sink into the ground, allowing the vehicle to pull forward as far as the second barrier. The first would rise again, trapping the vehicle until it was completely inspected, and only then would the inner barrier drop to allow entry to the courtyard in front of the station.

"It's a shit setup," said Juliana Hopkinson. It was twilight. Hopkinson, Saoirse, and Mwesigye stood in a small watchtower at the top of the wall, overlooking the gate and the road. "The flank positions on the wall cannot cover the gate and cannot support the center. Same way, the flank positions are basically isolated. Also, we do not have enough troops for the length of the wall. We are too thin."

"You've done the best you can with what you have," Mwesigye said. "If we had a lot more troops, we wouldn't have enough ammunition for all of them."

"It's better than not having a wall at all," Saoirse said.

"Some wall," Hopkinson snorted. "One howitzer, just one, would turn this to rubble in a snap." She snapped her fingers to emphasize the word.

"It would," Mwesigye said, "but there is no artillery on Daleko Bałtyckie. Mortars, yes, some RPGs. But that's about it."

"We don't have to hold forever," Saoirse said. "Just until the battalion can relieve us. Even if we can't use the comms, they'll notice a battle, and they have short-range drones."

Hopkinson was not deterred from her pessimistic appraisal. "That assumes, sir, that the legate doesn't decide it's more important for Strazdins to be Marshal, however he gets it, and for Daleko Bałtyckie to be certified as an independent member world. If that's what the legate wants, he might let the Guards overrun us."

"Daleko Bałtyckie doesn't qualify without this plant. As long as we hold it, he can't certify it and Strazdins can't hold power. Literally."

"As you say, sir." Hopkinson finally grinned. "We'll hold it."

Saoirse looked away down Pilsudski Road at the lights and skyglow from Sobieski. As she did, the lights went out. Cyber had found the Off switch. Here and there, some lights came back on, powered by backup batteries, but most of the land lay dark. Two sets of headlights were visible on Pilsudski Road, coming closer.

Those lights proved to be a passenger car and a small truck. They stopped on the road in front of the first barrier. Eight Guardsmen jumped out, all carrying rifles. One of them began shouting, although Saoirse had no idea what he was saying; her comm wasn't set to Translate.

"Need one of the militia," Mwesigye said softly.

"Hey, pretty boy!" Hopkinson yelled down. "This is the Thirty-second Peacers. Speak English."

The man switched at once. "You are ordered to open the barriers and surrender the station!"

"Get fucked!" said Hopkinson. "We don't take orders from you."

The man shouted something in the first language he had used, and the three in the watchtower ducked as rifles swung to cover them. The windows of the watchtower shattered as a stream of bullets hit them. Answering fire from the wall positions on the other side of the gate led to cries from below.

Hopkinson picked up a small handheld rocket launcher from the floor of the watchtower. She loaded, raised it to her shoulder, and fired. A streak of flame and smoke traced a path from the watchtower to the cab of the truck. It exploded. The fire in the blown-out cab burned swiftly until foam from cylinders on the truck smothered it. Below, they could see two men carrying a third back to the car.

"Let them go," Mwesigye said into his comm. "Save the ammunition."

The Guards squeezed into the car along with their wounded companion and turned it around to head back toward the city. Three bodies lay on the dirt in front of the gate.

"Tomorrow will be the real thing," Saoirse said. "Still, we'd better watch through the night, just in case."

"We'll take care of that, Lieutenant," said Mwesigye.

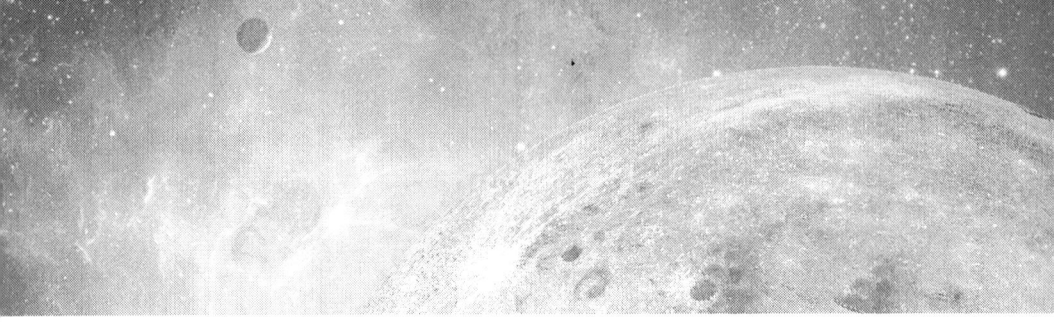

FORTY-FIVE

Saoirse woke with a start to the rattle of gunfire against the walls of the administration offices in the station building. A random round flew through a window now devoid of glass and put a hole in the wall six feet above where she lay on the floor. A few flakes of paint floated down onto her. She shook her head in an attempt to clear it. She did not remember going to sleep, did remember telling Mwesigye she was *not* going to sleep, did remember agreeing only to sit and rest for a moment. She must have fallen asleep on the tiled floor the moment she sat down.

How long had she slept? It was broad daylight now. A glance at her comm told her she had been out for a little over three hours. That was plenty—would have to be plenty. She sat up and had to stifle a groan. Every muscle throughout her body was stiff and sore and protested against being moved. She hadn't felt that way since she got past the first week of training with Sergeant Adelayo.

Three more bullets hit high up on the wall above her. She had obviously picked a poor room to sleep in. Three of the militia were positioned at the windows, banging away sporadically with their rifles—to what end, she had no idea. What was happening? She had no idea about that either, but she had to find out. She crawled to the door, taking care to stay below the level of the windows, and did not stand up until she was in the windowless corridor that led to the stairway.

Past the front door of the station, the driveway and courtyard looked like a junkyard. The vehicles that had been parked there were scorched wrecks of twisted metal and broken glass. Remnants of flame-smothering foam were everywhere. The little fern-clovers that had carpeted the ground between the station building and the wall were charred black, burned up by the explosions that had destroyed the cars. From the wall came a random but constant chatter of gunfire. What had wreaked such havoc in the enclosure? A shrill whistle sounded, followed by a blast over toward the river that threw dirt and rock into the air. Mortars! Saoirse dropped to the ground as another whistle ended in an explosion at one corner of the upper story and sent chunks of concrete tumbling to the ground.

She got up and ran for the watchtower at the gate. Another mortar shell burst off to her right. She ignored it. At the wall, she scrambled up the stairs to the watchtower where she had been with Mwesigye and Hopkinson. Juliana Hopkinson was there, as she had been the previous evening. She had piled concrete rubble on top of the wall where the windows had been shot out to extend the cover and create an improvised firing slot.

"Morning, Lieutenant," said Hopkinson. "Is breakfast coming around?"

"Only if I can get an omelet station," Saoirse answered. "What's going on?"

"Look through the slot. It's safer than sticking your head up. They've set up about four hundred yards off, in the cleared area before where the flexis take over. Machine guns mounted on trucks, mortars, some rockets. We've had a few casualties that I know of. Not bad. Mostly they're making us keep our heads down; they haven't done any real damage. Yet."

As Hopkinson finished speaking, the fire from the Guards picked up and turned into an almost continuous series of impacts against the wall and the razor wire on top of it. Saoirse glanced through the embrasure and saw a truck with metal sheeting on top headed for the gate. Hopkinson squeezed next to her and peered out.

"Figures," Hopkinson said.

Then they heard the same sound of a light plane that they'd heard on the Coastal Highway. Machine gunners in the open side doors of the plane raked the positions on the top of the wall with fire. Hopkinson and Saoirse squeezed into the corner of the front wall and the floor of the watchtower, trying to stay out of sight of the gunner above them.

"Shit," Hopkinson said. "The assholes up there are going to kill us or pin us down while the truck drives up to the gate and blows it open. We don't have anything like a SAM, not here."

"Is that fucking plane armored?" Saoirse asked.

"Doubt it."

"Good. Can you get it to fly toward us?" Saoirse asked. "The gunners in the doors can only fire to the side, so it has to fly past us or over us."

"It just headed toward the cliffside end of the wall," Hopkinson said. "I'll get their goddamn attention." She picked up the rocket launcher from the floor of the watchtower, took a deep breath, stood up, and fired at the back of the plane. She dropped flat as more bullets crashed into the walls of the watchtower.

The rocket flew toward the plane and missed. The occupants of the plane saw it shoot past, however, and the plane banked around, searching for the source of the rocket fire.

"Too much to hope I'd hit it with a dumb rocket," Hopkinson said, "but here comes your plane."

Saoirse looked up. The plane was flying over the top of the wall, headed toward the watchtower. Then it dipped a wing to turn and give the gunner an open shot at them. *Now*, Saoirse thought. She came up to one knee and sighted. She had the barest glimpse of the pilot in the cockpit. It was enough. She fired. The plane's nose dropped. A long dive followed, ending with the plane splashing into the Nowy Vistula and going over the falls.

"Jesus fucking Christ!" said Hopkinson. "You are the best fucking shot in the battalion. You are the best fucking shot I've ever seen."

"What about the fucking truck?" Saoirse shouted.

"I've got it," Hopkinson said.

The fall of the plane created a lull in the firing from the Guards' positions. It wasn't that they had to stop shooting, only that they had thought of the plane as invulnerable, and when it fell, they stopped to watch it.

Hopkinson took advantage of the slackened fire to reload the launcher. She jumped up, sighted on the truck, and fired. The rocket hit the truck's windshield and exploded.

Men leaped out of the back of the truck as the front caught fire. Sprays of foam blasted out to extinguish it. The truck had been just short of the gate when Hopkinson hit it, and the men who bailed out of it tried to shelter behind it while their compatriots unleashed another storm of fire at the defenders on the wall. Saoirse hunkered down and sighted through the firing slot. A man behind the truck shifted position and exposed a leg. She shot him, and he fell away from the cover of the truck. One of his mates tried to drag him back. That exposed the second man, and Saoirse shot him too. The others tried to escape back to the cover of their original positions, their assault on the gate abandoned. Only five of them made it.

. . .

The day passed more swiftly than Saoirse would have expected. She always had something to occupy her, even if it was just looking through the embrasure, waiting for a target to present himself. Knowing that the Guards had access to their comm codes and frequencies, the peacers and militia dared not use their comms to coordinate the defense. As a result, she made multiple trips back to the control station to confer with Mwesigye. She ran a gauntlet of sorts to do that, because the Guards continued to throw mortar shells at random into the courtyard and at the station building. A whistle would come out of the sky, and anyone crossing the compound would drop to the ground, or into a hole dug by a previous round, and seconds later, ten pounds of high explosive would blast the earth. All you could do when that happened was hope it didn't land too close.

The building showed the effect of the bombardment. By late morning, the upper floor was little more than a shell. One mortar round hit the top of the wall and blew off three feet of concrete. That led Saoirse and Mwesigye to rush four of their carefully husbanded reserve to take positions in the rubble and discourage the Guards from any thought of storming that point.

Saoirse made the rounds of all the positions along the wall. She made sure the best marksmen were posted there, although she also made certain to rotate them back after several hours for food, drink, and the tenuous respite the building provided from the bullets and the mortar shells. Not all of them wanted that break, because it meant running the gauntlet of the courtyard to reach the building, so Saoirse had to decide if they were, in fact, fit to stay at the wall. Some had to run the gauntlet anyway, because ammunition had to be brought to the wall. Not all of them made it.

Their worst loss came shortly before noon. A shell hit right in front of the entrance, badly wounding Stephenson, who had just returned from the wall. He fell outside and screamed for the medic, who rushed out to help him. Another shell fell and killed them both. That left them with no medic to care for the increasing number of wounded.

Through all of it, Saoirse kept moving. She was surprised that none of it bothered her. Not the explosions, not the bullets, not the cries, and not the blood. She didn't understand why that should be. In the occasional quiet interlude, she would wonder about whether it meant something else was wrong with her, but some crisis always demanded attention before she found any answers.

Thankfully, no more planes arrived over the station, despite Mwesigye's certainty that there were more light planes available. Whether the Guards were unwilling to risk losing another plane and pilot or whether they were simply confident of winning anyway wasn't clear, but Saoirse and Mwesigye were not going to complain. The Guards did try on two more occasions to run storming parties to the wall, using trucks with metal shielding welded on. Both were beaten off, leaving two more charred hulks and an additional twenty-six bodies in front of the wall.

As the day moved into midafternoon, Saoirse found a moment to wonder why the battalion had not arrived to relieve them. Her troops had spotted drones in the air, so even though the drones didn't last long, Venezelos had to know what was happening. She sighed. The reason didn't matter. The battalion wasn't coming down Pilsudski Road yet, and her troops would somehow need to hang on until it did, despite the dwindling ammunition and number of troops able to fight.

She sent Hopkinson back to the building and settled at the watchtower herself. She did not need to see much. All she needed was a little bit of a man above or outside of cover, or even blocking the light through a gap in cover. That was enough for her to put a bullet into him. She did it often enough that the Guards would watch for the muzzle flash at the watchtower and respond with a hail of fire. As soon as she shot, she would roll away from the embrasure and hug the floor, then wait for the storm to pass. It was a kind of game, she thought, and she was better at it than they were. The Guards acknowledged that later in the afternoon when the shooting all but stopped and they repositioned farther away.

Dusk was falling when one of the militia climbed up to the ruined watchtower and poked his head through the doorway. "Lieutenant Irish," he said, "they need you back in the control station."

"What's the problem? Can it wait?" Saoirse asked.

"I don't know," said the militiaman. "All I know is your Cyber said to get you."

Cyber? If Alves needed her, that put a different light on it. "Someone has to take this position," she said. "Can you shoot well enough to do it until I can send a peacer back here?"

"I can do that, Irish," the man said.

Saoirse decided she would need to take him at his word and crawled backward until she was through the doorway, with her feet on the stairs leading down. "Keep your goddamn head below any opening," she said. "They like shooting at this spot."

Then it was down to the ground and dash across the courtyard. As she reached the station entrance, an explosion sounded behind her. She turned to see smoke and flame shoot skyward from a direct hit on the watchtower she had quitted less than two minutes ago.

Chance. It was a funny thing, she thought. She was sorry for the militiaman who had stayed there at her order; then her mind shifted to the need to have Mwesigye find a couple of troopers to take a position in the mess the mortar shell had left and keep the gate covered. She found a second to wonder again at how coldly she was thinking, and then her mind went to whatever Alves needed. She needed to know that.

Alves was on the second floor, in the back corner of the building, in what had been the station director's office. The roof was mostly gone, and the windows had been blown out by an explosion that left the interior a shambles. The early-evening sky gave enough illumination through the hole in the roof that Saoirse could pick her way past the debris on the floor. Alves was standing in the outer corner, by an overturned desk. Mwesigye, Hopkinson, and Nnadi were with her. Saoirse held up her hand to Alves and spoke quickly with Mwesigye about the watchtower. He, in turn, told Nnadi to find another peacer and take care of it. Then they both turned to Alves.

"A shell hit here a little while ago," Alves said. "Blew the office apart. There was a safe in the concrete under the director's desk. The safe was explosion-proof, but its lock wasn't. Look what was inside."

Alves shone the light from her comm on a row of stacks of paper that had been neatly placed on the floor.

"What's this?" Saoirse asked.

"It's their records of the zombie trade." Alves almost spat the words out. "This is why we didn't find any of it when we searched the prezydent's offices. They knew we were coming. They wiped the one drive that must have had the vehicle information and moved the rest of it here. We talked to a couple of the employees from downstairs. This was brought here right before our raid. It's a logical place to hide it, when I think about it. And it's all *paper!*"

"You can't hack paper and ink," Saoirse said.

"You need to look at this." Alves knelt down and picked up a page from the top of one of the piles. "These papers, they show how much they shipped, what ships they use, how much *money* this is bringing. And it shows who they are paying off. Scan this with your comm and use Translate. It's Latvian." The sheet Alves was holding shook under the light.

Saoirse knelt down next to her and took the page. She saw that she held a neat listing of where Prezydent Strazdins dispersed the money from the zombie trade. At the top of the list, the recipient of the most money by far, was Solar Council Legate Liu. Captain Bronson's name was there as well. *Our intelligence was actually their intelligence*, Saoirse thought. *Bronson wasn't stupid, only working for the other side.*

"This explains a lot," she said. "This is why the legate is so hot to certify Daleko Bałtyckie as an independent world. That's why he ordered Venezelos to keep the battalion on base and why our staffing and supply were never right. That's how they've known what we were doing all along and why the battalion isn't outside right now."

"And why our comms are jammed," Alves added. "The legate's office has our codes and frequencies. Of course. They have battery backup, so they have power and can keep jamming us."

"We have to get this to Venezelos," Saoirse said.

"We can't use the comms," Alves pointed out.

"I know." Saoirse chewed on her lower lip. "I've got an idea. Cyber, can you digitize this stuff? Fast?"

Alves nodded. "The control room is two levels underground. Everything works."

"Good. I want three chips, each with a complete copy." She turned to Mwesigye. "Find Andrzej and two of his buddies. Have them meet us in the control room."

Mwesigye left immediately with Hopkinson. Alves started to gather up the pages. In the meantime, Saoirse looked through the summary pages she had scanned with her comm. She saw Cixin Wang's name from Titan Research Base. She also saw how the organization was structured at Titan Station. The person running it wasn't Abel Concannon.

It was Mom.

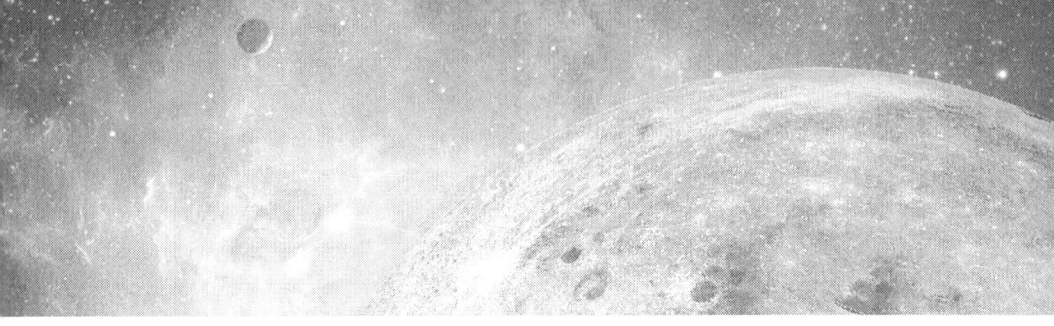

FORTY-SIX

Alves, Andrzej, two of Andrzej's friends, Nowak, and Mwesigye were in the basement control room of the station when Saoirse came down the stairs. She was in a haze, chiding herself for having taken so long to get there when matters were urgent and hung in the balance. Still, once she saw Mom's name in the Titan Station organization and on the money list, one thought had led inexorably to another. Her mind went over all the signals she had missed or refused to see, starting with how an alcoholic and a druggie with only a high school education could be filling the sysadmin role on Titan Station.

Oh sure, she was bright and oh-so-good with computer systems. Oh sure, she was Mom's pet. She had liked being someone's pet for once! Her mind circled over how she had sat with Mom and told her everything she'd found from snooping through Titan Station's system. She thought about the beautiful new comm Mom had given her, and how she had been tracked that last frantic day on the station. It was all so obvious, and she had been all so blind and even more stupid.

Worse, she had left Gusty on Titan Station with Mom.

You are a worthless piece of— Stop feeling sorry for yourself, Saoirse!

Arriving in the control room, Saoirse blinked and saw the others in front of her. This was no time to go off and have a pity party. Not now. Not ever.

"Are the chips ready?" she asked.

Alves held out a palm with three small chips embedded in plastic. "Each one has everything. I didn't put any encryption or protection. Didn't think you'd want it."

"I don't."

A light flashed next to a vid screen at the main console, and a ringtone echoed in the room. Saoirse looked at it, the unvoiced question evident on her face.

"Log says it's been signaling every twenty minutes for the last three hours," Alves said. "Nobody's been down here, with all of what's going on. I saw it when I came down and checked it. It's a direct landline to the prezydent's office. We wanted to check with you before we pick up."

Saoirse watched the signal light flash twice more. The others in the room were waiting for an answer. When had she become the font of all wisdom?

"Leave it alone," she said. "What we're doing is more important." Another snap decision, she thought, in a day of hundreds of them. How many right and how many wrong? Would she ever know?

"Cyber, give each of the boys a chip." Alves handed out the chips to Andrzej and his friends, and Saoirse turned to face the three of them. They were filthy and disheveled from first the climb and then the fighting, but their eyes were fixed on her, their faces alert. "Listen to me," she said. "There's a lot of information on those chips, but the most important piece is that Solar Council Legate Liu and Captain Bronson of the peacers are in the pay of Prezydent Strazdins." She paused and searched their faces to see that the words registered. Then she said, "Andrzej, you said that you had taken the cliff path at night."

He stood straighter. "Yes, Irish. I wasn't lying."

"Good. You and your friends, go down that trail to the branch point you showed me, where the trail splits and the new one goes off and comes out past the station wall. Get to there and then split up. Each of you go to the peacer base a different way. Only one of you has to make it there. Get to Lieutenant Colonel Dimitris Venezelos. He's in command. Give him the chip and tell him what I just told you. No matter what anybody says, the only person you speak to and give that chip to is Lieutenant Colonel Venezelos. Do you understand?" She saw three nods. "Then repeat it back to me." After each one of them had done so, she added, "You can also tell Venezelos that there is only one person on Titan Station in the solar system that he can trust. She's a peacer. Her name is Augusta Gray. Got that too?" Again the nods.

"We won't let you down, Irish," said Andrzej. "We'll see Venezelos. I can be there by daylight."

Saoirse looked at her comm. "We need to buy some hours," she said. "At least the Guards will be busy up here. That should help you get through. Now, get going."

The youngest of the three had no evidence of beard yet on his face. He stopped next to Nowak and they had a brief exchange of words, followed by a briefer embrace. Then the three were gone.

"I was only saying goodbye and good luck to my grandson," Nowak said. His voice sounded as tired as his face looked. "You know," he said to Saoirse, "these boys will do anything to impress you."

She nodded. She understood why, and she knew she was exploiting that in a completely cynical way. She did that because she had read all the books Tommie had downloaded to her, and that was what good commanders did. They took whatever edge they could find and used it to accomplish their mission, because, in the end, the mission was all that mattered. She had sent three. Was that enough? No answer to the question. It was done.

"Are you sure of Venezelos?" Mwesigye asked.

Saoirse shrugged. "As sure as I can be. His name is not in the papers we found, and I have to think that if he were working with Liu, things would have gone differently." In the end, she had made yet another decision and she would deal with the consequences.

After a short silence, she said, "We need to buy time for the boys to get to Venezelos. Cyber, if—no, *when* that line signals again, answer it. Find out who it is and what they want, but don't tell them anything. Don't tell them I'm in command. If they want whoever is in command, say they're not in the building, that they're out with the defenses. You can say you'll have the commander back here for a call in an hour. That will get us the first hour. Sergeant," she said to Mwesigye, "you and I should check our defenses. There's no way we're going to let Strazdins and his assholes take over Daleko Bałtyckie and keep shipping zombie to Earth and God knows where else. No way."

"Lieutenant," said Mwesigye, "that's a mission we'll all sign on for. Let's go have a look at what's out there now."

. . .

Saoirse and Mwesigye were back in the control room in considerably less than an hour.

"It was some flunky from the prezydent's office," Alves told them. "He was annoyed that we hadn't picked up before. I told him I was sorry but we had been busy."

"You're too polite, Cyber," Saoirse said. "Next time, tell him to fuck a sheep. Or himself."

Cyber almost smiled. "He wanted to know who was in command," she said. "I didn't tell him. Then he said that the prezydent wants a conference call immediately with whoever is in command and with Legate Liu."

"Yeah." Saoirse put her helmet on a console and ran her hands through her hair. "Liu is going to order us to surrender." Her tired brain didn't want to think, but an idea popped up regardless. She forced herself to focus on it and wondered if it would sound any good if she said it out loud. "Strazdins needs this plant back under his control and operating. Without it, he can't hold power no matter what he does with the Sejm, and Daleko Bałtyckie can't qualify as an independent world. He also knows his records are in this building but doesn't know if we've found them yet, so he'll want to prevent that. He'll want whatever gets us out of here the fastest. Makes sense?"

Both Alves and Mwesigye nodded.

"Okay. When the hour is up, call back and tell the flunky that we agree to talk, but not until dawn. We want a cease-fire until then so we can take care of wounded. Don't tell him who's in command, but tell him Venezelos has to be on the call as well."

"Why would he agree to that?" Alves looked puzzled.

Saoirse laughed. "He probably won't. But I'll bet Strazdins isn't the one sitting by the comm in the middle of the night. They'll have to call him. That's a bit more time. When the guy calls back and says no, tell him we'll destroy the plant if Strazdins doesn't agree."

"What!" Alves' jaw dropped and hung open, her eyebrows arched up above wide eyes, a face that said eloquently that she could not believe what she'd heard.

"Say it, and see what happens. And when he gives you shit, remember to tell him to fuck himself. Then hang up. He'll call back." Saoirse put both hands on the console next to her helmet and leaned forward as though holding herself up. "What do you think of our defenses, Sergeant?"

"We won't hold the wall for long," Mwesigye said. "Too low on troopers and ammunition. What we can do, when it's necessary, is pull everyone back into the station building. Make them fight us for it room by room. They'll take a lot of casualties, and maybe these Guards won't do it."

"Plan for it," Saoirse said. "Cyber, what I said about destroying the plant, can you do it?"

"What do you mean?" There was no mistaking the tremor in Alves' voice. "I mean, sure, I can stop the cooling system and block the safety overrides. The cores will melt down. But you don't really want that, do you?"

"No. Mass murder and suicide is not the idea. But you can do something to ruin it short of a meltdown, can't you?"

"Maybe," Alves said. "I'm not a nuclear engineer—not any kind of an engineer. But let me look at the system, at the overrides, what they are supposed to prevent. Maybe."

"Okay. Figure that you have until dawn. Or whenever this call happens. We need to be ready for an attack," she said to Mwesigye. "I'd bet either while we're arguing over the call or whenever we're supposed to have a cease-fire."

"Why would they do that?" Alves asked.

It was Mwesigye who answered. "Because they're assholes," he said, "and they'll call our bluff on destroying the plant."

"And if they can overrun us by surprise, they don't have to negotiate the call or wait," Saoirse added. "They will attack when they think we're not looking for it."

. . .

When the time came, Alves placed the call to the prezydent's office, and the conversation went as they had planned. The return call, thirty minutes later, agreed to add Venezelos but insisted that the conference had to take place in no more than an hour. Saoirse shook her head and Alves stuck to the script. After nearly an hour with no return call from the prezydent's office, shooting erupted along the wall as the Guards tried to rush the gateway with a shielded truck. That attack was beaten off easily. The call from the prezydent's office arrived as soon as the Guards retreated. The person calling informed them that the prezydent agreed to the dawn call and to the cease-fire.

"Any chance you'll be able to send the data from their records when this call happens?" Saoirse asked Alves after she broke the last connection.

"No." Alves shook her head. "This is a landline and it connects through the prezydent's office. They made sure I knew there would be a thirty-second delay between anything we say or send before it goes out to Venezelos. They will block anything they don't like or can't read. They were very clear. And the legate will be with Venezelos in person at the base."

"Yeah. That would have been too easy," Saoirse said. "Just make sure you can take this plant down by dawn. If none of the boys gets through to Venezelos, that may be the only way we can stop Strazdins."

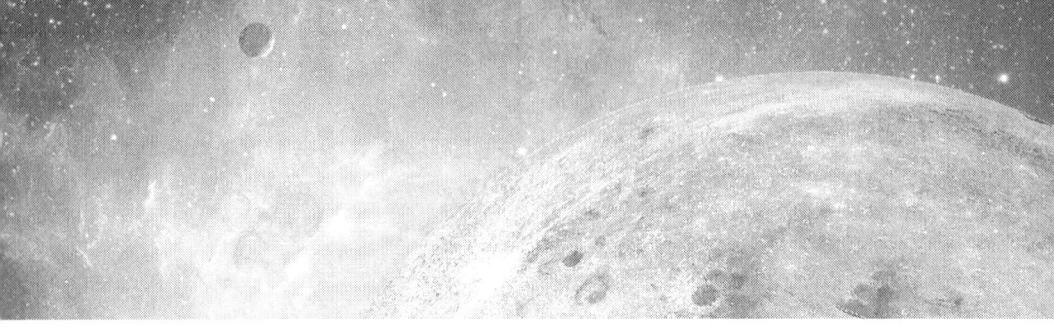

FORTY-SEVEN

Lieutenant Colonel Dimitris Venezelos was angry and unhappy in roughly equal measures. The dawn conference call was the least of it; late nights and early mornings that often merged together were part of his job description. Nor was it the physical presence of Legate Liu in his office, as irritating as that was—as though the man did not trust Venezelos to take the call independently.

His two missing platoons, which *had* to be the reason for the call, were the reason for his mood. Two platoons of peacers, along with a company of militia, seemed to have vanished in the swamp several days ago. An accusation had come from the prezydent's office that those peacers and militia had perpetrated a massacre in some village. No evidence was provided and the claim had not been repeated, but the platoons remained out of sight and out of contact. Then he was told his troops had been lost in one of the forest fires for which Daleko Bałtyckie was famous. A smoke plume had been visible from the base, so the fire had probably happened, but then *something* had definitely happened at the Nowy Vistula crossing. Again, no information was provided, although the City Guards had moved up outside the base, positioned as if to fight any move the battalion made.

Then yesterday, it sounded as though a pitched battle had taken place out toward Sobieski Point, where the nuclear plant was. The short-range drones he did have were sufficient to cover that area. The images and data they sent confirmed the fighting and showed that peacers were involved—at least until the drones were shot down. Then the Guards outside the base had vanished. Still, with all of that, all he had from the legate's office was a blunt refusal to allow his battalion off the base, coupled with a statement that the local government was handling it—as though Daleko Bałtyckie were already an independent world and member of the Assembly.

It was time for the call. Venezelos was standing behind his desk with his vid screen on, ready to give the legate a piece of his mind—several pieces, actually—when Liu walked in.

"I would like an explanation, Legate Liu, a real explanation and not some confabulated drivel, for what is going on."

Liu stopped in front of the desk, and the two men stared at each other across it. "I suspect this call will provide that and, I hope, a way to clean up the mess you have made."

"The mess I made?" Venezelos was incredulous.

"Yes. If you had not found, shall we say, a creative way to circumvent my order and sent your troops out, none of this would be happening. You have a rogue unit out there. I will be frank, Dimitris, you may have been technically correct in what you did, but I will not forget, and the consequences will be borne by you." Liu's customary, albeit superficial, cordiality was absent. "That is why my orders to you have become very specific. If that results in peacers killed out at that plant, the fault is yours."

"Strong words for a man who never faced an armed enemy," Venezelos said.

"Please." Liu bit the word off short, as if to swallow whatever else he was going to say. "I do not need to hear the story again about how you made your stars. Once was quite enough. Now, is this display of yours double-sided or will I need to literally stand over your shoulder?"

"It is not double-sided. I do not need anyone else to see what I am viewing in my office. You can bring one of the chairs around to my side of the desk. The weight should not be a problem for a man of your unquestioned strength."

Liu glared at him but dragged one of the chairs around to sit next to Venezelos, who adjusted the display so that they both showed in the Self window. As he finished, another window opened to show Prezydent Strazdins. His was a young face—broad, square, and tanned. Close-set brown eyes were so dark that they almost matched the black of his pupils.

"Where's the peacer?" Liu muttered.

They waited for a minute, then two minutes before a third window opened. Saoirse Kenneally looked out from the screen. She sat at a console, scored body armor over her camo, head bare.

Liu hit the Mute symbol on the screen. "You have a woman in command out there? On this world?" He sounded as though he did not believe his eyes. "And *that* woman? This is indeed one hell of a mess you have made, Dimitris."

"She wasn't in command when they left," Venezelos said. It was an effort to keep his tone mild as Liu leaned across him to get his entire face in the window. "Let's see what she has to say before we jump to conclusions." He unmuted the microphone to cut off any further side comment from Liu.

"I am Lieutenant Irish Kenneally, Third Platoon, C Company, Thirty-second Peacemaker Battalion. I am the officer in command at the Sobieski Point Power Station. Prezydent Strazdins' office requested this call. Please tell me what you want to talk about."

Venezelos glanced at Liu, who looked ready to have a stroke. Veins stood out at the side of his neck, his teeth were clenched, and a small muscle at the hinge of his jaw spasmed repetitively.

"I am Solar Council Legate Liu Honghui," he said through jaws that barely moved. "Confirm that you know who I am and that the Peacemakers on Daleko Bałtyckie report to me."

"Confirmed, sir." Kenneally said nothing beyond that.

Liu cleared his throat. "All right, then. You are ordered to immediately surrender your troops to the City Guards outside the plant. Send someone out through the gate with a white flag, leave the gateway open, and put down your weapons. Confirm that you are obeying."

"No, sir."

"What!" Liu's neck veins bulged even further. "You insubordinate little . . ."

"Little girl?" Kenneally suggested.

"Goddamn it! Bitch!" Liu seethed. "I gave you an order."

"Not a valid one, sir." Kenneally's face and tone remained neutral. "You are, as you say, the highest civilian authority on Daleko Bałtyckie, and the Peacemakers report to you. However, as a civilian, you cannot give direct orders to a Peacemaker unit in the field when it is actively engaged with the enemy. You can look it up. I did."

Liu turned in his seat and brought his hands up as if to give Venezelos a shove, then thought better of it and was left with his hands in the air. "Dimitris! You command this battalion. *You* are her superior officer. You are responsible directly to me. You order her to surrender."

Venezelos hesitated. There had to be a reason Kenneally was doing this. It must be obvious by this point that the battalion was not coming to relieve its troops at the Point. That disgusted him and might end his career regardless of anything Liu did, but Kenneally had to know it was true. So, why? "Are you concerned about the safety of your troops if you surrender?" he asked. "Both yours and the militia with you?"

"I can speak to that," Strazdins said, breaking into the conversation. "The Guards report to me, and unlike, I guess, the situation with Legate Liu, they always take my orders. I can guarantee your safety if you surrender."

"Really?" said Kenneally. "But then we are prisoners and there is always an afterward, you know."

"I am beginning to share Legate Liu's opinion of you." Strazdins stopped, held a hand up, half seen in the monitor window, and collected himself. "This should not be so difficult. I will tell you what I will do. Now, you and your men, they have fought hard; they have fought very well. I say that in front of your commander. You have fought well. But you have no chance and we should end the bloodshed on both sides. What I will do, to honor how well you have fought, is this: surrender now and you are free to go. Just leave the plant and your weapons and go. No imprisonment, no charges, no penalties. I am sure the legate will agree as well. Now, what do you say?"

"Free to go? With safe passage?" Kenneally asked.

"Yes," Strazdins said. "You are free to go. Safe passage to your base. Only, of course, if you give up your weapons."

"*Molon labe*," said Saoirse Kenneally. Her window closed.

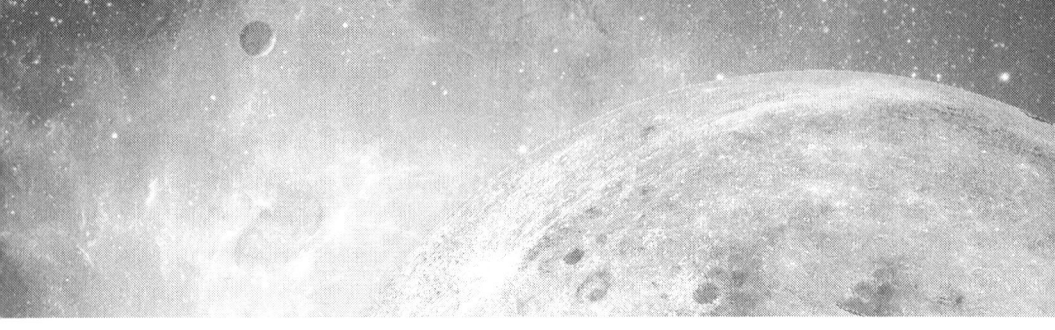

FORTY-EIGHT

"What the *fuck* was that!" Liu was on his feet as soon as the connection terminated, color rising in his face.

Venezelos pushed himself away from his desk and away from Liu. He stayed seated, elbows on the arms of his chair, fingers steepled in front of his chest. "It was a message, I think, to me specifically. One that would go through the thirty-second delay and the prezydent's filter because it is only two words, and Greek. Which she knows I understand."

"That was Greek at the end? She doesn't speak Greek! Tell me what it means and why it's a message."

"You don't need to speak Greek to know this," Venezelos said, "but I don't imagine you ever studied the origins of Western civilization."

"Don't be ridiculous," Liu said.

"Then I will tell you a short story." Venezelos paused. "It's now a little over twenty-seven hundred years since this happened, back when the Persian Empire under Xerxes invaded Greece. We were a collection of city-states back then that spent most of their time and effort fighting each other. When the Persians invaded, one of the city-states, Sparta, sent a force to block the invaders. It was, however, during an important religious festival, and the Spartans would not interrupt that—so they sent only three hundred men under Leonidas, one of their two kings."

Venezelos indicated his framed image of the statue of Leonidas. "That is his statue; I remember pointing it out to Kenneally the day she first reported. They picked up some allies on their way, but probably no more than six or seven thousand in all. The Persians numbered more than one hundred thousand. So Leonidas picked a place where the Persians couldn't make use of their numbers, a very narrow pass with a wall. That place is called Thermopylae." Venezelos paused. "I see you do not recognize the name. Anyway, Xerxes did what Prezydent Strazdins just did. He praised the Spartans and offered to let them walk away free, safe passage. All they had to do was give up their weapons."

"And?"

"Leonidas told Xerxes exactly what Kenneally just said. *Molon labe*."

"Which means?"

"'Come and take them.'"

"You said she sent you a message. I don't see any message in this," Liu said.

Venezelos sighed. "It took three days of fighting, and the Spartans fought to the last man. Quite literally to the last man. The three days they delayed the Persians gave the Greeks time to rally their fleet and then defeat the Persians at Salamis."

"And that's the message?" Liu retorted. "I'll tell you the message. You have a rogue unit with a crazy bitch who thinks she's in command. That's what this is telling you."

"No." Venezelos stood up. He was a head taller than Liu, and the shorter man had to step back to look up at him. "Men, and I assume women, do fight to the death of their own free will. Not what happened with chipped soldiers back in the war years. Thermopylae is far from the only example in history. But," Venezelos paused, "when they fight to the death, to the last man, they do it for a *reason*. What is the *reason* these men and women are willing to fight to the death?" The call signal on Venezelos' monitor was flashing. He ignored it. "The message is about the reason, and I don't know what it is. I wonder if you do, Legate Liu."

"I told you the reason. She's crazy, and so are the rest of her troops. If I trusted you to do it, I would order you to take your battalion over there and make her surrender."

Whatever reply Venezelos was going to make went unsaid as a loud banging came on his office door, followed by a male voice that asked, "Lieutenant Colonel, are you okay?"

"Yes," Venezelos replied. "Why?"

"We tried your comm, voice and message. You didn't pick up or respond."

"I am busy. Whatever it is, I'll deal with it later."

"I'm sorry, sir."

Venezelos heard steps going away from his door, but they stopped and returned. The fist knocked on the door again. "I'm sorry, sir, but this is important. Please, sir, could you come out by yourself so that I can tell you?"

Venezelos looked at Liu, who shrugged. Then Venezelos opened his desk drawer, withdrew a pistol, and went to the door. He opened it to find a nervous peacer in the hallway shifting his weight from foot to foot. The sight of the weapon did nothing to calm the man.

"What is it?" Venezelos closed the door behind him and stepped away from it with the peacer.

"A young man showed up at the perimeter. Said he needs to speak to you, only to you. We didn't know what to do with him, so we put him in the guardhouse. We know you're busy, sir, but I think you should talk to him."

Maybe it was having related the story of Thermopylae that did it, but Venezelos thought he could hear a whisper in his ear. It was one word from his ancestors: *kairos*, the critical time for action.

. . .

Saoirse's camo was soaking wet under her armpits by the time she broke the connection and pushed back from the console. She had not expected it to be so difficult and stressful, especially since the conversation had gone almost exactly as she had played it out in her head beforehand. Maybe the stress had come from keeping her emotions in check. Alves and Mwesigye, the only others in the room with her, waited for her to speak.

"None of the boys made it," she said after she explained what her concluding words had meant. "The call would not have gone the way it did if Venezelos had that information."

"One of them may still get through," Mwesigye said. "Delays happen, particularly in a war zone, and that's what this place is now."

Saoirse shrugged. "Anything is possible, but we can't bet on it. I'm hoping that from what I said, Venezelos will know what we are doing and what will happen. I hope that's enough for him to bring the battalion, no matter what the legate says, and then he'll see the documents. But if he won't defy the legate, the only way we stop Strazdins is to take the plant down. Can you do it, Cyber?"

"I'll get it," Alves said. "I've almost got it worked out, but I need more time."

"How much?"

"Not sure. Couple of hours, maybe."

"Okay," Saoirse said. "You work it out. We'll give you the time." She headed to the staircase with Mwesigye. She was halfway up the stairs when she said, over her shoulder, "I'm sorry I got you into this, Jeremiah."

Mwesigye's laugh surprised her. "I wouldn't say that, Lieutenant. Truth is, I don't see any way they would let us live, no matter what they promised or what we did, because we know what's in those papers. It's like that out here in the Reach. We have a saying where I come from that humanity went out to the stars, but civilization didn't. For myself, I'd rather go down fighting. If you're fighting, at least there's always a chance."

"Thank you, Sergeant," Saoirse said. "I'll remember that. As long as we're fighting, there's a chance."

The renewed assault on the control station began almost as soon as they reached the front entrance to the building. This time, the Guards had put more thought and preparation into the attack. On a world lacking any GPS or autonomous driving technology, three of the shielded trucks were outfitted with crude steering and engine controls, packed with high explosive, and launched at the center of the station's wall. As the trucks rolled in, machine gun and mortar rounds rained down on the defenders. The peacers' last rocket turned one truck into a blazing pyrotechnic display, but the other two rolled ahead. As the trucks closed on the wall, smoke canisters began to fall. In minutes, the battlefield disappeared in a smoky fogbank.

The trucks hit the wall with twin blasts and bursts of flame that could be seen even through the smoke. The detonations were followed by the sounds of falling concrete as parts of the wall collapsed. Hard on the heels of the explosions and under the cover of the smoke came the assault of the Guards.

The fighting along the wall was vicious but brief. Once the Guards were able to penetrate the wall and close with the defenders, there were not enough peacers and militia to throw them back or even hold a defense line. Mwesigye used the comms and pulled their troops back to the control station to avoid losing all the troops at the wall. It no longer mattered if anyone was monitoring the comms.

The attack on the building began almost immediately after the wall was abandoned. More smoke canisters fell in the courtyard, and the Guards tried to rush the front entrance. Saoirse positioned herself at an empty window frame near the door and fired at anything that suggested a solid form moving in the smoke. Sometimes a scream followed a shot. Flashes burst out of the smoke as well, and bullets dug into the concrete, flew through the openings, and sometimes led to cries as they pierced a target inside.

The attackers were too numerous. They made it to the building wall and front entrance. They fired through the windows and the door. A grenade was tossed through one window; a militiaman grabbed it and threw it back out. It exploded outside to an accompaniment of yells. The attackers pushed through the door and climbed through windows. Smoke from the outside drifted in and clouded the interior. The fight in the front rooms degenerated into a hand-to-hand melee, where a knife in the stomach was as likely as a bullet.

"Second line!" shouted Mwesigye above the din. "Second line!"

Saoirse echoed him as loudly as she could.

The remaining peacers and militia pulled back, as they had planned the previous night, to the building's back rooms and corridors. While the Guards sorted themselves out in the smoke-filled front rooms they had won at such cost, the peacers charged back through the interior doors and corridors, blasting into the Guards. In a few minutes, the front rooms were cleared of Guards. The floors were carpeted in bodies: Guards, peacers, militia. Saoirse saw Grandfather Nowak slumped dead against a wall, a line of bullet wounds across his chest, his shirt soaked in blood. A body on the floor was identifiable as Juliana Hopkinson only by the long braided ponytail down her back.

"We can't hold the front of the building," Mwesigye said. "Not enough of us left." He ordered the remaining peacers and militia again to the back rooms and corridors, so they could target the Guards when they attacked the front again.

Saoirse grabbed Mwesigye's arm to get his attention. "We need to block the way to the lower levels," she said. "The Guards will go around the building sooner or later and try to force their way in the back entrance."

Mwesigye nodded and they hurried down the same corridor that Saoirse had forced her way in two days before. The two peacers stationed at the back door were exchanging fire with unseen Guards behind the building. Saoirse and Mwesigye turned to the right. A small desk had been set up halfway down the hall, in front of the stairway that led down to the control room level.

"Are you ready, Cyber?" Saoirse yelled into the comm as she reached the desk.

No answer came. Instead, bullets and cries sounded in the corridor behind her. She looked back. A blow struck her below the left elbow and spun her halfway around. Blinding, shattering pain lanced through her left arm. A thunderclap exploded in her head; a gout of blood shot out of her mouth and across the desk. Uncomprehendingly, she looked at a tooth in the middle of the pool of blood on the desk. Through the loud, high-pitched ringing in her ears, she heard more gunshots. She thought she heard Cyber yelling, "It's okay! It's okay! It's okay!"

That was good, Saoirse thought. She needed to tell Cyber to blow the plant. They had held as long as they could. Cyber had to blow the plant. They couldn't hold any longer. But she couldn't make words come out of her mouth. She tried to move her jaw, to speak. Agony! Something warm and liquid rolled out of her mouth and down her chin. She saw blood dripping on the already bloodied desk. She had to tell Cyber to blow the plant, but she couldn't speak. That was all right. Cyber knew what she had to do. Cyber would do it. Saoirse only had to give her a few more minutes. Again, she heard Cyber yell that it was okay. A very few minutes, Saoirse, she told herself.

She propped herself up against the desk with her right arm, rifle still clutched in that hand. The left was useless. Her left sleeve was drenched in blood; she couldn't move the arm or the hand. It was only a pulsing, throbbing spasm of pain. She edged around the desk carefully to avoid falling, wondering the whole time why she hadn't been shot again. She saw the reason as she worked her way around the desk and looked up the corridor. Bodies lay by the open door. Mwesigye sat on the floor not far from the desk, a bloody smear on the wall above him. He looked at her through half-closed eyes and raised a hand to give a thumbs-up sign. The hand dropped down again after a few seconds.

Saoirse continued around the desk one labored foot at a time. Each movement caused fresh agony in her left arm. Finally, she dropped into the chair. Grim-faced, she maneuvered the rifle so that it rested on the desk. That way, she could point it down the corridor with only one hand. While she sat there and waited for the end, she took a certain satisfaction in the realization that she would again defy her family's expectations and, this time, even her own.

She was going to die sober.

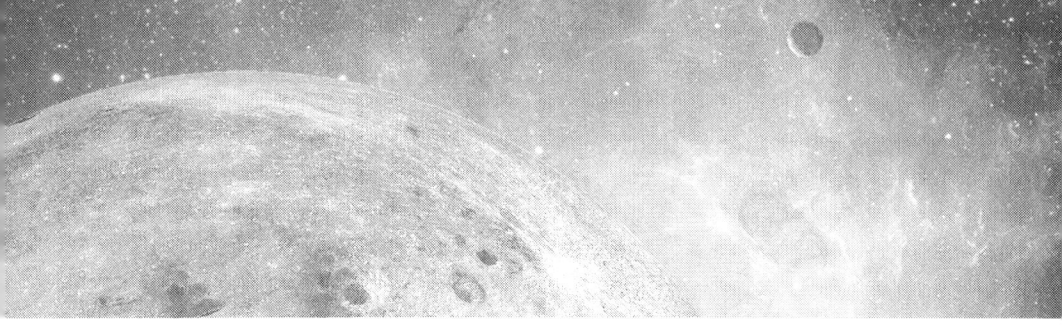

FORTY-NINE

It was a bright summer day in Chicagoland, the rare type, with a cloudless blue sky but without the baking heat. Saoirse had taken her little sister, Caitlyn, to Grant Park, where they would meet Saoirse's boyfriend, Tommie. Some of the girls from high school had been there, even though the school was in Dublin, and they had tried to be mean, but Saoirse's friend Gusty was there and made them stop. Caitlyn was dancing around the fountain, singing to the stuffed bunny in her arms, when she caught sight of Tommie coming up the path. She ran to him with a squeal and jumped into his arms. Saoirse was only a step behind, arms outstretched—

Pain! Pain, that was all she felt; the sunlit scene was gone. Then, no pain. Only blackness, no feeling at all.

Saoirse opened her eyes, saw a concrete room painted white. Sunlight, pouring through an open window, made little dust motes sparkle. She was in a bed, looking up at the ceiling. A sheet and a blanket covered her to her chin. Her head didn't want to move, resisted moving. A click and a squeak announced a door opening. She looked down, past her blanketed toes, and saw Lieutenant Colonel Venezelos step through the door.

"Good afternoon, Captain," Venezelos said. "The docs told me you were awake."

Saoirse tried to turn her head to find the captain Venezelos was speaking to, but her head and neck did not want to turn. Venezelos walked over to her bed and looked down at her. Waited.

"What happened?" Saoirse asked. Her jaw did not want to move. A rusty hinge would have been smoother. Her voice was strange in her ears. Raspy.

"At the Point, do you mean?" Venezelos paused. He might have been waiting for her to nod, but that movement was beyond her. "That's a story," he said finally, "but I will give you the condensed version for now. A young man named Andrzej reached our base with a chip and a story of his own to tell. Let us say that I considered Legate Liu's orders null and void from that point and put him and Bronson under arrest. The Thirty-second Battalion moved immediately to relieve you at the Point. We took the prezydent's offices and the legate's offices, and that restored communication. We were able to reach Cyber to let her know we were on the way. I will say that I took considerable pleasure in personally leading the attack. We took the Guards in the rear, and after what the fighting had already done to them—what *you* and your troops had done to them—they collapsed."

He shook his head. "The carnage up there shocked everyone. No one—city, highlands, swampers—no one was prepared for what happened. We rounded up the Sejm delegates and trucked them up there to see it before we cleaned up. We made them see it with the bodies still there. It was a rude and immediate education in what war is, and what going to war means. It's not that now they are suddenly in love with each other, but they are working together. Alicja Symanski and Henriks Ligas are working it out with the other delegates. Daleko Bałtyckie will get a just government, and the zombie trade will stop."

So that was what Cyber had been saying when Saoirse heard, *It's okay.* Thank God Cyber hadn't destroyed the plant before that point!

"Andrzej made it," Saoirse said. "Only Andrzej?"

"Yes." Venezelos paused again. "We found one boy dead, shot, on the way into Sobieski. We found another body at the base of the falls a couple of weeks later."

Saoirse looked up at the ceiling. She should have sent only Andrzej. Those two deaths were because she had thought she was smart. Although if that other boy hadn't been on the road to Sobieski, maybe Andrzej would have been caught, and probably they would have been killed in the fighting anyway. And if Cyber had destroyed the plant before the battalion contacted her . . .

No, Saoirse, you do the best you can with the situation you have, and you never know how it would have been if you chose differently.

"How many?" Saoirse croaked.

"Survived? Eight peacers, including you, and six militia."

"My God. Mwesigye?"

Venezelos nodded. "Medical retirement. We shipped him out on an interstellar to a specialized hospital and rehab about a month ago. Would have sent you, but you weren't stable enough then."

A month. Hold that, she thought. "Cyber?"

"She's fine."

"You said a month. What happened to me?"

"I notice you put yourself last." Venezelos smiled. "Our surgeon thinks your case should be written up. You took a bullet below your left ear, near the angle of the jaw. Took out your back molars, dug a channel across your tongue, and came out your mouth. It will leave an interesting scar. Took some doing to put your jaw back together, but they did it. Then there's your arm. I am sorry about the snake."

"My snake? What?"

"Two bullets to the left forearm. Shattered both of the bones, tore the artery. You almost bled out. We do have good surgeons here. They printed some new bones and put them together with some metal and some plastic. I thought you were going to need a cyborg exemption, but they saved the nerves too. Your arm will work as well as it ever did. Doc saved you a piece of one of the bullets he dug out. Has it in plastic for you. The only thing is the snake. There is a scar through part of it we couldn't do anything about."

She tried to look at her arm, but couldn't. It felt as if there was a soft cast on it anyway.

"How long? How long have I been here?"

"Over two months," Venezelos said. "More out than in. This is the first time the docs let you lighten up enough to talk."

"Lighten up?" A sudden panic gripped her. "What have they been giving me? You know my record. I can't—"

"Relax, Captain." Venezelos smiled again. "We know how to deal with people with your type of problems. If we didn't, we'd have even worse trouble filling our combat units than we do now."

"You said 'Captain,'" Saoirse said. "You said it before, and I thought there was someone else here. Why did you call me captain?"

"It is appropriate when you have been promoted to that rank."

Saoirse was silent for a moment. It was as though she heard the words that Venezelos had spoken, but they didn't make sense. She turned them over in her mind. Played them over again internally. It was wrong. Worse than a mistake.

"You can't, sir."

"Can't what?"

"You can't promote me, sir. Can't make me a captain." Saying that last word made the last crack in a dam that was ready to burst. She couldn't hold it in any longer, wouldn't hold it in. The whole web of lies and deceit tore open, and it all came tumbling out as fast as she could speak. "You can't promote me, because I wasn't even a lieutenant to begin with. It was all faked. I faked it!" Her jaw screamed in pain as she tried to shout the words. "I wasn't even a peacer. That's a lie too. I was nothing more than a scoppy specialist, that's all, and even then, if you want the truth, I was really just a drunk looking for a way out of jail. I'm worthless, that's what I am, worth less than the pig shit on a swamper's bootheel."

"Curious choice of words," Venezelos said when she paused for breath. "I know there were some falsifications in your records."

"You knew?"

"Well, some of it, if not in all the detail you just gave me. Your record failed validation at HQ on Earth, so a notice was sent to me with orders to investigate. Transit times into the Reach being what they are, the ship carrying the notice didn't drop into the Daleko Bałtyckie system and transmit until your unit had left for Wałęsa. Fortuitous timing, if you will. So."

Venezelos stopped, as if choosing his words. "The current situation is that the SC legate is in jail, the same jail as the prezydent of Sobieski. Martial law is in effect, and as a result, I am the supreme military and civil authority on the planet. I have examined the, ah, inconsistencies in your record that HQ flagged and concluded my investigation by placing waivers and corrections as needed. I have confirmed that your previous rank of lieutenant was correct and have promoted you to captain. I trust that is clear."

"Why?" Saoirse was having trouble talking, and it wasn't only due to her wound. "Why aren't you throwing me in jail, or kicking me out of the peacers, or both?"

Venezelos was back to smiling. "It would be difficult to promote you if I put you in jail. And then there's the matter of your Valor Star. The whole battalion voted on it. The militia asked to vote as well, and we let them, even if that part of it is unofficial. Well, as far as the SC is concerned, all Peacers' Stars are unofficial, so we do what we want. It was the most lopsided vote I've heard of. It would embarrass the unit if you went to jail."

"What!"

"Yes. There is also the matter of your PLM. Not many living who hold that honor. I signed off on that, since I am the highest authority on the planet. Therefore it would also embarrass me if you went to jail. It's better for everybody for you to be a captain." Venezelos seemed to be enjoying himself.

"I still don't understand," Saoirse said. "I lied. I cheated. I did—"

"Exactly." Venezelos cut her off. "Understand something, Captain. People don't join the peacers because they are leading wonderful lives. But what you did is what matters. What you did here." He let out a brief sigh. "The universe is an unforgiving place, and we humans have a way of making it worse. This planet was on the road to hell. We've seen it all before, and all too often the peacers make it worse. The zombie trade made this place a nightmare that reached all the way to Earth. This time, we were able to make it right, thanks to you. The peacers won't forget. A few ships have been through since this all happened, so you can be sure the story is all across the Reach, wherever the interstellars have taken it. They're calling it Kenneally at the Point. If we put everything you've done, the good and the bad, onto the scales, I know which way the balance will tip."

"Oh my God."

Venezelos waited.

"What happens next?" Saoirse asked.

"We have an agreement with the US Army to provide advanced training for our high-potential officers. There is going to be a combat peacer unit that will need a captain, count on it, and it would be a good idea if you learned your job. That will take you back to Earth for a while. What do you think of that?"

"I think that would be fine," Saoirse said. Then something occurred to her. "If I am going back to Earth, would I be able to attend to a few things?"

"I am certain we can arrange some leave for you." Venezelos straightened his stance. "With that, I am going to leave you, as I still have this planet to manage. There is someone else here who has been wanting to speak with you for a while, and I am going to let him in."

The man who replaced Venezelos in her hospital room was perhaps the last man Saoirse would have expected to see: Aleksander Szczechowicz. He was dressed exactly as he had been that day in the pole tree swamp forest, but he held his wide-brimmed sun hat in front of him, and his face was somber. Time passed while they looked at each other in silence.

"I buried my son after the Guards left," he said at last.

"I'm sorry, so sorry."

Aleksander shrugged. He started to twist the hat in his hands as though he were wringing out a dish towel. "What you did, all of you, my son and you, but especially you when you started shooting, you saved us. They were going to take our children as hostages, from villages all up and down the coast, to assure our Sejm votes and to make us harvest zombipterisin. Who knows what the final cost would have been, but you saved us from that. There is a hard lesson in this."

He fell silent for a moment, twisting his hat. "I buried him afterward on a small hillock near the rock pile with the thunder hole. I'm sure he played his little trick when he brought you there that day." Aleksander tried to smile. "He can see the sea from there and hear the thunder; he would like that. He was always a good sailor, even as a young boy. He will be safe from the sea, though, and our seas are dangerous here. He won't like that, of course. He never wanted to be safe. But this time he must defer to me."

"I'm sorry," Saoirse said again. "Did you . . . Were you able to talk with him . . . before . . ."

Aleksander shook his head. "No. My son and I were not much for talking to each other. I suppose he got that from me. He had left a letter for me in case—well, in case what happened would happen. I think he knew. He wrote much that he never said, that he never could say. Unfortunately, it is impossible for me to say anything in return." Aleksander looked down at his hat. He had torn the crown halfway off the brim. A tear rolled out of one eye and down one of the furrows in his cheek.

"What can I do?" Saoirse asked. "You came to see me."

"There is nothing for you to do," Aleksander said. "I came here because, in his letter, my son asked me to see you. He asked me to tell you that he loved you. Tomasz always had trouble speaking of his feelings." Aleksander was crying. The tears ran off his face and splashed on the floor.

"I loved him too." Saoirse's voice was a whisper amid her own tears.

PART V
THE BEGINNING

Today is victory over yourself of yesterday.
MIYAMOTO MUSASHI
Go Rin No Sho (*A Book of Five Rings*)

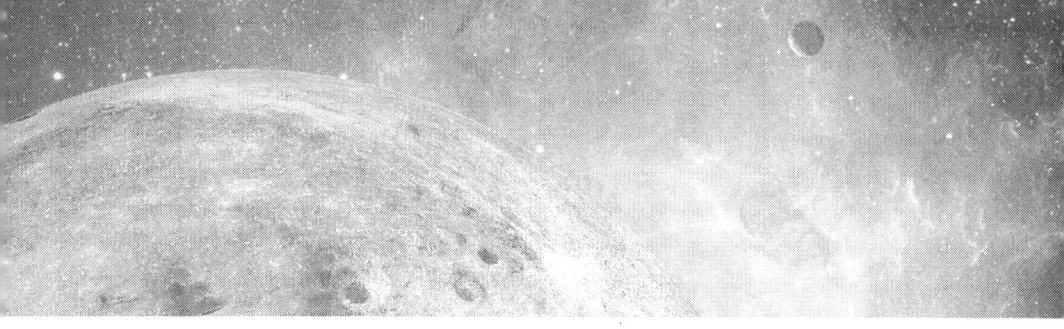

FIFTY

The passengers from the *Interstellar Reach Spaceship Suleiman the Magnificent* passed through the lock of the dock shuttle and queued up at the admission kiosks in the dock at Titan Station. Among them was a tall woman in the light-blue and gray dress uniform and beret of the Peacemakers. Where other passengers pressed close to one another in line to be that many inches and seconds closer to the kiosks, they left a wide berth around her. That could have been because of the sidearm she wore at her belt, but it could easily have been the way she held herself and the dark-blue eyes that dared anyone to meet them.

Saoirse was more than a little tense, and the kiosk acceptance did nothing to ease it. Yes, she had the message from Gusty, received minutes after the *Suleiman* had dropped through the wormhole and transmitted its manifest. The message said all was well, but Saoirse knew that computers and messages were not to be trusted—not by those who understood how those systems worked. Anxious, she scanned the crowd.

There was a commotion not far from her, people giving way quickly, as they would when an armed person in uniform was pushing through. Saoirse let out the breath she had been holding. Gusty!

Augusta Gray covered the remaining dozen feet with three long running strides. Her face wore a broad smile. At first she opened her arms, then caught sight of the uniform, came to attention, and saluted. Caught off guard, Saoirse paused a couple of seconds before returning it. Then she laughed and the two of them came together, with Gusty lifting Saoirse off the floor in a bear hug. The crowd in the dock moved to clear space around them on all sides, nearly every eye focused on them.

"My God, you look good!" Gusty said. "And captain now. Oh my God!"

Saoirse struggled to regain her footing and her breath. "You're looking damned good yourself, and those are sergeant's stripes, I see. Congratulations!"

"Thank you. Sergeant indeed, and for right now, acting head of StatSec."

Saoirse grabbed Gusty by the shoulders and looked her up and down. "Acting head of StatSec? There has to be a story there."

"Oh, there is," Gusty said.

Before she could go further, they were interrupted by a child's voice shouting, "Hey, Mandy, you wanted to see girl peacers. Here are two of them!"

Saoirse looked down and saw a boy of, she guessed, ten years standing a few feet away, pointing at them. A girl of about the same age ran to join him. They were dressed alike, and their faces were similar enough to be brother and sister. The main difference was that the girl's auburn hair was worn long and pulled back in a ponytail. Saoirse's mind flashed to Juliana Hopkinson.

The girl stepped in front of Saoirse, and her eyes went wide. "She's got stars!"

Now, what to do with this? Saoirse wondered. She could have turned her back on the girl and walked off to hear Gusty's story, but that didn't feel right. Instead, she squatted down to bring her face level with the girl's. "Your name is Mandy?"

"Amanda."

"Okay. So, Amanda, we say we 'make' the stars, not 'get' the stars. That's because they're not given to you. You have to earn them."

"I understand," Amanda said solemnly. "I'm going to be a peacer when I grow up." She was still staring at the stars. "Grandpa!" she called out. "She's wearing red and gold!"

That brought an older man over to join them. His pink scalp with only a fringe of white hair gave away his age, but otherwise his bearing was as erect as any trooper Saoirse had seen.

"Donald Dubois," he said. "Let me apologize for my grandchildren. Fraternal twins, but Amanda got the, ah, spine."

Before Saoirse could think of a reply, Gusty inserted herself. "May I present Captain Saoirse Kenneally," she said to Dubois.

That drew a sharp look and a step back from Dubois. "Captain Kenneally? As in Kenneally at the Point?"

Saoirse was sure she was blushing as red as her stars. She nodded.

He peered at the ribbon over her left breast. "That would be the PLM," he said. "I'm US Army—retired, obviously. I don't think I've ever seen anyone wearing the PLM. Amanda, do you realize whom you've met?"

"Yes," Amanda said. To Saoirse, she said, "You're Irish Kenneally." Her voice was not much above a whisper. "My grandpa lets me see the army and peacer newsfeeds he gets. I'm going to be a peacer, and I'm going to be just like you."

Just like me, Saoirse thought. *That might not be what you want to be, not if you have any choice in the matter.* She squatted down again. "Look, Amanda, there's a dark side to me you don't know about. I'm not sure anyone should be just like me." She paused. She didn't need to give this girl details, but walking away still didn't feel right. "What I will do, Amanda, is make you a promise. You're way too young now, but when you're grown, if you do come out into the Reach as a peacer, you find me and I'll show you how to fight. A peacer named Tomasz Szczechowicz did that for me, and I'll do it for you. It's a peacer tradition."

"Really?" The girl's eyes rounded. "Because I'll do that, Captain Kenneally. I'll remember you. But what if you don't remember me?"

Saoirse had the feeling that every time she opened her mouth, she dug a bigger hole for herself. But she was not going to walk away. She brushed down the side of her jacket with one hand and felt something in the pocket. She stuck her hand in and pulled out a thin plastic block with a metal fragment embedded in it.

"Here's what we'll do," Saoirse said. "The piece of metal in this plastic," she held it up in front of Amanda, "that's part of a bullet the doc dug out of my left arm after the fighting at the Point. You keep it." She pressed it into Amanda's hand. "What it's telling you is that if you go out into the Reach for glory, there's a price you might pay. You should think about that. But when you're grown, if you decide to go, you bring that and show it to me. I'll remember you and I'll teach you."

Amanda tried to give it back. "I shouldn't take this," she said. "It's your bullet."

Saoirse shook her head. "It left me plenty to remind me of it. I don't need the bullet. It's yours." She stood up again.

"Thank you," Dubois said. "Thank you very much." With an outstretched arm, he gathered up the two children and ushered them to the outbound kiosk.

After they walked away, Saoirse heard a sound that could have been a fist hitting an arm. Amanda's high voice carried as she said to her brother, "I will be a peacer like Captain Kenneally when I grow up, and all you're going to be is a stupid boy." Saoirse had to grin.

Gusty slung an arm over Saoirse's shoulder. "So, if we are done with the hero worship," she said, "why don't we go to Olga's and catch up?"

• • •

Something felt different about Olga's, although Saoirse couldn't see what it was. The plastic tables were the same as the last time she had been there. So were the chairs, save possibly for more stains on the seat cushions. The menu was unchanged. Maybe she had changed.

They both ordered coffee and leaned back in their chairs with the mugs.

"God, that's good," Saoirse said after her first gulp.

Gusty stared at her. "Did that bullet take out your taste buds? Olga's coffee is mediocre at best, and goes to downright awful on occasion. We like it 'cause it's cheap."

Saoirse grinned. "If you want truly awful coffee, come out into the Reach to Daleko Bałtyckie. This tastes like heaven." She took another swallow.

Gusty winced. "The solar system will be just fine for me," she said. "I've read and listened to all the stories of your adventures. I don't need to have them myself."

"But you had some adventures of your own."

"Oh yes." Gusty sipped her own coffee. "An interstellar docked a while back and I got a package from a Lieutenant Colonel Venezelos. Somebody you know, of course. It came with a message that the peacers had all kicked in and gotten me a box of the genuine Daleko Bałtyckie tobacco they knew I liked. Okay, I smoke tobacco, but I've never had any from Daleko Bałtyckie. I didn't even know the planet existed. So I went through it really carefully and found this little chip. And oh my." She stopped and looked at Saoirse over her cup.

"And?" Saoirse prompted.

"The guy they replaced S with was a lieutenant. We all thought he was Concannon's man, but once I saw the information on the chip, I knew better. I was careful, didn't try to transmit anything until I took care of business here. There were a few peacers here I was sure of—not many, but enough. Then I had a confrontation with the lieutenant, and thank you for all that time on the firing range. I shot straighter, and let me tell you, those exploding azide rounds do mess up a body.

"From there, my squad arrested Mom, and her whole business unraveled up here. There was a major detonation on Earth when we sent word. That's where she is now. Under lots of locks. Forever, I hope. I got promoted to sergeant, and they made me acting head until they assign an officer. When they do, I go to OCS and become a lieutenant." She leaned back and pointed a finger across the table. "I will catch you yet, Kenneally, in spite of your grossly unfair start."

"I'm sure you will," Saoirse said. "Plenty of opportunity in the Reach."

"That part I will leave to you," Gusty said. "No need for stars on my uniform. I predict that it will end up with you commanding general of the Peacemakers outside the solar system, and I'll settle for command of all of them here. How's that?"

"Done," said Saoirse. "The bad girls rule the Reach."

They smiled and bumped fists across the table.

* * *

Donal Kenneally sat at one of Tokyo Sushi's tables in the Chicago O'Hare International Airport concourse, waiting for his little sister and wondering whether he should be doing that. It had been nearly a year since he—or any member of the family, for that matter—had seen or heard from Saoirse. A spate of lurid stories involving her had come across the newsfeeds some months ago, but that was all old news from somewhere out in the Reach, so who knew how reliable it was. Then, out of the blue, or more accurately out of the black, had come a message from Titan Station. She would be inbound from the station on the *William the Conqueror* and would take a plane from the elevator port outside Quito to O'Hare.

So there he sat. What version of Saerie was going to show up? Her message had been very specific about when the ship would make orbit, when she would reach the port, which flight she would take, and when she would arrive in Chicago. That was all very unlike Saerie. "I'll get there kinda around sometime maybe," would have been more typical. And then . . . nothing. That was typical, and none of them had any way to reach *her*. The comm she'd had when she was last on Earth wasn't in operation.

What had happened to Saoirse in the year the family had tried to forget this baby sister existed—a stance he knew his parents were now regretting? She had gone out into the Reach; that was clear. Searches turned up references to a peacer named Saoirse Kenneally, which seemed incredible, and there were those newsfeeds about battles and medals that seemed even more incredible. They had nothing solid, though, and no details, at least none anyone would believe. Dad had plenty of connections, but none in the peacers. So much of what happened in the Reach stayed in the Reach. That brought him back to his original question: What version of Saerie was coming to see him now? Sweet Saerie? Mixed-up Saerie? Angry Saerie? Explosive Saerie? Thermonuclear Saerie? As long as it wasn't drunk Saerie, he told himself. Anything but that.

"Donnie!"

He looked up with a start. While he was lost in his musings, she had walked up, and there she was right in front of him. She looked good—so good that it was a second before he recognized her. Saerie was trim and fit, wearing black pants and a tight maroon short-sleeved shirt that showed off her muscular physique. Her black hair was cropped short over the ears and at the neck; he didn't ever recall seeing it that way. His eyes caught the tattoo of a rattlesnake that circled her arm from wrist to biceps. Where had that come from?

"Don't you recognize me?" Her voice had a rasp he didn't remember. While he was thinking about it, she pulled a chair from another table and sat down across from him.

"To be honest," he said, "I guess I was expecting a uniform."

"I'm on leave," she said. "Civvies for a few days."

"Are you still . . . drinking?"

"No." A shake of her head. "Haven't had anything since that last time you saw me on Earth."

Donal felt himself relax. "I'm glad you're past that."

"I'm not 'past that,' Donnie. It never goes away. It's always one day at a time."

The sharpness in her tone put him back on guard, the way he always had to be with Saerie. That rasp was still there in her voice. It was her voice, but different. "What happened to your voice?"

"Got shot in the head." She opened her mouth wide and stuck out her tongue so he could see the scar that ran diagonally across it from back to tip. "Doc said I've got nothing important up there anyway." She laughed. "Knocked out some teeth, messed up my jaw, and did something to my voice, but that's about it."

"Jesus." Laughing and smiling about being shot in the head, that was strange even for her. "Look, Saerie," he began, but she cut him off with a wave of her hand.

"I've told you not to call me that," she said in a voice gone hard. "Don't do it anymore."

Donal saw anger flash in her eyes, and while he waited for the explosion, he wondered why, of all the family, he had to deal with her. That was what he got, he assumed, for being the one who had always kept some degree of relationship with her, who went to the jails, who made the calls when the others were afraid of how a conversation might blow up.

No explosion came, however. "Okay," he started again cautiously, "what do they call you out there?"

"Irish, mostly," she said.

"Irish? Irish Kenneally? That's seriously redundant, you know."

She shrugged. "They also call me Captain Kenneally. Or *sir*."

Donal had the sensation that the conversation was veering off course and headed to a bad place. Still, she hadn't blown up yet. "Okay, Saoirse, if that's okay, what I wanted to say is that we'd like you to come home. Mom and Dad talked with everyone. We'd all like you to come home."

He felt her relax. She even smiled. "I'd like that, Donnie. I was hoping I could come by, maybe spend a few days, talk about . . . some things."

"It doesn't have to be just a few days," he said hastily. "We kept your room and your stuff—well, we had it all cleaned up, but it's still your room. You can come home."

She was shaking her head before he was halfway through his little speech. "I said I was on leave, Donnie. It's not that many days. Then I have to report to Fort Mattis. The peacers are sending me to an advanced officer training program run by the US Army."

The army? "But . . . but you don't have to do that. You can live at home for now. Dad said he'll pay for school. We'll get used to the, ah, snake. No one will say a word." He paused. "What happened there?" He pointed to the white scar that split the snake on her forearm.

"Snake took a bullet for me," she said. "Two, actually. I never was any good taking care of pets, was I?"

"Jesus. *Another* bullet. All the more reason to come home, Saoirse. Mom and Dad and I and all of us have been scared you were going to die out there, get killed somewhere, and you're sitting here talking about . . . My God, how many times *have* you been shot?"

Saoirse's face held a wan smile. "I can't come home to stay, Donnie. I'm on Earth for training, and when it's done, they'll send me back out into the Reach where the fighting is—and there's a lot of it. I'm what they call a combat peacer, and I'm actually good at it. That's what I *am*. Yes, that means there's a risk, maybe a pretty high risk, that someday I'm going to die violently out there. That's the way it is, and I'm at peace with it. All of you need to accept that."

Donal was quiet for a minute. Then he said, "If that's who you are and you're set on that, we'll be okay. Not happy about it, but Mom and Dad will accept it." He sighed. "Maybe you can wear long sleeves when you come home."

"I will," Saoirse said, "because I do want to come home. I need to talk to Mom and Dad—all of you, really. There's a lot I need to say, a lot of truth I need to tell, things you should know and apologies I need to make. I need to do this before there's a day I can't do it. That's another lesson I've had."

"Sounds like that might take a while," he said. "You're going to your army program now?"

"No," Saoirse said. "Let's go home first."

Made in United States
Troutdale, OR
04/27/2025